Praise fo...

'Diana Gabaldon is a born storyteller' *Los Angeles Daily News*

'A rich and pacey novel' *Woman's Own*

'History comes deliciously alive on the page'
New York Daily News

'Triumphant . . . Her use of historical detail and a truly adult love story confirm Gabaldon as a superior writer'
Publishers Weekly

'Capturing the lonely, tormented and courageous career of a man who fights for his crown, his honour and his own secrets, Gabaldon delivers breathtaking human drama, proving once again that she can bring history to life in a way few novelists ever have' *Sheffield Star*

'Gabaldon provides a rich, abundantly researched, entirely readable portrait of life among the English upper classes in the 1750s. From London's literary salons and political intrigue to fearsome battle scenes in the Seven Years' War, her writing is always vivid and often lyrical' *Washington Post*

'A blockbuster hit' *Wall Street Journal*

'One of the things that sets Gabaldon apart from other romance writers is exhaustive research of the times in which her characters live, so evident in her attention to period detail . . . plot lines and stand-alone yarns are expertly woven together'
Toronto Star

By Diana Gabaldon

Outlander
Dragonfly in Amber
Voyager
Drums of Autumn
The Fiery Cross
A Breath of Snow and Ashes
An Echo in the Bone
A Trail of Fire (short stories)

The Outlandish Companion
(non-fiction)

Lord John and the Hellfire Club (novella)
Lord John and the Private Matter
Lord John and the Succubus (novella)
Lord John and the Brotherhood of the Blade
Lord John and the Haunted Soldier (novella)
Custom of the Army (novella)
Lord John and the Hand of Devils (collected novellas)
The Scottish Prisoner
Plague of Zombies (novella)

Diana Gabaldon is the *New York Times* bestselling author of the wildly popular *Outlander* novels and one work of non-fiction, as well as the bestselling series featuring Lord John Grey, an important character from the original series. She lives with her family and a lot of other assorted wildlife in Scottsdale, Arizona. Visit her website at www.dianagabaldon.com

A Trail of Fire

Four Outlander Tales

DIANA GABALDON

An Orion paperback

First published in Great Britain in 2012
by Orion
This paperback edition published in 2013
by Orion Books,
an imprint of The Orion Publishing Group Ltd,
Orion House, 5 Upper St Martin's Lane,
London WC2H 9EA

An Hachette UK company

1 3 5 7 9 10 8 6 4 2

Copyright for this collection © Diana Gabaldon 2012

For further copyright information see page 380

A CIP catalogue record for this book
is available from the British Library.

ISBN 978-1-4091-0380-6

Typeset at The Spartan Press Ltd,
Lymington, Hants

Printed and bound by CPI Group (UK) Ltd,
Croydon, CRO 4YY

www.orionbooks.co.uk

This book is for Susan Pitman Butler,
without whom ten million necessary things would not get done

Contents

Acknowledgements

The author gratefully acknowledges . . .

. . . Maria Szybek, for invaluable advice in the matter of Polish vulgarities and WWII flying history . . .

. . . Douglas Watkins, for vivid descriptions of aerobatics (and crashing) in a small plane, technical information regarding the flying of small planes, and for coming up with a Really Good Reason for the crash that occurs in this book.

. . . Philippe Safavi, my French translator, who very graciously offered his services in translating the French bits in 'Plague of Zombies' and 'The Space Between', if only to save himself the pain of having to read my ungrammatical attempts. (Any misplaced or missing accent marks are my fault; any misspellings are undoubtedly the fault of Beastly Interfering Microsoft Word, which ought to be taken out and shot, if you ask me. (So should anyone who relies on its asinine suggestions re spelling or grammar.)

. . . Barbara Schnell (my German translator), Karen Henry (Nit-picker-in-Chief), Allene Edwards (Assistant Chief Nit-picker) and a number of other kind friends and acquaintances from the Compuserve Books and Writers Forum, where it's been my pleasure to hang out for the last thirty years, for drawing my attention to assorted things needing attention. (I am Not Good with dates.)

. . . Ivan Rendall, whose *Spitfire: Icon of a Nation* was my principal technical reference for 'A Leaf on the Wind of All Hallows', Wendy Moore, whose excellent biography of Dr John Hunter, *The Knife Man*, inadvertently inspired 'The Custom of the Army', Wade Davis, for his valuable book, *The Serpent and the Rainbow*, with its scientific information on making zombies, and Thomas Wentworth Higginson, whose *Black Rebellion: Five Slave Revolts* supplied much of the historical background for 'Plague of Zombies'.

. . . Catherine MacGregor, for advice on Gaelic inclusions, and for telling me about the two memorial plaques at the Plains of Abraham.

. . . George R.R. Martin and Gardner Dozois, who inadvertently set me on the path to writing short (well, sort of) pieces.

. . . John Joseph Adams and Jim Frenkel, for their graciousness in allowing me to publish 'The Space Between' in this volume. (This story will be available in the US in early 2013, in their anthology THE MAD SCIENTIST'S GUIDE TO WORLD DOMINATION, edited by John Joseph Adams, published by Tor.)

Mistress of the Bulge

When *The Scottish Prisoner* was published, a bookseller friend turned to me in delight and said, 'I think you've invented a new literary form – the bulge!' In other words, a story that is neither sequel nor prequel, but lives inside an existing body of work. Now, frankly, I wish she had thought of something more poetic to describe my efforts, but I have to admit that 'bulge' has a bit more punch – with its vivid imagery of a snake that's swallowed some large and squirming prey – than colourless terms like 'interpolation' or 'inclusion'.

I first wrote a short story fifteen years ago, mostly to see whether I *could* write something shorter than 300,000 words. It was an interesting technical challenge, but 'short' is not what you'd call one of my great natural skills. Still, I found the experience interesting, and since then have written the occasional short (well . . . sort of; it's all relative, isn't it?) piece when invited to contribute to an anthology now and then.

Even though these stories are relatively brief, they're almost all connected to (and integral parts of) the large series of novels that includes both the huge *Outlander* novels and the smaller historical mysteries focused on the character of Lord John Grey. These novellas too are bulges; stories that fill a lacuna in the main story or explore the life and times of secondary characters, while connecting with the existing parts of the series.

Now, an anthology is a collection of stories written by a number of different authors. It's a good way to sample the styles and voices of writers you might not usually encounter, or try an unfamiliar genre. Still, some readers may be chiefly interested in a particular favourite writer, and not want to buy an anthology for the sake of just one short story or novella.[1]

A few years ago, I collected three novellas about Lord John Grey (two of them previously published in anthologies, one written specifically for the new collection) into a single volume, and titled it *Lord John and the Hand of Devils*. Readers enjoyed having these pieces of Lord John's story conveniently to hand, and so I figured that whenever I had a few more short pieces, I'd publish another collection. This is it.

This volume includes two Lord John novellas: *The Custom of the Army*, and *Lord John and the Plague of Zombies*. In terms of the overall chronology of the novels and shorter pieces involving his lordship, *Custom* follows the novel *Brotherhood of the Blade* and precedes the novel *The Scottish Prisoner*. *Zombies* follows *The Scottish Prisoner* (though it was in fact written *while* I was writing *Prisoner*, and was published before the novel was finished, and if you don't think *that* was a swift bit of juggling . . .). You'll find an overall chronology of both the main *Outlander* novels and the Lord John novels and novellas at the back of this book.

The Custom of the Army is set in 1759, in London and Quebec, and while it probably *was* all the fault of the electric eel, Lord John finds himself obliged to leave London for the wilds of Canada and the dangerous proximity of James Wolfe, the British general besieging the

[1]According to the Science Fiction and Fantasy Writers of America, a short story is something containing fewer than 17,500 words, while a novella is a story between 17,501 and 40,000 words. Anything bigger than 40,000 words is technically a novel. By *some* people's standards. <cough>

Citadel of Quebec. (*'Melodramatic ass,' was what Hal had said, hastily briefing him before his departure. 'Showy, bad judgement, terrible strategist. Has the Devil's own luck, though, I'll give him that. Don't follow him into anything stupid.'*)

Plague of Zombies takes place in 1761, on the island of Jamaica, where Lord John is sent as commander of a battalion intended to suppress what seems to be a revolt of the escaped slaves called maroons. But things are not always what they seem. (*He rubbed the rest of the blood from his hand with the hem of his banyan, and the cold horror of the last few minutes faded into a glowing coal of anger, hot in the pit of his stomach. He'd been a soldier most of his life; he'd killed. He'd seen the dead on battlefields. And one thing he knew for a fact. Dead men don't bleed.*)

Now, you'll also find two other stories in this book: *A Leaf on the Wind of All Hallows*, and *The Space Between Leaf* is the story of Roger MacKenzie's parents, Jerry and Dolly, and takes place during WWII. (*It was cold in the room, and she hugged herself. She was wearing nothing but Jerry's string vest – he thought she looked erotic in it – 'lewd', he said, approving, his Highland accent making the word sound really dirty – and the thought made her smile. The thin cotton clung to her breasts, true enough, and her nipples poked out something scandalous, if only from the chill. She wanted to go crawl in next to him, longing for his warmth, longing to keep touching him for as long as they had.*)

The Space Between follows the events in the novel *An Echo in the Bone*, is set in Paris in 1778, and concerns Michael Murray (Young Ian Murray's elder brother), Joan MacKimmie (Marsali MacKimmie Fraser's younger sister), Master Raymond, Mother Hildegarde (yes, she's still alive), the Comte St Germain (ditto – surely you didn't think he was really dead, did you?), and a number of other interesting people. (*'What a waste of a wonderful arse,' Monsieur Brechin remarked in French, watching Joan's ascent from the far side of the cabin. 'And mon Dieu, those legs! Imagine those wrapped around your back, eh? Would you have her keep the striped stockings on? I would.' It hadn't occurred to Michael to imagine that, but he was now having a hard time dismissing the image. He coughed into his handkerchief to hide the reddening of his face.*)

I hope you'll enjoy the journey into so-far-uncharted territory, torches held aloft!

Diana Gabaldon

A Leaf on the Wind of All Hallows

Introduction to
A Leaf on the Wind of All Hallows

One of the interesting things you can do with a 'bulge' is to follow mysteries, hints, and loose ends from the main books of the series. One such trail follows the story of Roger MacKenzie's parents.

In *Outlander*, we learn that Roger was orphaned during World War II, and then adopted by his great-uncle, the Reverend Reginald Wakefield, who tells Claire and Frank that Roger's mother was killed in the Blitz, and that his father was a Spitfire pilot 'shot down over the Channel'.

In *Drums of Autumn*, Roger tells Brianna the moving story of his mother's death in the collapse of a Tube station during the bombing of London.

But in *An Echo in the Bone*, there is a poignant conversation in the moonlight between Claire and Roger, during which we encounter *this* little zinger:

> Her hands wrapped his, small and hard and smelling of medicine.
>
> 'I don't know what happened to your father,' she said. 'But it wasn't what they told you [. . .]
>
> 'Of course things happen,' she said, as though able to read his thoughts. 'Accounts get garbled, too, over time and distance. Whoever told your mother might have been mistaken; she might have said something that the reverend misconstrued. All those things are possible. But during the War, I had letters from Frank – he wrote as

3

often as he could, up until they recruited him into MI6. After that, I often wouldn't hear anything for months. But just before that, he wrote to me, and mentioned – just as casual chat, you know – that he'd run into something strange in the reports he was handling. A Spitfire had gone down, crashed – not shot down; they thought it must have been an engine failure – in Northumbria, and while it hadn't burned, for a wonder, there was no sign of the pilot. None. And he did mention the name of the pilot, because he thought Jeremiah rather an appropriately doomed sort of name.'

'Jerry,' Roger said, his lips feeling numb. 'My mother always called him Jerry.'

'Yes,' she said softly. 'And there are circles of standing stones scattered all over Northumbria.'

So what *really* happened to Jerry MacKenzie and his wife Dolly? Read on.

A Leaf on the Wind of All Hallows

It was two weeks yet to Hallowe'en, but the gremlins were already at work.

Jerry MacKenzie turned Dolly II onto the runway full-throttle, shoulder-hunched, blood-thumping, already half-way up Green leader's arse – pulled back on the stick and got a choking shudder instead of the giddy lift of take-off. Alarmed, he eased back, but before he could try again, there was a bang that made him jerk by reflex, smacking his head against the Perspex. It hadn't been a bullet, though; the off tyre had blown, and a sickening tilt looped them off the runway, bumping and jolting into the grass.

There was a strong smell of petrol, and Jerry popped the Spitfire's hood and hopped out in panic, envisioning imminent incineration, just as the last plane of Green flight roared past him and took wing, its engine fading to a buzz within seconds.

A mechanic was pelting down from the hangar to see what the trouble was, but Jerry'd already opened Dolly's belly and the trouble was plain: the fuel line was punctured. Well, thank Christ he hadn't got into the air with it, that was one thing, but he grabbed the line to see how bad the puncture was, and it came apart in his hands and soaked his sleeve nearly to the shoulder with high-test petrol. Good job the mechanic hadn't come loping up with a lit cigarette in his mouth.

5

He rolled out from under the plane, sneezing, and Gregory the mechanic stepped over him.

'Not flying her today, mate,' Greg said, squatting down to look up into the engine, and shaking his head at what he saw.

'Aye, tell me something I don't know.' He held his soaked sleeve gingerly away from his body. 'How long to fix her?'

Greg shrugged, eyes squinted against the cold wind as he surveyed Dolly's guts.

'Half an hour for the tyre. You'll maybe have her back up tomorrow, if the fuel line's the only engine trouble. Anything else we should be looking at?'

'Aye, the left wing-gun trigger sticks sometimes. Gie us a bit o' grease, maybe?'

'I'll see what the canteen's got in the way of leftover dripping. You best hit the showers, Mac. You're turning blue.'

He was shivering, right enough, the rapidly evaporating petrol wicking his body heat away like candlesmoke. Still, he lingered for a moment, watching as the mechanic poked and prodded, whistling through his teeth.

'Go on, then,' Greg said in feigned exasperation, backing out of the engine and seeing Jerry still there. 'I'll take good care of her.'

'Aye, I know. I just— aye, thanks.' Adrenaline from the aborted flight was still surging through him, thwarted reflexes making him twitch. He walked away, suppressing the urge to look back over his shoulder at his wounded plane.

Jerry came out of the pilots' WC half an hour later, eyes stinging with soap and petrol, backbone knotted. Half his mind was on Dolly, the other half with his mates. Blue

6

and Green were up this morning, Red and Yellow resting. Green flight would be out over Flamborough Head by now, hunting.

He swallowed, still restless, dry-mouthed by proxy, and went to fetch a cup of tea from the canteen. That was a mistake; he heard the gremlins laughing as soon as he walked in and saw Sailor Malan.

Malan was Group Captain and a decent bloke overall. South African, a great tactician – and the most ferocious, most persistent air fighter Jerry'd seen yet. Rat terriers weren't in it. Which was why he felt a beetle skitter briefly down his spine when Malan's deep-set eyes fixed on him.

'Lieutenant!' Malan rose from his seat, smiling. 'The very man I had in mind!'

The Devil he had, Jerry thought, arranging his face into a look of respectful expectancy. Malan couldn't have heard about Dolly's spot of bother yet, and without that, Jerry would have scrambled with Green flight on their way to hunt 109s over Flamborough Head. Malan hadn't been looking for Jerry; he just thought he'd do, for whatever job was up. And the fact that the Group Captain had called him by his rank, rather than his name, meant it probably wasn't a job anyone would volunteer for.

He didn't have time to worry about what that might be, though; Malan was introducing the other man, a tallish chap in army uniform with dark hair and a pleasant, if sharp, look about him. Eyes like a good sheep dog, he thought, nodding in reply to Captain Randall's greeting. Kindly, maybe, but he won't miss much.

'Randall's come over from Ops at Ealing,' Sailor was saying over his shoulder. He hadn't waited for them to exchange polite chat, but was already leading them out across the tarmac, heading for the Flight Command offices. Jerry grimaced and followed, casting a longing glance downfield at Dolly, who was being towed ignominiously

7

into the hangar. The rag-doll painted on her nose was blurred, the black curls partially dissolved by weather and spilled petrol. Well, he'd touch it up later, when he'd heard the details of whatever horrible job the stranger had brought.

His gaze rested resentfully on Randall's neck, and the man turned suddenly, glancing back over his shoulder as though he'd felt the stress of Jerry's regard. Jerry felt a qualm in the pit of his stomach, as half-recognised observations – the lack of insignia on the uniform, that air of confidence peculiar to men who kept secrets – gelled with the look in the stranger's eye.

Ops at Ealing, my Aunt Fanny, he thought. He wasn't even surprised, as Sailor waved Randall through the door, to hear the Group Captain lean close and murmur in his ear, 'Careful – he's a funny bugger.'

Jerry nodded, stomach tightening. Malan didn't mean Captain Randall was either humorous or a Freemason. 'Funny bugger' in this context meant only one thing. MI6.

Captain Randall *was* from the secret arm of British Intelligence. He made no bones about it, once Malan had deposited them in a vacant office and left them to it.

'We're wanting a pilot – a good pilot –' he added with a faint smile, 'to fly solo reconnaissance. A new project. Very special.'

'Solo? Where?' Jerry asked warily. Spitfires normally flew in four-plane flights, or in larger configurations, all the way up to an entire squadron, sixteen planes. In formation, they could cover each other to some extent against the heavier Heinkels and Messerschmitts. But they seldom flew alone by choice.

8

'I'll tell you that a bit later. First – are you fit, do you think?'

Jerry reared back a bit at that, stung. What did this bloody boffin think he— then he caught a glance at his reflection in the window pane. Eyes red as a mad boar's, his wet hair sticking up in spikes, a fresh red bruise spreading on his forehead and his blouson stuck to him in damp patches where he hadn't bothered to dry off before dressing.

'Extremely fit,' he snapped. 'Sir.'

Randall lifted a hand half an inch, dismissing the need for sirs.

'I meant your knee,' he said mildly.

'Oh,' Jerry said, disconcerted. 'That. Aye, it's fine.'

He'd taken two bullets through his right knee a year before, when he'd dived after a 109 and neglected to see another one that popped out of nowhere behind him and peppered his arse.

On fire, but terrified of bailing out into a sky filled with smoke, bullets, and random explosions, he'd ridden his burning plane down, both of them screaming as they fell out of the sky, Dolly I's metal skin so hot it had seared his left forearm through his jacket, his right foot squelching in the blood that filled his boot as he stamped the rudder pedal. Made it, though, and had been on the sick and hurt list for two months. He still limped very noticeably, but he didn't regret his smashed patella; he'd had his second month's sick leave at home – and wee Roger had come along nine months later.

He smiled broadly at the thought of his lad, and Randall smiled back in involuntary response.

'Good,' he said. 'You're all right to fly a long mission, then?'

Jerry shrugged. 'How long can it be in a Spitfire? Unless you've thought up a way to refuel in the air.' He'd meant

9

that as a joke, and was further disconcerted to see Randall's lips purse a little, as though thinking whether to tell him they *had*.

'It is a Spitfire ye mean me to fly?' he asked, suddenly uncertain. Christ, what if it was one of the experimental birds they heard about now and again? His skin prickled with a combination of fear and excitement. But Randall nodded.

'Oh, yes, certainly. Nothing else is manoeuvrable enough, and there may be a good bit of ducking and dodging. What we've done is to take a Spitfire II, remove one pair of wing-guns, and refit it with a pair of cameras.'

'One pair?'

Again that slight pursing of lips before Randall replied.

'You might need the second pair of guns.'

'Oh. Aye. Well, then . . .'

The immediate notion, as Randall explained it, was for Jerry to go to Northumberland, where he'd spend two weeks being trained in the use of the wing-cameras, taking pictures of selected bits of landscape at different altitudes. And where he'd work with a support team who were meant to be trained in keeping the cameras functioning in bad weather. They'd teach him how to get the film out without ruining it, just in case he had to. After which . . .

'I can't tell you yet exactly where you'll be going,' Randall had said. His manner through the conversation had been intent, but friendly, joking now and then. Now all trace of joviality had vanished; he was dead serious. 'Eastern Europe is all I can say just now.'

Jerry felt his inside hollow out a little and took a deep breath to fill the empty space. He could say no. But he'd signed up to be an RAF flier, and that's what he was.

'Aye, right. Will I— maybe see my wife once, before I go, then?'

Randall's face softened a little at that, and Jerry saw the

Captain's thumb touch his own gold wedding ring in reflex.

'I think that can be arranged.'

Marjorie MacKenzie – Dolly to her husband – opened the blackout curtains. No more than an inch . . . well, two inches. It wouldn't matter; the inside of the little flat was dark as the inside of a coal-scuttle. London outside was equally dark; she knew the curtains were open only because she felt the cold glass of the window through the narrow crack. She leaned close, breathing on the glass, and felt the moisture of her breath condense, cool near her face. Couldn't see the mist, but felt the squeak of her fingertip on the glass as she quickly drew a small heart there, the letter J inside.

It faded at once, of course, but that didn't matter; the charm would be there when the light came in, invisible but there, standing between her husband and the sky.

When the light came, it would fall just so, across his pillow. She'd see his sleeping face in the light: the jack-straw hair, the fading bruise on his temple, the deep-set eyes, closed in innocence. He looked so young, asleep. Almost as young as he really was. Only twenty-two; too young to have such lines in his face. She touched the corner of her mouth, but couldn't feel the crease the mirror showed her – her mouth was swollen, tender, and the ball of her thumb ran across her lower lip, lightly, to and fro.

What else, what else? What more could she do for him? He'd left her with something of himself. Perhaps there would be another baby – something he gave her, but something she gave him, as well. Another baby. Another child to raise alone?

'Even so,' she whispered, her mouth tightening, face raw from hours of stubbled kissing; neither of them had been able to wait for him to shave. 'Even so.'

At least he'd got to see Roger. Hold his little boy – and have said little boy sick up milk all down the back of his shirt. Jerry'd yelped in surprise, but hadn't let her take Roger back; he'd held his son and petted him until the wee mannie fell asleep, only then laying him down in his basket and stripping off the stained shirt before coming to her.

It was cold in the room, and she hugged herself. She was wearing nothing but Jerry's string vest – he thought she looked erotic in it, 'lewd', he said, approving, his Highland accent making the word sound really dirty – and the thought made her smile. The thin cotton clung to her breasts, true enough, and her nipples poked out something scandalous, if only from the chill.

She wanted to go crawl in next to him, longing for his warmth, longing to keep touching him for as long as they had. He'd need to go at eight, to catch the train back; it would barely be light then. Some puritanical impulse of denial kept her hovering there, though, cold and wakeful in the dark. She felt as though if she denied herself, her desire, offered that denial as sacrifice, it would strengthen the magic, help to keep him safe and bring him back. God knew what a minister would say to that bit of superstition, and her tingling mouth twisted in self-mockery. And doubt.

Still, she sat in the dark, waiting for the cold blue light of the dawn that would take him.

Baby Roger put an end to her dithering, though; babies did. He rustled in his basket, making the little waking-up grunts that presaged an outraged roar at the discovery of a wet nappy and an empty stomach, and she hurried across the tiny room to his basket, breasts swinging heavy, already letting down her milk. She wanted to keep him from waking Jerry, but stubbed her toe on the spindly chair, and sent it over with a bang.

There was an explosion of bedclothes as Jerry sprang up with a loud 'FUCK!' that drowned her own muffled 'damn!' and Roger topped them both with a shriek like an air-raid siren. Like clockwork, old Mrs Munns in the next flat thumped indignantly on the thin wall.

Jerry's naked shape crossed the room in a bound. He pounded furiously on the partition with his fist, making the wallboard quiver and boom like a drum. He paused, fist still raised, waiting. Roger had stopped screeching, impressed by the racket.

Dead silence from the other side of the wall, and Marjorie pressed her mouth against Roger's round little head to muffle her giggling. He smelled of baby-scent and fresh pee, and she cuddled him like a large hot-water bottle, his immediate warmth and need making her notions of watching over her men in the lonely cold seem silly.

Jerry gave a satisfied grunt and came across to her.

'Ha,' he said, and kissed her.

'What d'ye think you are?' she whispered, leaning into him. 'A gorilla?'

'Yeah,' he whispered back, taking her hand and pressing it against him. 'Want to see my banana?'

'Dzien dobry.'

Jerry halted in the act of lowering himself into a chair, and stared at a smiling Frank Randall.

'Oh, aye,' he said. 'Like that, is it? *Niech sie pan odpierdoli.*' It meant, 'Fuck off, sir,' in formal Polish, and Randall, taken by surprise, broke out laughing.

'Like that,' he agreed. He had a wodge of papers with

13

him, official forms, all sorts, the bumf, as the pilots called it – Jerry recognised the one you signed that named who your pension went to, and the one about what to do with your body if there was one and anyone had time to bother. He'd done all that when he signed up, but they made you do it again, if you went on special service. He ignored the forms, though, eyes fixed instead on the maps Randall had brought.

'And here's me thinkin' you and Malan picked me for my bonny face,' he drawled, exaggerating his accent. He sat and leaned back, affecting casualness. 'It is Poland, then?' So it hadn't been coincidence, after all – or only the coincidence of Dolly's mishap sending him into the building early. In a way, that was comforting; it wasn't the bloody Hand of Fate tapping him on the shoulder by puncturing the fuel line. The Hand of Fate had been in it a good bit earlier, putting him in Green flight with Andrzej Kolodziewicz.

Andrzej was a real guid yin, a good friend. He'd copped it a month before, spiralling up away from a Messerschmitt. Maybe he'd been blinded by the sun, maybe just looking over the wrong shoulder. Left wing shot to hell, and he'd spiralled right back down and into the ground. Jerry hadn't seen the crash, but he'd heard about it. And got drunk on vodka with Andrzej's brother after.

'Poland,' Randall agreed. 'Malan says you can carry on a conversation in Polish. That true?'

'I can order a drink, start a fight, or ask directions. Any of that of use?'

'The last one might be,' Randall said, very dry. 'But we'll hope it doesn't come to that.'

The MI6 agent had pushed aside the forms, and unrolled the maps. Despite himself, Jerry leaned forward, drawn as by a magnet. They were official maps, but with markings made by hand – circles, Xs.

14

'It's like this,' Randall said, flattening the maps with both hands. 'The Nazis have had labour camps in Poland for the last two years, but it's not common knowledge among the public, either home or abroad. It would be very helpful to the war effort if it *were* common knowledge. Not just the camps' existence, but the kind of thing that goes on there.' A shadow crossed the dark, lean face – anger, Jerry thought, intrigued. Apparently, Mr MI6 knew what kind of thing went on there, and he wondered how.

'If we want it widely known and widely talked about – and we do – we need documentary evidence,' Randall said matter-of-factly. 'Photographs.'

There'd be four of them, he said, four Spitfire pilots. A flight – but they wouldn't fly together. Each one of them would have a specific target, geographically separate, but all to be hit on the same day.

'The camps are guarded, but not with anti-aircraft ordnance. There are towers, though; machine-guns.' And Jerry didn't need telling that a machine-gun was just as effective in someone's hands as it was from an enemy plane. To take the sort of pictures Randall wanted would mean coming in low – low enough to risk being shot from the towers. His only advantage would be the benefit of surprise; the guards might spot him, but they wouldn't be expecting him to come diving out of the sky for a low pass just above the camp.

'Don't try for more than one pass, unless the cameras malfunction. Better to have fewer pictures than none at all.'

'Yes, sir.' He'd reverted to 'sir', as Group Captain Malan was present at the meeting, silent but listening intently. Got to keep up appearances.

'Here's the list of the targets you'll practise on in Northumberland. Get as close as you think reasonable, without risking—' Randall's face did change at that, breaking into a wry smile. 'Get as close as you can manage with a chance of coming back, all right? The cameras may be worth even more than you are.'

That got a faint chuckle from Malan. Pilots – especially trained pilots – were valuable. The RAF had plenty of planes now, but nowhere near enough pilots to fly them.

He'd be taught to use the wing-cameras and to unload the film safely. If he was shot down but was still alive and the plane didn't burn, he was to get the film out and try to get it back over the border.

'Hence the Polish.' Randall ran a hand through his hair, and gave Jerry a crooked smile. 'If you have to walk out, you may need to ask directions.' They had two Polish-speaking pilots, he said – one Pole and a Hungarian who'd volunteered, and an Englishman with a few words of the language, like Jerry.

'And it is a volunteer mission, let me reiterate.'

'Aye, I know,' Jerry said irritably. 'Said I'd go, didn't I? Sir.'

'You did.' Randall looked at him for a moment, dark eyes unreadable, then lowered his gaze to the maps again. 'Thanks,' he said softly.

The canopy snicked shut over his head. It was a dank, damp Northumberland day, and his breath condensed on the inside of the Perspex hood within seconds. He leaned forward to wipe it away, emitting a sharp yelp as several strands of his hair were ripped out. He'd forgotten to duck. Again. He shoved the canopy release with a muttered oath and the light brown strands caught in the seam where the Perspex closed flew away, caught up by the wind. He closed the canopy again, crouching, and waiting for the signal for take-off.

16

The signalman wig-wagged him and he turned up the throttle, feeling the plane begin to move.

He touched his pocket automatically, whispering, 'Love you, Dolly,' under his breath. Everyone had his little ritual, those last few moments before take-off. For Jerry MacKenzie, it was his wife's face and his lucky stone that usually settled the worms in his belly. She'd found it in a rocky hill on the Isle of Lewis, where they'd spent their brief honeymoon – a rough sapphire, she said, very rare.

'Like you,' he'd said, and kissed her.

No need for worms just now, but it wasn't a ritual if you only did it sometimes, was it? And even if it wasn't going to be combat today, he'd need to be paying attention.

He went up in slow circles, getting the feel of the new plane, sniffing to get her scent. He wished they'd let him fly Dolly II, her seat stained with his sweat, the familiar dent in the console where he'd slammed his fist in exultation at a kill – but they'd already modified this one with the wing-cameras and the latest thing in night-sights. It didn't do to get attached to the planes, anyway; they were almost as fragile as the men flying them, though the parts could be reused.

No matter; he'd sneaked out to the hangar the evening before and done a quick rag-doll on the nose to make it his. He'd know Dolly III well enough by the time they went into Poland.

He dived, pulled up sharp, and did Dutch rolls for a bit, wig-wagging through the cloud-layer, then complete rolls and Immelmanns, all the while reciting Malan's Rules to focus his mind and keep from getting air-sick.

The Rules were posted in every RAF barracks now: the Ten Commandments, the fliers called them – and not as a joke.

17

TEN OF MY RULES FOR AIR FIGHTING, the poster said in bold black type. Jerry knew them by heart.

'*Wait until you see the whites of his eyes,*' he chanted under his breath. '*Fire short bursts of one to two seconds only when your sights are definitely "ON".*' He glanced at his sights, suffering a moment's disorientation. The camera wizard had relocated them. Shite.

'*Whilst shooting think of nothing else, brace the whole of your body: have both hands on the stick: concentrate on your ring sight.*' Well, away to fuck, then. The buttons that operated the camera weren't on the stick; they were on a box connected to a wire that ran out the window; the box itself was strapped to his knee. He'd be bloody looking out the window anyway, not using sights – unless things went wrong and he had to use the guns. In which case . . .

'*Always keep a sharp lookout. "Keep your finger out."*' Aye, right, that one was still good.

'*Height gives you the initiative.*' Not in this case. He'd be flying low, under the radar, and not be looking for a fight. Always the chance one might find him, though. If any German craft found him flying solo in Poland, his best chance was likely to head straight for the sun and fall in. That thought made him smile.

'*Always turn and face the attack.*' He snorted and flexed his bad knee, which ached with the cold. Aye, if you saw it coming in time.

'*Make your decisions promptly. It is better to act quickly even though your tactics are not the best.*' He'd learned that one fast. His body often was moving before his brain had even notified his consciousness that he'd seen something. Nothing to see just now, nor did he expect to, but he kept looking by reflex.

'*Never fly straight and level for more than 30 seconds in the combat area.*' Definitely out. Straight and level was just what he was going to have to do. And slowly.

'*When diving to attack always leave a proportion of your formation above to act as a top guard.*' Irrelevant; he wouldn't have a formation – and that was a thought that gave him the cold grue. He'd be completely alone; no help coming if he got into bother.

'*INITIATIVE, AGGRESSION, AIR DISCIPLINE, and TEAM WORK are words that MEAN something in Air Fighting.*' Yeah, they did. What meant something in reconnaissance? Stealth, Speed, and Bloody Good Luck, more like. He took a deep breath, and dived, shouting the last of the Ten Commandments so it echoed in his Perspex shell.

'Go in quickly – Punch hard – GET OUT!'

❊

'Rubber-necking,' they called it, but Jerry usually ended a day's flying feeling as though he'd been cast in concrete from the shoulder-blades up. He bent his head forward now, ferociously massaging the base of his skull to ease the growing ache. He'd been practising since dawn, and it was nearly tea-time. *Ball-bearings, set, for the use of pilots, one*, he thought. Ought to add that to the standard equipment list. He shook his head like a wet dog, hunched his shoulders, groaning, then resumed the sector-by-sector scan of the sky around him that every pilot did religiously, three hundred and sixty degrees, every moment in the air. All the live ones, anyway.

Dolly'd given him a white silk scarf as a parting present. He didn't know how she'd managed the money for it and she wouldn't let him ask, just settled it round his neck inside his flight jacket. Somebody'd told her the Spitfire pilots all wore them, to save the constant collar-chafing, and she meant him to have one. It felt nice, he'd admit that. Made him think of her touch when she'd put it on

19

him. He pushed the thought hastily aside; the last thing he could afford to do was start thinking about his wife, if he ever hoped to get back to her. And he did mean to get back to her.

Where was that bugger? Had he given up?

No, he'd not; a dark spot popped out from behind a bank of cloud just over his left shoulder and dived for his tail. Jerry turned, a hard, high spiral, up and into the same clouds, the other after him like stink on shite. They played at dodgem for a few moments, in and out of the drifting clouds – he had the advantage in altitude, could play the coming-out-of-the-sun trick, if there were any sun, but it was autumn in Northumberland and there hadn't been any sun in days . . .

Gone. He heard the buzzing of the other plane, faintly, for a moment – or thought he had. Hard to tell above the dull roar of his own engine. Gone, though; he wasn't where Jerry'd expected him to be.

'Oh, like that, is it?' He kept on looking, ten degrees of sky every second; it was the only way to be sure you didn't miss any— A glimpse of something dark and his heart jerked along with his hand. Up and away. It was gone then, the black speck, but he went on climbing, slowly now, looking. Wouldn't do to get too low, and he wanted to keep the altitude . . .

The cloud was thin here, drifting waves of mist, but getting thicker. He saw a solid-looking bank of cloud moving slowly in from the west, but still a good distance away. It was cold, too; his face was chilled. He might be picking up ice if he went too hi— there.

The other plane, closer and higher than he'd expected. The other pilot spotted him at the same moment and came roaring down on him, too close to avoid. He didn't try.

'Aye, wait for it, ye wee bugger,' he murmured, hand

tight on the stick. One second, two, almost on him – and he buried the stick in his balls, jerked it hard left, turned neatly over and went off in a long, looping series of barrel rolls that put him right away out of range.

His radio crackled and he heard Paul Rakoczy chortling through his hairy nose.

'*Kurwa twoja mać!* Where you learn that, you Scotch fucker?'

'At my mammy's tit, *dupek*,' he replied, grinning. 'Buy me a drink, and I'll teach it to ye.'

A burst of static obscured the end of an obscene Polish remark, and Rakoczy flew off with a wig-wag of farewell. Ah, well. Enough sky-larking then; back to the fucking cameras.

Jerry rolled his head, worked his shoulders and stretched as well as could be managed in the confines of a II's cockpit – it had minor improvements over the Spitfire I, but roominess wasn't one of them – had a glance at the wings for ice – no, that was all right – and turned farther inland.

It was too soon to worry over it, but his right hand found the trigger that operated the cameras. His fingers twiddled anxiously over the buttons, checking, rechecking. He was getting used to them, but they didn't work like the gun-triggers; he didn't have them wired in to his reflexes yet. Didn't like the feeling, either. Tiny things, like typewriter keys, not the snug feel of the gun-triggers.

He'd only had the left-handed ones since yesterday; before that, he'd been flying a plane with the buttons on the right. Much discussion with Flight and the MI6 button-boffin, whether it was better to stay with the right, as he'd had practice already, or change for the sake of his cack-handedness. When they'd finally got round to asking him which he wanted, it had been too late in the day to fix

21

it straight off. So he'd been given a couple of hours' extra flying time today, to mess about with the new fix-up.

Right, there it was. The bumpy grey line that cut through the yellowing fields of Northumberland like a perforation, same as you might tear the countryside along it, separating north from south as neat as tearing a piece of paper. Bet the emperor Hadrian wished it was that easy, he thought, grinning as he swooped down along the line of the ancient wall.

The cameras made a loud *clunk-clunk* noise when they fired. *Clunk-clunk, clunk-clunk*! OK, sashay out, bank over, come down . . . *clunk-clunk, clunk-clunk* . . . he didn't like the noise, not the same satisfaction as the vicious short *Brrpt*! of his wing-guns. Made him feel wrong, like something gone with the engine . . . aye, there it was coming up, his goal for the moment.

Mile-castle 37.

A stone rectangle, attached to Hadrian's Wall like a snail on a leaf. The old Roman legions had made these small, neat forts to house the garrisons that guarded the wall. Nothing left now but the outline of the foundation, but it made a good target.

He circled once, calculating, then dived and roared over it at an altitude of maybe fifty feet, cameras clunking like an army of stampeding robots. Pulled up sharp and hared off, circling high and fast, pulling out to run for the imagined border, circling up again . . . and all the time his heart thumped and the sweat ran down his sides, imagining what it would be like when the real day came.

Mid-afternoon, it would be, like this. The winter light just going, but still enough to see clearly. He'd circle, find an angle that would let him cross the whole camp and please God, one that would let him come out of the sun. And then he'd go in.

One pass, Randall had said. Don't risk more than one, unless the cameras malfunction.

The bloody things did malfunction, roughly every third pass. The buttons were slippery under his fingers. Sometimes they worked on the next try, sometimes they didn't.

If they didn't work on the first pass over the camp, or didn't work often enough, he'd have to try again.

'*Niech to szlag*,' he muttered, Fuck the Devil, and pressed the buttons again, one-two, one-two. 'Gentle but firm, like you'd do it to a lady's privates,' the boffin had told him, illustrating a brisk twiddle. He'd never thought of doing that . . . would Dolly like it? he wondered. And where exactly did you do it? Aye, well, women did come with a button, maybe that was it – but then, two fingers? . . . *Clunk-clunk. Clunk-clunk. Crunch.*

He reverted to English profanity, and smashed both buttons with his fist. One camera answered with a startled *clunk*! but the other was silent.

He poked the button again and again, to no effect. 'Bloody fucking arse-buggering . . .' He thought vaguely that he'd have to stop swearing once this was over and he was home again – bad example for the lad.

'FUCK!' he bellowed, and ripping the strap free of his leg, he picked up the box and hammered it on the edge of the seat, then slammed it back onto his thigh – visibly dented, he saw with grim satisfaction – and pressed the balky button.

Clunk, the camera answered meekly.

'Aye, well, then, just you remember that!' he said, and puffing in righteous indignation, gave the buttons a good jabbing.

He'd not been paying attention during this small temper-tantrum, but had been circling upward – standard default for a Spitfire flier. He started back down for a

23

fresh pass at the mile-castle, but within a minute or two, began to hear a knocking sound from the engine.

'No!' he said, and gave it more throttle. The knocking got louder; he could feel it vibrating through the fuselage. Then there was a loud *clang!* from the engine compartment right by his knee, and with horror he saw tiny droplets of oil spatter on the Perspex in front of his face. The engine stopped.

'Bloody, bloody . . .' he was too busy to find another word. His lovely agile fighter had suddenly become a very clumsy glider. He was going down and the only question was whether he'd find a relatively flat spot to crash in.

His hand groped automatically for the landing-gear but then drew back – no time, belly-landing, where was the bottom? Jesus, he'd been distracted, hadn't seen that solid bank of cloud move in; it must have come faster than he . . . Thoughts flitted through his mind, too fast for words. He glanced at the altimeter, but what it told him was of limited use, because he didn't know what the ground under him was like: crags, flat meadow, water? He hoped and prayed for a road, a grassy flat spot, anything short of— God, he was at 500 feet and still in cloud!

'Christ!'

The ground appeared in a sudden burst of yellow and brown. He jerked the nose up, saw the rocks of a crag dead ahead, swerved, stalled, nose-dived, pulled back, pulled back, not enough, oh, God—

His first conscious thought was that he should have radioed base when the engine went.

'Stupid fucker,' he mumbled. *'Make your decisions promptly. It is better to act quickly even though your tactics are not the best.* Clot-heid.'

24

He seemed to be lying on his side. That didn't seem right. He felt cautiously with one hand – grass and mud. What, had he been thrown clear of the plane?

He had. His head hurt badly, his knee much worse. He had to sit down on the matted wet grass for a bit, unable to think through the waves of pain that squeezed his head with each heartbeat.

It was nearly dark, and rising mist surrounded him. He breathed deep, sniffing the dank, cold air. It smelled of rot and old mangel-wurzels – but what it didn't smell of was petrol and burning fuselage.

Right. Maybe she hadn't caught fire when she crashed, then. If not, and if her radio was still working . . .

He staggered to his feet, nearly losing his balance from a sudden attack of vertigo, and turned in a slow circle, peering into the mist. There was nothing *but* mist to his left and behind him, but to his right, he made out two or three large, bulky shapes, standing upright.

Making his way slowly across the lumpy ground, he found that they were stones. Remnants of one of those prehistoric sites that littered the ground in northern Britain. Only three of the big stones were still standing, but he could see a few more, fallen or pushed over, lying like bodies in the darkening fog. He paused to vomit, holding on to one of the stones. Christ, his head was like to split! And he had a terrible buzzing in his ears . . . he pawed vaguely at his ear, thinking somehow he'd left his headset on, but felt nothing but a cold, wet ear.

He closed his eyes again, breathing hard, and leaned against the stone for support. The static in his ears was getting worse, accompanied by a sort of whine. Had he burst an eardrum? He forced himself to open his eyes, and was rewarded with the sight of a large dark irregular shape, well beyond the remains of the stone circle. Dolly!

The plane was barely visible, fading into the swirling

dark, but that's what it had to be. Mostly intact, it looked like, though very much nose-down with her tail in the air – she must have ploughed into the earth. He staggered on the rock-strewn ground, feeling the vertigo set in again, with a vengeance. He waved his arms, trying to keep his balance, but his head spun, and Christ, the bloody *noise* in his head . . . he couldn't think, oh, Jesus, he felt as if his bones were dissolv—

It was full dark when he came to himself, but the clouds had broken and a three-quarter moon shone in the deep black of a country sky. He moved, and groaned. Every bone in his body hurt – but none was broken. That was something, he told himself. His clothes were sodden with damp, he was starving, and his knee was so stiff he couldn't straighten his right leg all the way, but that was all right; he thought he could make shift to hobble as far as a road.

Oh, wait. Radio. Yes, he'd forgotten. If Dolly's radio were intact, he could . . .

He stared blankly at the open ground before him. He'd have sworn it was— but he must have got turned round in the dark and fog— no.

He turned quite round, three times, before he stopped, afraid of becoming dizzy again. The plane was gone.

It *was* gone. He was sure it had lain about fifty feet beyond that one stone, the tallest one; he'd taken note of it as a marker, to keep his bearings. He walked out to the spot where he was sure Dolly had come down, walked slowly round the stones in a wide circle, glancing to one side and then the other in growing confusion.

Not only was the plane gone, it didn't seem ever to have been there. There was no trace, no furrow in the thick

26

meadow grass, let alone the kind of gouge in the earth that such a crash would have made. Had he been imagining its presence? Wishful thinking?

He shook his head to clear it – but in fact, it *was* clear. The buzzing and whining in his ears had stopped, and while he still had bruises and a mild headache, he was feeling much better. He walked slowly back around the stones, still looking, a growing sense of deep cold curling through his wame. It wasn't fucking there.

He woke in the morning without the slightest notion where he was. He was curled up on grass; that much came dimly to him – he could smell it. Grass that cattle had been grazing, because there was a large cow-pat just by him, and fresh enough to smell that, too. He stretched out a leg, cautious. Then an arm. Rolled onto his back, and felt a hair better for having something solid under him, though the sky overhead was a dizzy void.

It was a soft, pale blue void, too. Not a trace of cloud.

How long . . . ?! A jolt of alarm brought him up onto his knees, but a bright yellow stab of pain behind his eyes sat him down again, moaning and cursing breathlessly.

Once more. He waited 'til his breath was coming steady, then risked cracking one eye open.

Well, it was certainly still Northumbria, the northern part, where England's billowing fields crash onto the inhospitable rocks of Scotland. He recognised the rolling hills, covered with sere grass and punctuated by towering rocks that shot straight up into sudden toothy crags. He swallowed, and rubbed both hands hard over his head and face, assuring himself he was still real. He didn't feel real. Even after he'd taken a careful count of fingers, toes, and private bits – counting the last twice, just in case – he still

27

felt that something important had been misplaced, torn off somehow, and left behind.

His ears still rang, rather like they did after a specially active trip. Why, though? What had he heard?

He found that he could move a little more easily now, and managed to look all round the sky, sector by sector. Nothing up there. No memory of anything up there. And yet the inside of his head buzzed and jangled, and the flesh on his body rippled with agitation. He chafed his arms, hard, to make it go.

Horripilation. That's the proper word for gooseflesh; Dolly'd told him that. She kept a little notebook and wrote down words she came across in her reading; she was a great one for the reading. She'd already got wee Roger sitting in her lap to be read to after tea, round-eyed as Bonzo at the coloured pictures in his rag-book.

Thought of his family got him up onto his feet, swaying, but all right now, better, yes, definitely better, though he still felt as though his skin didn't quite fit. The plane, where was that?

He looked round him. No plane was visible. Anywhere. Then it came back to him, with a lurch of the stomach. Real, it was real. He'd been sure in the night that he was dreaming or hallucinating, had lain down to recover himself, and must have fallen asleep. But he was awake now, no mistake; there was a bug of some kind down his back, and he slapped viciously to try to squash it.

His heart was pounding unpleasantly and his palms were sweating. He wiped them on his trousers, and scanned the landscape. It wasn't flat, but neither did it offer much concealment. No trees, no bosky dells. There was a small lake off in the distance – he caught the shine of water – but if he'd ditched in water, surely to God he'd be wet?

Maybe he'd been unconscious long enough to dry out,

28

he thought. Maybe he'd imagined that he'd seen the plane near the stones. Surely he couldn't have walked this far from the lake and forgotten it? He'd started walking toward the lake, out of sheer inability to think of anything more useful to do. Clearly time had passed; the sky had cleared like magic. Well, they'd have little trouble finding him, at least; they knew he was near the wall. A truck should be along soon; he couldn't be more than two hours from the airfield.

'And a good thing, too,' he muttered. He'd picked a specially God-forsaken spot to crash – there wasn't a farmhouse or a paddock anywhere in sight, not so much as a sniff of chimney-smoke.

His head was becoming clearer now. He'd circle the lake – just in case – then head for the road. Might meet the support crew coming in.

'And tell them I've lost the bloody plane?' he asked himself aloud. 'Aye, right. Come on, ye wee idjit, think! Now, where did ye see it last?'

He walked for a long time. Slowly, because of the knee, but that began to feel easier after a while. His mind was not feeling easier. There was something wrong with the countryside. Granted, Northumbria was a ragged sort of place, but not *this* ragged. He'd found a road – but it wasn't the B road he'd seen from the air. It was a dirt track, pocked with stones and showing signs of being much travelled by hooved animals with a heavily fibrous diet.

Wished he hadn't thought of diet. His wame was flapping against his backbone. Thinking about breakfast was better than thinking about other things, though, and for a time, he amused himself by envisioning the powdered

29

eggs and soggy toast he'd have got in the mess, then going on to the lavish breakfasts of his youth in the Highlands: huge bowls of steaming parritch, slices of black pudding fried in lard, bannocks with marmalade, gallons of hot strong tea . . .

An hour later, he found Hadrian's Wall. Hard to miss, even grown over with grass and all-sorts like it was. It marched stolidly along, just like the Roman Legions who'd built it, stubbornly workmanlike, a grey seam stitching its way up hill and down dale, dividing the peaceful fields to the south from those marauding buggers up north. He grinned at the thought and sat down on the wall – it was less than a yard high, just here – to massage his knee.

He hadn't found the plane, or anything else, and was beginning to doubt his own sense of reality. He'd seen a fox, any number of rabbits, and a pheasant who'd nearly given him heart failure by bursting out from right under his feet. No people at all, though, and that was giving him a queer feeling in his water.

Aye, there was a war on, right enough, and many of the menfolk were gone, but the farmhouses hadn't been sacrificed to the war effort, had they? The women were running the farms, feeding the nation, all that – he'd heard the PM on the radio praising them for it only last week. So where the bloody hell was everybody?

The sun was getting low in the sky when at last he saw a house. It was flush against the wall, and struck him as somehow familiar, though he knew he'd never seen it before. Stone-built and squat, but quite large, with a ratty-looking thatch. There was smoke coming from the chimney, though, and he limped toward it as fast as he could go.

There was a person outside – a woman in a ragged long

dress and an apron, feeding chickens. He shouted, and she looked up, her mouth falling open at the sight of him.

'Hey,' he said, breathless from hurry. 'I've had a crash. I need help. Are ye on the phone, maybe?'

She didn't answer. She dropped the basket of chicken feed and ran right away, round the corner of the house. He sighed in exasperation. Well, maybe she'd gone to fetch her husband. He didn't see any sign of a vehicle, not so much as a tractor, but maybe the man was—

The man was tall, stringy, bearded, and snaggle-toothed. He was also dressed in a dirty shirt and baggy short pants that showed his hairy legs and bare feet – and accompanied by two other men in similar comic attire. Jerry instantly interpreted the looks on their faces, and didn't stay to laugh.

'Hey, nay problem, mate,' he said, backing up, hands out. 'I'm off, right?'

They kept coming, slowly, spreading out to surround him. He hadn't liked the looks of them to start with, and was liking them less by the second. Hungry, they looked, with a speculative glitter in their eyes.

One of them said something to him, a question of some kind, but the Northumbrian accent was too thick for him to catch more than a word. 'Who' was the word, and he hastily pulled his dog-tags from the neck of his blouson, waving the red and green disks at them. One of the men smiled, but not in a nice way.

'Look,' he said, still backing up. 'I didna mean to—'

The man in the lead reached out a horny hand and took hold of his forearm. He jerked back, but the man, instead of letting go, punched him in the belly.

He could feel his mouth opening and shutting like a fish's, but no air came in. He flailed wildly, but they all were on him then. They were calling out to each other, and he didn't understand a word, but the intent was plain as the nose he managed to butt with his head.

It was the only blow he landed. Within two minutes, he'd been efficiently beaten into pudding, had his pockets rifled, been stripped of his jacket and dog-tags, frog-marched down the road and heaved bodily down a steep, rocky slope.

He rolled, bouncing from one outcrop to the next, until he managed to fling out an arm and grab onto a scrubby thornbush. He came to a scraping halt and lay with his face in a clump of heather, panting and thinking incongruously of taking Dolly to the pictures, just before he'd joined up. They'd seen *The Wizard of Oz*, and he was beginning to feel creepily like the lass in that film – maybe it was the resemblance of the Northumbrians to scarecrows and lions.

'At least the fucking lion spoke English,' he muttered, sitting up. 'Jesus, now what?'

It occurred to him that it might be a good time to stop cursing and start praying.

London, two years later

She'd been home from her work no more than five minutes. Just in time to meet Roger's mad charge across the floor, shrieking 'MUMMY!', she pretending to be staggered by his impact – not so much a pretence; he was getting big. Just time to call out to her own mum, hear the muffled reply from the kitchen, sniff hopefully for the comforting smell of tea and catch a tantalising whiff of tinned sardines that made her mouth water – a rare treat.

Just time to sit down for what seemed the first time in days, and take off her high-heeled shoes, relief washing over her feet like seawater when the tide comes in. She noticed with dismay the hole in the heel of her stocking, though. Her last pair, too. She was just undoing her garter, thinking that she'd have to start using leg-tan like Maisie, drawing a careful seam up the back of each leg with an eyebrow pencil, when there came a knock at the door.

'Mrs MacKenzie?' The man who stood at the door of her mother's flat was tall, a dark silhouette in the dimness of the hall, but she knew at once he was a soldier.

'Yes?' She couldn't help the leap of her heart, the clench of her stomach. She tried frantically to damp it down, deny it, the hope that had sprung up like a struck match. A mistake. There'd been a mistake. He hadn't been killed, he'd been lost somehow, maybe captured, and now they'd found hi— then she saw the small box in the soldier's hand and her legs gave way under her.

Her vision sparkled at the edges, and the stranger's face swam above her, blurred with concern. She could hear, though – hear her mum rush through from the kitchen, slippers slapping in her haste, voice raised in agitation. Heard the man's name, Captain Randall, Frank Randall. Hear Roger's small husky voice warm in her ear, saying 'Mummy? Mummy?' in confusion.

Then she was on the swaybacked davenport, holding a cup of hot water that smelled of tea – they could only change the tea-leaves once a week, and this was Friday, she thought irrelevantly. He should have come on Sunday, her mum was saying, they could have given him a decent cuppa. But perhaps he didn't work on Sundays?

Her mum had put Captain Randall in the best chair, near the electric fire, and had switched on two bars as a sign of hospitality. Her mother was chatting with the captain, holding Roger in her lap. Her son was more interested in the little box sitting on the tiny pie-crust table; he kept reaching for it, but his grandmother wouldn't let him have it. Marjorie recognised the intent look on his face.

33

He wouldn't throw a fit – he hardly ever did – but he wouldn't give up, either.

He didn't look a lot like his father, save when he wanted something badly. She pulled herself up a bit, shaking her head to clear the dizziness, and Roger looked up at her, distracted by her movement. For an instant, she saw Jerry look out of his eyes, and the world swam afresh. She closed her own, though, and gulped her tea, scalding as it was.

Mum and Captain Randall had been talking politely, giving her time to recover herself. Did he have children of his own? Mum asked.

'No,' he said, with what might have been a wistful look at wee Roger. 'Not yet. I haven't seen my wife in two years.'

'Better late than never,' said a sharp voice, and she was surprised to discover that it was hers. She put down the cup, pulled up the loose stocking that had puddled round her ankle and fixed Captain Randall with a look. 'What have you brought me?' she said, trying for a tone of calm dignity. Didn't work; she sounded brittle as broken glass, even to her own ears.

Captain Randall eyed her cautiously, but took up the little box and held it out to her.

'It's Lieutenant MacKenzie's,' he said. 'An MID oakleaf cluster. Awarded posthumously for—'

With an effort, she pushed herself away, back into the cushions, shaking her head.

'I don't want it.'

'Really, Marjorie!' Her mother was shocked.

'And I don't like that word. Pos— posth— don't say it.'

She couldn't overcome the notion that Jerry was somehow inside the box – a notion that seemed dreadful at one moment, comforting the next. Captain Randall set it down, very slowly, as though it might blow up.

34

'I won't say it,' he said gently. 'May I say, though . . . I knew him. Your husband. Very briefly, but I did know him. I came myself, because I wanted to say to you how very brave he was.'

'Brave.' The word was like a pebble in her mouth. She wished she could spit it at him.

'Of course he was,' her mother said firmly. 'Hear that, Roger? Your dad was a good man, and he was a brave one. You won't forget that.'

Roger was paying no attention, struggling to get down. His gran set him reluctantly on the floor and he lurched over to Captain Randall, taking a firm grip on the captain's fresh-creased trousers with both hands – hands greasy, she saw, with sardine oil and toast crumbs. The captain's lips twitched, but he didn't try to detach Roger, just patted his head.

'Who's a good boy, then?' he asked.

'Fith,' Roger said firmly. 'Fith!'

Marjorie felt an incongruous impulse to laugh at the captain's puzzled expression, though it didn't touch the stone in her heart.

'It's his new word,' she said. 'Fish. He can't say "sardine".'

'Thar . . . DEEM!' Roger said, glaring at her. 'Fitttthhhhh!'

The captain laughed out loud, and pulling out a handkerchief, carefully wiped the spittle off Roger's face, casually going on to wipe the grubby little paws as well.

'Of course it's a fish,' he assured Roger. 'You're a clever lad. And a big help to your mummy, I'm sure. Here, I've brought you something for your tea.' He groped in the pocket of his coat and pulled out a small pot of jam. Strawberry jam. Marjorie's salivary glands contracted painfully. With the sugar rationing, she hadn't tasted jam in . . .

'He's a great help,' her mother put in stoutly, determined to keep the conversation on a proper plane despite her daughter's peculiar behaviour. She avoided Marjorie's eye. 'A lovely boy. His name's Roger.'

'Yes, I know.' He glanced at Marjorie, who'd made a brief movement. 'Your husband told me. He was—'

'Brave. You told me.' Suddenly something snapped. It was her half-hooked garter, but the pop of it made her sit up straight, fists clenched in the thin fabric of her skirt. 'Brave,' she repeated. 'They're all brave, aren't they? Every single one. Even you – or are you?'

She heard her mother's gasp, but went on anyway, reckless.

'You all have to be brave and noble and— and— perfect, don't you? Because if you were weak, if there were any cracks, if anyone looked like being not quite the thing, you know – well, it might all fall apart, mightn't it? So none of you will, will you? Or if somebody did, the rest of you would cover it up. You won't ever not do something, no matter what it is, because you can't not do it; all the other chaps would think the worse of you, wouldn't they, and we can't have that, oh, no, we can't have that!'

Captain Randall was looking at her intently, his eyes dark with concern. Probably thought she was a nutter – probably she was, but what did it matter?

'Marjie, Marjie, love,' her mother was murmuring, horribly embarrassed. 'You oughn't to say such things to—'

'You made him do it, didn't you?' She was on her feet now, looming over the captain, making him look up at her. 'He told me. He told me about you. You came and asked him to do— whatever it was that got him killed. Oh, don't trouble yourself, he didn't tell me your bloody precious secrets – not him, he wouldn't do that. He was a flier.' She was panting with rage and had to stop to draw breath. Roger, she saw dimly, had shrunk into himself

36

and was clinging to the captain's leg; Randall put an arm about the boy automatically, as though to shelter him from his mother's wrath. With an effort she made herself stop shouting, and to her horror, felt tears begin to course down her face.

'And now you come and bring me— and bring me . . .'

'Marjie.' Her mother came up close beside her, her body warm and soft and comforting in her worn old pinny. She thrust a tea-towel into Marjorie's hands, then moved between her daughter and the enemy, solid as a battleship.

'It's kind of you to've brought us this, captain,' Marjorie heard her saying, and felt her move away, bending to pick up the little box. Marjorie sat down blindly, pressing the tea-towel to her face, hiding.

'Here, Roger, look. See how it opens? See how pretty? It's called— what did you say it was again, captain? Oh, oakleaf cluster. Yes, that's right. Can you say "medal", Roger? Meh-dul. This is your dad's medal.'

Roger didn't say anything. Probably scared stiff, poor little chap. She had to pull herself together. But she'd gone too far. She couldn't stop.

'He cried when he left me,' she muttered the secret into the folds of the tea-towel. 'He didn't want to go.' Her shoulders heaved with a convulsive, unexpected sob and she pressed the towel hard against her eyes, whispering to herself. 'You said you'd come back, Jerry, you said you'd come *back*.'

She stayed hidden behind her flour-sacking fortress, while renewed offers of tea were made and, to her vague surprise, accepted. She'd thought Captain Randall would seize the chance of her retreat to make his own. But he stayed, chatting calmly with her mother, talking slowly to Roger while her mother fetched the tea, ignoring her embarrassing performance entirely, keeping up a quiet, companionable presence in the shabby room.

The rattle and bustle of the tea-tray's arrival gave her the opportunity to drop her cloth façade, and she meekly accepted a slice of toast spread with a thin scrape of margarine and a delectable spoonful of the strawberry jam.

'There, now,' her mother said, looking on with approval. 'You'll not have eaten anything since breakfast, I daresay. Enough to give anyone the wambles.'

Marjorie shot her mother a look, but in fact it was true; she hadn't had any luncheon because Maisie was off with 'female trouble' – a condition that afflicted her roughly every other week – and she'd had to mind the shop all day.

Conversation flowed comfortably around her, a soothing stream past an immoveable rock. Even Roger relaxed with the introduction of jam. He'd never tasted any before, and sniffed it curiously, took a cautious lick – and then took an enormous bite that left a red smear on his nose, his moss-green eyes round with wonder and delight. The little box, now open, sat on the pie-crust table, but no one spoke of it or looked in that direction.

After a decent interval, Captain Randall got up to go, giving Roger a shiny sixpence in parting. Feeling it the least she could do, Marjorie got up to see him out. Her stockings spiralled down her legs, and she kicked them off with contempt, walking bare-legged to the door. She heard her mother sigh behind her.

'Thank you,' she said, opening the door for him. 'I . . . appreciate—'

To her surprise, he stopped her, putting a hand on her arm.

'I've no particular right to say this to you – but I will,' he said, low-voiced. 'You're right; they're not all brave. Most of them – of us – we're just . . . there, and we do our best. Most of the time,' he added, and the corner of his mouth lifted slightly, though she couldn't tell whether it was in humour or bitterness.

'But your husband—' He closed his eyes for a moment and said, 'The bravest are surely those who have the clearest vision of what is before them, glory and danger alike, and yet notwithstanding, go out to meet it. He did that, every day, for a long time.'

'You sent him, though,' she said, her voice as low as his. 'You did.'

His smile was bleak.

'I've done such things every day . . . for a long time.'

The door closed quietly behind him, and she stood there swaying, eyes closed, feeling the draught come under it, chilling her bare feet. It was well into the autumn now, and the dark was smudging the windows, though it was just past tea-time.

I've done what I do every day for a long time, too, she thought. *But they don't call it brave when you don't have a choice.*

Her mother was moving through the flat, muttering to herself as she closed the curtains. Or not so much to herself.

'He liked her. Anyone could see that. So kind, coming himself to bring the medal and all. And how does she act? Like a cat that's had its tail stepped on, all claws and caterwauling, that's how. How does she ever expect a man to—'

'I don't want a man,' Marjorie said loudly. Her mother turned round, squat, solid, implacable.

'You need a man, Marjorie. And little Rog needs a father.'

'He has a father,' she said through her teeth. 'Captain Randall has a wife. And I don't need anyone.'

Anyone but Jerry.

39

He licked his lips at the smell. Hot pastry, steaming, juicy meat. There was a row of fat little pasties ranged along the sill, covered with a clean cloth in case of birds, but showing plump and rounded through it, the odd spot of gravy soaking through the napkin.

His mouth watered so fiercely that his salivary glands ached and he had to massage the underside of his jaw to ease the pain.

It was the first house he'd seen in two days. Once he'd got out of the ravine, he'd circled well away from the mile-castle and eventually struck a small cluster of cottages, where the people were no more understandable, but did give him some food. That had lasted him a little while; beyond that, he'd been surviving on what he could glean from hedges and the odd vegetable patch. He'd found another hamlet, but the folk there had driven him away.

Once he'd got enough of a grip of himself to think clearly, it became obvious that he needed to go back to the standing stones. Whatever had happened to him had happened there, and if he really *was* somewhere in the past – and hard as he'd tried to find some alternative explanation, none was forthcoming – then his only chance of getting back where he belonged seemed to lie there, too.

He'd come well away from the drover's track, though, seeking food, and as the few people he met didn't understand him any more than he understood them, he'd had some difficulty in finding his way back to the wall. He thought he was quite close, now, though – the ragged country was beginning to seem familiar, though perhaps that was only delusion.

Everything else had faded into unimportance, though, when he smelled food.

He circled the house at a cautious distance, checking for dogs. No dog. Aye, fine, then. He chose an approach from the side, out of view of any of the few windows. Darted swiftly from bush to ploughshare to midden to house, and plastered himself against the grey stone wall, breathing hard – and breathing in that delicious, savoury aroma. Shite, he was drooling. He wiped his sleeve hastily across his mouth, slithered round the corner, and reached out a hand.

As it happened, the farmstead did boast a dog, which had been attending its absent master in the barn. Both these worthies returning unexpectedly at this point, the dog at once spotted what it assumed to be jiggery-pokery taking place, and gave tongue in an altogether proper manner. Alerted in turn to felonious activity on his premises, the householder instantly joined the affray, armed with a wooden spade, with which he batted Jerry over the head.

As he staggered back against the wall of the house, he had just wit enough left to notice that the farmwife – now sticking out of her window and shrieking like the Glasgow Express – had knocked one of the pasties to the ground, where it was being devoured by the dog, who wore an expression of piety and rewarded virtue that Jerry found really offensive.

Then the farmer hit him again, and he stopped being offended.

It was a well-built byre, the stones fitted carefully and mortared. He wore himself out with shouting and kicking at the door until his gammy leg gave way and he collapsed onto the earthen floor.

'Now bloody what?' he muttered. He was damp with

sweat from his effort, but it was cold in the byre, with that penetrating damp cold peculiar to the British Isles, that seeps into your bones and makes the joints ache. His knee would give him fits in the morning. The air was saturated with the scent of manure and chilled urine. 'Why would the bloody Jerries want the damn place?' he said, and sitting up, huddled into his shirt. It was going to be a frigging long night.

He got up onto his hands and knees and felt carefully round inside the byre, but there was nothing even faintly edible – only a scurf of mouldy hay. Not even the rats would have that; the inside of the place was empty as a drum and silent as a church.

What had happened to the cows? he wondered. Dead of a plague, eaten, sold? Or maybe just not yet back from the summer pastures – though it was late in the year for that, surely.

He sat down again, back against the door, as the wood was marginally less cold than the stone walls. He'd thought about being captured in battle, made prisoner by the Germans – they all had, now and then, though chaps mostly didn't talk about it. He thought about POW camps, and those camps in Poland, the ones he'd been meant to photograph. Were they as bleak as this? Stupid thing to think of, really.

But he'd got to pass the time 'til morning one way or another, and there were lots of things he'd rather not think about just now. Like what would happen once morning came. He didn't think breakfast in bed was going to be part of it.

The wind was rising. Whining past the corners of the cow-byre with a keening noise that set his teeth on edge. He still had his silk scarf; it had slipped down inside his shirt when the bandits in the mile-castle had attacked him. He fished it out now and wrapped it round his neck, for comfort, if not warmth.

He'd brought Dolly breakfast in bed now and then. She woke up slow and sleepy, and he loved the way she scooped her tangled curly black hair off her face, peering out slit-eyed, like a small, sweet mole blinking in the light. He'd sit her up and put the tray on the table beside her, and then he'd shuck his own clothes and crawl in bed, too, cuddling close to her soft warm skin. Sometimes sliding down in the bed, and her pretending not to notice, sipping tea or putting marmite on her toast while he burrowed under the covers and found his way up through the cottony layers of sheets and nightie. He loved the smell of her, always, but especially when he'd made love to her the night before, and she bore the strong musky scent of him between her legs.

He shifted a little, roused by the memory, but the subsequent thought – that he might never see her again – quelled him at once.

Still thinking of Dolly, though, he put his hand automatically to his pocket, and was alarmed to find no lump there. He slapped at his thigh, but failed to find the small hard bulge of the sapphire. Could he have put it in the other pocket by mistake? He delved urgently, shoving both hands deep into his pockets. No stone – but there was something in his right-hand pocket. Something powdery, almost greasy . . . what the devil?

He brought his fingers out, peering as closely at them as he could, but it was too dark to see more than a vague outline of his hand, let alone anything on it. He rubbed his fingers gingerly together; it felt something like the thick soot that builds up inside a chimney.

'Jesus,' he whispered, and put his fingers to his nose. There was a distinct smell of combustion. Not petrol-ish, at all, but a scent of burning so intense he could taste it on

43

the back of his tongue. Like something out of a volcano. What in the name of God Almighty could burn a rock and leave the man who carried it alive?

The sort of thing he'd met among the standing stones, that was what.

He'd been doing all right with the not feeling too afraid until now, but . . . he swallowed hard, and sat down again, quietly.

'Now I lay me down to sleep,' he whispered to the knees of his trousers. 'I pray the Lord my soul to keep . . .'

He did in fact sleep eventually, in spite of the cold, from simple exhaustion. He was dreaming about wee Roger, who for some reason was a grown man now, but still holding his tiny blue bear, minuscule in a broad-palmed grasp. His son was speaking to him in Gaelic, saying something urgent that he couldn't understand, and he was growing frustrated, telling Roger over and over for Christ's sake to speak English, couldn't he?

Then he heard another voice through the fog of sleep and realised that someone was in fact talking somewhere close by.

He jerked awake, struggling to grasp what was being said, and failing utterly. It took him several seconds to realise that whoever was speaking – there seemed to be two voices, hissing and muttering in argument – really was speaking in Gaelic.

He had only a smattering of it himself; his mother had had it, but— he was moving before he could complete the thought, panicked at the notion that potential assistance might get away.

'Hoy!' he bellowed, scrambling – or trying to scramble – to his feet. His much-abused knee wasn't having any, though, and gave way the instant he put weight on it, catapulting him face-first toward the door.

He twisted as he fell and hit it with his shoulder. The

44

booming thud put paid to the argument; the voices fell silent at once.

'Help! Help me!' he shouted, pounding on the door. 'Help!'

'Will ye for God's sake hush your noise?' said a low, annoyed voice on the other side of the door. 'Ye want to have them all down on us? Here, then, bring the light closer.'

This last seemed to be addressed to the voice's companion, for a faint glow shone through the gap at the bottom of the door. There was a scraping noise as the bolt was drawn, and a faint grunt of effort, then a *thunk!* as the bolt was set down against the wall. The door swung open, and Jerry blinked in a sudden shaft of light as the slide of a lantern grated open.

He turned his head aside and closed his eyes for an instant, deliberate, as he would if flying at night and momentarily blinded by a flare or by the glow of his own exhaust. When he opened them again, the two men were in the cow-byre with him, looking him over with open curiosity.

Biggish buggers, both of them, taller and broader than he was. One fair, one black-haired as Lucifer. They didn't look much alike, and yet he had the feeling that they might be related – some fleeting glimpse of bone, a similarity of expression, maybe.

'What's your name, mate?' said the dark chap, softly. Jerry felt the nip of wariness at his nape, even as he felt a thrill in the pit of his stomach. It was regular speech, perfectly understandable. A Scots accent, but—

'MacKenzie, J.W.,' he said, straightening up to attention. 'Lieutenant, Royal Air Force. Service number—'

An indescribable expression flitted across the dark bloke's face. An urge to laugh, of all bloody things, and a flare of excitement in his eyes – really striking eyes, a vivid green

45

that flashed sudden in the light. None of that mattered to Jerry; what was important was that the man plainly knew. He *knew*.

'Who are you?' he asked, urgent. 'Where d'ye come from?'

The two exchanged an unfathomable glance, and the other answered.

'Inverness.'

'Ye know what I mean!' He took a deep breath. '*When?*'

The two strangers were much of an age, but the fair one had plainly had a harder life; his face was deeply weathered and lined.

'A lang way from you,' he said quietly, and despite his own agitation, Jerry heard the note of desolation in his voice. 'From now. Lost.'

Lost. Oh, God. But still—

'Jesus. And where are we now? Wh-when?'

'Northumbria,' the dark man answered briefly, 'and I don't bloody know for sure. Look, there's no time. If anyone hears us—'

'Aye, right. Let's go, then.'

The air outside was wonderful after the smells of the cow-byre, cold and full of dying heather and turned earth. He thought he could even smell the moon, a faint green sickle above the horizon; he tasted cheese at the thought, and his mouth watered. He wiped a trickle of saliva away, and hurried after his rescuers, hobbling as fast as he could.

The farmhouse was black, a squatty black blot on the landscape. The dark bloke grabbed him by the arm as he was about to go past it, quickly licked a finger and held it up to test the wind.

'The dogs,' he explained in a whisper. 'This way.'

They circled the farmhouse at a cautious distance, and found themselves stumbling through a ploughed field.

Clods burst under Jerry's boots as he hurried to keep up, lurching on his bad knee with every step.

'Where we going?' he panted, when he thought it safe to speak.

'We're taking ye back to the stones near the lake,' the dark man said tersely. 'That has to be where ye came through.' The fair one just snorted, as though this wasn't his notion – but he didn't argue.

Hope flared up in Jerry like a bonfire. They knew what the stones were, how it worked. They'd show him how to get back!

'How— how did ye find me?' He could hardly breathe, such a pace they kept up, but had to know. The lantern was shut and he couldn't see their faces, but the dark man made a muffled sound that might have been a laugh.

'I met an auld wifie wearing your dog-tags. Very proud of them, she was.'

'Ye've got them?' Jerry gasped.

'Nay, she wouldna give them up.' It was the fair man, sounding definitely amused. 'Told us where she'd got them, though, and we followed your trail backward. Hey!' He caught Jerry's elbow, just as his foot twisted out from under him. The sound of a barking dog broke the night – some way away, but distinct. The fair man's hand clenched tight on his arm. 'Come on, then – hurry!'

Jerry had a bad stitch in his side, and his knee was all but useless by the time the little group of stones came in sight, a pale huddle in the light of the waning moon. Still, he was surprised at how near the stones were to the farmhouse; he must have circled round more than he thought in his wanderings.

'Right,' said the dark man, coming to an abrupt halt. 'This is where we leave you.'

'Ye do?' Jerry panted. 'But— but you—'

'When ye came . . . through. Did ye have anything on you? A gemstone, any jewellery?'

'Aye,' Jerry said, bewildered. 'I had a raw sapphire in my pocket. But it's gone. It's like it—'

'Like it burned up,' the blond man finished for him, grim-voiced. 'Aye. Well, so?' This last was clearly addressed to the dark man, who hesitated. Jerry couldn't see his face, but his whole body spoke of indecision. He wasn't one to dither, though – he stuck a hand into the leather pouch at his waist, pulled something out, and pressed it into Jerry's hand. It was faintly warm from the man's body, and hard in his palm. A small stone of some kind. Faceted, like the stone in a ring.

'Take this; it's a good one. When ye go through,' the dark man was speaking urgently to him, 'think about your wife, about Marjorie. Think hard; see her in your mind's eye, and walk straight through. Whatever the hell ye do, though, don't think about your son. Just your wife.'

'What?' Jerry was gob-smacked. 'How the bloody hell do you know my wife's name? And where've ye heard about my son?'

'It doesn't matter,' the man said, and Jerry saw the motion as he turned his head to look back over his shoulder.

'Damn,' said the fair one, softly. 'They're coming. There's a light.'

There was: a single light, bobbing evenly over the ground, as it would if someone carried it. But look as he might, Jerry could see no one behind it, and a violent shiver ran over him.

'*Tannasg*,' said the other man under his breath. Jerry knew that word well enough – spirit, it meant. And usually an ill-disposed one. A haunt.

'Aye, maybe.' The dark man's voice was calm. 'And maybe not. It's near Samhain, after all. Either way, ye need to go, man, and now. Remember, think of your wife.'

Jerry swallowed, his hand closing tight around the stone.

'Aye. Aye . . . right. Thanks, then,' he added awkwardly, and heard the breath of a rueful laugh from the dark man.

'Nay bother, mate,' he said. And with that, they were both off, making their way across the stubbled meadow, two lumbering shapes in the moonlight.

Heart thumping in his ears, Jerry turned toward the stones. They looked just like they'd looked before. Just stones. But the echo of what he'd heard in there . . . he swallowed. It wasn't like there was much choice.

'Dolly,' he whispered, trying to summon up a vision of his wife. 'Dolly. Dolly, help me!'

He took a hesitant step toward the stones. Another. One more. Then nearly bit his tongue off as a hand clamped down on his shoulder. He whirled, fist up, but the dark man's other hand seized his wrist.

'I love you,' the dark man said, his voice fierce. Then he was gone again, with the shoof-shoof sounds of boots in dry grass, leaving Jerry with his mouth agape.

He caught the other man's voice from the darkness, irritated, half-amused. He spoke differently from the dark man, a much thicker accent, but Jerry understood him without difficulty.

'Why did ye tell him a daft thing like that?'

And the dark one's reply, soft-spoken, in a tone that terrified him more than anything had, so far.

'Because he isn't going to make it back. It's the only chance I'll ever have. Come on.'

The day was dawning when he came to himself again, and the world was quiet. No birds sang and the air was cold with the chill of November and winter coming on. When

49

he could stand up, he went to look, shaky as a newborn lamb.

The plane wasn't there, but there was still a deep gouge in the earth where it had been. Not raw earth, though; furred over with grass and meadow plants – not just furred, he saw, limping over to have a closer look. Matted. Dead stalks from earlier years' growth.

If he'd been where he thought he'd been, if he'd truly gone . . . back . . . then he'd come forward again, but not to the same place he'd left. How long? A year, two? He sat down on the grass, too drained to stand up any longer. He felt as though he'd walked every second of the time between then and now.

He'd done what the green-eyed stranger had said. Concentrated fiercely on Dolly. But he hadn't been able to keep from thinking of wee Roger, not altogether. How could he? The picture he had most vividly of Dolly was her holding the lad, close against her breast; that's what he'd seen. And yet he'd made it. He thought he'd made it. Maybe.

What might have happened? he wondered. There hadn't been time to ask. There'd been no time to hesitate, either; more lights had come bobbing across the dark, with uncouth Northumbrian shouts behind them, hunting him, and he'd hurled himself into the midst of the standing stones and things went pear-shaped again, even worse. He hoped the strangers who'd rescued him had got away.

Lost, the fair man had said, and even now, the word went through him like a bit of jagged metal. He swallowed.

He thought he wasn't where he had been, but was he still lost, himself? Where was he now? Or rather, when?

He stayed for a bit, gathering his strength. In a few minutes, though, he heard a familiar sound – the low growl of engines, and the swish of tyres on asphalt. He swallowed hard, and standing up, turned away from the stones, toward the road.

He was lucky – for once, he thought wryly. There was a line of troop transports passing, and he swung aboard one without difficulty. The soldiers looked startled at his appearance – he was rumpled and stained, bruised and torn about and with a two-week beard – but they instantly assumed he'd been off on a tear and was now trying to sneak back to his base without being detected. They laughed and nudged him knowingly, but were sympathetic, and when he confessed he was skint, had a quick whip-round for enough cash to buy a train ticket from Salisbury, where the transport was headed.

He did his best to smile and go along with the ragging, but soon enough they tired of him and turned to their own conversations, and he was allowed to sit swaying on the bench, feeling the thrum of the engine through his legs, surrounded by the comfortable presence of comrades.

'Hey, mate,' he said casually to the young soldier beside him. 'What year is it?'

The boy – he couldn't be more than seventeen, and Jerry felt the weight of the five years between them as though they were fifty – looked at him wide-eyed, then whooped with laughter.

'What've you been having to drink, Dad? Bring any away with you?'

That led to more ragging, and he didn't try asking again.

Did it matter?

He remembered almost nothing of the journey from Salisbury to London. People looked at him oddly, but no one tried to stop him. It didn't matter; nothing mattered but getting to Dolly. Everything else could wait.

London was a shock. There was bomb damage everywhere. Streets were scattered with shattered glass from shop windows, glinting in the pale sun, other streets blocked off by barriers. Here and there a stark black notice: Do Not Enter – UNEXPLODED BOMB.

He made his way from St Pancras on foot, needing to see, his heart rising into his throat fit to choke him as he did see what had been done. After a while, he stopped seeing the details, perceiving bomb-craters and debris only as blocks to his progress, things stopping him from reaching home.

And then he did reach home.

The rubble had been pushed off the street into a heap, but not taken away. Great blackened lumps of shattered stone and concrete lay like a cairn where Montrose Terrace had once stood.

All the blood in his heart stopped dead, congealed by the sight. He groped, pawing mindlessly for the wrought-iron railing to keep himself from falling, but it wasn't there.

Of course not, his mind said, quite calmly. It's gone for the war, hasn't it? Melted down, made into planes. Bombs.

His knee gave way without warning, and he fell, landing hard on both knees, not feeling the impact, the crunch of pain from his badly mended kneecap quite drowned out by the blunt small voice inside his head.

Too late. Ye went too far.

'Mr MacKenzie, Mr MacKenzie!' He blinked at the blurred thing above him, not understanding what it was.

Something tugged at him, though, and he breathed, the rush of air in his chest ragged and strange.

'Sit up, Mr MacKenzie, do.' The anxious voice was still there, and hands – yes, it was hands – tugging at his arm. He shook his head, screwed his eyes shut hard, then opened them again, and the round thing became the hound-like face of old Mr Wardlaw, who kept the corner shop.

'Ah, there you are.' The old man's voice was relieved, and the wrinkles in his baggy old face relaxed their anxious lines. 'Had a bad turn, did you?'

'I—' Speech was beyond him, but he flapped his hand at the wreckage. He didn't think he was crying, but his face was wet. The wrinkles in Wardlaw's face creased deeper in concern, then the old grocer realised what he meant, and his face lit up.

'Oh, dear!' he said. 'Oh, no! No, no, no – they're all right, sir, your family's all right! Did you hear me?' he asked anxiously. 'Can you breathe? Had I best fetch you some salts, do you think?'

It took Jerry several tries to make it to his feet, hampered both by his knee and by Mr Wardlaw's fumbling attempts to help him, but by the time he'd got all the way up, he'd regained the power of speech.

'Where?' he gasped. 'Where are they?'

'Why – your missus took the little boy and went to stay with her mother, sometime after you left. I don't recall quite where she said . . .' Mr Wardlaw turned, gesturing vaguely in the direction of the river. 'Camberwell, was it?'

'Bethnal Green.' Jerry's mind had come back, though it felt still as though it was a pebble rolling round the rim of some bottomless abyss, its balance uncertain. He tried to dust himself off, but his hands were shaking. 'She lives in Bethnal Green. You're sure – you're sure, man?'

'Yes, yes.' The grocer was altogether relieved, smiling

53

and nodding so hard that his jowls trembled. 'She left – must be more than a year ago, soon after she – soon after she . . .' The old man's smile faded abruptly and his mouth slowly opened, a flabby dark hole of horror.

'But you're dead, Mr MacKenzie,' he whispered, backing away, hands held up before him. 'Oh, God. You're dead.'

'The fuck I am, the fuck I am, the *fuck* I am!' He caught sight of a woman's startled face and stopped abruptly, gulping air like a landed fish. He'd been weaving down the shattered street, fists pumping, limping and staggering, muttering his private motto under his breath like the Hail Marys of a rosary. Maybe not as far under his breath as he'd thought.

He stopped, leaning against the marble front of the Bank of England, panting. He was streaming with sweat and the right leg of his trousers was heavily streaked with dried blood from the fall. His knee was throbbing in time with his heart, his face, his hands, his thoughts. *They're alive. So am I.*

The woman he'd startled was down the street, talking to a policeman; she turned, pointing at him. He straightened up at once, squaring his shoulders. Braced his knee and gritted his teeth, forcing it to bear his weight as he strode down the street, officer-like. The very last thing he wanted just now was to be taken up as drunk.

He marched past the policeman, nodding politely, touching his forehead in lieu of cap. The policeman looked taken aback, made to speak but couldn't quite decide what to say, and a moment later, Jerry was round the corner and away.

It was getting dark. There weren't many cabs in this

54

area at the best of times – none at all, now, and he hadn't any money, anyway. The Tube. If the lines were open, it was the fastest way to Bethnal Green. And surely he could cadge the fare from someone. Somehow. He went back to limping, grimly determined. He had to reach Bethnal Green by dark.

It was so much changed. Like the rest of London. Houses damaged, halfway repaired, abandoned, others no more than a blackened depression or a heap of rubble. The air was thick with coal dust, stone dust, and the smells of paraffin and cooking grease, the brutal, acrid smell of cordite.

Half the streets had no signs, and he wasn't so familiar with Bethnal Green to begin with. He'd visited Dolly's mother just twice, once when they went to tell her they'd run off and got married – she hadn't been best pleased, Mrs Wakefield, but she'd put a good face on it, even if the face had a lemon-sucking look to it.

The second time had been when he signed up with the RAF; he'd gone alone to tell her, to ask her to look after Dolly while he was gone. Dolly's mother had gone white. She knew as well as he did what the life-expectancy was for fliers. But she'd told him she was proud of him, and held his hand tight for a long moment before she let him leave, saying only, 'Come back, Jeremiah. She needs you.'

He soldiered on, skirting craters in the street, asking his way. It was nearly full dark, now; he couldn't be on the streets much longer. His anxiety began to ease a little as he started to see things he knew, though. Close, he was getting close.

And then the sirens began, and people began to pour out of the houses.

55

He was being buffeted by the crowd, borne down the street as much by their barely controlled panic as by their physical impact. There was shouting, people calling for separated family members, wardens bellowing directions, waving their torches, their flat white helmets pale as mushrooms in the gloom. Above it, through it, the air-raid siren pierced him like a sharpened wire, thrust him down the street on its spike, ramming him into others likewise skewered by fright.

The tide of it swept round the next corner and he saw the red circle with its blue line over the entrance to the Tube station, lit up by a warden's flashlight. He was sucked in, propelled through sudden bright lights, hurtling down the stair, the next, onto a platform, deep into the earth, into safety. And all the time the whoop and moan of the sirens still filling the air, barely muffled by the dirt above.

There were wardens moving among the crowd, pushing people back against the walls, into the tunnels, away from the edge of the track. He brushed up against a woman with two toddlers, picked one – a little girl with round eyes and a blue teddy-bear – out of her arms and turned his shoulder into the crowd, making a way for them. He found a small space in a tunnel-mouth, pushed the woman into it and gave her back the little girl. Her mouth moved in thanks, but he couldn't hear her above the noise of the crowd, the sirens, the creaking, the—

A sudden monstrous thud from above shook the station, and the whole crowd was struck silent, every eye on the high arched ceiling above them.

The tiles were white, and as they looked, a dark crack appeared suddenly between two rows of them. A gasp rose from the crowd, louder than the sirens. The crack seemed to stop, to hesitate – and then it zig-zagged suddenly, parting the tiles, in different directions.

He looked down from the growing crack, to see who was below it – the people still on the stair. The crowd at the bottom was too thick to move, everyone stopped still by horror. And then he saw her, partway up the stair.

Dolly. *She's cut her hair*, he thought. It was short and curly, black as soot – black as the hair of the little boy she held in her arms, close against her, sheltering him. Her face was set, jaw clenched. And then she turned a bit, and saw him.

Her face went blank for an instant and then flared like a lit match, with a radiant joy that struck him in the heart and flamed through his being.

There was a much louder *thud!* from above, and a scream of terror rose from the crowd, louder, much louder than the sirens. Despite the shrieking, he could hear the fine rattle, like rain, as dirt began to pour from the crack above. He shoved with all his might, but couldn't get past, couldn't reach them. Dolly looked up, and he saw her jaw set hard again, her eyes blaze with determination. She shoved the man in front of her, who stumbled and fell down a step, squashing into the people in front of him. She swung Roger down into the little space she'd made, and with a twist of shoulders and the heave of her whole body, hurled the little boy up, over the rail – toward Jerry.

He saw what she was doing and was already leaning, pushing forward, straining to reach . . . the boy struck him high in the chest like a lump of concrete, little head smashing painfully into Jerry's face, knocking his head back. He had one arm round the child, falling back on the people behind him, struggling to find his footing, get a firmer hold – and then something gave way in the crowd around him, he staggered into an open space, and then his knee gave way and he plunged over the lip of the track.

He didn't hear the crack of his head against the rail or

the screams of the people above; it was all lost in a roar like the end of the world as the roof over the stair fell in.

The little boy was still as death, but he wasn't dead; Jerry could feel his heart beat, thumping fast against his own chest. It was all he could feel. Poor little bugger must have had his wind knocked out.

People had stopped screaming, but there was still shouting, calling out. There was a strange silence underneath all the racket. His blood had stopped pounding through his head, his own heart no longer hammering. Perhaps that was it.

The silence underneath felt alive, somehow. Peaceful, but like sunlight on water, moving, glittering. He could still hear the noises above the silence, feet running, anxious voices, bangs and creakings – but he was sinking gently into the silence; the noises grew distant, though he could still hear voices.

'Is that one—?'

'Nay, he's gone – look at his head, poor chap, caved in something horrid. The boy's well enough, I think, just bumps and scratches. Here, lad, come up . . . no, no, let go, now. It's all right, just let go. Let me pick you up, yes, that's good, it's all right now, hush, hush, there's a good boy . . .'

'What a look on that bloke's face. I never saw anything like—'

'Here, take the little chap. I'll see if the bloke's got any identification.'

'Come on, big man, yeah, that's it, that's it, come with me. Hush now, it's all right, it's all right . . . is that your daddy, then?'

'No tags, no service book. Funny, that. He's RAF, though, isn't he? AWOL, d'ye think?'

He could hear Dolly laughing at that, felt her hand stroke his

58

hair. He smiled and turned his head to see her smiling back, the radiant joy spreading round her like rings in shining water . . .

'Rafe! The rest of it's going! Run! *Run!*'

AUTHOR'S NOTES

Before y'all get tangled up in your underwear about it being All Hallow's Eve when Jeremiah leaves, and 'nearly Samhain (aka All Hallow's Eve)' when he returns – bear in mind that Great Britain changed from the Julian to the Gregorian calendar in 1752, this resulting in a 'loss' of twelve days. And for those of you who'd like to know more about the two men who rescue him, more of their story can be found in *An Echo in the Bone*.

'Never have so many owed so much to so few.' This was Winston Churchill's acknowledgement to the RAF pilots who protected Britain during World War II – and he was about right.

Adolph Gysbert Malan – known as 'Sailor' (probably because 'Adolph' was not a popular name at the time) – was a South African flying ace who became the leader of the famous No. 74 Squadron RAF. He was known for sending German bomber pilots home with dead crews, to demoralise the Luftwaffe, and I would have mentioned this gruesomely fascinating detail in the story, had there been any good way of getting it in, but there wasn't. His 'Ten Commandments' for Air Fighting are as given in the text.

59

While the mission that Captain Frank Randall recruits Jerry MacKenzie for is fictional, the situation wasn't. The Nazis did have labour camps in Poland long before anyone in the rest of Europe became aware of them, and the eventual revelation did much to rally anti-Nazi feeling.

I'd like particularly to acknowledge the assistance of Maria Szybek in the delicate matter of Polish vulgarities (any errors in grammar, spelling, or accent marks are entirely mine), and of Douglas Watkins in the technical descriptons of small-plane manoeuvres (also the valuable suggestion of the malfunction that brought Jerry's Spitfire down).

The Custom of the Army

Introduction to
The Custom of the Army

One of the pleasures of writing historical fiction is that the best parts aren't made up. This particular story came about as the result of my having read Wendy Moore's excellent biography of Dr John Hunter, *The Knife Man* – and my having read at the same time a brief facsimile book printed by the National Park Service, detailing regulations of the British Army during the American Revolution.

I wasn't *looking* for anything in particular in either of these books, just reading for background, general information on the period – and the always-alluring chance of stumbling across something fascinating, like electric eel parties in London (these, along with Dr Hunter himself – who appears briefly in this story – are a matter of historical record).

As for British Army regulations, a little of that stuff goes a long way; as a novelist, you want to resist the temptation to tell people things just because you happen to know them. Still, that book too had its little nuggets, such as the information that the word 'bomb' was common in the eighteenth century, and what they meant by that: in addition to merely meaning 'an explosive device', it referred also to a wrapped and tarred parcel of shrapnel shot from a cannon (though we must be careful not to use the word 'shrapnel', as it's derived from Lt Henry Shrapnel of the Royal Artillery, who took the original 'bomb' concept and developed the 'shrapnel shell', a debris-filled bomb filled also with gunpowder and designed to explode in mid-air after being fired from a cannon. Unfortunately, he did this in 1784, which was inconvenient, as 'shrapnel' is a pretty good word to have when writing about warfare).

Among the other bits of interesting trivia, though, I was struck by a brief description of the procedure for courts-martial: *'The custom of the army is that a court-martial be presided over by a senior officer and such a number of other officers as he shall think fit to serve as council, these being generally four in number, but can be more but not generally less than three . . . The person accused shall have the right to call witnesses in his support, and the council shall question these, as well as any other persons whom they may wish, and shall thus determine the circumstances, and if conviction ensue, the sentence to be imposed.'*

And that was it. No elaborate procedures for the introduction of evidence, no standards for conviction, no sentencing guidelines, no requirements for who could or should serve as 'council' to a court-martial, just 'the custom of the army'. The phrase – rather obviously – stuck in my head.

The Custom of the Army

All things considered, it was probably the fault of the electric eel. John Grey could – and for a time, did – blame the Honourable Caroline Woodford as well. And the surgeon. And certainly that blasted poet. Still . . . no, it was the eel's fault.

The party had been at Lucinda Joffrey's house. Sir Richard was absent; a diplomat of his stature could not have countenanced something so frivolous. Electric eel parties were a mania in London just now, but owing to the scarcity of the creatures, a private party was a rare occasion. Most such parties were held at public theatres, with the fortunate few selected for encounter with the eel summoned onstage, there to be shocked and sent reeling like nine-pins for the entertainment of the audience.

'The record is forty-two at once!' Caroline had told him, her eyes wide and shining as she looked up from the creature in its tank.

'Really?' It was one of the most peculiar things he'd seen, though not very striking. Nearly three feet long, it had a heavy, squarish body with a blunt head that looked to have been inexpertly moulded out of sculptor's clay, and tiny eyes like dull glass beads. It had little in common with the lashing, lithesome eels of the fish-market – and certainly did not seem capable of felling forty-two people at once.

The thing had no grace at all, save for a small thin ruffle

of a fin that ran the length of its lower body, undulating as a gauze curtain does in the wind. Lord John expressed this observation to the Honourable Caroline, and was accused in consequence of being poetic.

'Poetic?' said an amused voice behind him. 'Is there no end to our gallant major's talents?'

Lord John turned, with an inward grimace and an outward smile and bowed to Edwin Nicholls.

'I should not think of trespassing upon your province, Mr Nicholls,' he said politely.

Nicholls wrote execrable verse, mostly upon the subject of love, and was much admired by young women of a certain turn of mind. The Honourable Caroline wasn't one of them; she'd written a very clever parody of his style, though Grey thought Nicholls had not heard about it. He hoped not.

'Oh, don't you?' Nicholls raised one honey-coloured brow at him, and glanced briefly but meaningfully at Miss Woodford. His tone was jocular, but his look was not, and Grey wondered just how much Mr Nicholls had had to drink. Nicholls was flushed of cheek and glittering of eye, but that might be only the heat of the room, which was considerable, and the excitement of the party.

'Do you think of composing an ode to our friend?' Grey asked, ignoring Nicholls's allusion and gesturing toward the large tank that contained the eel.

Nicholls laughed, too loudly – yes, quite a bit the worse for drink – and waved a dismissive hand.

'No, no, Major. How could I think of expending my energies upon such a gross and insignificant creature, when there are angels of delight such as this to inspire me?' He leered – Grey did not wish to impugn the fellow, but he undeniably leered – at Miss Woodford, who smiled – with compressed lips – and tapped him rebukingly with her fan.

Where was Caroline's uncle? Grey wondered. Simon Woodford shared his niece's interest in natural history, and would certainly have escorted her . . . Oh, there. Simon Woodford was deep in discussion with Mr Hunter, the famous surgeon – what had possessed Lucinda to invite *him*? Then he caught sight of Lucinda, viewing Mr Hunter over her fan with narrowed eyes, and realised that she *hadn't* invited him.

John Hunter was a famous surgeon – and an infamous anatomist. Rumour had it that he would stop at nothing to bag a particularly desirable body, whether human or not. He did move in society, but not in the Joffreys' circles.

Lucinda Joffrey had most expressive eyes. Her one claim to beauty, they were almond-shaped, amber in colour, and capable of sending remarkably minatory messages across a crowded room.

Come here! they said. Grey smiled and lifted his glass in salute to her, but made no move to obey. The eyes narrowed further, gleaming dangerously, then cut abruptly toward the surgeon, who was edging toward the tank, his face alight with curiosity and acquisitiveness.

The eyes whipped back to Grey.

Get rid of him! they said.

Grey glanced at Miss Woodford. Mr Nicholls had seized her hand in his and appeared to be declaiming something; she looked as though she wanted the hand back. Grey looked back at Lucinda and shrugged, with a small gesture toward Mr Nicholls's ochre-velvet back, expressing regret that social responsibility prevented his carrying out her order.

'Not only the face of an angel,' Nicholls was saying, squeezing Caroline's fingers so hard that she squeaked, 'but the skin as well.' He stroked her hand, the leer

67

intensifying. 'What do angels smell like in the morning, I wonder?'

Grey measured him up thoughtfully. One more remark of that sort, and he might be obliged to invite Mr Nicholls to step outside. Nicholls was tall and heavily built, outweighed Grey by a couple of stone, and had a reputation for bellicosity. *Best try to break his nose first*, Grey thought, shifting his weight, *then run him head-first into a hedge. He won't come back in if I make a mess of him.*

'What are you looking at?' Nicholls inquired unpleasantly, catching Grey's gaze upon him.

Grey was saved from reply by a loud clapping of hands – the eel's proprietor calling the party to order. Miss Woodford took advantage of the distraction to snatch her hand away, cheeks flaming with mortification. Grey moved at once to her side, and put a hand beneath her elbow, fixing Nicholls with an icy stare.

'Come with me, Miss Woodford,' he said. 'Let us find a good place from which to watch the proceedings.'

'Watch?' said a voice beside him. 'Why surely you don't mean to *watch*, do you, sir? Are you not curious to try the phenomenon yourself?'

It was Hunter himself, bushy hair tied carelessly back, though decently dressed in a damson-red suit, and grinning up at Grey; the surgeon was broad-shouldered and muscular, but quite short – barely five foot two, to Grey's five-six. Evidently he had noted Grey's wordless exchange with Lucinda.

'Oh, I think—' Grey began, but Hunter had his arm and was tugging him toward the crowd gathering round the tank. Caroline, with an alarmed glance at the glowering Nicholls, hastily followed him.

'I shall be most interested to hear your account of the sensation,' Hunter was saying chattily. 'Some people report a remarkable euphoria, a momentary disorientation . . .

shortness of breath, or dizziness – sometimes pain in the chest. You have not a weak heart, I hope, Major? Or you, Miss Woodford?'

'Me?' Caroline looked surprised.

Hunter bowed to her.

'I should be particularly interested to see your own response, ma'am,' he said respectfully. 'So few women have the courage to undertake such an adventure.'

'She doesn't want to,' Grey said hurriedly.

'Well, perhaps I *do*,' she said, and gave him a little frown, before glancing at the tank and the long grey form inside it. She gave a little shiver – but Grey recognised it, from long acquaintance with the lady, as a shiver of anticipation, rather than revulsion.

Mr Hunter recognised it, too. He grinned more broadly, and bowed again, extending his arm to Miss Woodford.

'Allow me to secure you a place, ma'am.'

Grey and Nicholls both moved purposefully to prevent him, collided, and were left scowling at each other as Mr Hunter escorted Caroline to the tank and introduced her to the eel's owner, a dark-looking little creature named Horace Suddfield.

Grey nudged Nicholls aside and plunged into the crowd, elbowing his way ruthlessly to the front. Hunter spotted him and beamed.

'Have you any metal remaining in your chest, Major?'

'Have I— what?'

'Metal,' Hunter repeated. 'Arthur Longstreet described to me the operation in which he removed thirty-seven pieces of metal from your chest – most impressive. If any bits remain, though, I must advise you against trying the eel. Metal conducts electricity, you see, and the chance of burns—'

Nicholls had made his way through the throng as well, and gave an unpleasant laugh, hearing this.

69

'A good excuse, Major,' he said, a noticeable jeer in his voice. He was very drunk indeed, Grey thought. Still—

'No, I haven't,' he said abruptly.

'Excellent,' Suddfield said, politely. 'A soldier, I understand you are, sir? A bold gentleman, I perceive – who better to take first place?'

And before Grey could protest, he found himself next to the tank, Caroline Woodford's hand clutching his, her other held by Nicholls, who was glaring malevolently.

'Are we all arranged, ladies and gentlemen?' Suddfield cried. 'How many, Dobbs?'

'Forty-five!' came a call from his assistant from the next room, through which the line of participants snaked, joined hand to hand and twitching with excitement, the rest of the party standing well back, agog.

'All touching, all touching?' Suddfield cried. 'Take a firm grip of your friends, please, a very firm grip!' He turned to Grey, his small face alight. 'Go ahead, sir! Grip it tightly, please – just there, just there before the tail!'

Disregarding his better judgement and the consequences to his lace cuff, Grey set his jaw and plunged his hand into the water.

In the split second when he grasped the slimy thing, he expected something like the snap one got from touching a Leiden jar and making it spark. Then he was flung violently backward, every muscle in his body contorted, and he found himself on the floor, thrashing like a landed fish, gasping in a vain attempt to recall how to breathe.

The surgeon, Mr Hunter, squatted next to him, observing him with bright-eyed interest.

'How do you feel?' he inquired. 'Dizzy, at all?'

Grey shook his head, mouth opening and closing like a goldfish's, and with some effort, thumped his chest. Thus invited, Mr Hunter leaned down at once, unbuttoned Grey's waistcoat and pressed an ear to his shirtfront.

Whatever he heard – or didn't – seemed to alarm him, for he jerked up, clenched both fists together and brought them down on Grey's chest with a thud that reverberated to his backbone.

This blow had the salutary effect of forcing breath out of his lungs; they filled again by reflex, and suddenly, he remembered how to breathe. His heart also seemed to have been recalled to a sense of its duty, and began beating again. He sat up, fending off another blow from Mr Hunter, and sat blinking at the carnage around him.

The floor was filled with bodies. Some still writhing, some lying still, limbs outflung in abandonment, some already recovered and being helped to their feet by friends. Excited exclamations filled the air, and Suddfield stood by his eel, beaming with pride and accepting congratulations. The eel itself seemed annoyed; it was swimming round in circles, angrily switching its heavy body.

Edwin Nicholls was on hands and knees, Grey saw, rising slowly to his feet. He reached down to grasp Caroline Woodford's arms and help her to rise. This she did, but so awkwardly that she lost her balance and fell face-first into Mr Nicholls. He in turn lost his own balance and sat down hard, the Honourable Caroline atop him. Whether from shock, excitement, drink, or simple boorishness, he seized the moment – and Caroline – and planted a hearty kiss upon her astonished lips.

Matters thereafter were somewhat confused. He had a vague impression that he *had* broken Nicholls's nose – and there was a set of burst and swollen knuckles on his right hand to give weight to the supposition. There was a lot of noise, though, and he had the disconcerting feeling of not being altogether firmly confined within his own body. Parts of him seemed to be constantly drifting off, escaping the outlines of his flesh.

What *was* still inside was distinctly jangled. His hearing

– still somewhat impaired from the cannon explosion a few months before – had given up entirely under the strain of electric shock. That is, he could still hear, but what he heard made no sense. Random words reached him through a fog of buzzing and ringing, but he could not connect them sensibly to the moving mouths around him. He wasn't at all sure that his own voice was saying what he meant it to, for that matter.

He was surrounded by voices, faces – a sea of feverish sound and movement. People touched him, pulled him, pushed him. He flung out an arm, trying as much to discover where it was, as to strike anyone, but felt the impact of flesh. More noise. Here and there a face he recognised: Lucinda, shocked and furious; Caroline, distraught, her red hair dishevelled and coming down, all its powder lost.

The net result of everything was that he was not positive whether he had called Nicholls out, or the reverse. Surely Nicholls must have challenged him? He had a vivid recollection of Nicholls, gore-soaked handkerchief held to his nose and a homicidal light in his narrowed eyes. But then he'd found himself outside, in his shirt-sleeves, standing in the little park that fronted the Joffreys' house, with a pistol in his hand. He wouldn't have chosen to fight with a strange pistol, would he?

Maybe Nicholls had insulted him, and he had called Nicholls out without quite realising it?

It had rained earlier, was chilly now; wind was whipping his shirt round his body. His sense of smell was remarkably acute; it seemed to be the only thing working properly. He smelled smoke from the chimneys, the damp green of the plants, and his own sweat, oddly metallic. And something faintly foul – something redolent of mud and slime. By reflex, he rubbed the hand that had touched the eel against his breeches.

72

Someone was saying something to him. With difficulty, he fixed his attention on Dr Hunter, standing by his side, still with that look of penetrating interest. *Well, of course. They'd need a surgeon*, he thought dimly. *Have to have a surgeon at a duel.*

'Yes,' he said, seeing Hunter's eyebrows raised in inquiry of some sort. Then, seized by a belated fear that he had just promised his body to the surgeon were he killed, grasped Hunter's coat with his free hand.

'You . . . don't . . . touch me,' he said. 'No . . . knives. Ghoul,' he added for good measure, finally locating the word. Hunter nodded, seeming unoffended.

The sky was overcast, the only light that shed by the distant torches at the house's entrance. Nicholls was a whitish blur, coming closer.

Suddenly someone grabbed Grey, turned him forcibly about, and he found himself back to back with Nicholls, the bigger man's heat startling, so near.

Shit, he thought suddenly. *Is he any kind of a shot?*

Someone spoke and he began to walk – he thought he was walking – until an outthrust arm stopped him, and he turned in answer to someone pointing urgently behind him.

Oh, hell, he thought wearily, seeing Nicholls's arm come down. *I don't care.*

He blinked at the muzzle-flash – the report was lost in the shocked gasp from the crowd – and stood for a moment, wondering whether he'd been hit. Nothing seemed amiss, though, and someone nearby was urging him to fire.

Frigging poet, he thought. *I'll delope and have done. I want to go home.* He raised his arm, aiming straight up into the air, but his arm lost contact with his brain for an instant, and his wrist sagged. He jerked, correcting it, and his hand

73

tensed on the trigger. He had barely time to jerk the barrel aside, firing wildly.

To his surprise, Nicholls staggered a bit, then sat down on the grass. He sat propped on one hand, the other clutched dramatically to his shoulder, head thrown back.

It was raining quite hard by now. Grey blinked water off his lashes, and shook his head. The air tasted sharp, like cut metal, and for an instant, he had the impression that it smelled . . . purple.

'That can't be right,' he said aloud, and found that his ability to speak seemed to have come back. He turned to speak to Hunter, but the surgeon had, of course, darted across to Nicholls, was peering down the neck of the poet's shirt. There was blood on it, Grey saw, but Nicholls was refusing to lie down, gesturing vigorously with his free hand. Blood was running down his face from his nose; perhaps that was it.

'Come away, sir,' said a quiet voice at his side. 'It'll be bad for Lady Joffrey, else.'

'What?' He looked, surprised, to find Richard Tarleton, who had been his ensign in Germany, now in the uniform of a Lancers lieutenant. 'Oh. Yes, it will.' Duelling was illegal in London; for the police to arrest Lucinda's guests before her house would be a scandal – not something that would please her husband, Sir Richard, at all.

The crowd had already melted away, as though the rain had rendered them soluble. The torches by the door had been extinguished. Nicholls was being helped off by Hunter and someone else, lurching away through the increasing rain. Grey shivered. God knew where his coat or cloak was.

'Let's go, then,' he said.

74

Grey opened his eyes.

'Did you say something, Tom?'

Tom Byrd, his valet, had produced a cough like a chimney sweep's, at a distance of approximately one foot from Grey's ear. Seeing that he had obtained his employer's attention, he presented the chamber pot at port arms.

'His Grace is downstairs, me lord. With her ladyship.'

Grey blinked at the window behind Tom, where the open drapes showed a dim square of rainy light.

'Her ladyship? What, the duchess?' What could have happened? It couldn't be past nine o'clock. His sister-in-law never paid calls before afternoon, and he had never known her to go anywhere with his brother during the day.

'No, me lord. The little 'un.'

'The little— oh. My god-daughter?' He sat up, feeling well but strange, and took the utensil from Tom.

'Yes, me lord. His Grace said as he wants to speak to you about "the events of last night".' Tom had crossed to the window and was looking censoriously at the remnants of Grey's shirt and breeches, these stained with grass, mud, blood and powder stains, and flung carelessly over the back of the chair. He turned a reproachful eye on Grey, who closed his own, trying to recall exactly what the events of last night had been.

He felt somewhat odd. Not drunk, he hadn't been drunk; he had no headache, no uneasiness of digestion . . .

'Last night,' he repeated, uncertain. Last night had been confused, but he did remember it. The eel party. Lucinda Joffrey, Caroline . . . why on earth ought Hal to be concerned with . . . what, the duel? Why should his brother care about such a silly affair – and even if he did, why appear at Grey's door at the crack of dawn with his six-month-old daughter?

It was more the time of day than the child's presence

75

that was unusual; his brother often did take his daughter out, with the feeble excuse that the child needed air. His wife accused him of wanting to show the baby off – she was beautiful – but Grey thought the cause somewhat more straightforward. His ferocious, autocratic, dictatorial brother, colonel of his own regiment, terror of both his own troops and his enemies – had fallen in love with his daughter. The regiment would leave for its new posting within a month's time. Hal simply couldn't bear to have her out of his sight.

Thus, he found the Duke of Pardloe seated in the morning room, Lady Dorothea Jacqueline Benedicta Grey cradled in his arm, gnawing on a rusk her father held for her. Her wet silk bonnet, her tiny rabbit-fur bunting, and two letters, one open, one still sealed, lay upon the table at the Duke's elbow.

Hal glanced up at him.

'I've ordered your breakfast. Say hallo to Uncle John, Dottie.' He turned the baby gently round. She didn't remove her attention from the rusk, but made a small chirping noise.

'Hallo, sweetheart.' John leaned over and kissed the top of her head, covered with a soft blonde down and slightly damp. 'Having a nice outing with Daddy in the pouring rain?'

'We brought you something.' Hal picked up the opened letter, and raising an eyebrow at his brother, handed it to him.

Grey raised an eyebrow back and began to read.

'What?!' He looked up from the sheet, mouth open.

'Yes, that's what I said,' Hal agreed cordially, 'when it was delivered to my door, just before dawn.' He reached for the sealed letter, carefully balancing the baby. 'Here, this one's yours. It came just after dawn.'

Grey dropped the first letter as though it was on fire, and seized the second, ripping it open.

Oh, John, it read without preamble, *forgive me, I couldn't stop him, I really couldn't, I'm SO sorry. I told him, but he wouldn't listen. I'd run away, but I don't know where to go. Please, please do something!*

It wasn't signed, but didn't need to be. He'd recognised the Honourable Caroline Woodford's writing, scribbled and frantic as it was. The paper was blotched and puckered – with tearstains?

He shook his head violently, as though to clear it, then picked up the first letter again. It was just as he'd read it the first time – a formal demand from Alfred, Lord Enderby to his Grace the Duke of Pardloe, for satisfaction regarding the injury to the honour of his sister, the Honourable Caroline Woodford, by the agency of his Grace's brother, Lord John Grey.

Grey glanced from one document to the other, several times, then looked at his brother.

'What the devil?'

'I gather you had an eventful evening,' Hal said, grunting slightly as he bent to retrieve the rusk Dottie had dropped on the carpet. 'No, darling, you don't want that anymore.'

Dottie disagreed violently with this assertion, and was distracted only by Uncle John picking her up and blowing in her ear.

'Eventful,' he repeated. 'Yes, it was, rather. But I didn't do anything to Caroline Woodford save hold her hand whilst being shocked by an electric eel, I swear it. Gleeglgleeglgleegl-ppppppssssshhhhh,' he added to Dottie, who shrieked and giggled in response. He glanced up to find Hal staring at him.

'Lucinda Joffrey's party,' he amplified. 'Surely you and Minnie were invited?'

77

Hal grunted. 'Oh. Yes, we were, but I had a prior engagement. Minnie didn't mention the eel. What's this I hear about you fighting a duel over the girl, though?'

'What? It wasn't—' He stopped, trying to think. 'Well, perhaps it was, come to think. Nicholls – you know, that swine who wrote the ode to Minnie's feet? – he kissed Miss Woodford, and she didn't want him to, so I punched him. Who told you about the duel?'

'Richard Tarleton. He came into White's card-room late last night, and said he'd just seen you home.'

'Well, then, you likely know as much about it as I do. Oh, you want Daddy back now, do you?' He handed Dottie back to his brother and brushed at a damp patch of saliva on the shoulder of his coat.

'I suppose that's what Enderby's getting at.' Hal nodded at the earl's letter. 'That you made the poor girl publicly conspicuous and compromised her virtue by fighting a scandalous duel over her. I suppose he's got a point.'

Dottie was now gumming her father's knuckle, making little growling noises. Hal dug in his pocket and came out with a silver teething ring, which he offered her in lieu of his finger, meanwhile giving Grey a sidelong look.

'You don't want to marry Caroline Woodford, do you? That's what Enderby's demand amounts to.'

'God, no.' Caroline was a good friend – bright, pretty, and given to mad escapades, but marriage? Him?

Hal nodded.

'Lovely girl, but you'd end up in Newgate or Bedlam within a month.'

'Or dead,' Grey said, gingerly picking at the bandage Tom had insisted on wrapping round his knuckles. 'How's Nicholls this morning, do you know?'

'Ah.' Hal rocked back a little, drawing a deep breath. 'Well . . . dead, actually. I had rather a nasty letter from his father, accusing you of murder. That one came over breakfast; didn't think to bring it. Did you mean to kill him?'

Grey sat down quite suddenly, all the blood having left his head.

'No,' he whispered. His lips felt stiff and his hands had gone numb. 'Oh, Jesus. No.'

Hal swiftly pulled his snuff-box from his pocket, one-handed, dumped out the vial of smelling-salts he kept in it and handed it to his brother. Grey was grateful; he hadn't been going to faint, but the assault of ammoniac fumes gave him excuse for watering eyes and congested breathing.

'Jesus,' he repeated, and sneezed explosively several times in a row. 'I didn't aim to kill— I swear it, Hal. I deloped. Or tried to,' he added honestly.

Lord Enderby's letter suddenly made more sense, as did Hal's presence. What had been a silly affair that should have disappeared with the morning dew had become – or would, directly the gossip had time to spread – not merely a scandal, but quite possibly something worse. It was not unthinkable that he *might* be arrested for murder. Quite without warning, the figured carpet yawned at his feet, an abyss into which his life might vanish.

Hal nodded, and gave him his own handkerchief.

'I know,' he said quietly. 'Things . . . happen sometimes. That you don't intend – that you'd give your life to have back.'

Grey wiped his face, glancing at his brother under cover of the gesture. Hal looked suddenly older than his years, his face drawn by more than worry over Grey.

'Nathaniel Twelvetrees, you mean?' Normally, he wouldn't have mentioned that matter, but both men's guards were down.

Hal gave him a sharp look, then looked away.

'No, not Twelvetrees. I hadn't any choice about that.

79

And I did mean to kill him. I meant . . . what led to that duel.' He grimaced. 'Marry in haste, repent at leisure.' He looked at the note on the table and shook his head. His hand passed gently over Dottie's head. 'I won't have you repeat my mistakes, John,' he said quietly.

Grey nodded, wordless. Hal's first wife had been seduced by Nathaniel Twelvetrees. Hal's mistakes notwithstanding, Grey had never intended marriage with anyone, and didn't now.

Hal frowned, tapping the folded letter on the table in thought. He darted a glance at John, and sighed, then set the letter down, reached into his coat, and withdrew two further documents, one clearly official, from its seal.

'Your new commission,' he said, handing it over. 'For Crefeld,' he said, raising an eyebrow at his brother's look of blank incomprehension. 'You were brevetted lieutenant-colonel. You didn't remember?'

'I— well . . . not exactly.' He had a vague feeling that someone – probably Hal – had told him about it, soon after Crefeld, but he'd been badly wounded then, and in no frame of mind to think about the army, let alone to care about battlefield promotion. Later—

'Wasn't there some confusion over it?' Grey took the commission and opened it, frowning. 'I thought they'd changed their minds.'

'Oh, you do remember, then,' Hal said, eyebrow still cocked. 'General Wiedman gave it you after the battle. The confirmation was held up, though, because of the enquiry into the cannon explosion, and then the . . . ah . . . kerfuffle over Adams.'

'Oh.' Grey was still shaken by the news of Nicholls's death, but mention of Adams started his brain functioning again. 'Adams. Oh. You mean Twelvetrees held up the commission?' Colonel Reginald Twelvetrees, of the Royal Artillery – brother to Nathaniel, and cousin to Bernard

Adams, the traitor awaiting trial in the Tower, as a result of Grey's efforts the preceding autumn.

'Yes. Bastard,' Hal added dispassionately. 'I'll have him for breakfast, one of these days.'

'Not on my account, I hope,' Grey said dryly.

'Oh, no,' Hal assured him, jiggling his daughter gently to prevent her fussing. 'It will be a purely personal pleasure.'

Grey smiled at that, despite his disquiet, and put down the commission. 'Right,' he said, with a glance at the fourth document, which still lay folded on the table. It was an official-looking letter, and had been opened; the seal was broken. 'A proposal of marriage, a denunciation for murder, and a new commission – what the devil's that one? A bill from my tailor?'

'Ah, that. I didn't mean to show it to you,' Hal said, leaning carefully to hand it over without dropping Dottie. 'But under the circumstances . . .'

He waited, noncommittal, as Grey opened the letter and read it. It was a request – or an order, depending how you looked at it – for the attendance of Major Lord John Grey at the court-martial of one Captain Charles Carruthers, to serve as witness of character for the same. In . . .

'In Canada?' John's exclamation startled Dottie, who crumpled up her face and threatened to cry.

'Hush, sweetheart.' Hal jiggled faster, hastily patting her back. 'It's all right; only Uncle John being an ass.'

Grey ignored this, waving the letter at his brother.

'What the devil is Charlie Carruthers being court-martialled for? And why on earth am I being summoned as a character witness?'

'Failure to suppress a mutiny,' Hal said. 'As to why you – he asked for you, apparently. An officer under charges is allowed to call his own witnesses, for whatever purpose. Didn't you know that?'

Grey supposed that he had, in an academic sort of way. But he had never attended a court-martial himself; it wasn't a common proceeding, and he had no real idea of the shape of the proceedings. He glanced sideways at Hal.

'You say you didn't mean to show it to me?'

Hal shrugged, and blew softly over the top of his daughter's head, making the short blonde hairs furrow and rise like wheat in the wind.

'No point. I meant to write back and say that as your commanding officer, I required you here; why should you be dragged off to the wilds of Canada? But given your talent for awkward situations . . . what did it feel like?' he inquired curiously.

'What did— oh, the eel.' Grey was accustomed to his brother's lightning shifts of conversation, and made the adjustment easily. 'Well, it was rather a shock.'

He laughed – if tremulously – at Hal's glower, and Dottie squirmed round in her father's arms, reaching out her own plump little arms appealingly to her uncle.

'Flirt,' he told her, taking her from Hal. 'No, really, it was remarkable. You know how it feels when you break a bone? That sort of jolt before you feel the pain, that goes right through you, and you go blind for a moment and feel like someone's driven a nail through your belly? It was like that, only much stronger, and it went on for longer. Stopped my breath,' he admitted. 'Quite literally. And my heart, too, I think. Dr Hunter – you know, the anatomist? – was there, and pounded on my chest to get it started again.'

Hal was listening with close attention, and asked several questions, which Grey answered automatically, his mind occupied with this latest surprising communiqué.

Charlie Carruthers. They'd been young officers together, though from different regiments. Fought beside one another in Scotland, gone round London together for a bit on their next leave. They'd had – well, you couldn't call it an affair. Three or four brief encounters – sweating, breathless quarters of an hour in dark corners that could be conveniently forgotten in daylight, or shrugged off as the result of drunkennness, not spoken of by either party.

That had been in the Bad Time, as he thought of it; those years after Hector's death, when he'd sought oblivion wherever he could find it – and found it often – before slowly recovering himself.

Likely he wouldn't have recalled Carruthers at all, save for the one thing.

Carruthers had been born with an interesting deformity – he had a double hand. While Carruthers's right hand was normal in appearance and worked quite as usual, there was another, dwarf hand that sprang from his wrist and nestled neatly against its larger partner. Dr Hunter would probably pay hundreds for that hand, Grey thought, with a mild lurch of the stomach.

The dwarf hand had only two short fingers and a stubby thumb, but Carruthers could open and close it, though not without also opening and closing the larger one. The shock when Carruthers had closed both of them simultaneously on Grey's prick had been nearly as extraordinary as had the electric eel's.

'Nicholls hasn't been buried yet, has he?' he asked abruptly, the thought of the eel party and Dr Hunter causing him to interrupt some remark of Hal's.

Hal looked surprised.

'Surely not. Why?' He narrowed his eyes at Grey. 'You don't mean to attend the funeral, surely?'

'No, no,' Grey said hastily. 'I was only thinking of Dr Hunter. He, um, has a certain reputation . . . and Nicholls did go off with him. After the duel.'

'A reputation as what, for God's sake?' Hal demanded impatiently.

'As a body-snatcher,' Grey blurted.

There was a sudden silence, awareness dawning in Hal's face. He'd gone pale.

'You don't think— no! How could he?'

'A . . . um . . . hundredweight or so of stones being substituted just prior to the coffin's being nailed shut is the usual method – or so I've heard,' Grey said, as well as he could with Dottie's fist being poked up his nose.

Hal swallowed. Grey could see the hairs rise on his wrist.

'I'll ask Harry,' Hal said, after a short silence. 'The funeral can't have been arranged yet, and if . . .'

Both brothers shuddered reflexively, imagining all too exactly the scene as an agitated family member insisted upon raising the coffin lid, to find . . .

'Maybe better not,' Grey said, swallowing. Dottie had left off trying to remove his nose, and was patting her tiny hand over his lips as he talked. The feel of it on his skin . . .

He peeled her gently off and gave her back to Hal.

'I don't know what use Charles Carruthers thinks I might be to him – but all right, I'll go.' He glanced at Lord Enderby's note, Caroline's crumpled missive. 'After all, I suppose there are worse things than being scalped by Red Indians.'

Hal nodded, sober.

'I've arranged your sailing. You leave tomorrow.' He stood and lifted Dottie. 'Here, sweetheart. Kiss your Uncle John goodbye.'

A month later, Grey found himself, Tom Byrd at his side, climbing off the *Harwood* and into one of the small boats that would land them and the battalion of Louisbourg

84

grenadiers with whom they had been travelling on a large island near the mouth of the St Lawrence River.

He had never seen anything like it. The river itself was larger than any he had ever seen, nearly half a mile across, running wide and deep, a dark blue-black under the sun. Great cliffs and undulating hills rose on either side of the river, so thickly forested that the underlying stone was nearly invisible. It was hot, and the sky arched brilliant overhead, much brighter and much wider than any sky he had seen before. A loud hum echoed from the lush growth – insects, he supposed, birds, and the rush of the water, though it felt as though the wilderness were singing to itself, in a voice heard only in his blood. Beside him, Tom was fairly vibrating with excitement, his eyes out on stalks, not to miss anything.

'Cor, is that a Red Indian?' he whispered, leaning close to Grey in the boat.

'I don't suppose he can be anything else,' Grey replied, as the gentleman loitering by the landing was naked save for a breech-clout, a striped blanket slung over one shoulder, and a coating of what – from the shimmer of his limbs – appeared to be grease of some kind.

'I thought they'd be redder,' Tom said, echoing Grey's own thought. The Indian's skin was considerably darker than Grey's own, to be sure, but a rather pleasant soft brown in colour, something like dried oak leaves. The Indian appeared to find them nearly as interesting as they had found him; he was eyeing Grey in particular with intent consideration.

'It's your hair, me lord,' Tom hissed in Grey's ear. 'I told you you ought to have worn a wig.'

'Nonsense, Tom.' At the same time, Grey experienced an odd frisson up the back of the neck, constricting his scalp. Vain of his hair, which was blond and thick, he didn't commonly wear a wig, choosing instead to bind and powder his own for formal occasions. The present occasion wasn't formal in the least. With the advent of fresh water aboard, Tom had insisted upon washing his hair that morning, and it was still spread loose upon his shoulders, though it had long since dried.

The boat crunched on the shingle, and the Indian flung aside his blanket and came to help the men run it up the shore. Grey found himself next to the man, close enough to smell him. He smelled quite unlike anyone Grey had ever encountered; gamy, certainly – he wondered, with a small thrill, whether the grease the man wore might be bear-fat – but with the tang of herbs and a sweat like fresh-sheared copper.

Straightening up from the gunwale, the Indian caught Grey's eye and smiled.

'You be careful, Englishman,' he said, in a voice with a noticeable French accent, and reaching out, ran his fingers quite casually through Grey's loose hair. 'Your scalp would look good on a Huron's belt.'

This made the soldiers from the boat all laugh, and the Indian, still smiling, turned to them.

'They are not so particular, the Abenaki who work for the French. A scalp is a scalp – and the French pay well for one, no matter what colour.' He nodded genially to the grenadiers, who had stopped laughing. 'You come with me.'

There was a small camp on the island already, a detachment of infantry under a Captain Woodford – whose name gave Grey a slight wariness, but who turned out to be no relation, thank God, to Lord Enderby's family.

'We're fairly safe on this side of the island,' he told Grey, offering him a flask of brandy outside his own tent after supper. 'But the Indians raid the other side regularly – I lost four men last week, three killed and one carried off.'

'You have your own scouts, though?' Grey asked, slapping at the mosquitoes that had begun to swarm in the dusk. He had not seen the Indian who had brought them to the camp again, but there were several more in camp, mostly clustered together around their own fire, but one or two squatting among the Louisbourg grenadiers who had crossed with Grey on the *Harwood*, bright-eyed and watchful.

'Yes, and trustworthy for the most part,' Woodford said, answering Grey's unasked question. He laughed, though not with any humour. 'At least we hope so.'

Woodford gave him supper, and they had a hand of cards, Grey exchanging news of home for gossip of the current campaign.

General Wolfe had spent no little time at Montmorency, below the town of Quebec, but had nothing but disappointment from his attempts there, and so had abandoned that post, re-gathering the main body of his troops some miles upstream from the Citadel of Quebec. A so-far impregnable fortress, it perched on sheer cliffs above the river, commanding both the river and the plains to the west with her cannon, obliging English warships to steal past under cover of night – and not always successfully.

'Wolfe'll be champing at the bit, now his grenadiers are come,' Woodford predicted. 'He puts great store by those fellows, fought with 'em at Louisbourg. Here, colonel, you're being eaten alive – try a bit of this on your hands and face.' He dug about in his campaign chest and came up with a tin of strong-smelling grease, which he pushed across the table.

87

'Bear-grease and mint,' he explained. 'The Indians use it – that, or cover themselves with mud.'

Grey helped himself liberally; the scent wasn't quite the same as what he had smelled earlier on the scout, but it was very similar, and he felt an odd sense of disturbance in its application. Though it did discourage the biting insects.

He had made no secret of the reason for his presence, and now asked openly about Carruthers.

'Where is he held, do you know?'

Woodford frowned and poured more brandy.

'He's not. He's paroled; has a billet in the town at Gareon, where Wolfe's headquarters are.'

'Ah?' Grey was mildly surprised – but then, Carruthers was not charged with mutiny, but rather with failure to suppress one – a rare charge. 'Do you know the particulars of the case?'

Woodford opened his mouth, as though to speak, but then drew a deep breath, shook his head, and drank brandy. From which Grey deduced that probably everyone knew the particulars, but that there was something fishy about the affair. Well, time enough. He'd hear about the matter directly from Carruthers.

Conversation became general, and after a time, Grey said goodnight. The grenadiers had been busy; a new little city of canvas tents had sprung up at the edge of the existing camp, and the appetising smells of fresh meat roasting and brewing tea were rising on the air.

Tom had doubtless managed to raise his own tent, somewhere in the mass. He was in no hurry to find it, though; he was enjoying the novel sensations of firm footing and solitude, after weeks of crowded shipboard life. He cut outside the orderly rows of new tents, walking just beyond the glow of the firelight, feeling pleasantly invisible, though still close enough for safety – or at least he hoped so. The forest stood only a few yards beyond, the outlines of trees and bushes still just visible, the dark not quite complete.

A drifting spark of green drew his eye, and he felt delight well up in him. There was another . . . another . . . ten, a dozen, and the air was suddenly full of fireflies, soft green sparks that winked on and off, glowing like tiny, distant candles among the dark foliage. He'd seen fireflies once or twice before, in Germany, but never in such abundance. They were simple magic, pure as moonlight.

He could not have said how long he watched them, wandering slowly along the edge of the encampment, but at last he sighed and turned toward the centre, full-fed, pleasantly tired, and with no immediate responsibility to do anything. He had no troops under his command, no reports to write . . . nothing, really, to do until he reached Gareon and Charlie Carruthers.

With a sigh of peace, he closed the flap of his tent and shucked his outer clothing.

He was roused abruptly from the edge of sleep by screams and shouts, and sat bolt upright. Tom, who had been asleep on his bedsack at Grey's feet, sprang up like a frog onto hands and knees, scrabbling madly for pistol and shot in the chest.

Not waiting, Grey seized the dagger he had hung on the tent-peg before retiring, and flinging back the flap, peered out. Men were rushing to and fro, colliding with tents, shouting orders, yelling for help. There was a glow in the sky, a reddening of the low-hanging clouds.

'Fire-ships!' someone shouted. Grey shoved his feet into his shoes and joined the throng of men now rushing toward the water.

Out in the centre of the broad dark river stood the bulk of the *Harwood*, at anchor. And coming slowly down upon her were one, two, and then three blazing vessels – a raft, stacked with flammable waste, doused with oil and set afire. A small boat, its mast and sail flaming bright against the night. Something else – an Indian canoe, with a heap of burning grass and leaves? Too far to see, but it was coming closer.

He glanced at the ship and saw movement on deck – too far to make out individual men, but things were happening. The ship couldn't raise anchor and sail away, not in time – but she was lowering her boats, sailors setting out to try to deflect the fire-ships, keep them away from the *Harwood*.

Absorbed in the sight, he had not noticed the shrieks and shouts still coming from the other side of the camp. But now, as the men on the shore fell silent, watching the fire-ships, they began to stir, realising belatedly that something else was afoot.

'Indians,' the man beside Grey said suddenly, as a particularly high, ululating screech split the air. 'Indians!'

This cry became general, and everyone began to rush in the other direction.

'Stop! Halt!' Grey flung out an arm, catching a man across the throat and knocking him flat. He raised his voice in the vain hope of stopping the rush. 'You! You and you – seize your neighbour, come with me!' The man he had knocked down bounced up again, white-eyed in the starlight.

'It may be a trap!' Grey shouted. 'Stay here! Stand to your arms!'

'Stand! Stand!' A short gentleman in his nightshirt took up the cry in a cast-iron bellow, adding to its effect by seizing a dead branch from the ground and laying about himself, turning back those trying to get past him to the encampment.

Another spark grew upstream, and another beyond it; more fire-ships. The boats were in the water now, mere dots in the darkness. If they could fend off the fire-ships, the *Harwood* might be saved from immediate destruction; Grey's fear was that whatever was going on in the rear of the encampment was a ruse designed to pull men away from the shore, leaving the ship protected only by her marines, should the French then send down a barge loaded with explosives, or a boarding craft, hoping to elude detection whilst everyone was dazzled or occupied by the blazing fire-ships and the raid.

The first of the fire-ships had drifted harmlessly on to the far shore, and was burning itself out on the sand, brilliant and beautiful against the night. The short gentleman with the remarkable voice – clearly he was a sergeant, Grey thought – had succeeded in rallying a small group of soldiers, whom he now presented to Grey with a brisk salute.

'Will they go and fetch their muskets, all orderly, sir?'

'They will,' Grey said. 'And hurry. Go with them, sergeant – it is sergeant?'

'Sergeant Aloysius Cutter, sir,' the short gentleman replied with a nod, 'and pleased to know an officer what has a brain in his head.'

'Thank you, sergeant. And fetch back as many more men as fall conveniently to hand, if you please. With arms. A rifleman or two, if you can find them.'

Matters thus momentarily attended to, he turned his attention once more to the river, where two of the *Harwood*'s small boats were herding one of the fire-ships away from the transport, circling it and pushing water with their oars; he caught the splash of their efforts, and the shouts of the sailors.

'Me lord?'

The voice at his elbow nearly made him swallow his tongue. He turned with an attempt at calmness, ready to reproach Tom for venturing out into the chaos, but before he could summon words, his young valet stooped at his feet, holding something.

'I've brought your breeches, me lord,' Tom said, voice trembling. 'Thought you might need 'em, if there was fighting.'

'Very thoughtful of you, Tom,' he assured his valet, fighting an urge to laugh. He stepped into the breeches and pulled them up, tucking in his shirt. 'What's been happening in the camp, do you know?'

He could hear Tom swallow hard.

'Indians, me lord,' Tom said. 'They came screaming through the tents, set one or two afire. They killed one man I saw, and . . . and scalped him.' His voice was thick, as though he might be about to vomit. 'It was nasty.'

'I daresay.' The night was warm, but Grey felt the hairs rise on arms and neck. The chilling screams had stopped, and while he could still hear considerable hubbub in the camp, it was of a different tone now; no random shouting, just the calls of officers, sergeants and corporals ordering the men, beginning the process of assembly, of counting noses and reckoning damage.

Tom, bless him, had brought Grey's pistol, shot-bag, and powder, as well as his coat and stockings. Aware of the dark forest and the long, narrow trail between the shore and the camp, Grey didn't send Tom back, but merely told him to keep out of the way as Sergeant Cutter – who with good military instinct, had also taken time to put his breeches on – came up with his armed recruits.

'All present, sir,' Cutter said, saluting. ''Oom 'ave I the honour of h'addressing, sir?'

'I am Lieutenant-Colonel Grey. Set your men to watch the ship, please, sergeant, with particular attention to dark craft coming downstream, and then come back to report what you know of matters in camp.'

Cutter saluted and promptly vanished with a shout of 'Come on, you shower o' shit! Look lively, look lively!'

Tom gave a brief, strangled scream, and Grey whirled, drawing his dagger by reflex, to find a dark shape directly behind him.

'Don't kill me, Englishman,' said the Indian who had led them to the camp earlier. He sounded mildly amused. '*Le capitaine* sent me to find you.'

'Why?' Grey asked shortly. His heart was still pounding from the shock. He disliked being taken at a disadvantage, and disliked even more the thought that the man could easily have killed him before Grey knew he was there.

'The Abenaki set your tent on fire; he supposed they might have dragged you and your servant into the forest.'

Tom uttered an extremely coarse expletive, and made as though to dive directly into the trees, but Grey stopped him with a hand on his arm.

'Stay, Tom. It doesn't matter.'

'The bloody hell you say,' Tom replied heatedly, agitation depriving him of his normal manners. 'I daresay I can find you more smallclothes, not as that will be easy, but what about your cousin's painting of her and the little 'un she sent for Captain Stubbs? What about your good hat with the gold lace?!?'

Grey had a brief moment of alarm – his young cousin Olivia had sent a miniature of herself and her newborn son, charging him to deliver this to her husband, Captain Malcolm Stubbs, presently with Wolfe's troops. He clapped a hand to his side, though, and felt with relief the oval shape of the miniature in its wrappings, safe in his pocket.

'That's all right, Tom; I've got it. As to the hat . . . we'll worry about that later, I think. Here – what is your name, sir?' he inquired of the Indian, unwilling to address him simply as 'you'.

93

'Manoke,' said the Indian, still sounding amused.

'Quite. Will you take my servant back to the camp?' He saw the small, determined figure of Sergeant Cutter appear at the mouth of the trail, and firmly overriding Tom's protests, shooed him off in care of the Indian.

In the event, all five fire-ships either drifted or were steered away from the *Harwood*. Something that might – or might not – have been a boarding craft did appear upstream, but was frightened off by Grey's impromptu troops on the shore, firing volleys – though the range was woefully short; there was no possibility of hitting anything.

Still, the *Harwood* was secure, and the camp had settled into a state of uneasy watchfulness. Grey had seen Woodford briefly upon his return, near dawn, and learned that the raid had resulted in the deaths of two men and the capture of three more, dragged off into the forest. Three of the Indian raiders had been killed, another wounded – Woodford intended to interview this man before he died, but doubted that any useful information would result.

'They never talk,' he'd said, rubbing at his smoke-reddened eyes. His face was pouchy and grey with fatigue. 'They just close their eyes and start singing their damned deathsongs. Not a blind bit of difference what you do to 'em – they just keep singing.'

Grey had heard it, or thought he had, as he crawled wearily into his borrowed shelter toward daybreak. A faint, high-pitched chant, that rose and fell like the rush of the wind in the trees overhead. It kept up for a bit, then stopped abruptly, only to resume again, faint and interrupted, as he teetered on the edge of sleep.

What was the man saying? he wondered. Did it matter

that none of the men hearing him knew what he said? Perhaps the scout – Manoke, that was his name – was there; perhaps he would know.

Tom had found Grey a small tent at the end of a row. Probably he had ejected some subaltern, but Grey wasn't inclined to object. It was barely big enough for the canvas bedsack that lay on the ground and a box that served as table, on which stood an empty candlestick, but it was shelter. It had begun to rain lightly as he walked up the trail to camp, and the rain was now pattering busily on the canvas overhead, raising a sweet, musty scent. If the deathsong continued, it was no longer audible over the sound of the rain.

Grey turned over, the grass stuffing of the bedsack rustling softly beneath him, and fell at once into sleep.

He woke abruptly, face to face with an Indian. His reflexive flurry of movement was met with a low chuckle and a slight withdrawal, rather than a knife across the throat, though, and he broke through the fog of sleep in time to avoid doing serious damage to the scout Manoke.

'What?' he muttered, and rubbed the heel of his hand across his eyes. 'What is it?' *And why the devil are you lying on my bed?*

In answer to this, the Indian put a hand behind his head, drew him close, and kissed him. The man's tongue ran lightly across his lower lip, darted like a lizard's into his mouth, and then was gone.

So was the Indian.

He rolled over onto his back, blinking. A dream. It was still raining, harder now. He breathed in deeply; he could smell bear-grease, of course, on his own skin, and mint – was there any hint of metal? The light was stronger – it

95

must be day; he heard the drummer passing through the aisles of tents to rouse the men, the rattle of his sticks blending with the rattle of the rain, the shouts of corporals and sergeants – but still faint and grey. He could not have been asleep for more than half an hour, he thought.

'Christ,' he muttered, and turning himself stiffly over, pulled his coat over his head and sought sleep once again.

The *Harwood* tacked slowly upriver, with a sharp eye out for French marauders. There were a few alarms, including another raid by hostile Indians while camped on shore. This one ended more happily, with four marauders killed, and only one cook wounded, not seriously. They were obliged to loiter for a time, waiting for a cloudy night, in order to steal past the fortress of Quebec, menacing on its cliffs. They were spotted, in fact, and one or two cannon fired in their direction, but to no effect. And at last they came into port at Gareon, the site of General Wolfe's headquarters.

The town itself had been nearly engulfed by the growing military encampment that surrounded it, acres of tents spreading upward from the settlement on the riverbank, the whole presided over by a small French Catholic mission, whose tiny cross was just visible at the top of the hill that lay behind the town. The French inhabitants, with the political indifference of merchants everywhere, had given a Gallic shrug and set about happily overcharging the occupying forces.

The general himself was elsewhere, Grey was informed, fighting inland, but would doubtless return within the month. A lieutenant-colonel without brief or regimental affiliation was simply a nuisance; he was provided with suitable quarters and politely shooed away. With no

96

immediate duties to fulfil, he gave a shrug of his own and set out to discover the whereabouts of Captain Carruthers.

It wasn't difficult to find him. The *patron* of the first tavern Grey visited directed him at once to the habitat of *le capitaine*, a room in the house of a widow named Lambert, near the mission church. Grey wondered whether he would have received the information as readily from any other tavern-keeper in the village. Charlie had liked to drink when Grey had known him, and evidently still did, judging from the genial attitude of the *patron* when Carruthers's name was mentioned. Not that Grey could blame him, under the circumstances.

The widow – young, chestnut-haired, and quite attractive – viewed the English officer at her door with a deep suspicion, but when he followed his request for Captain Carruthers by mentioning that he was an old friend of the captain's, her face relaxed.

'*Bon*,' she said, swinging the door open abruptly. 'He needs friends.'

He ascended two flights of narrow stairs to Carruthers's attic, feeling the air about him grow warmer. It was pleasant at this time of day, but must grow stifling by mid-afternoon. He knocked, and felt a small shock of pleased recognition at hearing Carruthers's voice bid him enter.

Carruthers was seated at a rickety table in shirt and breeches, writing, an inkwell made from a gourd at one elbow, a pot of beer at the other. He looked at Grey blankly for an instant, then joy washed across his features, and he rose, nearly upsetting both.

'John!'

Before Grey could offer his hand, he found himself embraced – and returned the embrace wholeheartedly, a wash of memory flooding through him as he smelled Carruthers's hair, felt the scrape of his unshaven cheek against Grey's own. Even in the midst of this sensation,

97

though, he felt the slightness of Carruthers's body, the bones that pressed through his clothes.

'I never thought you'd come,' Carruthers was repeating, for perhaps the fourth time. He let go and stepped back, smiling as he dashed the back of his hand across his eyes, which were unabashedly wet.

'Well, you have an electric eel to thank for my presence,' Grey told him, smiling himself.

'A what?' Carruthers stared at him blankly.

'Long story – tell you later. For the moment, though – what the devil have you been doing, Charlie?'

The happiness faded somewhat from Carruthers's lean face, but didn't disappear altogether.

'Ah. Well. That's a long story, too. Let me send Martine for more beer.' He waved Grey toward the room's only stool, and went out before Grey could protest. He sat, gingerly, lest the stool collapse, but it held his weight. Besides the stool and table, the attic was very plainly furnished; a narrow cot, a chamber pot, and an ancient washstand with an earthenware basin and ewer completed the ensemble. It was very clean, but there was a faint smell of something in the air – something sweet and sickly, which he traced at once to a corked bottle standing at the back of the washstand.

Not that he had needed the smell of laudanum; one look at Carruthers's gaunt face told him enough. Returning to the stool, he glanced at the papers Carruthers had been working on. They appeared to be notes in preparation for the court-martial; the one on top was an account of an expedition undertaken by troops under Carruthers's command, on the orders of a Major Gerald Siverly.

Our orders instructed us to march to a village called Beaulieu, some ten miles to the east of Montmorency,

98

there to ransack and fire the houses, driving off such animals as we encountered. This we did. Some men of the village offered us resistance, armed with scythes and other implements. Two of these were shot, the others fled. We returned with two wagons filled with flour, cheeses, and small household goods, three cows and two good mules.

Grey got no further before the door opened. Carruthers came in and sat on the bed, nodding toward the papers.

'I thought I'd best write everything down. Just in case I don't live long enough for the court-martial.' He spoke matter-of-factly, and seeing the look on Grey's face, smiled faintly. 'Don't be troubled, John. I've always known I'd not make old bones. This—' He turned his right hand upward, letting the drooping cuff of his shirt fall back, '—isn't all of it.' He tapped his chest gently with his left hand.

'More than one doctor's told me I have some gross defect of the heart. Don't know, quite, if I have two of those, too—' he grinned at Grey, the sudden, charming smile he remembered so well, '—or only half of one, or what. Used to be, I just went faint now and then, but it's getting worse. Sometimes I feel it stop beating and just flutter in my chest, and everything begins to go all black and breathless. So far, it's always started beating again – but one of these days it isn't going to.'

Grey's eyes were fixed on Charlie's hand, the small dwarf hand curled against its larger fellow, looking as though Charlie held a strange flower cupped in his palm. As he watched, both hands opened slowly, the fingers moving in strangely beautiful synchrony.

'All right,' he said quietly. 'Tell me.'

Failure to suppress a mutiny was a rare charge, difficult to prove, and thus unlikely to be brought, unless other

99

factors were involved. Which in the present instance, they undoubtedly were.

'Know Siverly, do you?' Carruthers asked, taking the papers onto his knee.

'Not at all. I gather he's a bastard.' Grey gestured at the papers. 'What kind of bastard, though?'

'A corrupt one.' Carruthers tapped the pages square, carefully evening the edges, eyes fixed on them. 'That – what you read – it wasn't Siverly. It's General Wolfe's directive. I'm not sure whether the point is to deprive the fortress of provisions, in hopes of starving them out eventually, or to put pressure on Montcalm to send out troops to defend the countryside, where Wolfe could get at them – possibly both. But he means deliberately to terrorise the settlements on both sides of the river. No, we did this under the general's orders.' His face twisted a little, and he looked up suddenly at Grey. 'You remember the Highlands, John?'

'You know that I do.' No one involved in Cumberland's cleansing of the Highlands would ever forget. He had seen many Scottish villages like Beaulieu.

Carruthers took a deep breath.

'Yes. Well. The trouble was that Siverly took to appropriating the plunder we took from the countryside, under the pretext of selling it in order to make an equitable distribution among the troops.'

'What?' This was contrary to the normal custom of the army, whereby any soldier was entitled to what plunder he took. 'Who does he think he is, an admiral?' The navy did divide shares of prize-money among the crew, according to formula – but the navy was the navy; crews acted much more as single entities than did army companies, and there were Admiralty courts set up to deal with the sale of captured prize-ships.

Carruthers laughed at the question.

'His brother's a commodore. Perhaps that's where he got the notion. At any rate,' he added, sobering, 'he never did distribute the funds. Worse – he began withholding the soldiers' pay. Paying later and later, stopping pay for petty offences, claiming that the paychest hadn't been delivered – when several men had seen it unloaded from the coach with their own eyes.

'Bad enough, but the soldiers were still being fed and clothed adequately. But then he went too far.'

Siverly began to steal from the commissary, diverting quantities of supplies and selling them privately.

'I had my suspicions,' Carruthers explained, 'but no proof. I'd begun to watch him, though – and he knew I was watching him, so he trod carefully for a bit. But he couldn't resist the rifles.'

A shipment of a dozen new rifles, vastly superior to the ordinary Brown Bess musket, and very rare in the army.

'I think it must have been a clerical oversight that sent them to us in the first place. We hadn't any riflemen, and there was no real need for them. That's probably what made Siverly think he could get away with it.'

But he hadn't. Two private soldiers had unloaded the box, and curious at the weight, had opened it. Excited word had spread – and excitement had turned to disgruntled surprise when instead of new rifles, muskets showing considerable wear were later distributed. The talk – already angry – had escalated.

'Egged on by a hogshead of rum we confiscated from a tavern in Levi,' Carruthers said with a sigh. 'They drank all night – it was January, the nights are damned long in January here – and made up their minds to go and find the rifles. Which they did – under the floor in Siverly's quarters.'

'And where was Siverly?'

'In his quarters. He was rather badly used, I'm afraid.' A

muscle by Carruthers's mouth twitched. 'Escaped through a window, though, and made his way through the snow to the next garrison. It was twenty miles. Lost a couple of toes to frostbite, but survived.'

'Too bad.'

'Yes, it was.' The muscle twitched again.

'What happened to the mutineers?'

Carruthers blew out his cheeks, shaking his head.

'Deserted, most of them. Two were caught and hanged pretty promptly; three more rounded up later; they're in prison here.'

'And you—'

'And I,' Carruthers nodded. 'I was Siverly's second-in-command. I didn't know about the mutiny – one of the ensigns ran to fetch me when the men started to move toward Siverly's quarters – but I did arrive before they'd finished.'

'Not a great deal you could do under those circumstances, was there?'

'I didn't try,' Carruthers said bluntly.

'I see,' Grey said.

'Do you?' Carruthers gave him a crooked smile.

'Certainly. I take it Siverly is still in the army, and still holds a command? Yes, of course. He might have been furious enough to prefer the original charge against you, but you know as well as I do that under normal circumstances, the matter would likely have been dropped as soon as the general facts were known. You insisted on a court-martial, didn't you? So that you can make what you know public.' Given Carruthers's state of health, the knowledge that he risked a long imprisonment if convicted apparently didn't trouble him.

The smile straightened, and became genuine.

'I knew I chose the right man,' Carruthers said.

'I am exceeding flattered,' Grey said dryly. 'Why me, though?'

Carruthers had laid aside his papers, and now rocked back a little on the cot, hands linked around one knee.

'Why you, John?' The smile had vanished, and Carruthers's grey eyes were level on his. 'You know what we do. Our business is chaos, death, destruction. But you know why we do it, too.'

'Oh? Perhaps you'd have the goodness to tell me, then. I've always wondered.'

Humour lighted Charlie's eyes, but he spoke seriously.

'Someone has to keep order, John. Soldiers fight for all kinds of reasons, most of them ignoble. You and your brother, though . . .' He broke off, shaking his head. Grey saw that his hair was streaked with grey, though he knew Carruthers was no older than him.

'The world is chaos and death and destruction. But people like you – you don't stand for that. If there is any order in the world, any peace – it's because of you, John, and those very few like you.'

Grey felt he should say something, but was at a loss as to what that might be. Carruthers rose and came to Grey, putting a hand – the left – on his shoulder, the other gently against his face.

'What is it the Bible says?' Carruthers said quietly. 'Blessed are they that hunger and thirst for justice, for they shall be satisfied? I hunger, John,' he whispered. 'And you thirst. You won't fail me.' The fingers of Charlie's secret moved on his skin, a plea, a caress.

The custom of the army is that a court-martial be presided over by a senior officer and such a number of other officers as he shall think fit to serve as council, these being generally four in number, but can be more but not generally less than three. The person accused shall have the right to

103

call witnesses in his support, and the council shall question these, as well as any other persons whom they may wish, and shall thus determine the circumstances, and if conviction ensue, the sentence to be imposed.

That rather vague statement was evidently all that existed in terms of written definition and directive regarding the operations of courts-martial – or was all that Hal had turned up for him in the brief period prior to his departure. There were no formal laws governing such courts, nor did the law of the land apply to them. In short, the army was – as always, Grey thought – a law unto itself.

That being so, he might have considerable leeway in accomplishing what Charlie Carruthers wanted – or not, depending upon the personalities and professional alliances of the officers who composed the court. It would behove him to discover these men as soon as possible.

In the meantime, he had another small duty to discharge.

'Tom,' he called, rummaging in his trunk, 'have you discovered Captain Stubbs's billet?'

'Yes, me lord. And if you'll give over ruining your shirts, there, I'll tell you.' With a censorious look at his master, Tom nudged him deftly aside. 'What you a-looking for in there, anyway?'

'The miniature of my cousin and her child.' Grey stood back, permitting Tom to bend over the open chest, tenderly patting the abused shirts back into their tidy folds. The chest itself was rather scorched, but the soldiers had succeeded in rescuing it – and Grey's wardrobe, to Tom's relief.

'Here, me lord.' Tom withdrew the little packet, and handed it gently to Grey. 'Give me best to Captain Stubbs.

Reckon he'll be glad to get that. The little 'un's got quite the look of him, don't he?'

It took some little time, even with Tom's direction, to discover Malcolm Stubbs's billet. The address – insofar as it could be called one – lay in the poorer section of the town, somewhere down a muddy lane that ended abruptly at the river. Grey was surprised at this; Stubbs was a most sociable sort, and a conscientious officer. Why was he not billeted in an inn, or a good private house, near his troops?

By the time he found the lane, he had an uneasy feeling; this grew markedly, as he poked his way through the ramshackle sheds and the knots of filthy, polyglot children that broke from their play, brightening at the novel sight, and followed him, hissing unintelligible speculations to each other, but who stared blankly at him, mouths open, when he asked after Captain Stubbs, pointing at his own uniform by way of illustration, with a questioning wave at their surroundings.

He had made his way all the way down the lane, and his boots were caked with mud, dung, and a thick plastering of the leaves that sifted in a constant rain from the giant trees, before he discovered someone willing to answer him. This was an ancient Indian, sitting peacefully on a rock at the river's edge, wrapped in a striped British trade blanket, fishing. The man spoke a mixture of three or four languages, only two of which Grey understood, but this basis of understanding was adequate.

'*Un, deux, trois*, in back,' the ancient told him, pointing a thumb up the lane, then jerking this appendage sideways. Something in an aboriginal tongue followed, in which Grey thought he detected a reference to a woman – doubtless the owner of the house where Stubbs was billeted. A concluding reference to '*le bon capitaine*' seemed to reinforce this impression, and thanking the gentleman in both French and English, Grey retraced his steps to the

105

third house up the lane, still trailing a line of curious urchins, like the ragged tail of a kite.

No one answered his knock, but he went round the house – followed by the children – and discovered a small hut behind it, smoke coming from its grey stone chimney.

The day was beautiful, with a sky the colour of sapphires, and the air was suffused with the tang of early autumn. The door of the hut was ajar, to admit the crisp, fresh air, but he did not push it open. Instead, he drew his dagger from his belt and knocked with the hilt – to admiring gasps from his audience at the appearance of the knife. He repressed the urge to turn round and bow to them.

He heard no footsteps from within, but the door opened suddenly, revealing a young Indian woman, whose face blazed with sudden joy at beholding him.

He blinked, startled, and in that blink of an eye, the joy disappeared and the young woman clutched at the doorjamb for support, her other hand fisted into her chest.

'Batinse!?' she gasped, clearly terrified. 'Que se passe-t-il?'

'Rien,' he replied, equally startled. 'Ne vous inquiétez pas, madame. Le Capitaine Stubbs habite ici?' Don't perturb yourself, madame. Does Captain Stubbs live here?

Her eyes, already huge, rolled back in her head, and he seized her arm, fearing lest she faint at his feet. The largest of the urchins following him rushed forward and pushed the door open, and he put an arm round the woman's waist and half-dragged, half-carried her into the house.

Taking this as invitation, the rest of the children crowded in behind him, murmuring in what appeared to be sympathy, as he lugged the young woman to the bed and deposited her thereon. A small girl, wearing little more than a pair of drawers snugged round her insubstantial waist with a piece of string, pressed in beside him and said something to the young woman. Not receiving an answer, the girl behaved as though she had, turning and racing out of the door.

Grey hesitated, not sure what to do. The woman was breathing, though pale, and her eyelids fluttered.

'*Voulez-vous un peu d'eau?*' he inquired, turning about in search of water. He spotted a bucket of water near the hearth, but his attention was distracted from this by an object propped beside it. A cradle-board, with a swaddled infant bound to it, blinking large, curious eyes in his direction.

He knew already, of course, but kneeled down before the infant and waggled a tentative forefinger at it. The baby's eyes were big and dark, like its mother's, and the skin a paler shade of her own. The hair, though, was not straight, thick and black. It was the colour of cinnamon, and exploded from the child's skull in a nimbus of the same curls that Malcolm Stubbs kept rigorously clipped to his scalp and hidden beneath his wig.

'Wha' happen with *le capitaine*?' a peremptory voice demanded behind him. He turned on his heels, and finding a rather large woman looming over him, rose to his feet and bowed.

'Nothing whatever, madame,' he assured her. *Not yet, it hasn't.* 'I was merely seeking Captain Stubbs, to give him a message.'

'Oh.' The woman – French, but plainly the younger woman's mother or aunt – left off glowering at him, and seemed to deflate somewhat, settling back into a less threatening shape. 'Well, then. *D'un urgence*, this message?' She eyed him; clearly other British officers were not in the habit of visiting Stubbs at home. Most likely Stubbs had an official billet elsewhere, where he conducted his regimental business. No wonder they thought he'd come to say that Stubbs was dead or injured. *Not yet*, he added grimly to himself.

'No,' he said, feeling the weight of the miniature in his pocket. 'Important, but not urgent.' He left then. None of the children followed him.

Normally, it was not difficult to discover the whereabouts of a particular soldier, but Malcolm Stubbs seemed to have disappeared into thin air. Over the course of the next week, Grey combed headquarters, the military encampment, and the village, but no trace of his disgraceful cousin-by-marriage could be found. Still odder, no one appeared to have missed the captain. The men of Stubbs's immediate company merely shrugged in confusion, and his superior officer had evidently gone off upriver to inspect the state of various postings. Frustrated, Grey retired to the riverbank to think.

Two logical possibilities presented themselves – no, three. One, that Stubbs had heard about Grey's arrival, supposed that Grey would discover exactly what he had discovered, and had in consequence panicked and deserted. Two, he'd fallen foul of someone in a tavern or back alley, been killed, and was presently decomposing quietly under a layer of leaves in the woods. Or three – he'd been sent somewhere to do something, quietly.

Grey doubted the first exceedingly; Stubbs wasn't prone to panic, and if he had heard of Grey's arrival, Malcolm's first act would have been to come and find him, thus preventing his poking about in the village and finding what he'd found. He dismissed that possibility accordingly.

He dismissed the second still more promptly. Had Stubbs been killed, either deliberately or by accident, the alarm would have been raised. The army did generally know where its soldiers were, and if they weren't where they were meant to be, steps were taken. The same held true for desertion.

Right, then. If Stubbs was gone and no one was looking for him, it naturally followed that the army had sent him to wherever he'd gone. Since no one seemed to know where that was, his mission was presumably secret. And given Wolfe's current position and present obsession, that almost certainly meant that Malcolm Stubbs had gone downriver, searching for some way to attack Quebec. Grey sighed, satisfied with his deductions. Which in turn meant that – barring his being caught by the French, scalped or abducted by hostile Indians, or eaten by a bear – Stubbs would be back, eventually. There was nothing to do but wait.

He leaned against a tree, watching a couple of fishing canoes make their way slowly downstream, hugging the bank. The sky was overcast and the air light on his skin, a pleasant change from the summer heat. Cloudy skies were good for fishing; his father's gamekeeper had told him that. He wondered why – were the fish dazzled by sun, and thus sought murky hiding places in the depths, but rose toward the surface in dimmer light?

He thought suddenly of the electric eel, which Suddfield had told him lived in the silt-choked waters of the Amazon. The thing did have remarkably small eyes, and its proprietor had opined that it was able to use its remarkable electrical abilities in some way to discern, as well as to electrocute, its prey.

He couldn't have said what made him raise his head at that precise moment, but he looked up to find one of the canoes hovering in the shallow water a few feet from him. The Indian paddling the canoe gave him a brilliant smile.

'Englishman!' he called. 'You want to fish with me?'

A small jolt of electricity ran through him and he straightened up. Manoke's eyes were fixed on his, and he felt in memory the touch of lips and tongue, and the scent of fresh-sheared copper. His heart was racing – go off in company with an Indian he barely knew? It might easily be a trap. He could end up scalped or worse. But electric eels were not the only ones to discern things by means of a sixth sense, he thought.

'Yes!' he called. 'Meet you at the landing!'

Two weeks later, he stepped out of Manoke's canoe onto the landing, thin, sunburned, cheerful, and still in possession of his hair. Tom Byrd would be beside himself, he reflected; he'd left word as to what he was doing, but naturally had been able to give no estimate of his return. Doubtless poor Tom would be thinking he'd been captured and dragged off into slavery or scalped, his hair sold to the French.

In fact, they had drifted slowly downriver, pausing to fish wherever the mood took them, camping on sandbars and small islands, grilling their catch and eating their supper in smoke-scented peace, beneath the leaves of oak and alder. They had seen other craft now and then – not only canoes, but many French packet boats and brigs, as well as two English warships, tacking slowly up the river, sails bellying, the distant shouts of the sailors foreign to him just then as the tongues of the Iroquois.

And in the late summer dusk of the first day, Manoke had wiped his fingers after eating, stood up, casually untied his breech-clout and let it fall. Then waited, grinning, while Grey fought his way out of shirt and breeches.

They'd swum in the river to refresh themselves before eating; the Indian was clean, his skin no longer greasy. And yet he seemed to taste of wild game, the rich, uneasy tang of venison. Grey had wondered whether it was the man's race that was responsible, or only his diet?

'What do I taste like?' he'd asked, out of curiosity.

Manoke, absorbed in his business, had said something that might have been, 'Cock,' but might equally have been some expression of mild disgust, so Grey thought better of pursuing this line of inquiry. Besides, if he *did* taste of beef and biscuit or Yorkshire pudding, would the Indian recognise that? For that matter, did he really want to know, if he did? He did not, he decided, and they enjoyed the rest of the evening without benefit of conversation.

He scratched the small of his back where his breeches rubbed, uncomfortable with mosquito bites and the peel of fading sunburn. He'd tried the native style of dress, seeing its convenience, but had scorched his bum by lying too long in the sun one afternoon, and thereafter resorted to breeches, not wishing to hear any further jocular remarks regarding the whiteness of his arse.

Thinking such pleasant but disjointed thoughts, he'd made his way halfway through the town before noticing that there were many more soldiers in evidence than there had been before. Drums were pattering up and down the sloping, muddy streets, calling men from their billets, the rhythm of the military day making itself felt. His own steps fell naturally into the beat of the drums, he straightened, and felt the army reach out suddenly, seizing him, shaking him out of his sunburned bliss.

He glanced involuntarily up the hill and saw the flags fluttering above the large inn that served as field headquarters. Wolfe had returned.

Grey found his own quarters, reassured Tom as to his well-being, submitted to having his hair forcibly untangled, combed, powdered and tightly bound up in a formal queue, and with his clean uniform chafing his sunburned skin, went to present himself to the general, as courtesy demanded. He knew James Wolfe by sight; Wolfe was his own age, had fought at Culloden, been a junior officer under Cumberland during the Highland campaign – but did not know him personally. He'd heard a great deal about him, though.

'Grey, is it? Pardloe's brother, are you?' Wolfe lifted his long nose in Grey's direction, as though sniffing at him, in the manner of one dog inspecting another's backside. Grey trusted he would not be required to reciprocate, and instead bowed politely.

'My brother's compliments, sir.'

Actually, what his brother had had to say had been far from complimentary.

'Melodramatic ass,' was what Hal had said, hastily briefing him before his departure. 'Showy, bad judgement, terrible strategist. Has the Devil's own luck, though, I'll give him that. *Don't* follow him into anything stupid.'

Wolfe nodded amiably enough.

'And you've come as a witness for . . . who is it – Captain Carruthers?'

'Yes, sir. Has a date been set for the court-martial?'

'Dunno. Has it?' Wolfe asked his adjutant, a tall, spindly creature with a beady eye.

'No, sir. Now that his lordship is here, though, we can proceed. I'll tell Brigadier Lethbridge-Stewart; he's to chair the proceeding.'

Wolfe waved a hand.

'No, wait a bit. The brigadier will have other things on his mind. 'Til after . . .'

The adjutant nodded and made a note.

'Yes, sir.'

Wolfe was eyeing Grey, in the manner of a small boy bursting to share some secret.

'D'you understand Highlanders, colonel?'

Grey blinked, surprised.

'Insofar as such a thing is possible, sir,' he replied politely, and Wolfe brayed with laughter.

'Good man.' The general turned his head to one side and eyed Grey, appraising him. 'I've got a hundred or so of the creatures; been thinking what use they might be. I think I've found one – a small adventure.'

The adjutant smiled, despite himself, then quickly erased the smile.

'Indeed, sir?' Grey said cautiously.

'Somewhat dangerous,' Wolfe went on carelessly. 'But then, it's the Highlanders . . . no great mischief should they fall. Would you care to join us?'

Don't follow him into anything stupid. Right, Hal, he thought. Any suggestions on how to decline an offer like that from one's titular commander?

'I should be pleased, sir,' he said, feeling a brief ripple of unease down his spine. 'When?'

'In two weeks – at the dark of the moon.' Wolfe was all but wagging his tail in enthusiasm.

'Am I permitted to know the nature of the . . . er . . . expedition?'

Wolfe exchanged a look of anticipation with his adjutant, then turned eyes shiny with excitement on Grey.

'We're going to take Quebec, colonel.'

So Wolfe thought he had found his *point d'appui*. Or rather, his trusted scout, Malcolm Stubbs, had found it for him. Grey returned briefly to his quarters, put the miniature of

113

Olivia and little Cromwell in his pocket, and went to find Stubbs.

He didn't bother thinking what to say to Malcolm. It was as well, he thought, that he hadn't found Stubbs immediately after his discovery of the Indian mistress and her child; he might simply have knocked Stubbs down, without the bother of explanation. But time had elapsed, and his blood was cooler now. He was detached.

Or so he thought, until he entered a prosperous tavern – Malcolm had elevated tastes in wine – and found his cousin-by-marriage at a table, relaxed and jovial among his friends. Stubbs was aptly named, being approximately five foot four in both dimensions, a fair-haired fellow with an inclination to become red in the face when deeply entertained or deep in drink.

At the moment, he appeared to be experiencing both conditions, laughing at something one of his companions had said, waving his empty glass in the barmaid's direction. He turned back, spotted Grey coming across the floor, and lit up like a beacon. He'd been spending a good deal of time out of doors, Grey saw; he was nearly as sunburned as Grey himself.

'Grey!' he cried. 'Why, here's a sight for sore eyes! What the devil brings you to the wilderness?' Then he noticed Grey's expression, and his joviality faded slightly, a puzzled frown growing between his thick brows.

It hadn't time to grow far. Grey lunged across the table, scattering glasses, and seized Stubbs by the shirtfront.

'You come with me, you bloody swine,' he whispered, face shoved up against the younger man's, 'or I'll kill you right here, I swear it.'

He let go then, and stood, blood hammering in his temples. Stubbs rubbed at his chest, affronted, startled – and afraid. He could see it in the wide blue eyes. Slowly, Stubbs got up, motioning to his companions to stay.

'No bother, chaps,' he said, making a good attempt at casualness. 'My cousin – family emergency, what?'

Grey saw two of the men exchange knowing glances, then look at Grey, wary. They knew, all right.

Stiffly, he gestured for Stubbs to precede him, and they passed out of the door in a pretence of dignity. Once outside, though, he grabbed Stubbs by the arm and dragged him round the corner into a small alleyway. He pushed Stubbs hard, so that he lost his balance and fell against the wall; Grey kicked his legs out from under him, then kneeled on his thigh, digging his knee viciously into the thick muscle. Stubbs uttered a strangled noise, not quite a scream.

Grey dug in his pocket, hand trembling with fury, and brought out the miniature, which he showed briefly to Stubbs, before grinding it into the man's cheek. Stubbs yelped, grabbed at it, and Grey let him have it, rising unsteadily off the man.

'How dare you?' he said, low-voiced and vicious. 'How dare you dishonour your wife, your son?'

Malcolm was breathing hard, one hand clutching his abused thigh, but was regaining his composure.

'It's nothing,' he said. 'Nothing to do with Olivia at all.' He swallowed, wiped a hand across his mouth, and took a cautious glance at the miniature in his hand. 'That the sprat, is it? Good . . . good-looking lad. Looks like me, don't he?'

Grey kicked him brutally in the stomach.

'Yes, and so does your *other* son,' he hissed. 'How could you do such a thing?'

Malcolm's mouth opened, but nothing came out. He struggled for breath like a landed fish. Grey watched without pity. He'd have the man split and grilled over charcoal before he was done. He bent and took the miniature from Stubbs's unresisting hand, tucking it back in his pocket.

After a long moment, Stubbs achieved a whining gasp, and his face, which had gone puce, subsided back toward its normal brick colour. Saliva had collected at the corners of his mouth; he licked his lips, spat, then sat back, breathing heavily, and looked up at Grey.

'Going to hit me again?'

'Not just yet.'

'Good.' He stretched out a hand, and Grey took it, grunting as he helped Stubbs to his feet. Malcolm leaned against the wall, still panting, and eyed him.

'So, who made you God, Grey? Who are you, to sit in judgement of me, eh?'

Grey nearly hit him again, but desisted.

'Who am *I*?' he echoed. 'Olivia's fucking cousin, that's who! The nearest male relative she's got on this continent! And you, need I remind you – and evidently I do – are her fucking husband. Judgement? What the devil d'you mean by that, you filthy lecher?'

Malcolm coughed, and spat again.

'Yes. Well. I said, it's nothing to do with Olivia – and so it's nothing to do with you.' He spoke with apparent calmness, but Grey could see the pulse hammering in his throat, the nervous shiftiness of his eyes. 'It's nothing out of the ordinary – it's the bloody custom, for God's sake. Everybody—'

He kneed Stubbs in the balls.

'Try again,' he advised Stubbs, who had fallen down and was curled into a foetal position, moaning. 'Take your time; I'm not busy.'

Aware of eyes upon him, he turned to see several soldiers gathered at the mouth of the alley, hesitating. He was still wearing his dress uniform, though – somewhat the worse for wear, but still clearly displaying his rank – and when he gave them an evil look, they hastily dispersed.

'I should kill you here and now, you know,' he said to Stubbs after a few moments. The rage that had propelled him was draining away, though, as he watched the man retch and heave at his feet, and he spoke wearily. 'Better for Olivia to have a dead husband – and whatever property you leave – than a live scoundrel, who will betray her with her friends – likely with her own maid.'

Stubbs muttered something indistinguishable, and Grey bent, grasping him by the hair, and pulled his head up.

'What was that?'

'Wasn't . . . like that.' Groaning and clutching himself, Malcolm manoeuvred himself gingerly into a sitting position, knees drawn up. He gasped for a bit, head on his knees, before being able to go on.

'You don't know, do you?' He spoke low-voiced, not raising his head. 'You haven't seen the things I've seen. Not . . . done what I've had to do.'

'What do you mean?'

'The . . . the killing. Not . . . battle. Not an honourable thing. Farmers. Women . . .' He saw Stubbs's heavy throat move, swallowing. 'I— we— for months now. Looting the countryside, burning farms, villages.' He sighed, broad shoulders slumping. 'The men, they don't mind. Half of them are brutes to begin with.' He breathed. 'Think . . . nothing of shooting a man on his doorstep and taking his wife next to his body.' He swallowed. ''Tisn't only Montcalm who pays for scalps,' he said, in a low voice. Grey couldn't avoid hearing the rawness in his voice, a pain that wasn't physical.

'Every soldier's seen such things, Malcolm,' he said after a short silence, almost gently. 'You're an officer. It's your job to keep them in check.' *And you know damn well it isn't always possible*, he thought.

'I know,' Malcolm said, and began to cry. 'I couldn't.'

Grey waited while he sobbed, feeling increasingly

foolish and uncomfortable. At last, the broad shoulders heaved and subsided. After a moment, Malcolm said, in a voice that quivered only a little, 'Everybody finds a way, don't they? And there're not that many ways. Drink, cards, or women.' He raised his head and shifted a little, grimacing as he eased into a more comfortable position. 'But you don't go in much for women, do you?' he added, looking up.

Grey felt the bottom of his stomach drop, but realised in time that Malcolm had spoken matter-of-factly, with no tone of accusation.

'No,' he said, and drew a deep breath. 'Drink, mostly.'

Malcolm nodded, wiping his nose on his sleeve.

'Drink doesn't help me,' he said. 'I fall asleep, but I don't forget. I just dream about . . . things. And whores— I— well, I didn't want to get poxed and maybe . . . well, Olivia,' he muttered, looking down. 'No good at cards,' he said, clearing his throat. 'But sleeping in a woman's arms— I can sleep, then.'

Grey leaned against the wall, feeling nearly as battered as Malcolm Stubbs. Bright green leaves drifted through the air, whirling round them, settling in the mud.

'All right,' he said, eventually. 'What do you mean to do?'

'Dunno,' Stubbs said, in a tone of flat resignation. 'Think of something, I suppose.'

Grey bent and offered a hand; Stubbs got carefully to his feet, and nodding to Grey, shuffled toward the alley's mouth, bent over and holding himself as though his insides might fall out. Halfway there, though, he stopped and looked back over his shoulder. There was an anxious look on his face, half-embarrassed.

'Can I— the miniature? They are still mine, Olivia and the . . . my son.'

Grey heaved a sigh that went to the marrow of his bones; he felt a thousand years old.

'Yes, they are,' he said, and digging the miniature out of his pocket, tucked it carefully into Stubbs's coat. 'Remember it, will you?'

Two days later, a convoy of troop ships arrived, under the command of Admiral Holmes. The town was flooded afresh with men hungry for unsalted meat, fresh baked bread, liquor, and women. And a messenger arrived at Grey's quarters, bearing a parcel for him from his brother, with the admiral's compliments.

It was small, but packaged with care, wrapped in oilcloth and tied about with twine, the knot sealed with his brother's crest. That was unlike Hal, whose usual communiqués consisted of hastily dashed-off notes, generally employing slightly fewer than the minimum number of words necessary to convey his message. They were seldom signed, let alone sealed.

Tom Byrd appeared to think the package slightly ominous, too; he had set it by itself, apart from the other mail, and weighted it down with a large bottle of brandy, apparently to prevent it escaping. That, or he suspected Grey might require the brandy to sustain him in the arduous effort of reading a letter consisting of more than one page.

'Very thoughtful of you, Tom,' he murmured, smiling to himself and reaching for his pen-knife.

In fact, the letter within occupied less than a page, bore neither salutation nor signature, and was completely Hal-like.

Minnie wishes to know whether you are starving, though I don't know what she proposes to do about it, should the

119

answer be yes. The boys wish to know whether you have taken any scalps – they are confident that no Red Indian would succeed in taking yours; I share this opinion. You had better bring three tommyhawks when you come home.

Here is your paperweight; the jeweller was most impressed by the quality of the stone. The other thing is a copy of Adams's confession. They hanged him yesterday.

The other contents of the parcel consisted of a small wash-leather pouch, and an official-looking document on several sheets of good parchment, this folded and sealed – this time with the seal of George II. Grey left it lying on the table, fetched one of the pewter cups from his campaign chest, and filled it to the brim with brandy, wondering anew at his valet's perspicacity.

Thus fortified, he sat down and took up the little pouch, from which he decanted a small, heavy gold paperweight, made in the shape of a half-moon set among ocean waves, into his hand. It was set with a faceted – and very large – sapphire, that glowed like the evening star in its setting. Where had James Fraser acquired such a thing? he wondered.

He turned it in his hand, admiring the workmanship, but then set it aside. He sipped his brandy for a bit, watching the official document as though it might explode. He was reasonably sure it would.

He weighed the document in his hand, and felt the breeze from his window lift it a little, like the flap of a sail, just before it fills and bellies with a snap.

Waiting wouldn't help. And Hal plainly knew what it said, anyway; he'd tell Grey eventually, whether he wanted to know or not. Sighing, he put by his brandy and broke the seal.

I, Bernard Donald Adams, do make this confession of my own free will . . .

Was it? he wondered. He did not know Adams's handwriting, could not tell whether the document had been written or dictated— no, wait. He flipped over the sheets and examined the signature. Same hand. All right, he had written it himself.

He squinted at the writing. It seemed firm. Probably not extracted under torture, then. Perhaps it was the truth.

'Idiot,' he said under his breath. 'Read the god-damned thing and have done with it!'

He drank the rest of his brandy at a gulp, flattened the pages upon the stone of the parapet and read, at last, the story of his father's death.

The duke had suspected the existence of a Jacobite ring for some time, and had identified three men whom he thought involved in it. Still, he made no move to expose them, until the warrant was issued for his own arrest, upon the charge of treason. Hearing of this, he had sent at once to Adams, summoning him to the duke's country home at Earlingden.

Adams did not know how much the duke knew of his own involvement, but did not dare to stay away, lest the duke, under arrest, denounce him. So he armed himself with a pistol, and rode by night to Earlingden, arriving just before dawn.

He had come to the conservatory's outside doors, and been admitted by the duke. Whereupon 'some conversation' had ensued.

I had learned that day of the issuance of a warrant for arrest upon the charge of treason, to be served upon the body of the Duke of Pardloe. I was uneasy at this, for the duke had questioned both myself and some colleagues previously, in a manner that suggested to me that he suspected the existence of a secret movement to restore the Stuart throne.

I argued against the duke's arrest, as I did not know the extent of his knowledge or suspicions, and feared that if placed in exigent danger himself, he might be able to point a finger at myself or my principal colleagues, these being Joseph Arbuthnot, Lord Creemore, and Sir Edwin Bellman. Sir Edwin was urgent upon the point, though, saying that it would do no harm; any accusations made by Pardloe could be dismissed as simple attempts to save himself, with no grounding in fact – while the fact of his arrest would naturally cause a widespread assumption of guilt, and would distract any attentions that might at present be directed toward us.

The duke, hearing of the warrant, sent to my lodgings that evening, and summoned me to call upon him at his country home, immediately. I dared not spurn this summons, not knowing what evidence he might possess, and therefore rode by night to his estate, arriving soon before dawn.

Adams had met the duke there, in the conservatory. Whatever the form of this conversation, its result had been drastic.

I had brought with me a pistol, which I had loaded outside the house. I meant this only for protection, as I did not know what the duke's demeanour might be.

Dangerous, evidently. Gerard Grey, Duke of Pardloe, had also come armed to the meeting. According to Adams, the duke had withdrawn his own pistol from the recesses of his jacket – whether to attack or merely threaten was not clear – whereupon Adams had drawn his own pistol in panic. Both men fired; Adams thought the duke's pistol had misfired, since the duke could not have missed, at the distance.

Adams's shot did not misfire, nor did it miss its target, and seeing the blood upon the duke's bosom, Adams had panicked and run. Looking back, he had seen the duke, mortally stricken but still upright, seize the branch of the peach tree beside him for support, whereupon the duke had used the last of his strength to hurl his own useless weapon at Adams before collapsing.

John Grey sat still, slowly rubbing the parchment sheets between his fingers. He wasn't seeing the neat strokes in which Adams had set down his bloodless account. He saw the blood. A dark red, beautiful as a jewel where the sun through the glass of the roof struck it suddenly. His father's hair, tousled as it might be after hunting. And the peach, fallen to those same tiles, its perfection spoiled and ruined.

He set the papers down on the table; the wind stirred them, and by reflex, he reached for his new paperweight to hold them down.

What was it Carruthers had called him? Someone who keeps order. You and your brother, he'd said. You don't stand for it. If the world has peace and order, it's because of men like you.

Perhaps. He wondered if Carruthers knew the cost of peace and order – but then recalled Charlie's haggard face, its youthful beauty gone, nothing left in it now save the bones and the dogged determination that kept him breathing.

Yes, he knew.

Just after full dark, they boarded the ships. The convoy included Admiral Holmes's flagship, the *Lowestoff*, three men of war: the *Squirrel*, *Sea Horse*, and *Hunter*, a number of armed sloops, others loaded with ordnance, powder and ammunition, and a number of transports for the troops – 1,800 men in all. The *Sutherland* had been left below, anchored just out of firing range of the fortress, to keep an eye on the enemy's motions; the river there was littered with floating batteries and prowling small French craft.

He travelled with Wolfe and the Highlanders aboard *Sea Horse*, and spent the journey on deck, too keyed up to bear being below.

His brother's warning kept recurring in the back of his mind – *Don't follow him into anything stupid* – but it was much too late to think of that, and to block it out, he challenged one of the other officers to a whistling contest – each party to whistle the entirety of 'The Roast Beef of Old England', the loser the man who laughed first. He lost, but did not think of his brother again.

Just after midnight, the big ships quietly furled their sails, dropped anchor, and lay like slumbering gulls on the dark river. Anse au Foulon, the landing spot that Malcolm Stubbs and his scouts had recommended to General Wolfe, lay seven miles downriver, at the foot of sheer and crumbling slate cliffs that led upward to the Heights of Abraham.

'Is it named for the Biblical Abraham, do you think?' Grey had asked curiously, hearing the name, but had been informed that in fact, the cliff top comprised a farmstead belonging to an ex-pilot named Abraham Martin.

On the whole, he thought this prosaic origin just as

124

well. There was likely to be drama enough enacted on that ground, without thought of ancient prophets, conversations with God, nor any calculation of how many just men might be contained within the fortress of Quebec.

With a minimum of fuss, the Highlanders and their officers, Wolfe and his chosen troops – Grey among them – debarked into the small *bateaux* that would carry them silently down to the landing point.

The sounds of oars were mostly drowned by the river's rushing, and there was little conversation in the boats. Wolfe sat in the prow of the lead boat, facing his troops, looking now and then over his shoulder at the shore. Quite without warning, he began to speak. He didn't raise his voice, but the night was so still that those in the boat had little trouble in hearing him. To Grey's astonishment, he was reciting 'Elegy in a Country Churchyard'.

Melodramatic ass, Grey thought – and yet could not deny that the recitation was oddly moving. Wolfe made no show of it. It was as though he were simply talking to himself, and a shiver went over Grey as he reached the last verse.

The boast of heraldry, the pomp of pow'r,
And all that beauty, all that wealth e'er gave,
Awaits alike the inexorable hour.

'*The paths of glory lead but to the grave,*' Wolfe ended, so low-voiced that only the three or four men closest heard him. Grey was close enough to hear him clear his throat with a small 'hem' noise, and saw his shoulders lift.

'Gentlemen,' Wolfe said, lifting his voice as well, 'I should rather have written those lines than have taken Quebec.'

There was a faint stir, and a breath of laughter among the men.

125

So would I, Grey thought. *The poet who wrote them is likely sitting by his cosy fire in Cambridge eating buttered crumpets, not preparing to fall from a great height or get his arse shot off.*

He didn't know whether this was simply more of Wolfe's characteristic drama. Possibly – possibly not, he thought. He'd met Colonel Walsing by the latrines that morning, and Walsing had mentioned that Wolfe had given him a pendant the night before, with instructions to deliver it to Miss Landringham, to whom Wolfe was engaged.

But then, it was nothing out of the ordinary for men to put their personal valuables into the care of a friend before a hot battle. Were you killed or badly injured, your body might be looted before your comrades managed to retrieve you, and not everyone had a trustworthy servant with whom to leave such items. He himself had often carried snuffboxes, pocket-watches or rings into battle for friends – he'd had a reputation for luck, prior to Crefeld. No one had asked him to carry anything tonight.

He shifted his weight by instinct, feeling the current change, and Simon Fraser, next to him, swayed in the opposite direction, bumping him.

'*Pardon*,' Fraser murmured. Wolfe had made them all recite poetry in French round the dinner table the night before, and it was agreed that Fraser had the most authentic accent, he having fought with the French in Holland some years prior. Should they be hailed by a sentry, it would be his job to reply. Doubtless, Grey thought, Fraser was now thinking frantically in French, trying to saturate his mind with the language, lest any stray bit of English escape in panic.

'*Ce n'est rien*,' Grey murmured back, and Fraser chuckled, deep in his throat.

It was cloudy, the sky streaked with the shredded remnants of retreating rain-clouds. That was good; the surface of the river was broken, patched with faint light, fractured by stones and drifting tree-branches. Though even so, a decent sentry could scarcely fail to spot a train of boats.

Cold numbed his face, but his palms were sweating. He touched the dagger at his belt again; he was aware that he touched it every few minutes, as if needing to verify its presence, but couldn't help it, and didn't worry about it. He was straining his eyes, looking for anything – the glow of a careless fire, the shifting of a rock that was not a rock . . . nothing.

How far? he wondered. Two miles, three? He'd not yet seen the cliffs himself, was not sure how far below Gareon they lay.

The rush of water and the easy movement of the boat began to make him sleepy, tension notwithstanding, and he shook his head, yawning exaggeratedly to throw it off.

'*Quel est ce bateau?*' What boat is that? The shout from the shore seemed anticlimactic when it came, barely more remarkable than a night bird's call. But the next instant, Simon Fraser's hand crushed his, grinding the bones together as Fraser gulped air and shouted '*Celui de la Reine!*'

Grey clenched his teeth, not to let any blasphemous response escape. If the sentry demanded a password, he'd likely be crippled for life, he thought. An instant later, though, the sentry shouted, '*Passez!*' and Fraser's death-grip relaxed. Simon was breathing like a bellows, but nudged him and whispered '*Pardon,*' again.

'*Ce n'est* fucking *rien,*' he muttered, rubbing his hand and tenderly flexing the fingers.

They were getting close. Men were shifting to and fro in anticipation, more than Grey checking their weapons, straightening coats, coughing, spitting over the side, readying themselves. Still, it was a nerve-racking quarter-hour more before they began to swing toward shore – and another sentry called from the dark.

Grey's heart squeezed like a fist, and he nearly gasped with the twinge of pain from his old wounds.

'*Qui êtes-vous? Quels sont ces bateaux?*' a French voice demanded suspiciously. Who are you? What boats are those?

This time, he was ready, and seized Fraser's hand himself. Simon held on and leaning out toward the shore, called hoarsely, '*Des bateaux de ravitaillement! Taisez-vous – les anglais sont proches*! Provision boats! Be quiet – the British are nearby! Grey felt an insane urge to laugh, but didn't. In fact, the *Sutherland was* nearby, lurking out of cannon shot downstream, and doubtless the frogs knew it. In any case, the guard called, more quietly, '*Passez!*', and the train of boats slid smoothly past and round the final bend.

The bottom of the boat grated on sand, and half the men were over at once, tugging it further up. Wolfe half-leaped, half-fell over the side in eagerness, all trace of sombreness gone. They'd come aground on a small sandbar, just offshore, and the other boats were beaching now, a swarm of black figures gathering like ants.

Twenty-four of the Highlanders were meant to try the ascent first, finding – and insofar as possible, clearing, for the cliff was defended not only by its steepness but by abatis, nests of sharpened logs – a trail for the rest. Simon's bulky form faded into the dark, his French accent changing at once into the sibilant Gaelic as he hissed the men into position. Grey rather missed his presence.

He was not sure whether Wolfe had chosen the Highlanders for their skill at climbing, or because he preferred to risk them rather than his other troops. The latter, he thought. Like most English officers, Wolfe regarded the Highlanders with distrust and a certain contempt. Those officers, at least, who'd never fought with them – or against them.

From his spot at the foot of the cliff, he couldn't see them, but he could hear them; the scuffle of feet, now and then a wild scrabble and a clatter of falling small stones, loud grunts of effort and what he recognised as Gaelic invocations of God, His mother, and assorted saints. One man near him pulled a string of beads from the neck of his shirt and kissed the tiny cross attached to it, then tucked it back, and seizing a small sapling that grew out of the rock-face, leaped upward, kilt swinging, broadsword swaying from his belt in brief silhouette, before the darkness took him. Grey touched his dagger's hilt again, his own talisman against evil.

It was a long wait in the darkness; to some extent, he envied the Highlanders, who, whatever else they might be encountering – and the scrabbling noises and half-strangled whoops as a foot slipped and a comrade grabbed a hand or arm suggested that the climb was just as impossible as it seemed – were not dealing with boredom.

A sudden rumble and crashing came from above, and the shore-party scattered in panic as several sharpened logs plunged out of the dark above, dislodged from an abatis. One of them had struck point down no more than six feet from Grey, and stood quivering in the sand. With no discussion, the shore-party retreated to the sandbar.

The scrabblings and gruntings grew fainter, and suddenly ceased. Wolfe, who had been sitting on a boulder, stood up suddenly, straining his eyes upward.

'They've made it,' he whispered, and his fists curled in an excitement that Grey shared. 'God, they've made it!'

Well enough, and the men at the foot of the cliff held their breaths; there was a guard post at the top of the cliff. Silence, bar the everlasting noise of tree and river. And then a shot.

Just one. The men below shifted, touching their weapons, ready, not knowing for what.

Were there sounds above? He could not tell, and out of sheer nervousness, turned aside to urinate against the side of the cliff. He was fastening his flies when he heard Simon Fraser's voice above.

'Got 'em, by God!' he said. 'Come on, lads – the night's not long enough!'

The next few hours passed in a blur of the most arduous endeavour Grey had seen since he'd crossed the Scottish Highlands with his brother's regiment, bringing cannon to General Cope. No, actually, he thought, as he stood in darkness, one leg wedged between a tree and the rock-face, thirty feet of invisible space below him, and rope burning through his palms with an unseen deadweight of two hundred pounds or so on the end, this was worse.

The Highlanders had surprised the guard, shot their fleeing captain in the heel, and made all of them prisoner. That was the easy part. The next thing was for the rest of the landing party to ascend to the cliff top, now that the trail – if there was such a thing – had been cleared, where they would make preparations to raise not only the rest of the troops now coming down the river aboard the transports, but also seventeen battering cannon, twelve howitzers, three mortars, and all of the necessary encumbrances in terms of shell, powder, planks and limbers necessary to make this artillery effective. At least, Grey reflected, by the time they were done, the vertical trail up the cliffside would likely have been trampled into a simple cowpath.

As the sky lightened, Grey looked up for a moment from his spot at the top of the cliff, where he was now overseeing the last of the artillery as it was heaved over the edge, and saw the *bateaux* coming down again like a flock of swallows, they having crossed the river to collect an additional 1,200 troops that Wolfe had directed to march to Levi on the opposite shore, there to lie hidden in the woods until the Highlanders' expedient should have been proved.

A head, cursing freely, surged up over the edge of the cliff. Its attendant body lunged into view, tripped, and sprawled at Grey's feet.

'Sergeant Cutter!' Grey said, grinning as he bent to yank the little sergeant to his feet. 'Come to join the party, have you?'

'Jesus Fuck,' replied the sergeant, belligerently brushing dirt from his coat. 'We'd best win, that's all I can say.' And without waiting for reply, turned round to bellow down the cliff, 'Come ON, you bloody rascals! 'Ave you all eaten lead for breakfast, then? Shit it out and step lively! CLIMB, God damn your eyes!'

The net result of this monstrous effort being that as dawn spread its golden glow across the Plains of Abraham, the French sentries on the walls of the Citadel of Quebec gaped in disbelief at the sight of more than four thousand British troops, drawn up in battle array before them.

Through his telescope, Grey could see the sentries. The distance was too great to make out their facial expressions, but their attitudes of alarm and consternation were easy to read, and he grinned, seeing one French officer clutch his head briefly, then wave his arms like one dispelling a flock of chickens, sending his subordinates rushing off in all directions.

Wolfe was standing on a small hillock, long nose lifted as though to sniff the morning air. Grey thought he probably considered his pose noble and commanding; he reminded Grey of a dachshund scenting a badger; the air of alert eagerness was the same.

Wolfe wasn't the only one. Despite the labours of the night, skinned hands, battered shins, twisted knees and ankles, and a lack of food and sleep, a gleeful excitement ran through the troops like wine. Grey thought they were all giddy with fatigue.

The sound of drums came faintly to him on the wind; the French, beating hastily to quarters. Within minutes, he saw horsemen streaking away from the fortress, and smiled grimly. They were going to rally whatever troops Montcalm had within summoning distance, and he felt a tightening of the belly at the sight.

The matter hadn't really been in doubt; it was September, and winter was coming on. The town and fortress had been unable to provision themselves for a long siege, owing to Wolfe's scorched-earth policies. The French were there, the English before them – and the simple fact, apparent to both sides, was that the French would starve long before the English did. Montcalm would fight; he had no choice.

Many of the men had brought canteens of water, some a little food. They were allowed to relax sufficiently to eat, to ease their muscles – though none of them ever took their attention from the gathering French, massing before the fortress. Employing his telescope further, Grey could see that while the mass of milling men was growing, they were by no means all trained troops; Montcalm had called his militias from the countryside – farmers, fishermen, and *coureurs du bois*, by the look of them – and his Indians. Grey eyed the painted faces and oiled topknots warily, but his acquaintance with Manoke had deprived the Indians of much of their terrifying aspect – and they would not be nearly so effective on open ground, against cannon, as they were sneaking through the forest.

It took surprisingly little time for Montcalm to ready his troops, impromptu as they might be. The sun was no more than halfway up the sky when the French lines began their advance.

'HOLD your fucking fire, you villains! Fire before you're

ordered, and I'll give your fuckin' heads to the artillery to use for cannonballs!' He heard the unmistakable voice of Sergeant Aloysius Cutter, some distance back, but clearly audible. The same order was being echoed, if less picturesquely, through the British lines, and if every officer on the field had one eye firmly on the French, the other was fixed on General Wolfe, standing on his hillock, aflame with anticipation.

Grey felt his blood twitch, and moved restlessly from foot to foot, trying to ease a cramp in one leg. The advancing French line stopped, kneeled, and fired a volley. Another from the line standing behind them. Too far, much too far to have any effect. A deep rumble came from the British troops – something visceral and hungry.

Grey's hand had been on his dagger for so long that the wire-wrapped hilt had left its imprint on his fingers. His other hand was clenched upon a sabre. He had no command here, but the urge to raise his sword, gather the eyes of his men, hold them, focus them, was overwhelming. He shook his shoulders to loosen them and glanced at Wolfe.

Another volley, close enough this time that several British soldiers in the front lines fell, knocked down by musket fire.

'Hold, hold!' The order rattled down the lines like gunfire. The brimstone smell of slowmatch was thick, pungent above the scent of powder-smoke; the artillerymen held their fire as well.

French cannon fired, and balls bounced murderously across the field, but they seemed puny, ineffectual despite the damage they did. How many French? he wondered. Perhaps twice as many, but it didn't matter. It wouldn't matter.

Sweat ran down his face, and he rubbed a sleeve across to clear his eyes.

'Hold!'

Closer, closer. Many of the Indians were on horseback; he could see them in a knot on the left, milling. Those would bear watching . . .

'*Hold*!'

Wolfe's arm rose slowly, sword in hand, and the army breathed deep. His beloved grenadiers were next to him, solid in their companies, wrapped in sulphurous smoke from the matchtubes at their belts.

'Come on, you buggers,' the man next to Grey was muttering. 'Come on, come on!'

Smoke was drifting over the field, low white clouds. Forty paces. Effective range.

'Don't fire, don't fire, don't fire . . .' Someone was chanting to himself, struggling against panic.

Through the British lines, sun glinted on the rising swords, the officers echoing Wolfe's order.

'*Hold . . . hold . . .*'

The swords fell as one.

'FIRE!' and the ground shook.

A shout rose in his throat, part of the roar of the army, and he was charging with the men near him, swinging his sabre with all his might, finding flesh.

The volley had been devastating; bodies littered the ground. He leaped over a fallen Frenchman, brought his sabre down upon another, caught halfway in the act of loading, took him in the cleft between neck and shoulder, yanked his sabre free of the falling man and went on.

The British artillery was firing as fast as the guns could be served. Each boom shook his flesh. He gritted his teeth, squirmed aside from the point of a half-seen bayonet, and found himself panting, eyes watering from the smoke, standing alone.

Chest heaving, he turned round in a circle, disoriented. There was so much smoke around him that he could not for a moment tell where he was. It didn't matter.

An enormous blur of something passed him, shrieking, and he dodged by instinct and fell to the ground as the horse's feet churned past, hearing as an echo the Indian's grunt, the rush of the tomahawk blow that had missed his head.

'Shit,' he muttered, and scrambled to his feet.

The grenadiers were hard at work nearby; he heard their officers' shouts, the bang and pop of their explosions as they worked their way stolidly through the French like the small mobile batteries they were.

A grenade struck the ground a few feet away, and he felt a sharp pain in his thigh; a metal fragment had sliced through his breeches, drawing blood.

'Christ,' he said, belatedly becoming aware that being in the vicinity of a company of grenadiers was not a good idea. He shook his head to clear it and made his way away from them.

He heard a familiar sound that made him recoil for an instant from the force of memory – wild Highland screams, filled with rage and berserk glee. The Highlanders were hard at work with their broadswords – he saw two of them appear from the smoke, bare legs churning beneath their kilts, pursuing a pack of fleeing Frenchmen, and felt laughter bubble up through his heaving chest.

He didn't see the man in the smoke. His foot struck something heavy and he fell, sprawling across the body. The man screamed, and Grey scrambled hastily off him.

'Sorry. Are you— Christ, Malcolm!'

He was on his knees, bending low to avoid the smoke. Stubbs was gasping, grasping desperately at his coat.

'Jesus.' Malcolm's right leg was gone below the knee, flesh shredded and the white bone splintered, butcher-stained with spurting blood. Or . . . no. It wasn't gone. It – the foot, at least – was lying a little way away, still clad in shoe and tattered stocking.

Grey turned his head and threw up.

Bile stinging the back of his nose, he choked and spat, turned back, and grappled with his belt, wrenching it free.

'Don't . . .' Stubbs gasped, putting out a hand as Grey began wrapping the belt round his thigh. His face was whiter than the bone of his leg. 'Don't. Better . . . Better if I die.'

'The devil you will,' Grey replied briefly.

His hands were shaking, slippery with blood. It took three tries to get the end of the belt through the buckle, but it went, at last, and he jerked it tight, eliciting a yell from Stubbs.

'Here,' said an unfamiliar voice by his ear. 'Let's get him off. I'll— shit!' He looked up, startled, to see a tall British officer lunge upward, blocking the musket butt that would have brained Grey. Without thinking, he drew his dagger and stabbed the Frenchman in the leg. The man screamed, his leg buckling, and the strange officer pushed him over, kicked him in the face, and stamped on his throat, crushing it.

'I'll help,' the man said calmly, bending to take hold of Malcolm's arm, pulling him up. 'Take the other side; we'll get him to the back.' They got Malcolm up, his arms round their shoulders, and dragged him, paying no heed to the Frenchman thrashing and gurgling on the ground behind them.

Malcolm lived long enough to make it to the rear of the lines, where the army surgeons were already at work. By the time Grey and the other officer had turned him over to the surgeons, the battle was over.

Grey turned to see the French scattered and demoralised, fleeing toward the fortress. British troops were flooding across the trampled field, cheering, overrunning the abandoned French cannon.

The entire battle had lasted less than a quarter of an hour.

He found himself sitting on the ground, his mind quite blank, with no notion how long he had been there, though he supposed it couldn't have been much time at all.

He noticed an officer standing near him, and thought vaguely that the man seemed familiar. Who . . Oh, yes. Wolfe's adjutant. He'd never learned the man's name.

He stood up slowly, stiff as a nine-day pudding.

The adjutant was simply standing there. His eyes were turned in the direction of the fortress and the fleeing French, but Grey could tell that he wasn't really seeing either. Grey glanced over his shoulder, toward the hillock where Wolfe had stood earlier, but the general was nowhere in sight.

'General Wolfe . . . ?' he said.

'The general . . .' the adjutant said, and swallowed thickly. 'He was struck.'

Of course he was, silly ass, Grey thought uncharitably. *Standing up there like a bloody target, what could he expect?* But then he saw the tears standing in the adjutant's eyes, and understood.

'Dead, then?' he asked, stupidly, and the adjutant – why had he never thought to ask the man's name? – nodded, rubbing a smoke-stained sleeve across a smoke-stained countenance.

'He . . . in the wrist, first. Then in the body. He fell, and crawled – then he fell again. I turned him over . . . told him the battle was won; the French were scattered.'

'He understood?'

The adjutant nodded and took a deep breath that rattled in his throat. 'He said—' He stopped and coughed, then went on, more firmly. 'He said that in knowing he had conquered, he was content to die.'

'Did he?' Grey said blankly. He'd seen men die, often,

and imagined it much more likely that if James Wolfe had managed anything beyond an inarticulate groan, his final word had likely been either 'Shit,' or 'Oh, God,' depending upon the general's religious leanings, of which Grey had no notion. 'Yes, good,' he said, meaninglessly, and turned toward the fortress himself. Ant-trails of men were streaming toward it, and in the midst of one such stream he saw Montcalm's colours, fluttering in the wind. Below the colours, small in the distance, a man in general's uniform rode his horse, hatless, hunched and swaying in the saddle, his officers bunched close on either side, anxious lest he fall.

The British lines were reorganising, though it was clear no further fighting would be required. Not today. Nearby, he saw the tall officer who had saved his life and helped him to drag Malcolm Stubbs to safety, limping back toward his troops.

'The major over there,' he said, nudging the adjutant and nodding. 'Do you know his name?'

The adjutant blinked, then firmed his shoulders.

'Yes, of course. That's Major Siverly.'

'Oh. Well, it would be, wouldn't it?'

Admiral Holmes, third in command after Wolfe, accepted the surrender of Quebec three days later, Wolfe and his second, Brigadier Monckton, having perished in battle. Montcalm was dead, too – had died the morning following the battle. There was no way out for the French save surrender; winter was coming on, and the fortress and its city would starve long before its besiegers.

Two weeks after the battle, John Grey returned to Gareon, and found that smallpox had swept through the village like an autumn wind. The mother of Malcolm

Stubbs's son was dead; her mother offered to sell him the child. He asked her politely to wait.

Charlie Carruthers had perished, too, the smallpox not waiting for the weakness of his body to overcome him. Grey had the body burned, not wishing Carruthers's hand to be stolen, for both the Indians and the local *habitants* regarded such things superstitiously. He took a canoe by himself, and on a deserted island in the St Lawrence, scattered his friend's ashes to the wind.

He returned from this expedition to discover a letter, forwarded by Hal, from Mr John Hunter, surgeon. He checked the level of brandy in the decanter, and opened it with a sigh.

My dear Lord John,

I have heard some recent conversation regarding the unfortunate death of Mr Nicholls earlier this year, including comments indicating a public perception that you were responsible for his death. In case you shared this perception, I thought it might ease your mind to know that in fact you were not.

Grey sank slowly onto a stool, eyes glued to the sheet.

It is true that your ball did strike Mr Nicholls, but this accident contributed little or nothing to his demise. I saw you fire upward into the air – I said as much, to those present at the time, though most of them did not appear to take much notice. The ball apparently went up at a slight angle, and then fell upon Mr Nicholls from above. At this point, its power was quite spent, and the missile itself being negligible in size and weight, it barely penetrated the skin above his collar bone, where it lodged against the bone, doing no further damage.

The true cause of his collapse and death was an aortic

aneurysm, a weakness in the wall of one of the great vessels emergent from the heart; such weaknesses are often congenital. The stress of the electric shock and the emotion of the duello that followed apparently caused this aneurysm to rupture. Such an occurrence is untreatable, and invariably fatal, I am afraid. There is nothing that could have saved him.

Your servant,

John Hunter, Surgeon

Grey was conscious of a most extraordinary array of sensations. Relief, yes, there was a sense of profound relief, as of one waking from a nightmare. There was also a sense of injustice, coloured by the beginnings of indignation; by God, he had nearly been married! He might, of course, also have been maimed or killed as a result of the imbroglio, but that seemed relatively inconsequent; he was a soldier, after all – such things happened.

His hand trembled slightly as he set the note down. Beneath relief, gratitude, and indignation was a growing sense of horror.

I thought it might ease your mind . . . He could see Hunter's face, saying this; sympathetic, intelligent, and cheerful. It was a straightforward remark, but one fully cognisant of its own irony.

Yes, he was pleased to know he had not caused Edwin Nicholls's death. But the means of that knowledge . . . gooseflesh rose on his arms and he shuddered involuntarily, imagining . . .

'Oh, God,' he said. He'd been once to Hunter's house – to a poetry reading, held under the auspices of Mrs Hunter, whose salons were famous. Doctor Hunter did not attend these, but sometimes would come down from his part of the house to greet guests. On this occasion, he had done so, and falling into conversation with Grey and

140

a couple of other scientifically minded gentlemen, had invited them up to see some of the more interesting items of his famous collection: the rooster with a transplanted human tooth growing in its comb, the child with two heads, the foetus with a foot protruding from its stomach.

Hunter had made no mention of the walls of jars, these filled with eyeballs, fingers, sections of livers . . . or of the two or three complete human skeletons that hung from the ceiling, fully articulated and fixed by a bolt through the tops of their skulls. It had not occurred to Grey at the time to wonder where – or how – Hunter had acquired these.

Nicholls had had an eyetooth missing, the front tooth beside the empty space badly chipped. If he ever visited Hunter's house again, might he come face to face with a skull with a missing tooth?

He seized the brandy decanter, uncorked it, and drank directly from it, swallowing slowly and repeatedly, until the vision disappeared.

His small table was littered with papers. Among them, under his sapphire paperweight, was the tidy packet that the widow Lambert had handed him, her face blotched with weeping. He put a hand on it, feeling Charlie's doubled touch, gentle on his face, soft around his heart.

You won't fail me.

'No,' he said softly. 'No, Charlie, I won't.'

With Manoke's help as translator, he bought the child, after prolonged negotiation, for two golden guineas, a brightly coloured blanket, a pound of sugar and a small keg of rum. The grandmother's face was sunken, not with grief, he thought, but with dissatisfaction and weariness. With her daughter dead of the smallpox, her life would be harder. The English, she conveyed to Grey through Manoke, were cheap bastards; the French were much more generous. He resisted the impulse to give her another guinea.

It was full autumn now, and the leaves had all fallen. The bare branches of the trees spread black ironwork flat against a pale blue sky as he made his way upward through the town, to the small French mission. There were several small buildings surrounding the tiny church, with children playing outside; some of them paused to look at him, but most of them ignored him; British soldiers were nothing new.

Father LeCarré took the bundle gently from him, turning back the blanket to look at the child's face. The boy was awake; he pawed at the air, and the priest put out a finger for him to grasp.

'Ah,' he said, seeing the clear signs of mixed blood, and Grey knew the priest thought the child was his. He started to explain, but after all, what did it matter?

'We will baptise him as a Catholic, of course,' Father LeCarré said, looking up at him. The priest was a young man, rather plump, dark and clean-shaven, but with a gentle face. 'You do not mind that?'

'No.' Grey drew out a purse. 'Here: for his maintenance. I will send an additional five pounds each year, if you will advise me once a year of his continued welfare. Here – the address to which to write.' A sudden inspiration struck him – not that he did not trust the good father, he assured himself, only . . . 'Send me a lock of his hair,' he said. 'Every year.'

He was turning to go when the priest called him back, smiling.

'Has the infant a name, sir?'

'A—' He stopped dead. His mother had surely called him something, but Malcolm Stubbs hadn't thought to

142

tell him what it was before being shipped back to England. What should he call the child? Malcolm, for the father who had abandoned him? Hardly.

Charles, maybe, in memory of Carruthers . . .

. . . one of these days, it isn't going to.

'His name is John,' he said abruptly, and cleared his throat. 'John Cinnamon.'

'*Mais oui,*' the priest said, nodding. '*Bon voyage, monsieur – et allez avec le Bon Dieu.*'

'Thank you,' he said politely, and went away, not looking back, down to the riverbank where Manoke waited to bid him farewell.

AUTHOR'S NOTES

The Battle of Quebec is justly famous, as one of the great military triumphs of the eighteenth-century British Army. If you go today to the battlefield at the Plains of Abraham (in spite of this poetic name, it really was just named for the farmer who owned the land, one Abraham Martin), you'll see a plaque at the foot of the cliff there, commemorating the heroic achievement of the Highland troops who climbed this sheer cliff from the river below, clearing the way for the entire army – *and* their cannon, mortars, howitzers and accompanying impedimenta – to make a harrowing overnight ascent and confront General Montcalm with a jaw-dropping spectacle by the dawn's early light.

If you go up onto the field itself, you'll find another plaque, this one put up by the French, explaining (in French) what a dirty, unsportsmanlike trick this was for those British lowlifes to have played on the noble troops defending the Citadel. Ah, perspective.

General James Wolfe, along with Montcalm, was of course a real historical character, as was Brigadier Simon Fraser (whom you will have met – or will meet later – in *An Echo in the Bone*). My own rule of thumb when dealing with historical persons in the context of fiction is to try not to portray them as having done anything worse than what I *know* they did, according to the historical record.

In General Wolfe's case, Hal's opinion of his character and abilities is one commonly held and recorded by a number of contemporary military commentators. And there is documentary proof of his attitude toward the Highlanders whom he used for this endeavour, in the form of the letter quoted in the story: '. . . no great mischief if they fall.' (Allow me to recommend a wonderful novel by Alistair McLeod, titled *No Great Mischief*. It isn't about Wolfe; it's a novelised history of a family of Scots who settle in Nova Scotia, beginning in the eighteenth century and carrying on through the decades, but it is from Wolfe's letter that the book takes its title, and he's mentioned.)

Wolfe's policy with regard to the *habitant* villages surrounding the Citadel (looting, burning, general terrorising of the populace) is a matter of record. It wasn't an unusual thing for an invading army to do.

General Wolfe's dying words are also a matter of historical record, but like Lord John, I take leave to doubt that that's really what he said. He *is* reported by several sources to have recited Grey's 'Elegy written in a Country Churchyard' in the boat on the way to battle – and I think that's a sufficiently odd thing to have done that the reports are probably true.

144

As for Simon Fraser, he's widely reported to have been the British officer who fooled the French lookouts by calling out to them in French as the boats went by in the darkness – and he undoubtedly spoke excellent French, having campaigned in France. As to the details of exactly what he said – accounts vary, and that's not really an important detail, so I rolled my own.

I am greatly indebted to Philippe Safavi, who translates my novels into French, for checking and correcting the French inclusions, both in *The Custom of the Army* and *The Space Between*.

Lord John and the Plague of Zombies

Introduction to
Lord John and the Plague of Zombies

The thing about Lord John's situation and career – unmarried, no fixed establishment, discreet political connections, fairly high-ranking officer – is that he can easily take part in far-flung adventures, rather than being bound to a pedestrian daily life. To be honest, once I started doing 'bulges' involving him, I just looked at which year it was, and then consulted one of my historical time-line references to see what kinds of interesting events happened in that year. That's how he happened to find himself in Quebec for the battle there.

In terms of this story, though, the impetus came from two different sources, both 'trails' leading back from the main books of the series – *Voyager*, in this case. To wit: I knew that Lord John was the Governor of Jamaica in 1766, when Claire meets him aboard the *Porpoise*; it wasn't impossible for a man with connections and no experience to be appointed to such a post – but it was more likely for a man who *had* had experience in the territory to which he was appointed. I knew also that Geillis Duncan wasn't dead, and where she was. And after all, with a story set in Jamaica, how could I possibly resist zombies?

Lord John and the Plague of Zombies

There was a snake on the drawing-room table. A small snake, but still. Lord John Grey wondered whether to say anything about it.

The governor picked up a cut-crystal decanter that stood not six inches from the coiled reptile, appearing quite oblivious. Perhaps it was a pet, or perhaps the residents of Jamaica were accustomed to keep a tame snake in residence, to kill rats. Judging from the number of rats he'd seen since leaving the ship, this seemed sensible – though this particular snake didn't appear large enough to take on even your average mouse.

The wine was decent, but served at body heat, and it seemed to pass directly through Grey's gullet and into his blood. He'd had nothing to eat since before dawn, and felt the muscles of his lower back begin to tingle and relax. He put the glass down; he wanted a clear head.

'I cannot tell you, sir, how happy I am to receive you,' said the governor, putting down his own glass, empty. 'The position is acute.'

'So you said in your letter to Lord North. The situation has not changed appreciably since then?' It had been nearly three months since that letter was written; a lot could change in three months.

He thought Governor Warren shuddered, despite the temperature in the room.

'It has become worse,' the governor said, picking up the decanter. 'Much worse.'

Grey felt his shoulders tense, but spoke calmly.

'In what way? Have there been more—' He hesitated, searching for the right word. 'More demonstrations?' It was a mild word to describe the burning of cane fields, the looting of plantations, and the wholesale liberation of slaves.

Warren gave a hollow laugh. His handsome face was beading with sweat. There was a crumpled handkerchief on the arm of his chair, and he picked it up to mop at his skin. He hadn't shaved this morning – or, quite possibly, yesterday; Grey could hear the faint rasp of his dark whiskers on the cloth.

'Yes. More destruction. They burned a sugar press last month, though still in the remoter parts of the island. Now, though . . .' He paused, licking dry lips as he poured more wine. He made a cursory motion toward Grey's glass, but Grey shook his head.

'They've begun to move toward King's Town,' Warren said. 'It's deliberate, you can see it. One plantation after another, in a line coming straight down the mountain.' He sighed. 'I shouldn't say straight. Nothing in this bloody place is straight, starting with the landscape.'

That was true enough; Grey had admired the vivid green peaks that soared up from the centre of the island, a rough backdrop for the amazingly blue lagoon and the white sand shore.

'People are terrified,' Warren went on, seeming to get a grip on himself, though his face was once again slimy with sweat, and his hand shook on the decanter. It occurred to Grey, with a slight shock, that the governor himself was terrified. 'I have merchants – and their wives – in my office every day, begging, demanding protection from the blacks.'

'Well, you may assure them that protection will be provided them,' Grey said, sounding as reassuring as possible. He had half a battalion with him – three hundred infantry troops, and a company of artillery, equipped with small cannon. Enough to defend King's Town, if necessary. But his brief from Lord North was not merely to defend and reassure the merchants and shipping of King's Town and Spanish Town – nor even to provide protection to the larger sugar plantations. He was charged with putting down the slave rebellion entirely. Rounding up the ringleaders and putting a stop to the violence altogether.

The snake on the table moved suddenly, uncoiling itself in a languid manner. It startled Grey, who had begun to think it was a decorative sculpture. It was exquisite: only seven or eight inches long, and a beautiful pale yellow marked with brown, a faint iridescence in its scales like the glow of good Rhenish wine.

'It's gone farther now, though,' Warren was going on. 'It's not just burning and property destruction. Now it's come to murder.'

That brought Grey back with a jerk.

'Who has been murdered?' he demanded.

'A planter named Abernathy. Murdered in his own house, last week. His throat cut.'

'Was the house burned?'

'No, it wasn't. The maroons ransacked it, but were driven off by Abernathy's own slaves before they could set fire to the place. His wife survived by submerging herself in a spring behind the house, concealed by a patch of reeds.'

'I see.' He could imagine the scene all too well. 'Where is the plantation?'

'About ten miles out of King's Town. Rose Hall, it's called. Why?' A bloodshot eye swivelled in Grey's direction, and he realised that the glass of wine the governor had invited him to share had not been his first of the day. Nor, likely, his fifth.

Was the man a natural sot? he wondered. Or was it only the pressure of the current situation that had caused him to take to the bottle in such a blatant manner? He surveyed the governor covertly; the man was perhaps in his late thirties, and while plainly drunk at the moment, showed none of the signs of habitual indulgence. He was well-built and attractive; no bloat, no soft belly straining at his silk waistcoat, no broken veins in cheeks or nose . . .

'Have you a map of the district?' Surely it hadn't escaped Warren that if indeed the maroons were burning their way straight toward King's Town, it should be possible to predict where their next target lay and await them with several companies of armed infantry?

Warren drained the glass and sat panting gently for a moment, eyes fixed on the tablecloth, then seemed to pull himself together.

'Map,' he repeated. 'Yes, of course. Dawes . . . my secretary . . . he'll— he'll find you one.'

Motion caught Grey's eye. Rather to his surprise, the tiny snake, after casting to and fro, tongue tasting the air, had started across the table in what seemed a purposeful, if undulant, manner, headed straight for him. By reflex, he put up a hand to catch the little thing, lest it plunge to the floor.

The governor saw it, uttered a loud shriek, and flung himself back from the table. Grey looked at him in astonishment, the tiny snake curling over his fingers.

'It's not venomous,' he said, as mildly as he could. At least he didn't *think* so. His friend Oliver Gwynne was a natural philosopher and mad for snakes; Gwynne had shown him all the prizes of his collection during the course of one hair-raising afternoon, and he seemed to recall Gwynne telling him that there were no venomous reptiles at all on the island of Jamaica. Besides, the nasty ones all had triangular heads, while the harmless kinds were blunt, like this little fellow.

Warren was indisposed to listen to a lecture on the physiognomy of snakes. Shaking with terror, he backed against the wall.

'Where?' he gasped. 'Where did it come from?'

'It's been sitting on the table since I came in. I . . . um . . . thought it was . . .' Well, plainly it wasn't a pet, let alone an intended part of the table décor. He coughed, and got up, meaning to put the snake outside through the French doors that led onto the terrace.

Warren mistook his intent, though, and seeing him come closer, snake writhing through his fingers, burst through the French doors himself, crossed the terrace in a mad leap, and pelted down the flagstoned walk, coat-tails flying as though the Devil himself were in pursuit.

Grey was still staring after him in disbelief when a discreet cough from the inner door made him turn.

'Gideon Dawes, sir.' The governor's secretary was a short, tubby man with a round, pink face that probably was rather jolly by nature. At the moment, it bore a look of profound wariness. 'You are Lieutenant-Colonel Grey?'

Grey thought it unlikely that there was a plethora of men wearing the uniform and insignia of a lieutenant-colonel on the premises of King's House at that very moment, but nonetheless bowed, murmuring, 'Your servant, Mr Dawes. I'm afraid Mr Warren has been taken . . . er . . .' He nodded toward the open French doors. 'Perhaps someone should go after him?'

Mr Dawes closed his eyes with a look of pain, then sighed and opened them again, shaking his head.

'He'll be all right,' he said, though his tone lacked any real conviction. 'I've just been discussing commissary and billeting requirements with your Major Fettes; he wishes you to know that all the arrangements are quite in hand.'

'Oh. Thank you, Mr Dawes.' In spite of the unnerving nature of the governor's departure, he felt a sense of pleasure. He'd been a major himself for years; it was astonishing how pleasant it was to know that someone else was now burdened with the physical management of troops. All *he* had to do was give orders.

That being so, he gave one, though it was phrased as a courteous request, and Mr Dawes promptly led him through the corridors of the rambling house to a small clerk's hole near the governor's office, where maps were made available to him.

He could see at once that Warren had been right regarding both the devious nature of the terrain, and the trail of attacks. One of the maps was marked with the names of plantations, and small notes indicated where maroon raids had taken place. It was far from being a straight line, but nonetheless, a distinct sense of direction was obvious.

The room was warm, and he could feel sweat trickling down his back. Still, a cold finger touched the base of his neck lightly, when he saw the name 'Twelvetrees' on the map.

'Who owns this plantation?' he asked, keeping his voice level as he pointed at the paper.

'What?' Dawes had fallen into a sort of dreamy trance, looking out the window into the green of the jungle, but blinked and pushed his spectacles up, bending to peer at the map. 'Oh, Twelvetrees. It's owned by Philip Twelvetrees – a young man, inherited the place from a cousin only recently. Killed in a duel, they say – the cousin, I mean,' he amplified helpfully.

'Ah. Too bad.' Grey's chest tightened unpleasantly. He could have done without *that* complication. If . . . 'The cousin – was he named Edward Twelvetrees, by chance?'

Dawes looked mildly surprised.

'I do believe that was the name. I didn't know him, though; no one here did. He was an absentee owner, ran the place through an overseer.'

'I see.' He wanted to ask whether Philip Twelvetrees had come from London to take possession of his inheritance, but didn't. He didn't want to draw any attention by seeming to single out the Twelvetrees family. Time enough for that.

He asked a few more questions regarding the timing of the raids, which Mr Dawes answered promptly, but when it came to an explanation of the inciting causes of the rebellion, the secretary proved suddenly unhelpful – which Grey thought interesting.

'Really, sir, I know almost nothing of such matters,' Mr Dawes protested, when pressed on the subject. 'You would be best advised to speak with Captain Cresswell. He's the superintendent in charge of the maroons.'

Grey was surprised at this.

'Escaped slaves? They have a superintendent?'

'Oh. No, sir.' Dawes seemed relieved to have a more straightforward question with which to deal. 'The maroons are not escaped slaves. Or rather,' he corrected himself, 'they are *technically* escaped slaves, but it is a pointless distinction. These maroons are the descendants of slaves who escaped during the last century, and took to the mountain uplands. They have settlements up there. But as there is no way of identifying any current owner . . .' And as the government lacked any means of finding them and dragging them back, the Crown had wisely settled for installing a white superintendent, as was usual for dealing with native populations. The superintendent's business was to be in contact with the maroons, and deal with any matter that might arise pertaining to them.

Which raised the question, Grey thought, why had this

Captain Cresswell not been brought to meet him at once? He had sent word of his arrival as soon as the ship docked at daylight, not wishing to take Derwent Warren unawares.

'Where is Captain Cresswell presently?' he asked, still polite. Mr Dawes looked unhappy.

'I, um, am afraid I don't know, sir,' he said, casting down his gaze behind his spectacles.

There was a momentary silence, in which Grey could hear the calling of some bird from the jungle nearby.

'Where is he, *normally*?' Grey asked, with slightly less politesse.

Dawes blinked.

'I don't know, sir. I believe he has a house near the base of Guthrie's Defile – there is a small village there. But he would of course go up into the maroon settlements from time to time, to meet with the . . .' He waved a small, fat hand, unable to find a suitable word. 'The headmen. He did buy a new hat in Spanish Town earlier this month,' Dawes added, in the tones of someone offering a helpful observation.

'A *hat*?'

'Yes. Oh— but of course you would not know. It is customary among the maroons, when some agreement of importance is made, that the persons making the agreement shall exchange hats. So you see . . .'

'Yes, I do,' Grey said, trying not to let annoyance show in his voice. 'Will you be so kind, Mr Dawes, as to send to Guthrie's Defile, then – and to any other place in which you think Captain Cresswell might be discovered? Plainly I must speak with him, and as soon as possible.'

Dawes nodded vigorously, but before he could speak, the rich sound of a small gong came from somewhere in the house below. As though it had been a signal, Grey's stomach emitted a loud gurgle.

'Dinner in half an hour,' Mr Dawes said, looking happier than Grey had yet seen him. He almost scurried out the door, Grey in his wake.

'Mr Dawes,' he said, catching up at the head of the stair. 'Governor Warren. Do you think—'

'Oh, he will be present at dinner,' Dawes assured him. 'I'm sure he is quite recovered now; these small fits of excitement never last very long.'

'What causes them?' A savoury smell, rich with currants, onion, and spice, wafted up the stair, making Grey hasten his step.

'Oh . . .' Dawes, hastening along with him, glanced sideways at him. 'It is nothing. Only that his Excellency has a, um, somewhat morbid fancy concerning reptiles. Did he see a snake in the drawing room, or hear something concerning one?'

'He did, yes – though a remarkably small and harmless one.' Vaguely, Grey wondered what had happened to the little yellow snake. He thought he must have dropped it in the excitement of the governor's abrupt exit, and hoped it hadn't been injured.

Mr Dawes looked troubled, and murmured something that sounded like, 'Oh, dear, oh, dear . . .' but he merely shook his head and sighed.

Grey made his way to his room, meaning to freshen himself before dinner; the day was warm, and he smelled strongly of ship's reek – this composed in equal parts of sweat, sea-sickness, and sewage, well marinated in salt-water – and horse, having ridden up from the harbour to Spanish Town. With any luck, his valet would have clean linen aired for him by now.

King's House, as all royal governors' residences were

known, was a shambling old wreck of a mansion, perched on a high spot of ground on the edge of Spanish Town. Plans were afoot for an immense new Palladian building, to be erected in the town's centre, but it would be another year at least before construction could commence. In the meantime, efforts had been made to uphold His Majesty's dignity by means of beeswax-polish, silver, and immaculate linen, but the dingy printed wallpaper peeled from the corners of the rooms, and the dark-stained wood beneath exhaled a mouldy breath that made Grey want to hold his own whenever he walked inside.

One good feature of the house, though, was that it was surrounded on all four sides by a broad terrace, and overhung by large, spreading trees that cast lacy shadows on the flagstones. A number of the rooms opened directly onto this terrace – Grey's did – and it was therefore possible to step outside and draw a clean breath, scented by the distant sea or the equally distant upland jungles. There was no sign of his valet, but there *was* a clean shirt on the bed. He shucked his coat, changed his shirt, and then threw the French doors open wide.

He stood for a moment in the centre of the room, mid-afternoon sun spilling through the open doors, enjoying the sense of a solid surface under his feet after seven weeks at sea and seven hours on horseback. Enjoying even more the transitory sense of being alone. Command had its prices, and one of those was a nearly complete loss of solitude. He therefore seized it when he found it, knowing it wouldn't last for more than a few moments, but valuing it all the more for that.

Sure enough, it didn't last more than two minutes this time. He called out, 'Come,' at a rap on the doorframe, and turning, was struck by a visceral sense of attraction such as he had not experienced in months.

The man was young, perhaps twenty, and slender in his

blue and gold livery, but with a breadth of shoulder that spoke of strength, and a head and neck that would have graced a Greek sculpture. Perhaps because of the heat, he wore no wig, and his tight-curled hair was clipped so close that the finest modelling of his skull was apparent.

'Your servant, sah,' he said to Grey, bowing respectfully. 'The governor's compliments, and dinner will be served in ten minutes. May I see you to the dining room?'

'You may,' Grey said, reaching hastily for his coat. He didn't doubt that he could find the dining room unassisted, but the chance to watch this young man walk . . .

'You *may*,' Tom Byrd corrected, entering with his hands full of grooming implements, 'once I've put his lordship's hair to rights.' He fixed Grey with a minatory eye. 'You're not a-going in to dinner like that, me lord, and don't you think it. You sit down there.' He pointed sternly to a stool, and Lieutenant-Colonel Grey, commander of His Majesty's forces in Jamaica, meekly obeyed the dictates of his twenty-one-year-old valet. He didn't *always* allow Tom free rein, but in the current circumstance, was just as pleased to have an excuse to sit still in the company of the young black servant.

Tom laid out all his implements neatly on the dressing-table, from a pair of silver hairbrushes to a box of powder and a pair of curling tongs, with the care and attention of a surgeon arraying his knives and saws. Selecting a hairbrush, he leaned closer, peering at Grey's head, then gasped. 'Me lord! There's a big huge spider – walking right up your temple!'

Grey smacked his temple by reflex, and the spider in question – a clearly visible brown thing nearly a half-inch long – shot off into the air, striking the looking-glass with an audible tap before dropping to the surface of the dressing-table and racing for its life.

Tom and the black servant uttered identical cries of

horror and lunged for the creature, colliding in front of the dressing-table and falling over in a thrashing heap. Grey, strangling an almost irresistible urge to laugh, stepped over them and dispatched the fleeing spider neatly with the back of his other hairbrush.

He pulled Tom to his feet and dusted him off, allowing the black servant to scramble up by himself. He brushed off all apologies as well, but asked whether the spider had been a deadly one.

'Oh, yes, sah,' the servant assured him fervently. 'Should one of those bite you, sah, you would suffer excruciating pain at once. The flesh around the wound would putrefy, you would commence to be fevered within an hour, and in all likelihood, you would not live past dawn.'

'Oh, I see,' Grey said mildly, his flesh creeping briskly. 'Well, then. Perhaps you would not mind looking about the room while Tom is at his work? In case such spiders go about in company?'

Grey sat and let Tom brush and plait his hair, watching the young man as he assiduously searched under the bed and dressing-table, pulled out Grey's trunk, and pulled up the trailing curtains and shook them.

'What is your name?' he asked the young man, noting that Tom's fingers were trembling badly, and hoping to distract him from thoughts of the hostile wildlife with which Jamaica undoubtedly teemed. Tom was fearless in the streets of London, and perfectly willing to face down ferocious dogs or foaming horses. Spiders, though, were quite another matter.

'Rodrigo, sah,' said the young man, pausing in his curtain-shaking to bow. 'Your servant, sah.'

He seemed quite at ease in company, and conversed with them about the town, the weather – he confidently predicted rain in the evening, at about ten o'clock –

leading Grey to think that he had likely been employed as a servant in good families for some time. Was the man a slave? he wondered, or a free black?

His admiration for Rodrigo was, he assured himself, the same that he might have for a marvellous piece of sculpture, an elegant painting. And one of his friends did in fact possess a collection of Greek amphorae decorated with scenes that gave him quite the same sort of feeling. He shifted slightly in his seat, crossing his legs. He would be going into dinner soon. He resolved to think of large, hairy spiders, and was making some progress with this subject when something huge and black dropped down the chimney and rushed out of the disused hearth.

All three men shouted and leaped to their feet, stamping madly. This time it was Rodrigo who felled the intruder, crushing it under one sturdy shoe.

'What the devil was that?' Grey asked, bending over to peer at the thing, which was a good three inches long, gleamingly black, and roughly ovoid, with ghastly long, twitching antennae.

'Only a cockroach, sah,' Rodrigo assured him, wiping a hand across a sweating ebony brow. 'They will not harm you, but they *are* most disagreeable. If they come into your bed, they feed upon your eyebrows.'

Tom uttered a small strangled cry. The cockroach, far from being destroyed, had merely been inconvenienced by Rodrigo's shoe. It now extended thorny legs, heaved itself up and was proceeding about its business, though at a somewhat slower pace. Grey, the hairs prickling on his arms, seized the ash-shovel from among the fireplace implements and, scooping up the insect on its blade, jerked open the door and flung the nasty creature as far as he could – which, given his state of mind, was some considerable distance.

Tom was pale as custard when Grey came back in, but

picked up his employer's coat with trembling hands. He dropped it, though, and with a mumbled apology, bent to pick it up again, only to utter a strangled shriek, drop it again, and run backwards, slamming so hard against the wall that Grey heard a crack of laths and plaster.

'What the devil?' He bent, reaching gingerly for the fallen coat.

'Don't touch it, me lord!' Tom cried, but Grey had seen what the trouble was: a tiny yellow snake slithered out of the blue-velvet folds, head moving to and fro in slow curiosity.

'Well, hallo, there.' He reached out a hand, and as before, the little snake tasted his skin with a flickering tongue, then wove its way up into the palm of his hand. He stood up, cradling it carefully.

Tom and Rodrigo were standing like men turned to stone, staring at him.

'It's quite harmless,' he assured them. 'At least I think so. It must have fallen into my pocket earlier.'

Rodrigo was regaining a little of his nerve. He came forward and looked at the snake, but declined an offer to touch it, putting both hands firmly behind his back.

'That snake likes you, sah,' he said, glancing curiously from the snake to Grey's face, as though trying to distinguish a reason for such odd particularity.

'Possibly.' The snake had made its way upward and was now wrapped round two of Grey's fingers, squeezing with remarkable strength. 'On the other hand, I believe he may be attempting to kill and eat me. Do you know what his natural food might be?'

Rodrigo laughed at that, displaying very beautiful white teeth, and Grey had such a vision of those teeth, those soft mulberry lips, applied to— he coughed, hard, and looked away.

'He would eat anything that did not try to eat him first,

163

sah,' Rodrigo assured him. 'It was probably the sound of the cockroach that made him come out. He would hunt those.'

'What a very admirable sort of snake. Could we find him something to eat, do you think? To encourage him to stay, I mean.'

Tom's face suggested strongly that if the snake was staying, he was not. On the other hand . . . he glanced toward the door, whence the cockroach had made its exit, and shuddered. With great reluctance, he reached into his pocket and extracted a rather squashed bread-roll, containing ham and pickle.

This object being placed on the floor before it, the snake inspected it gingerly, ignored bread and pickle, but twining itself carefully about a chunk of ham, squeezed it fiercely into limp submission, then, opening its jaw to an amazing extent, engulfed its prey, to general cheers. Even Tom clapped his hands, and – if not ecstatic at Grey's suggestion that the snake might be accommodated in the dark space beneath the bed for the sake of preserving Grey's eyebrows – uttered no objections to this plan, either. The snake being ceremoniously installed and left to digest its meal, Grey was about to ask Rodrigo further questions regarding the natural fauna of the island, but was forestalled by the faint sound of a distant gong.

'Dinner!' he exclaimed, reaching for his now snakeless coat.

'Me lord! Your hair's not even powdered!' He refused to wear a wig, to Tom's ongoing dismay, but was obliged in the present instance to submit to powder. This toiletry accomplished in haste, he shrugged into his coat and fled, before Tom could suggest any further refinements to his appearance.

The governor appeared, as Mr Dawes had predicted, calm and dignified at the dinner table. All trace of sweat, hysteria and drunkenness had vanished, and beyond a brief word of apology for his abrupt disappearance, no reference was made to his earlier departure.

Major Fettes and Grey's adjutant, Captain Cherry, also appeared at table. A quick glance at them assured Grey that all was well with the troops. Fettes and Cherry couldn't be more diverse physically, the latter resembling a ferret and the former a block of wood – but both were extremely competent, and well-liked by the men.

There was little conversation to begin with; the three soldiers had been eating ship's biscuit and salt-beef for weeks. They settled down to the feast before them with the single-minded attention of ants presented with a loaf of bread; the magnitude of the challenge had no effect upon their earnest willingness. As the courses gradually slowed, though, Grey began to instigate conversation – his prerogative, as senior guest and commanding officer.

'Mr Dawes explained to me the position of super-intendent,' he said, keeping his attitude superficially pleasant. 'How long has Captain Cresswell held this position, sir?'

'For approximately six months, colonel,' the governor replied, wiping crumbs from his lips with a linen napkin. The governor was quite composed, but Grey had Dawes in the corner of his eye, and thought the secretary stiffened a little. That was interesting; he must get Dawes alone again, and go into this matter of superintendents more thoroughly.

'And was there a superintendent before Captain Cresswell?'

'Yes . . . in fact, there were two of them, were there not, Mr Dawes?'

'Yes, sir. Captain Ludgate and Captain Perriman.' Dawes was assiduously not meeting Grey's eye.

'I should like very much to speak with those gentlemen,' Grey said pleasantly.

Dawes jerked as though someone had run a hatpin into his buttock. The governor finished chewing a grape, swallowed, and said, 'I'm so sorry, colonel. Both Ludgate and Perriman have left Jamaica.'

'Why?' John Fettes asked bluntly. The governor hadn't been expecting that, and blinked.

'I expect Major Fettes wishes to know whether they were replaced in their offices because of some peculation or corrupt practice,' Bob Cherry put in chummily. 'And if that be the case, were they allowed to leave the island rather than face prosecution? And if so—'

'Why?' Fettes put in neatly. Grey repressed a smile. Should peace break out on a wide scale and an army career fail them, Fettes and Cherry could easily make a living as a music-hall knockabout cross-talk act. As interrogators, they could reduce almost any suspect to incoherence, confusion, and confession in nothing flat.

Governor Warren, though, appeared to be made of tougher stuff than the usual regimental miscreant. Either that, or he had nothing to hide, Grey thought, watching him explain with tired patience that Ludgate had retired because of ill health, and that Perriman had inherited money and gone back to England.

No, he thought, watching the governor's hand twitch and hover indecisively over the fruit bowl. *He's got something to hide. And so does Dawes. Is it the same thing, though? And has it got anything to do with the present trouble?*

The governor could easily be hiding some peculation or corruption of his own – and likely was, Grey thought dispassionately, taking in the lavish display of silver on the sideboard. Such corruption was – within limits –

considered more or less a perquisite of office. But if that was the case, it was not Grey's concern – unless it was in some way connected to the maroons and their rebellion.

Entertaining as it was to watch Fettes and Cherry at their work, he cut them off with a brief nod, and turned the conversation firmly back to the rebellion.

'What communications have you had from the rebels, sir?' he asked the governor. 'For I think in these cases, rebellion arises usually from some distinct source of grievance. What is it?'

Warren looked at him, jaw agape. He closed his mouth, slowly, and thought for a moment before replying. Grey rather thought he was considering how much Grey might discover from other avenues of inquiry.

Everything I bloody can, Grey thought, assuming an expression of neutral interest.

'Why, as to that, sir . . . the incident that began the . . . um . . . the difficulties . . . was the arrest of two young maroons, accused of stealing from a warehouse in King's Town.' The two had been whipped in the town square, and committed to prison, after which—

'Following a trial?' Grey interrupted. The governor's gaze rested on him, red-rimmed but cool.

'No, colonel. They had no right to a trial.'

'You had them whipped and imprisoned on the word of . . . who? The affronted merchant?'

Warren drew himself up a little and lifted his chin. Grey saw that he had been shaved, but a patch of black whisker had been overlooked; it showed in the hollow of his cheek like a blemish, a hairy mole.

'*I* did not, no, sir,' he said, coldly. 'The sentence was imposed by the magistrate in King's Town.'

'Who is?'

Dawes had closed his eyes with a small grimace.

'Judge Samuel Peters.'

167

Grey nodded thanks.

'Captain Cherry will visit Mr Judge Peters tomorrow,' he said pleasantly. 'And the prisoners, as well. I take it they are still in custody?'

'No, they aren't,' Mr Dawes put in, suddenly emerging from his impersonation of a dormouse. 'They escaped, within a week of their capture.'

The governor shot a brief, irritated glance at his secretary, but nodded reluctantly. With further prodding, it was admitted that the maroons had sent a protest at the treatment of the prisoners, via Captain Cresswell. The prisoners having escaped before the protest was received, though, it had not seemed necessary to do anything about it.

Grey wondered briefly whose patronage had got Warren his position, but dismissed the thought in favour of further explorations. The first violence had come without warning, he was told, with the burning of cane fields on a remote plantation. Word of it had reached Spanish Town several days later, by which time, another plantation had suffered similar depredation.

'Captain Cresswell rode at once to investigate the matter, of course,' Warren said, lips tight.

'And?'

'He didn't return. The maroons have not demanded ransom for him, nor have they sent word that he is dead. He may be with them; he may not. We simply don't know.'

Grey could not help looking at Dawes, who looked unhappy, but gave the ghost of a shrug. It wasn't his place to tell more than the governor wanted told, was it?

'Let me understand you, sir,' Grey said, not bothering to hide the edge in his voice. 'You have had *no* communication with the rebels since their initial protest? And you have taken no action to achieve any?'

Warren seemed to swell slightly, but replied in an even tone.

'In fact, colonel, I have. I sent for you.' He smiled, very slightly, and reached for the decanter.

The evening air hung damp and viscid, trembling with distant thunder. Unable to bear the stifling confines of his uniform any longer, Grey flung it off, not waiting for Tom's ministrations, and stood naked in the middle of the room, eyes closed, enjoying the touch of air from the terrace on his bare skin.

There was something remarkable about the air. Warm as it was, and even indoors, it had a silken touch that spoke of the sea and clear blue water. He couldn't see the water from his room; even had it been visible from Spanish Town, his room faced a hillside covered with jungle. He could feel it, though, and had a sudden longing to wade out through surf and immerse himself in the clean coolness of the ocean. The sun had nearly set now, and the cries of parrots and other birds were growing intermittent.

He peered underneath the bed, but didn't see the snake. Perhaps it was far back in the shadows; perhaps it had gone off in search of more ham. He straightened, stretched luxuriously, then shook himself and stood blinking, feeling stupid from too much wine and food, and lack of sleep – he had slept barely three hours out of the preceding four-and-twenty, what with the arrival, disembarkation, and the journey to King's House.

His mind appeared to have taken French leave for the moment; no matter; it would be back shortly. Meanwhile, though, its abdication had left his body in charge; not at all a responsible course of action.

He felt exhausted, but restless, and scratched idly at his

169

chest. The wounds there were solidly healed, slightly raised pink weals under his fingers, criss-crossing through the blond hair. One had passed within an inch of his left nipple; he'd been lucky not to lose it.

An immense pile of gauze cloth lay upon his bed. This must be the mosquito netting described to him by Mr Dawes at dinner – a draped contraption meant to enclose the entire bed, thus protecting its occupant from the depredations of bloodthirsty insects.

He'd spent some time with Fettes and Cherry after dinner, laying plans for the morrow. Cherry would call upon Judge Peters and obtain details of the maroons who had been captured. Fettes would send men into King's Town in a search for the location of the retired Mr Ludgate, erstwhile superintendent; if he could be found, Grey would like to know this gentleman's opinion of his successor. As for that successor – if Dawes did not manage to unearth Captain Cresswell by the end of tomorrow . . . Grey yawned involuntarily, then shook his head, blinking. Enough.

The troops would all be billeted by now, some granted their first liberty in months. He spared a glance at the small sheaf of maps and reports he had extracted from Mr Dawes earlier, but those could wait till morning, and better light. He'd think better after a good night's sleep.

He leaned against the frame of the open door, after a quick glance down the terrace showed him that the rooms nearby seemed unoccupied. Clouds were beginning to drift in from the sea, and he remembered what Rodrigo had said about the rain at night. He thought perhaps he could feel a slight coolness in the air, whether from rain or oncoming night, and the hair on his body prickled and rose.

From here, he could see nothing but the deep green of a jungle-clad hill, glowing like a sombre emerald in the twilight. From the other side of the house, though, as he left dinner, he'd seen the sprawl of Spanish Town below, a puzzle of narrow, aromatic streets. The taverns and the brothels would be doing a remarkable business tonight, he thought.

The thought brought with it a rare feeling of something that wasn't quite resentment. Any one of the soldiers he'd brought, from lowliest private soldier to Fettes himself, could walk into any brothel in Spanish Town – and there were a good many, Cherry had told him – and relieve the stresses caused by a long voyage without the slightest comment, or even the slightest attention. Not him.

His hand had dropped lower as he watched the light fade, idly kneading his flesh. There were accommodations for men such as himself in London, but it had been many years since he'd had recourse to such a place.

He had lost one lover to death, another to betrayal. The third . . . his lips tightened. Could you call a man your lover, who would never touch you – would recoil from the very thought of touching you? No. But at the same time, what would you call a man whose *mind* touched yours, whose prickly friendship was a gift, whose character, whose very existence, helped to define your own?

Not for the first time – and surely not for the last – he wished briefly that Jamie Fraser was dead. It was an automatic wish, though, at once dismissed from mind. The colour of the jungle had died to ash, and insects were beginning to whine past his ears.

He went in, and began to worry the folds of the gauze on his bed, until Tom came in to take it away from him, hang the mosquito-netting, and ready him for the night.

He couldn't sleep. Whether it was the heavy meal, the unaccustomed place, or simply the worry of his new and

171

so-far-unknown command, his mind refused to settle, and so did his body. He didn't waste time in useless thrashing, though; he'd brought several books. Reading a bit of *The Story of Tom Jones, A Foundling* would distract his mind, and let sleep steal in upon him.

The French doors were covered with sheer muslin curtains, but the moon was nearly full, and there was enough light by which to find his tinder-box, striker, and candlestick. The candle was good beeswax, and the flame rose pure and bright – and instantly attracted a small cloud of inquisitive gnats, mosquitoes, and tiny moths. He picked it up, intending to take it to bed with him, but then thought better.

Was it preferable to be gnawed by mosquitoes, or incinerated? Grey debated the point for all of three seconds, then set the lit candlestick back on the desk. The gauze netting would go up in a flash, if the candle fell over in bed.

Still, he needn't face death by bloodletting or be covered in itching bumps, simply because his valet didn't like the smell of bear-grease. He wouldn't get it on his clothes, in any case.

He flung off his nightshirt and kneeled to rummage in his trunk, with a guilty look over his shoulder. Tom, though, was safely tucked up somewhere amid the attics or outbuildings of King's House, and almost certainly sound asleep. Tom suffered badly with sea-sickness, and the voyage had been hard on him.

The heat of the Indies hadn't done the battered tin of bear-grease any good, either; the rancid fat nearly overpowered the scent of the peppermint and other herbs mixed into it. Still, he reasoned, if it repelled him, how much more a mosquito? and rubbed it into as much of his flesh as he could reach. Despite the stink, he found it not unpleasant. There was enough of the original smell left

172

as to remind of his usage of the stuff in Canada. Enough to remind him of Manoke, who had given it to him. Anointed him with it, in a cool blue evening on a deserted sandy isle in the St Lawrence River.

Finished, he put down the tin and touched his rising prick. He didn't suppose he'd ever see Manoke again. But he did remember. Vividly.

A little later, he lay gasping on the bed under his netting, heart thumping slowly in counterpoint to the echoes of his flesh. He opened his eyes, feeling pleasantly relaxed, his head finally clear. The room was close; the servants had shut the windows, of course, to keep out the dangerous night air, and sweat misted his body. He felt too slack to get up and open the French doors onto the terrace, though; in a moment would do.

He closed his eyes again – then opened them abruptly and leaped out of bed, reaching for the dagger he'd laid on the table. The servant called Rodrigo stood pressed against the door, the whites of his eyes showing in his black face.

'What do you want?' Grey put the dagger down, but kept his hand on it, his heart still racing.

'I have a message for you, sah,' the young man said. He swallowed audibly.

'Yes? Come into the light, where I can see you.' Grey reached for his banyan and slid into it, still keeping an eye on the man.

Rodrigo peeled himself off the door with evident reluctance, but he'd come to say something, and say it he would. He advanced into the dim circle of candlelight, hands at his sides, nervously clutching air.

'Do you know, sah, what an Obeah-man is?'

'No.'

That disconcerted Rodrigo visibly. He blinked, and twisted his lips, obviously at a loss as how to describe this entity. Finally, he shrugged his shoulders helplessly and gave up.

'He says to you, beware.'

'Does he?' Grey says dryly. 'Of anything specific?'

That seemed to help; Rodrigo nodded vigorously.

'You don't be close to the governor. Stay right away, as far as you can. He's going to – I mean . . . something bad might happen. Soon. He—' The servant broke off suddenly, apparently realising that he could be dismissed – if not worse – for talking about the governor in this loose fashion. Grey was more than curious, though, and sat down, motioning to Rodrigo to take the stool, which he did with obvious reluctance.

Whatever an Obeah-man was, Grey thought, he clearly had considerable power, to force Rodrigo to do something he so plainly didn't want to do. The young man's face shone with sweat and his hands clenched mindlessly on the fabric of his coat.

'Tell me what the Obeah-man said,' Grey said, leaning forward, intent. 'I promise you, I will tell no one.'

Rodrigo gulped, but nodded. He bent his head, looking at the table as though he might find the right words written in the grain of the wood.

'Zombie,' he muttered, almost inaudibly. 'The zombie come for him. For the governor.'

Grey had no notion what a zombie might be, but the word was spoken in such a tone as to make a chill flicker over his skin, sudden as distant lightning.

'Zombie,' he said carefully. Mindful of the governor's reaction earlier, he asked, 'Is a zombie perhaps a snake of some kind?'

Rodrigo gasped, but then seemed to relax a little.

'No, sah,' he said seriously. 'Zombie are dead people.' He stood up then, bowed abruptly and left, his message delivered.

Not surprisingly, Grey did not fall asleep immediately in the wake of this visit.

Having encountered German night-hags, Indian ghosts, and having spent a year or two in the Scottish Highlands, he had more acquaintance than most with picturesque superstition. While he wasn't inclined to give instant credence to local custom and belief, neither was he inclined to discount such belief out of hand. Belief made people do things that they otherwise wouldn't – and whether the belief had substance or not, the consequent actions certainly did.

Obeah-men and zombies notwithstanding, plainly there was some threat to Governor Warren – and he rather thought the governor knew what it was.

How exigent was the threat, though? He pinched out the candle-flame and sat in darkness for a moment, letting his eyes adjust themselves, then rose and went soft-footed to the French doors through which Rodrigo had vanished.

The guest bedchambers of King's House were merely a string of boxes, all facing onto the long terrace, and each opening directly on to it through a pair of French doors. These had been curtained for the night, long pale drapes of muslin drawn across them. He paused for a moment, hand on the drape; if anyone was watching his room, they would see the curtain being drawn aside.

Instead, he turned and went to the inner door of the room. This opened onto a narrow service corridor, completely dark at the moment – and completely empty, if his senses could be trusted. He closed the door quietly. It was interesting, he thought, that Rodrigo had come to the front door, so to speak, when he could have approached Grey unseen.

But he'd said the Obeah-man had sent him. Plainly he wanted it to be seen that he had obeyed his order. Which in turn meant that someone was likely watching to see that he had.

The logical conclusion would be that the same someone – or someones – was watching to see what Grey might do next.

His body had reached its own conclusions already, and was reaching for breeches and shirt before he had quite decided that if something was about to happen to Warren, it was clearly his duty to stop it, zombies or not. He stepped out of the French doors onto the terrace, moving quite openly.

There was an infantryman posted at either end of the terrace, as he'd expected; Robert Cherry was nothing if not meticulous. On the other hand, the bloody sentries had plainly not seen Rodrigo entering his room, and he wasn't at all pleased about that. Recriminations could wait, though; the nearer sentry saw *him* and challenged him with a sharp, 'Who goes there?'

'It's me,' Grey said briefly, and without ceremony, dispatched the sentry with orders to alert the other soldiers posted around the house, then send two men into the house, where they should wait in the hall until summoned.

Grey himself then went back into his room, through the inner door, and down the dark service corridor. He found a dozing black servant behind a door at the end of it, minding the fire under the row of huge coppers that supplied hot water to the household.

The man blinked and stared when shaken awake, but eventually nodded in response to Grey's demand to be taken to the governor's bedchamber, and led him into the main part of the house and up a darkened stair lit only by the moonlight streaming through the tall casements. Everything was quiet on the upper floor, save for slow, regular snoring coming from what the slave said was the governor's room.

The man was swaying with weariness; Grey dismissed him, with orders to let in the soldiers who should now be at the door, and send them up. The man yawned hugely, and Grey watched him stumble down the stairs into the murk of the hall below, hoping he would not fall and break his neck. The house was very quiet. He was beginning to feel somewhat foolish. And yet . . .

The house seemed to breathe around him, almost as though it were a sentient thing, and aware of him. He found the fancy unsettling.

Ought he to wake Warren? he wondered. Warn him? Question him? No, he decided. There was no point in disturbing the man's rest. Questions could wait for the morning.

The sound of feet coming up the stair dispelled his sense of uneasiness, and he gave his orders quietly. The sentries were to keep guard on this door until relieved in the morning; at any sound of disturbance within, they were to enter at once. Otherwise—

'Stay alert. If you see or hear *anything*, I wish to know about it.'

He paused, but Warren continued to snore, so he shrugged and made his way downstairs, out into the silken night, and back to his own room.

He smelled it first. For an instant, he thought he had left the tin of bear-grease ointment uncovered – and then the reek of sweet decay took him by the throat, followed instantly by a pair of hands that came out of the dark and fastened on said throat.

He fought back in blind panic, striking and kicking wildly, but the grip on his windpipe didn't loosen, and bright lights began to flicker at the corners of what would have been his vision if he'd had any. With a tremendous effort of will, he made himself go limp. The sudden weight surprised his assailant, and jerked Grey free of the throttling grasp as he fell. He hit the floor and rolled.

Bloody hell, where was the man? If it was a man. For even as his mind reasserted its claim to reason, his more visceral faculties were recalling Rodrigo's parting statement: *Zombie are dead people, sah.* And whatever was here in the dark with him seemed to have been dead for several days, judging from its smell.

He could hear the rustling of something moving quietly toward him. Was it breathing? He couldn't tell, for the rasp of his own breath, harsh in his throat, and the blood-thick hammering of his heart in his ears.

He was lying at the foot of a wall, his legs half under the dressing table's bench. There was light in the room, now his eyes were accustomed; the French doors were pale rectangles in the dark, and he could make out the shape of the thing that was hunting him. It was man-shaped, but oddly hunched, and swung its head and shoulders from side to side, almost as though it meant to smell him out. Which wouldn't take it more than two more seconds, at most.

He sat up abruptly, seized the small padded bench, and threw it as hard as he could at the thing's legs. It made a startled *Oof!* noise that was undeniably human and staggered, waving its arms to keep its balance. The noise reassured him, and he rolled up onto one knee and launched himself at the creature, bellowing incoherent abuse.

He butted it around chest-height, felt it fall backward, then lunged for the pool of shadow where he thought the table was. It was there, and feeling frantically over the surface, he found his dagger, still where he'd left it. He snatched it up, and turned just in time to face the thing, which closed with him at once, reeking and making a disagreeable gobbling noise. He slashed at it, and felt his knife skitter down the creature's forearm, bouncing off bone. It screamed, releasing a blast of foul breath directly into his face, then turned and rushed for the French doors, bursting them open in a shower of glass and flying muslin.

Grey charged after it, onto the terrace, shouting for the sentries. But the sentries, as he recalled belatedly, were in the main house, keeping watch over the governor, lest that worthy's rest be disturbed by . . . whatever sort of thing this was. Zombie?

Whatever it was, it was gone.

He sat down abruptly on the stones of the terrace, shaking with reaction. No one had come out in response to the noise. Surely no one could have slept through that; perhaps no one else was housed on this side of the mansion.

He felt ill and breathless, and rested his head for a moment on his knees, before jerking it up to look round, lest something else be stealing up on him. But the night was still and balmy. The only noise was an agitated rustling of leaves in a nearby tree, which he thought for a shocked moment might be the creature, climbing from branch to branch in search of refuge. Then he heard soft chitterings and hissing squeaks. *Bats*, said the calmly rational part of his mind – what was left of it.

He gulped and breathed, trying to get clean air into his lungs, to replace the disgusting stench of the creature. He'd been a soldier most of his life; he'd seen the dead on battlefields, and smelled them, too. Had buried fallen comrades in trenches and burned the bodies of his enemies. He knew what graves smelled like, and rotting flesh. And the thing that had had its hands round his throat had almost certainly come from a recent grave.

He was shivering violently, despite the warmth of the

night. He rubbed a hand over his left arm, aching from the struggle; he had been badly wounded two years before, at Crefeld, and had nearly lost the arm. It worked, but was still a good deal weaker than he liked. Glancing at it, though, he was startled. Dark smears befouled the pale sleeve of his banyan, and turning over his right hand, he found it wet and sticky.

'Jesus,' he murmured, and brought it gingerly to his nose. No mistaking *that* smell, even overlaid as it was by grave-reek and the incongruous scent of night-blooming jasmine from the vines that grew in tubs by the terrace. Rain was beginning to fall, pungent and sweet – but even that could not obliterate the smell.

Blood. Fresh blood. Not his, either.

He rubbed the rest of the blood from his hand with the hem of his banyan, and the cold horror of the last few minutes faded into a glowing coal of anger, hot in the pit of his stomach.

He'd been a soldier most of his life; he'd killed. He'd seen the dead on battlefields. And one thing he knew for a fact. Dead men don't bleed.

Fettes and Cherry had to know, of course. So did Tom, as the wreckage of his room couldn't be explained as the result of a nightmare. The four of them gathered in Grey's room, conferring by candlelight as Tom went about tidying the damage, white to the lips.

'You've never heard of zombie – or zombies? I have no idea whether the term is plural or not.' Heads were shaken all round. A large square bottle of excellent Scotch whisky had survived the rigours of the voyage in the bottom of his trunk, and he poured generous tots of this, including Tom in the distribution.

'Tom – will you ask among the servants tomorrow? Carefully, of course. Drink that; it will do you good.'

'Oh, I'll be careful, me lord,' Tom assured him fervently. He took an obedient gulp of the whisky before Grey could warn him. His eyes bulged and he made a noise like a bull that has sat on a bumblebee, but managed somehow to swallow the mouthful, after which he stood still, opening and closing his mouth in a stunned sort of way.

Bob Cherry's mouth twitched, but Fettes maintained his usual stolid imperturbability.

'Why the attack upon you, sir, do you suppose?'

'If the servant who warned me about the Obeah-man was correct, I can only suppose that it was a consequence of my posting sentries to keep guard upon the governor. But you're right,' he nodded at Fettes's implication. 'That means that whoever was responsible for this – ' he waved a hand to indicate the disorder of his chamber, which still smelled of its recent intruder, despite the rain-scented wind that came through the shattered doors and the burned-honey smell of the whisky, ' – either was watching the house closely, or—'

'Or lives here,' Fettes said, and took a meditative sip. 'Dawes, perhaps?'

Grey's eyebrows rose. That small, tubby, genial man? And yet he'd known a number of small, wicked men.

'Well,' he said slowly, 'it was not he who attacked me; I can tell you that much. Whoever it was, was taller than I am, and of a very lean build – not corpulent at all.'

Tom made a hesitant noise, indicating that he had had a thought, and Grey nodded at him, giving permission to speak.

'You're quite sure, me lord, as the man who went for you . . . er . . . *wasn't* dead? Because by the smell of him, he's been buried for a week, at least.'

A reflexive shudder went through all of them, but Grey shook his head.

'I am positive,' he said, as firmly as he could. 'It was a live man – though certainly a peculiar one,' he added, frowning.

'Ought we to search the house, sir?' Cherry suggested.

Grey shook his head, reluctantly.

'He – or it – came from the garden, and went away in the same direction. He left discernible foot-marks.' He did not add that there had been sufficient time for the servants – if they were involved – to hide any traces of the creature by now. If there was involvement there, he thought the servant Rodrigo was his best avenue of inquiry – and it would not serve his purposes to alarm the house and focus attention on the young man ahead of time.

'Tom,' he said, turning to his valet. 'Does Rodrigo appear to be approachable?'

'Oh, yes, me lord. He was friendly to me over supper,' Tom assured him, brush in hand. 'D'ye want me to talk to him?'

'Yes, if you will. Beyond that . . .' He rubbed a hand over his face, feeling the sprouting beard-stubble on his jaw. 'I think we will proceed with the plans for tomorrow. But Major Cherry – will you also find time to question Mr Dawes? You may tell him what transpired here tonight; I should find his response to that most interesting.'

'Yes, sir.' Cherry sat up and finished his whisky, coughed and sat blinking for a moment, then cleared his throat. 'The, um, the governor, sir . . . ?'

'I'll speak to him myself,' Grey said. 'And then I propose to ride up into the hills, to pay a visit to a couple of plantations, with an eye to defensive postings. For we must be seen to be taking prompt and decisive action. If there's offensive action to be taken against the maroons, it will wait until we see what we're up against.' Fettes and

182

Cherry nodded; lifelong soldiers, they had no urgent desire to rush into combat.

The meeting dismissed, Grey sat down with a fresh glass of whisky, sipping it as Tom finished his work in silence.

'You're sure as you want to sleep in this room tonight, me lord?' he said, putting the dressing-table bench neatly back in its place. 'I could find you another place, I'm sure.'

Grey smiled at him with affection.

'I'm sure you could, Tom. But so could our recent friend, I expect. No, Major Cherry will post a double guard on the terrace, as well as in the main house. It will be perfectly safe.' And even if it wasn't, the thought of hiding, skulking away from whatever the thing was that had visited him . . . no. He wouldn't allow them – whoever they were – to think they had shaken his nerve.

Tom sighed and shook his head, but reached into his shirt and drew out a small cross, woven of wheat stalks and somewhat battered, suspended on a bit of leather string.

'All right, me lord. But you'll wear this, at least.'

'What is it?'

'A charm, me lord. That Ilsa gave it to me, in Germany. She said it would protect me against evil – and so it has.'

'Oh, no, Tom – surely you must keep—'

Mouth set in an expression of obstinacy that Grey knew well, Tom leaned forward and put the leather string over Grey's head. The mouth relaxed.

'There, me lord. Now *I* can sleep, at least.'

Grey's plan to speak to the governor at breakfast was foiled, as that gentleman sent word that he was indisposed. Grey, Cherry, and Fettes all exchanged looks across the breakfast table, but Grey said merely, 'Fettes?

And you, Major Cherry, please.' They nodded, a look of subdued satisfaction passing between them. He hid a smile; they loved questioning people.

The secretary, Dawes, was present at breakfast, but said little, giving all his attention to the eggs and toast on his plate. Grey inspected him carefully, but he showed no sign, either of nocturnal excursions or of clandestine knowledge. He gave Cherry an eye. Both Fettes and Cherry brightened perceptibly.

For the moment, though, his own path lay clear. He needed to make a public appearance, as soon as possible, and to take such action as would make it apparent to the public that the situation was under control – and would make it apparent to the maroons that attention was being paid and that their destructive activities would no longer be allowed to pass unchallenged.

He summoned one of his other captains after breakfast, and arranged for an escort. Twelve men should make enough of a show, he decided.

'And where will you be going, sir?' Captain Lossey asked, squinting as he made mental calculations regarding horses, pack mules, and supplies.

Grey took a deep breath and grasped the nettle.

'A plantation called Twelvetrees,' he said. 'Twenty miles or so into the uplands above King's Town.'

Philip Twelvetrees was young, perhaps in his mid-twenties, and good-looking in a sturdy sort of way. He didn't stir Grey personally, but nonetheless Grey felt a tightness through his body as he shook hands with the man, studying his face carefully for any sign that Twelvetrees recognised his name, or attributed any importance to his presence beyond the present political situation.

184

Not a flicker of unease or suspicion crossed Twelvetrees's face, and Grey relaxed a little, accepting the offer of a cooling drink. This turned out to be a mixture of fruit juices and wine, tart but refreshing.

'It's called *sangria*,' Twelvetrees remarked, holding up his glass so the soft light fell glowing through it. 'Blood, it means. In Spanish.'

Grey did not speak much Spanish, but did know that. However, blood seemed as good a *point d'appui* as any, concerning his business.

'So you think we might be next?' Twelvetrees paled noticeably beneath his tan. He hastily swallowed a gulp of sangria and straightened his shoulders, though. 'No, no. I'm sure we'll be all right. Our slaves are loyal, I'd swear to that.'

'How many have you? And do you trust them with arms?'

'One hundred and sixteen,' Twelvetrees replied, automatically. Plainly he was contemplating the expense and danger of arming some fifty men — for at least half his slaves must be women or children – and setting them essentially at liberty upon his property. And the vision of an unknown number of maroons, also armed, coming suddenly out of the night with torches. He drank a little more sangria. 'Perhaps . . . what did you have in mind?' he asked abruptly, setting down his glass.

Grey had just finished laying out his suggested plans, which called for the posting of two companies of infantry at the plantation, when a flutter of muslin at the door made him lift his eyes.

'Oh, Nan!' Philip put a hand over the papers Grey had spread out on the table, and shot Grey a quick warning look. 'Here's Colonel Grey come to call. Colonel, my sister, Nancy.'

'Miss Twelvetrees.' Grey had risen at once, and now

took two or three steps toward her, bowing over her hand. Behind him, he heard the rustle as Twelvetrees hastily shuffled maps and diagrams together.

Nancy Twelvetrees shared her brother's genial sturdiness. Not pretty in the least, she had intelligent dark eyes – and these sharpened noticeably at her brother's introduction.

'Colonel Grey,' she said, waving him gracefully back to his seat as she took her own. 'Would you be connected with the Greys of Ilford, in Sussex? Or perhaps your family are from the London branch . . . ?'

'My brother has an estate in Sussex, yes,' he said hastily. Forbearing to add that it was his half-brother Paul, who was not in fact a Grey, having been born of his mother's first marriage. Forbearing also to mention that his elder full brother was the Duke of Pardloe, and the man who had shot one Nathaniel Twelvetrees twenty years before. Which would logically expose the fact that Grey himself . . .

Philip Twelvetrees rather obviously did not want his sister alarmed by any mention of the present situation. Grey gave him the faintest of nods in acknowledgement, and Twelvetrees relaxed visibly, settling down to exchange polite social conversation.

'And what is it that brings you to Jamaica, Colonel Grey?' Miss Twelvetrees asked eventually. Knowing this was coming, Grey had devised an answer of careful vagueness, having to do with the Crown's concern for shipping. Halfway through this taraddle, though, Miss Twelvetrees gave him a very direct look and demanded, 'Are you here because of the governor?'

'Nan!' said her brother, shocked.

'Are you?' she repeated, ignoring her brother. Her eyes were very bright, and her cheeks flushed.

Grey smiled at her.

186

'What makes you think that that might be the case, may I ask, ma'am?'

'Because if you haven't come to remove Derwent Warren from his office, then *someone* should!'

'Nancy!' Philip was nearly as flushed as his sister. He leaned forward, grasping her wrist. 'Nancy, please!'

She made as though to pull away, but then, seeing his pleading face, contented herself with a simple, 'Hmph!' and sat back in her chair, mouth set in a thin line.

Grey would dearly have liked to know what lay behind Miss Twelvetrees's animosity for the governor, but he couldn't well inquire directly, and instead guided the conversation smoothly away, inquiring of Philip regarding the operations of the plantation, and of Miss Twelvetrees regarding the natural history of Jamaica, for which she seemed to have some feeling, judging by the rather good watercolours of plants and animals that hung about the room, all neatly signed 'N. T.'

Gradually, the sense of tension in the room relaxed, and Grey became aware that Miss Twelvetrees was focusing her attentions upon him. Not quite flirting; she was not built for flirtation. But definitely going out of her way to make him aware of her as a woman. He didn't quite know what she had in mind – he was presentable enough, but didn't think she was truly attracted to him. Still, he made no move to stop her; if Philip should leave them alone together, he might be able to find out why she had said that about Governor Warren.

A quarter-hour later, a mulatto man in a well-made suit put his head in at the door to the drawing room and asked if he might speak with Philip. He cast a curious eye toward Grey, but Twelvetrees made no move to introduce them, instead excusing himself and taking the visitor – who, Grey conceived, must be an overseer of some kind –

to the far end of the large, airy room, where they conferred in low voices.

He at once seized the opportunity to fix his attention on Miss Nancy, in hopes of turning the conversation to his own ends.

'I collect you are acquainted with the governor, Miss Twelvetrees?' he asked, to which she gave a short laugh.

'Better than I might wish, sir.'

'Really?' he said, in as inviting a tone as possible.

'Really,' she said, and smiled unpleasantly. 'But let us not waste time in discussing a . . . a person of such low character.' The smile altered, and she leaned toward him, touching his hand, which surprised him. 'Tell me, colonel, does your wife accompany you? Or does she remain in London, from fear of fevers and slave uprisings?'

'Alas, I am unmarried, ma'am,' he said, thinking that she likely knew a good deal more than her brother wished her to.

'Really,' she said again, in an altogether different tone.

Her touch lingered on his hand, a fraction of a moment too long. Not long enough to be blatant, but long enough for a normal man to perceive it – and Grey's reflexes in such matters were much better developed than a normal man's, from necessity.

He barely thought consciously, but smiled at her, then glanced at her brother, then back, with the tiniest of regretful shrugs. He forbore to add the lingering smile that would have said, 'Later.'

She sucked her lower lip in for a moment, then released it, wet and reddened, and gave him a look under lowered lids that said 'Later,' and a good deal more. He coughed, and out of the sheer need to say *something* completely free of suggestion, asked abruptly, 'Do you by chance know what an Obeah-man is, Miss Twelvetrees?'

Her eyes sprang wide, and she lifted her hand from his

arm. He managed to move out of her easy reach without actually appearing to shove his chair backward, and thought she didn't notice; she was still looking at him with great attention, but the nature of that attention had changed. The sharp vertical lines between her brows deepened into a harsh eleven.

'Where did you encounter that term, colonel, may I ask?' Her voice was quite normal, her tone light – but she also glanced at her brother's turned back, and she spoke quietly.

'One of the governor's servants mentioned it. I see you are familiar with the term – I collect it is to do with Africans?'

'Yes.' Now she was biting her upper lip, but the intent was not sexual. 'The Koromantyn slaves – you know what those are?'

'No.'

'Negroes from the Gold Coast,' she said, and putting her hand once more on his sleeve, pulled him up and drew him a little away, toward the far end of the room. 'Most planters want them, because they're big and strong, and usually very well-formed.' Was it— no, he decided, it was *not* his imagination; the tip of her tongue had darted out and touched her lip in the fraction of an instant before she'd said 'well-formed.' He thought Philip Twelvetrees had best find his sister a husband, and quickly.

'Do you have Koromantyn slaves here?'

'A few. The thing is, Koromantyns tend to be intractable. Very aggressive, and hard to control.'

'Not a desirable trait in a slave, I collect,' he said, making an effort to keep any edge out of his tone.

'Well, it can be,' she said, surprising him. She smiled briefly. 'If your slaves are loyal – and ours are, I'd swear it – then you don't mind them being a bit bloody-minded

189

toward . . . anyone who might want to come and cause trouble.'

He was sufficiently shocked at her language that it took him a moment to absorb her meaning. The tongue-tip flickered out again, and had she had dimples, she would certainly have employed them.

'I see,' he said carefully. 'But you were about to tell me what an Obeah-man is. Some figure of authority, I take it, among the Koromantyns?'

The flirtatiousness vanished abruptly, and she frowned again.

'Yes. *Obi* is what they call their . . . religion, I suppose one must call it. Though from what little I know of it, no minister or priest would allow it that name.'

Loud screams came from the garden below, and he glanced out, to see a flock of small, brightly coloured parrots swooping in and out of a big, lacy tree with yellowish fruit. Like clockwork, two small black children, naked as eggs, shot out of the shrubbery and aimed slingshots at the birds. Rocks spattered harmlessly among the branches, but the birds rose in a feathery vortex of agitation and flapped off, shrieking their complaints.

Miss Twelvetrees ignored the interruption, resuming her explanation directly the noise subsided.

'An Obeah-man talks to the spirits. He, or she – there are Obeah-women, too – is the person that one goes to, to . . . arrange things.'

'What sorts of things?'

A faint hint of her former flirtatiousness reappeared.

'Oh . . . to make someone fall in love with you. To get with child. To get *without* child . . .' and here she looked to see whether she had shocked him again, but he merely nodded, '—or to curse someone. To cause them ill-luck, or ill-health. Or death.'

This was promising.

'And how is this done, may I ask? Causing illness or death?'

Here, however, she shook her head.

'I don't know. It's really not safe to ask,' she added, lowering her voice still further, and now her eyes were serious. 'Tell me – the servant who spoke to you; what did he say?'

Aware of just how quickly gossip spreads in rural places, Grey wasn't about to reveal that threats had been made against Governor Warren. Instead he asked, 'Have you ever heard of zombies?'

She went quite white.

'No,' she said abruptly. It was a risk, but he took her hand to keep her from turning away.

'I cannot tell you why I need to know,' he said, very low-voiced, 'but please believe me, Miss Twelvetrees – Nancy – ' callously, he pressed her hand, 'it's extremely important. Any help that you can give me would be— well, I should appreciate it extremely.' Her hand was warm; the fingers moved a little in his, and not in an effort to pull away. Her colour was coming back.

'I truly don't know much,' she said, equally low-voiced. 'Only that zombies are dead people, who have been raised by magic, to do the bidding of the person who made them.'

'The person who made them – this would be an Obeah-man?'

'Oh! No,' she said, surprised. 'The Koromantyns don't make zombies. In fact, they think it quite an unclean practice.'

'I'm entirely of one mind with them,' he assured her. 'Who *does* make zombies?'

'Nancy!' Philip had concluded his conversation with the overseer, and was coming toward them, a hospitable smile on his broad, perspiring face. 'I say, can we not have something to eat? I'm sure the colonel must be famished, and I'm most extraordinarily clemmed myself.'

'Yes, of course,' Miss Twelvetrees said, with a quick warning glance at Grey. 'I'll tell Cook.' Grey tightened his grip momentarily on her fingers, and she smiled at him.

'As I was saying, colonel, you must call on Mrs Abernathy at Rose Hall. She would be the person best equipped to inform you.'

'Inform you?' Twelvetrees, curse him, chose this moment to become inquisitive. 'About what?'

'Customs and beliefs among the Ashanti, my dear,' his sister said blandly. 'Colonel Grey has a particular interest in such things.'

Twelvetrees snorted briefly.

'Ashanti, my left foot! Ibo, Fulani, Koromantyn . . . baptise 'em all proper Christians and let's hear no more about what heathen beliefs they may have brought with 'em. From the little *I* know, you don't want to hear about that sort of thing, colonel. Though if you *do*, of course,' he added hastily, recalling that it was not his place to tell the lieutenant-colonel who would be protecting Twelvetrees's life and property his business, 'then my sister's quite right – Mrs Abernathy would be best placed to advise you. Almost all her slaves are Ashanti. She . . . er . . . she's said to . . . um . . . take an interest.'

To Grey's own interest, Twelvetrees's face went a deep red, and he hastily changed the subject, asking Grey fussy questions about the exact disposition of his troops. Grey evaded direct answers beyond assuring Twelvetrees that two companies of infantry would be dispatched to his plantation as soon as word could be sent to Spanish Town.

He wished to leave at once, for various reasons, but was obliged to remain for tea, an uncomfortable meal of heavy, stodgy food, eaten under the heated gaze of Miss Twelvetrees. For the most part, he thought he had handled her with tact and delicacy – but toward the end of the meal she began to give him little pursed-mouth jabs. Nothing one could – or should – overtly notice, but he saw Philip blink at her once or twice in frowning bewilderment.

'Of course, I could not pose as an authority regarding any aspect of life on Jamaica,' she said, fixing him with an unreadable look. 'We have lived here barely six months.'

'Indeed,' he said politely, a wodge of undigested Savoy cake settling heavily in his stomach. 'You seem very much at home – and a very lovely home it is, Miss Twelvetrees. I perceive your most harmonious touch throughout.'

This belated attempt at flattery was met with the scorn it deserved; the eleven was back, hardening her brow.

'My brother inherited the plantation from his cousin, Edward Twelvetrees. Edward lived in London, himself.' She levelled a look like the barrel of a musket at him. 'Did you know him, colonel?'

And just what would the bloody woman do if he told her the truth? he wondered. Clearly, she thought she knew something, but . . . no, he thought, watching her closely. She couldn't know the truth, but had heard some rumour. So this poking at him was an attempt – and a clumsy one – to get him to say more.

'I know several Twelvetrees casually,' he said, very amiably. 'But if I met your cousin, I do not think I had the pleasure of speaking with him at any great length.' *You bloody murderer!* and *Fucking sodomite!* not really constituting conversation, if you asked Grey.

Miss Twelvetrees blinked at him, surprised, and he realised what he should have seen much earlier. She was drunk. He had found the sangria light, refreshing – but had drunk only one glass himself. He had not noticed her refill her own, and yet the pitcher stood nearly empty.

'My dear,' said Philip, very kindly. 'It is warm, is it not? You look a trifle pale and indisposed.' In fact, she was flushed, her hair beginning to come down behind her rather large ears – but she did indeed look indisposed. Philip rang the bell, rising to his feet, and nodded to the black maid who came in.

'I am not indisposed,' Nancy Twelvetrees said, with some dignity. 'I'm— I simply— that is—' But the black maid, evidently used to this office, was already hauling Miss Twelvetrees toward the door, though with sufficient skill as to make it look as though she merely assisted her mistress.

Grey rose himself, perforce, and took Miss Nancy's hand, bowing over it.

'Your servant, Miss Twelvetrees,' he said. 'I hope—'

'We know,' she said, staring at him from large, suddenly tear-filled eyes. 'Do you hear me? *We know.*' Then she was gone, the sound of her unsteady steps a ragged drumbeat on the parquet floor.

There was a brief, awkward silence between the two men. Grey cleared his throat just as Philip Twelvetrees coughed.

'Didn't really like cousin Edward,' he said.

'Oh,' said Grey.

They walked together to the yard where Grey's horse browsed under a tree, its sides streaked with parrot-droppings.

'Don't mind Nancy, will you?' Twelvetrees said quietly, not looking at him. 'She had . . . a disappointment, in London. I thought she might get over it more easily here, but— well, I made a mistake, and it's not easy to unmake.' He sighed, and Grey had a sudden strong urge to pat him sympathetically on the back.

Instead, he made an indeterminate noise in his throat, nodded, and mounted.

'The troops will be here the day after tomorrow, sir,' he said. 'You have my word upon it.'

Grey had intended to return to Spanish Town, but instead paused on the road, pulled out the chart Dawes had given him, and calculated the distance to Rose Hall. It would mean camping on the mountain overnight, but they were prepared for that – and beyond the desirability of hearing at first-hand the details of a maroon attack, he was now more than curious to speak with Mrs Abernathy regarding zombies.

He called his aide, wrote out instructions for the dispatch of troops to Twelvetrees, then sent two men back to Spanish Town with the message, and sent two more on before, to discover a good campsite. They reached this as the sun was beginning to sink, glowing like a flaming pearl in a soft pink sky.

'What is that?' he asked, looking up abruptly from the cup of gunpowder tea Corporal Sansom had handed him. Sansom looked startled, too, and looked up the slope where the sound had come from.

'Don't know, sir,' he said. 'It sounds like a horn of some kind.'

It did. Not a trumpet, or anything of a standard military nature. Definitely a sound of human origin, though. The men stood quiet, waiting. A moment or two, and the sound came again.

'That's a different one,' Sansom said, sounding alarmed. 'It came from over there—' pointing up the slope, '—didn't it?'

'Yes, it did,' Grey said absently. 'Hush!'

The first horn sounded again, a plaintive bleat almost lost in the noises of the birds settling for the night, and then fell silent.

Grey's skin tingled, his senses alert. They were not

alone in the jungle. Someone – some*ones* – were out there in the oncoming night, signalling to each other. Quietly, he gave orders for the building of a hasty fortification, and the camp fell at once into the work of organising defence. The men with him were mostly veterans, and while wary, not at all panicked. Within a very short time, a redoubt of stone and brush had been thrown up, sentries posted in pairs around camp, and every man's weapon was loaded and primed, ready for an attack.

Nothing came, though, and while the men lay on their arms all night, there was no further sign of human presence. Such presence was there, though; Grey could feel it. Them. Watching.

He ate his supper and sat with his back against an outcrop of rock, dagger in his belt and loaded musket to hand. Waiting.

But nothing happened, and the sun rose. They broke camp in an orderly fashion, and if horns sounded in the jungle, the sound was lost in the shriek and chatter of the birds.

He had never been in the presence of anyone who repelled him so acutely. He wondered why that was; there was nothing overtly ill-favoured or ugly about her. If anything, she was a handsome Scotchwoman of middle age, fair-haired and buxom. And yet, the widow Abernathy chilled him, despite the warmth of the air on the terrace where she had chosen to receive him at Rose Hall.

She was not dressed in mourning, he saw, nor did she make any obvious acknowledgement of the recent death of her husband. She wore white muslin, embroidered in blue about the hems and cuffs.

'I understand that I must congratulate you upon your

survival, madam,' he said, taking the seat she gestured him to. It was a somewhat callous thing to say, but she looked hard as nails; he didn't think it would upset her, and he was right.

'Thank you,' she said, leaning back in her own wicker chair and looking him frankly up and down in a way that he found unsettling. 'It was bloody cold in that spring, I'll tell ye that for nothing. Like to died myself, frozen right through.'

He inclined his head courteously.

'I trust you suffered no lingering ill-effects from the experience? Beyond, of course, the lamentable death of your husband,' he hurried to add.

She laughed coarsely.

'Glad to get shot o' the wicked sod.'

At a loss how to reply to this, Grey coughed and changed the subject.

'I am told, madam, that you have an interest in some of the rituals practised by slaves.'

Her somewhat bleared green glance sharpened at that.

'Who told you that?'

'Miss Nancy Twelvetrees.' There was no reason to keep the identity of his informant secret, after all.

'Oh, wee Nancy, was it?' She seemed amused by that, and shot him a sideways look. 'I expect she liked *you*, no?'

He couldn't see what Miss Twelvetrees's opinion of him might have to do with the matter, and said so, politely. Mrs Abernathy merely smirked at that, waving a hand.

'Aye, well. What is it ye want to know, then?'

'I want to know how zombies are made.'

Shock wiped the smirk off her face, and she blinked at him stupidly for a moment, before picking up her glass and draining it.

'Zombies,' she said, and looked at him with a certain wary interest. 'Why?'

He told her. From careless amusement, her attitude changed, interest sharpening. She made him repeat the story of his encounter with the thing in his room, asking sharp questions regarding its smell, particularly.

'Decayed flesh,' she said. 'Ye'd ken what that smells like, would ye?'

It must have been her accent that brought back the battlefield at Culloden, and the stench of burning corpses. He shuddered, unable to stop himself.

'Yes,' he said abruptly. 'Why?'

She pursed her lips in thought.

'There are different ways to go about it, aye? One way is to give the *afile* powder to the person, wait until they drop, and then bury them atop a recent corpse. Ye just spread the earth lightly over them,' she explained, catching his look. 'And make sure to put leaves and sticks over the face afore sprinkling the earth, so as the person can still breathe. When the poison dissipates enough for them to move again, and sense things, they see they're buried, they smell the reek, and so they ken they must be dead.' She spoke as matter-of-factly as though she had been telling him her private receipt for apple pan-dowdy or treacle-cake. Weirdly enough, that steadied him, and he was able to speak past his revulsion, calmly.

'Poison. That would be the *afile* powder? What sort of poison is it, do you know?'

Seeing the spark in her eye, he thanked the impulse that had led him to add 'Do you know?' to that question – for if not for pride, he thought she might not have told him. As it was, she shrugged and answered off-hand.

'Oh . . . herbs. Ground bones – bits o' other things. But the main thing, the one thing ye *must* have, is the liver of a *fugu* fish.'

He shook his head, not recognising the name. 'Describe it, if you please.' She did; from her description, he thought it must be one of the odd puffer-fish that blew themselves up like bladders if disturbed. He made a silent resolve never to eat one. In the course of the conversation, though, something was becoming apparent to him.

'But what you are telling me – your pardon, madam – is that in fact a zombie is *not* a dead person at all? That they are merely drugged?'

Her lips curved; they were still plump and red, he saw, younger than her face would suggest.

'What good would a dead person be to anyone?'

'But plainly the widespread belief is that zombies *are* dead.'

'Aye, of course. The zombies think they're dead, and so does everyone else. It's not true, but it's effective. Scares folk rigid. As for "merely drugged", though . . .' She shook her head. 'They don't come back from it, ye ken. The poison damages their brains, and their nervous systems. They can follow simple instructions, but they've no real capacity for thought anymore – and they mostly move stiff and slow.'

'Do they?' he murmured. The creature – well, the man, he was now sure of that – who had attacked him had not been stiff and slow, by any means. Ergo . . .

'I'm told, madam, that most of your slaves are Ashanti. Would any of them know more about this process?'

'No,' she said abruptly, sitting up a little. 'I learned what I ken from a *houngan* – that would be a sort of . . . practitioner, I suppose ye'd say. He wasna one of my slaves, though.'

'A practitioner of *what*, exactly?'

Her tongue passed slowly over the tips of her sharp teeth, yellowed, but still sound.

'Of magic,' she said, and laughed softly, as though to herself. 'Aye, magic. African magic. Slave magic.'

199

'You believe in magic?' He asked it as much from curiosity as anything else.

'Don't you?' Her brows rose, but he shook his head.

'I do not. And in fact, from what you have just told me yourself, the process of creating – if that's the word – a zombie is *not* in fact magic, but merely the administration of poison over a period of time, added to the power of suggestion.' Another thought struck him. 'Can a person recover from such poisoning? You say it does not kill them.'

She shook her head.

'The poison doesn't, no. But they always die. They starve, for one thing. They lose all notion of will, and canna do anything save what the *houngan* tells them to do. Gradually, they waste away to nothing, and—' Her fingers snapped silently.

'Even were they to survive,' she went on practically, 'the people would kill them. Once a person's been made a zombie, there's nay way back.'

Throughout the conversation, Grey had been becoming aware that Mrs Abernathy spoke from what seemed a much closer acquaintance with the notion than one might acquire from an idle interest in natural philosophy. He wanted to get away from her, but obliged himself to sit still and ask one more question.

'Do you know of any particular significance attributed to snakes, madam? In African magic, I mean.'

She blinked, somewhat taken aback by that.

'Snakes,' she repeated slowly. 'Aye. Well . . . snakes ha' wisdom, they say. And some o' the *loas* are snakes.'

'*Loas*?'

She rubbed absently at her forehead, and he saw, with a small prickle of revulsion, the faint stippling of a rash. He'd seen that before; the sign of advanced syphilitic infection.

'I suppose ye'd call them spirits,' she said, and eyed him appraisingly. 'D'ye see snakes in your dreams, colonel?'

'Do I— no. I don't.' He didn't, but the suggestion was unspeakably disturbing. She smiled.

'A *loa* rides a person, aye? Speaks through them. And I see a great huge snake, lyin' on your shoulders, colonel.' She heaved herself abruptly to her feet.

'I'd be careful what ye eat, Colonel Grey.'

They returned to Spanish Town two days later. The ride back gave Grey time for thought, from which he drew certain conclusions. Among these conclusions was the conviction that maroons had not, in fact, attacked Rose Hall. He had spoken to Mrs Abernathy's overseer, who seemed reluctant and shifty, very vague on the details of the presumed attack. And later . . .

After his conversations with the overseer and several slaves, he had gone back to the house to take formal leave of Mrs Abernathy. No one had answered his knock, and he had walked round the house in search of a servant. What he had found instead was a path leading downward from the house, with a glimpse of water at the bottom.

Out of curiosity, he had followed this path, and found the infamous spring in which Mrs Abernathy had presumably sought refuge from the murdering intruders. Mrs Abernathy was in the spring, naked, swimming with slow composure from one side to the other, white-streaked fair hair streaming out behind her.

The water was crystalline; he could see the fleshy pumping of her buttocks, moving like a bellows that propelled her movements – and glimpse the purplish hollow of her sex, exposed by the flexion. There were no banks of concealing reeds or other vegetation; no one could have failed

201

to see the woman if she'd been in the spring – and plainly, the temperature of the water was no dissuasion to her.

So she'd lied about the maroons. He had a cold certainty that Mrs Abernathy had murdered her husband, or arranged it – but there was little he was equipped to do with that conclusion. Arrest her? There were no witnesses – or none who could legally testify against her, even if they wanted to. And he rather thought that none of her slaves would want to; those he had spoken with had displayed extreme reticence with regard to their mistress. Whether that was the result of loyalty or fear, the effect would be the same.

What the conclusion *did* mean to him was that the maroons were in fact likely not guilty of murder, and that was important. So far, all reports of mischief involved only property damage – and that, only to fields and equipment. No houses had been burned, and while several plantation owners had claimed that their slaves had been taken, there was no proof of this; the slaves in question might simply have taken advantage of the chaos of an attack to run.

This spoke to him of a certain amount of care on the part of whoever led the maroons. Who did? he wondered. What sort of man? The impression he was gaining was not that of a rebellion – there had been no declaration, and he would have expected that – but of the boiling over of a long-simmering frustration. He *had* to speak with Captain Cresswell. And he hoped that bloody secretary had managed to find the superintendent by the time he reached King's House.

In the event, he reached King's House long after dark, and was informed by the governor's butler – appearing like a

202

black ghost in his nightshirt – that the household were asleep.

'All right,' he said wearily. 'Call my valet, if you will. And tell the governor's servant in the morning that I will require to speak to his Excellency after breakfast, no matter what his state of health may be.'

Tom was sufficiently pleased to see Grey in one piece as to make no protest at being awakened, and had him washed, nightshirted, and tucked up beneath his mosquito-netting before the church-bells of Spanish Town tolled midnight. The doors of his room had been repaired, but Grey made Tom leave the window open, and fell asleep with a silken wind caressing his cheeks and no thought of what the morning might bring.

He was roused from an unusually vivid erotic dream by an agitated banging. He pulled his head out from under the pillow, the feel of rasping red hairs still rough on his lips, and shook his head violently, trying to reorient himself in space and time. Bang, bang, bang, bang, *bang!* Bloody hell . . . ? Oh. Door.

'What? Come in, for God's sake! What the devil— oh. Wait a moment, then.' He struggled out of the tangle of bedclothes and discarded nightshirt – good Christ, had he really been doing what he'd been dreaming about doing? – and flung his banyan over his rapidly detumescing flesh.

'What?' he demanded, finally getting the door open. To his surprise, Tom stood there, saucer-eyed and trembling, next to Major Fettes.

'Are you all right, me lord?' Tom burst out, cutting off Major Fettes's first words.

'Do I appear to be spurting blood or missing any necessary appendages?' Grey demanded, rather irritably. 'What's happened, Fettes?'

Now that he'd got his eyes properly open, he saw that Fettes looked almost as disturbed as Tom. The major –

veteran of a dozen major campaigns, decorated for valour, and known for his coolness – swallowed visibly and braced his shoulders.

'It's the governor, sir. I think you'd best come and see.'

❦

'Where are the men who were assigned to guard him?' Grey asked calmly, stepping out of the governor's bedroom and closing the door gently behind him. The doorknob slid out of his fingers, slick under his hand. He knew the slickness was his own sweat, and not blood, but his stomach gave a lurch and he rubbed his fingers convulsively against the leg of his breeches.

'They're gone, sir.' Fettes had got his voice, if not quite his face, back under control. 'I've sent men to search the grounds.'

'Good. Would you please call the servants together? I'll need to question them.'

Fettes took a deep breath.

'They're gone, too.'

'What? All of them?'

'Yes, sir.'

He took a deep breath himself – and let it out again, fast. Even outside the room, the stench was gagging. He could feel the smell, thick on his skin, and rubbed his fingers on his breeches once again, hard. He swallowed, and holding his breath, jerked his head to Fettes – and Cherry, who had joined them, shaking his head mutely in answer to Grey's raised brow. No sign of the vanished sentries, then. God damn it; a search would have to be made for their bodies. The thought made him cold, despite the growing warmth of the morning.

He went down the stairs, his officers only too glad to follow. By the time he reached the foot, he had decided

204

where to begin, at least. He stopped and turned to Fettes and Cherry.

'Right. The island is under military law as of this moment. Notify the officers, but tell them there is to be no public announcement yet. And *don't* tell them why.' Given the flight of the servants, it was more than likely that news of the governor's death would reach the inhabitants of Spanish Town within hours – if it hadn't already. But if there was the slightest chance that the populace might remain in ignorance of the fact that Governor Warren had been killed and partially devoured in his own residence, while under the guard of His Majesty's army . . . Grey was taking it.

'What about the secretary?' he asked abruptly, suddenly remembering. 'Dawes. Is he gone, too? Or dead?'

Fettes and Cherry exchanged a guilty look.

'Don't know, sir,' Cherry said gruffly. 'I'll go and look.'

'Do that, if you please.'

He nodded in return to their salutes, and went outside, shuddering in relief at the touch of the sun on his face, the warmth of it through the thin linen of his shirt. He walked slowly toward his room, where Tom had doubtless already managed to assemble and clean his uniform.

Now what? Dawes, if the man was still alive – and he hoped to God he was . . . A sudden surge of saliva choked him, and he spat several times on the terrace, unable to swallow for the memory of that throat-clenching smell.

'Tom,' he said urgently, coming into the room. 'Did you have an opportunity to speak to the other servants? To Rodrigo?'

'Yes, me lord.' Tom waved him onto the stool and kneeled to put his stockings on. 'They all knew about zombies – said they were dead people, just like Rodrigo said. A *houngan* – that's a . . . well, I don't quite know, but folk are right scared of 'em. Anyway, one of those who takes against somebody – or what's paid to do so, I reckon – will take the somebody, and kill them, then raise 'em up again, to be his servant, and that's a zombie. They were all dead scared of the notion, me lord,' he said earnestly, looking up.

'I don't blame them in the slightest. Did any of them know about my visitor?'

Tom shook his head.

'They said not, but I think they did, me lord. They weren't a-going to say, though. I got Rodrigo off by himself, and he admitted he knew about it, but he said he didn't think it was a zombie what came after you, because I told him how you fought it, and what a mess it made of your room.' He narrowed his eyes at the dressing-table, with its cracked mirror.

'Really? What did he think it was?'

'He wouldn't really say, but I pestered him a bit, and he finally let on as it might have been a *houngan*, just pretending to be a zombie.'

Grey digested that possibility for a moment. Had the creature who attacked him meant to kill him? If so – why? But if not . . . the attack might only have been meant to pave the way for what had now happened, by making it seem that there were zombies lurking about King's House in some profusion. That made a certain amount of sense, save for the fact . . .

'But I'm told that zombies are slow and stiff in their movements. Could one of them have done what . . . was done to the governor?' He swallowed.

'I dunno, me lord. Never met one.' Tom grinned briefly at him, rising from fastening his knee-buckles. It was a nervous grin, but Grey smiled back, heartened by it.

'I suppose I will have to go and look at the body again,' he said, rising. 'Will you come with me, Tom?' His valet was young, but very observant, especially in matters pertaining to the body, and had been of help to him before in interpreting post-mortem phenomena.

Tom paled noticeably, but gulped and nodded, and squaring his shoulders, followed Lord John out onto the terrace.

On their way to the governor's room, they met Major Fettes, gloomily eating a slice of pineapple scavenged from the kitchen.

'Come with me, major,' Grey ordered. 'You can tell me what discoveries you and Cherry have made in my absence.'

'I can tell you one such, sir,' Fettes said, putting down the pineapple and wiping his hands on his waistcoat. 'Judge Peters has gone to Eleuthera.'

'What the devil for?' That was a nuisance; he'd been hoping to discover more about the original incident that had incited the rebellion, and as he was obviously not going to learn anything from Warren . . . he waved a hand at Fettes; it hardly mattered why Peters had gone.

'Right. Well, then— ' Breathing through his mouth as much as possible, Grey pushed open the door. Tom, behind him, made an involuntary sound, but then stepped carefully up and squatted beside the body.

Grey squatted beside him. He could hear thickened breathing behind him.

'Major,' he said, without turning round. 'If Captain Cherry has found Mr Dawes, would you be so kind as to fetch him in here?'

They were hard at it when Dawes came in, accompanied by both Fettes and Cherry, and Grey ignored all of them.

'The bitemarks *are* human?' he asked, carefully turning one of Warren's lower legs toward the light from the

207

window. Tom nodded, wiping the back of his hand across his mouth.

'Sure of it, me lord. I been bitten by dogs – nothing like this. Besides—' He inserted his forearm into his mouth and bit down fiercely, then displayed the results to Grey. 'See, me lord? The teeth go in a circle, like.'

'No doubt of it.' Grey straightened and turned to Dawes, who was sagging at the knees to such an extent that Captain Cherry was obliged to hold him up. 'Do sit down, please, Mr Dawes, and give me your opinion of matters here.'

Dawes's round face was blotched, his lips pale. He shook his head and tried to back away, but was prevented by Cherry's grip on his arm.

'I know nothing, sir,' he gasped. 'Nothing at all. Please, may I go? I, I . . . really, sir, I grow faint!'

'That's all right,' Grey said pleasantly. 'You can lie down on the bed if you can't stand up.'

Dawes glanced at the bed, went white, and sat down heavily on the floor. Saw what was on the floor beside him and scrambled hurriedly to his feet, where he stood swaying and gulping.

Grey nodded at a stool, and Cherry propelled the little secretary, not ungently, onto it.

'What's he told you, Fettes?' Grey asked, turning back toward the bed. 'Tom, we're going to wrap Mr Warren up in the counterpane then lay him on the floor and roll him up in the carpet. To prevent leakage.'

'Right, me lord.' Tom and Captain Cherry set gingerly about this process, while Grey walked over and stood looking down at Dawes.

'Pled ignorance, for the most part,' Fettes said, joining Grey and giving Dawes a speculative look. 'He did tell us that Derwent Warren had seduced a woman called Nancy

208

Twelvetrees, in London. Threw her over, though, and married the heiress to the Atherton fortune.'

'Who had better sense than to accompany her husband to the West Indies, I take it? Yes. Did he know that Miss Twelvetrees and her brother had inherited a plantation on Jamaica, and were proposing to emigrate here?'

'No, sir.' It was the first time Dawes had spoken, and his voice was little more than a croak. He cleared his throat, and spoke more firmly. 'He was entirely surprised to meet the Twelvetrees at his first assembly.'

'I daresay. Was the surprise mutual?'

'It was. Miss Twelvetrees went white, then red, then removed her shoe and set about the governor with the heel of it.'

'I wish I'd seen that,' Grey said, with real regret. 'Right. Well, as you can see, the governor is no longer in need of your discretion. I, on the other hand, am in need of your loquacity. You can start by telling me why he was afraid of snakes.'

'Oh.' Dawes gnawed his lower lip. 'I cannot be sure, you understand—'

'Speak up, you lump,' growled Fettes, leaning menacingly over Dawes, who recoiled.

'I— I—' he stammered. 'Truly, I don't know the details. But it— it had to do with a young woman. A young black woman. He— the governor, that is— women were something of a weakness for him . . .'

'And?' Grey prodded.

The young woman, it appeared, was a slave in the household. And not disposed to accept the governor's attentions. The governor was not accustomed to take 'no' for an answer – and didn't. The young woman had vanished the next day, run away, and had not been recaptured as yet. But the day after, a black man in a turban and loincloth had come to King's House, and had requested audience.

'He wasn't admitted, of course. But he wouldn't go away, either.' Dawes shrugged. 'Just squatted at the foot of the front steps and waited.'

When Warren had at length emerged, the man had risen, stepped forward, and in formal tones, informed the governor that he was herewith cursed.

'Cursed?' said Grey, interested. 'How?'

'Well, now, there my knowledge reaches its limits, sir,' Dawes replied. He had recovered some of his self-confidence by now, and straightened up a little. 'For having pronounced the fact, he then proceeded to speak in an unfamiliar tongue – though I think some of it may have been Spanish, it wasn't all like that. I must suppose that he was, er, administering the curse, so to speak?'

'I'm sure I don't know.' By now, Tom and Captain Cherry had completed their disagreeable task, and the governor reposed in an innocuous cocoon of carpeting. 'I'm sorry, gentlemen, but there are no servants to assist us. We're going to take him down to the garden shed. Come, Mr Dawes; you can be assistant pall-bearer. And tell us on the way where the snakes come into it.'

Panting and groaning, with the occasional near-slip, they manhandled the unwieldy bundle down the stairs. Mr Dawes, making ineffectual grabs at the carpeting, was prodded by Captain Cherry into further discourse.

'Well, I *thought* that I caught the word "snake" in the man's tirade,' he said. 'And then . . . the snakes began to come.'

Small snakes, large snakes. A snake was found in the governor's bath. Another appeared under the dining-table, to the horror of a merchant's lady who was dining with the governor, and who had hysterics all over the dining room before fainting heavily across the table. Mr

Dawes appeared to find something amusing in this, and Grey, perspiring heavily, gave him a glare that returned him more soberly to his account.

'Every day, it seemed, and in different places. We had the house searched, repeatedly. But no one could – or would, perhaps – detect the source of the reptiles. And while no one was bitten, still the nervous strain of not knowing whether you would turn back your coverlet to discover something writhing amongst your bedding . . .'

'Quite. Ugh!' They paused and set down their burden. Grey wiped his forehead on his sleeve. 'And how did you make the connection, Mr Dawes, between this plague of snakes, and Mr Warren's mistreatment of the slave girl?'

Dawes looked surprised, and pushed his spectacles back up his sweating nose.

'Oh, did I not say? The man – I was told later that he was an Obeah-man, whatever that may be – spoke her name, in the midst of his denunciation. Azeel, it was.'

'I see. All right – ready? One, two, three – up!'

Dawes had given up any pretence of helping, but scampered down the garden path ahead of them to open the shed door. He had quite lost any lingering reticence, and seemed anxious to provide any information he could.

'He did not tell me directly, but I believe he had begun to dream of snakes, and of the girl.'

'How do— you know?' Grey grunted. 'That's my foot, major!'

'I heard him . . . er . . . speaking to himself. He had begun to drink rather heavily, you see. Quite understandable, under the circumstances, don't you think?'

Grey wished he could drink heavily, but had no breath left with which to say so.

There was a sudden cry of startlement from Tom, who had gone in to clear space in the shed, and all three officers dropped the carpet with a thump, reaching for nonexistent weapons.

'Me lord, me lord! Look who I found, a-hiding in the shed!' Tom was leaping up the path toward him, face abeam with happiness, the youth Rodrigo coming warily behind him. Grey's heart leaped at the sight, and he felt a most unaccustomed smile touch his face.

'Your servant, sah.' Rodrigo, very timid, made a deep bow.

'I'm very pleased to see you, Rodrigo. Tell me – did you see anything of what passed here last night?'

The young man shuddered, and turned his face away.

'No, sah,' he said, so low-voiced Grey could barely hear him. 'It was zombies. They . . . eat people. I heard them, but I know better than to look. I ran down into the garden, and hid myself.'

'You heard them?' Grey said sharply. 'What did you hear, exactly?'

Rodrigo swallowed, and if it had been possible for a green tinge to show on skin such as his, would undoubtedly have turned the shade of a sea-turtle.

'Feet, sah,' he said. 'Bare feet. But they don't walk, step-step, like a person. They only shuffle, sh-sh, sh-sh.' He made small pushing motions with his hands in illustration, and Grey felt a slight lifting of the hairs on the back of his neck.

'Could you tell how many . . . men . . . there were?'

Rodrigo shook his head.

'More than two, from the sound.'

Tom pushed a little forward, round face intent.

'Was there anybody else with 'em, d'you think? Somebody with a regular step, I mean?'

Rodrigo looked startled, and then horrified.

'You mean a *houngan*? I don't know.' He shrugged. 'Maybe. I didn't hear shoes. But . . .'

'Oh. Because—' Tom stopped abruptly, glanced at Grey, and coughed. 'Oh.'

Despite more questions, this was all that Rodrigo could contribute, and so the carpet was picked up again – this time, with the servant helping – and bestowed in its temporary resting place. Fettes and Cherry chipped away a bit more at Dawes, but the secretary was unable to offer any further information regarding the governor's activities, let alone speculate as to what malign force had brought about his demise.

'Have you heard of zombies before, Mr Dawes?' Grey inquired, mopping his face with the remains of his handkerchief.

'Er . . . yes,' the secretary replied cautiously. 'But surely you don't believe what the servant . . . oh, surely not!' He cast an appalled glance at the shed.

'Are zombies in fact reputed to devour human flesh?' Dawes resumed his sickly pallor.

'Well, yes. But . . . oh, dear!'

'Sums it up nicely,' muttered Cherry, under his breath. 'I take it you don't mean to make a public announcement of the governor's demise, then, sir?'

'You are correct, captain. I don't want public panic over a plague of zombies at large in Spanish Town, whether that is actually the case, or not. Mr Dawes, I believe we need trouble you no more for the moment; you are excused.' He watched the secretary stumble off, before beckoning his officers closer. Tom moved a little away, discreet as always, and took Rodrigo with him.

'Have you discovered anything else that might have bearing on the present circumstance?'

They glanced at each other, and Fettes nodded to Cherry, wheezing gently. Cherry strongly resembled that eponymous fruit, but being younger and more slender than Fettes, had more breath.

213

'Yes, sir. I went looking for Ludgate, the old superintendent. Didn't find him – he's buggered off to Canada, they said – but I got a right earful concerning the present superintendent.'

Grey groped for a moment for the name.

'Cresswell?'

'That's him.'

'Corruption and peculations' appeared to sum up the subject of Captain Cresswell's tenure as superintendent very well, according to Cherry's informants in Spanish Town and King's Town. Amongst other abuses, he had arranged trade between the maroons on the uplands and the merchants below, in the form of birdskins, snakeskins and other exotica, timber from the upland forests, and so on – but had, by report, accepted payment on behalf of the maroons but failed to deliver it.

'Had he any part in the arrest of the two young maroons accused of theft?'

Cherry's teeth flashed in a grin.

'Odd you should ask, sir. Yes, they said – well, some of them did – that the two young men had come down to complain about Cresswell's behaviour, but the governor wouldn't see them. They were heard to declare they would take back their goods by force – so when a substantial chunk of the contents of one warehouse went missing, it was assumed that was what they'd done.

'They – the maroons – insisted they hadn't touched the stuff, but Cresswell seized the opportunity and had them arrested for theft.'

Grey closed his eyes, enjoying the momentary coolness of a breeze from the sea.

'The governor wouldn't see the young men, you said. Is there any suggestion of an improper connection between the governor and Captain Cresswell?'

'Oh, yes,' said Fettes, rolling his eyes. 'No proof yet – but we haven't been looking long, either.'

'I see. And we still do not know the whereabouts of Captain Cresswell?'

Cherry and Fettes shook their heads in unison.

'The general conclusion is that Accompong scragged him,' Cherry said.

'Who?'

'Oh. Sorry, sir,' Cherry apologised. 'That's the name of the maroon's headman, so they say. *Captain* Accompong, he calls himself, if you please.' Cherry's lips twisted a little.

Grey sighed.

'All right. No reports of any further depredations by the maroons, by whatever name?'

'Not unless you count murdering the governor,' said Fettes.

'Actually,' Grey said slowly, 'I don't think that the maroons are responsible for this particular death.' He was somewhat surprised to hear himself say so, in truth – and yet he found that he *did* think it.

Fettes blinked, this being as close to an expression of astonishment as he ever got, and Cherry looked openly sceptical. Grey did not choose to go into the matter of Mrs Abernathy, nor yet to explain his conclusions about the maroons' disinclination for violence. Strange, he thought. He had heard Captain Accompong's name only moments before, but with that name, his thoughts began to coalesce around a shadowy figure. Suddenly, there was a mind out there, someone with whom he might engage.

In battle, the personality and temperament of the commanding officer was nearly as important as the number of troops he commanded. So. He needed to know more about Captain Accompong, but that could wait for the moment.

He nodded to Tom, who approached respectfully, Rodrigo behind him.

'Tell them what you discovered, Tom.'

Tom cleared his throat and folded his hands at his waist.

'Well, we . . . er . . . disrobed the governor—' Fettes flinched, and Tom cleared his throat again before going on, '—and had a close look. And the long and the short of it, sir, and sir,' he added, with a nod to Cherry, 'is that Governor Warren was stabbed in the back.'

Both officers looked blank.

'But— the place is covered with blood and filth and nastiness,' Cherry protested. 'It smells like that place where they put the bloaters they drag out of the Thames!'

'Footprints,' Fettes said, giving Tom a faintly accusing look. 'There were footprints. Big, bloody, *bare* footprints.'

'I do not deny that something objectionable was present in that room,' Grey said dryly. 'But whoever – or whatever – gnawed the governor probably did not kill him. He was almost certainly dead when the . . . er . . . subsequent damage occurred.'

Rodrigo's eyes were huge. Fettes was heard to observe under his breath that he would be damned, but both Fettes and Cherry were good men, and did not argue with Grey's conclusions, any more than they had taken issue with his order to hide Warren's body – they could plainly perceive the desirability of suppressing rumour of a plague of zombies.

'The point, gentlemen, is that after several months of incident, there has been nothing for the last month. Perhaps Mr Warren's death is meant to be incitement – but if it was not the work of the maroons, then the question is – what are the maroons waiting for?'

Tom lifted his head, eyes wide.

'Why, me lord, I'd say – they're waiting for *you*. What else?'

What else, indeed. Why had he not seen that at once? Of course Tom was right. The maroons' protest had gone unanswered, their complaint unremedied. So they had set out to attract attention in the most noticeable – if not the best – way open to them. Time had passed, nothing was done in response, and then they had heard that soldiers were coming. Lieutenant-Colonel Grey had now appeared. Naturally, they were waiting to see what he would do.

What had he done so far? Sent troops to guard the plantations that were the most likely targets of a fresh attack. That was not likely to encourage the maroons to abandon their present plan of action, though it might cause them to direct their efforts elsewhere.

He walked to and fro in the wilderness of the King's House garden, thinking, but there were few alternatives.

He summoned Fettes, and informed him that he, Fettes, was, until further notice, acting governor of the island of Jamaica.

Fettes looked more like a block of wood than usual.

'Yes, sir,' he said. 'If I might ask, sir . . . where are you going?'

'I'm going to talk to Captain Accompong.'

'Alone, sir?' Fettes was appalled. 'Surely you cannot mean to go up there *alone*!'

'I won't be,' Grey assured him. 'I'm taking my valet,

217

and the servant boy. I'll need someone who can translate for me, if necessary.'

Seeing the mulish cast settling upon Fettes's brow, he sighed.

'To go there in force, major, is to invite battle, and that is not what I want.'

'No, sir,' Fettes said dubiously, 'but surely a proper escort . . . !'

'No, major.' Grey was courteous, but firm. 'I wish to make it clear that I am coming to *speak* with Captain Accompong, and nothing more. I go alone.'

'Yes, sir.' Fettes was beginning to look like a block of wood that someone had set about with a hammer and chisel.

'As you wish, sir.'

Grey nodded, and turned to go into the house, but then paused and turned back.

'Oh, there is one thing that you might do for me, major.'

Fettes brightened slightly.

'Yes, sir?'

'Find me a particularly excellent hat, would you? With gold lace, if possible.'

They rode for nearly two days before they heard the first of the horns. A high, melancholy sound in the twilight, it seemed far away, and only a sort of metallic note made Grey sure that it was not in fact the cry of some large, exotic bird.

'Maroons,' Rodrigo said under his breath, and crouched a little, as though trying to avoid notice, even in the saddle. 'That's how they talk to each other. Every group has a horn; they all sound different.'

Another long, mournful falling note. Was it the same horn? Grey wondered. Or a second, answering the first?

'Talk to each other, you say. Can you tell what they're saying?'

Rodrigo had straightened up a little in his saddle, putting a hand automatically behind him to steady the leather box that held the most ostentatious hat available in Spanish Town.

'Yes, sah. They're telling each other we're here.'

Tom muttered something under his own breath, that sounded like, 'Could have told you that meself for free,' but declined to repeat or expand upon his sentiment when invited to do so.

They camped for the night under the shelter of a tree, so tired that they merely sat in silence as they ate, watching the nightly rainstorm come in over the sea, then crawled into the canvas tent Grey had brought. The young men fell asleep instantly to the pattering of rain above them.

Grey lay awake for a little, fighting tiredness, his mind reaching upward. He had worn uniform, though not full-dress, so that his identity would be apparent. And his gambit so far had been accepted; they had not been challenged, let alone attacked. Apparently Captain Accompong would receive him.

Then what? He wasn't sure. He did hope that he might recover his men – the two sentries who had disappeared on the night of Governor Warren's murder. Their bodies had not been discovered, nor had any of their uniform or equipment turned up – and Captain Cherry had had the whole of Spanish Town *and* King's Town turned over in the search. If they had been taken alive, though, that reinforced his impression of Accompong – and gave him some hope that this rebellion might be resolved in some manner not involving a prolonged military campaign fought through jungles and rocks, and ending in chains and executions. But if . . . Sleep overcame him, and he lapsed into incongruous dreams of bright birds, whose feathers brushed his cheeks as they flew silently past.

Grey woke in the morning to the feel of sun on his face. He blinked for a moment, confused, and then sat up. He was alone. Truly alone.

He scrambled to his feet, heart thumping, reaching for his dagger. It was there in his belt, but that was the only thing still where it should be. His horse – all the horses – were gone. So was his tent. So was the pack-mule and its panniers. And so were Tom and Rodrigo.

He saw this at once – the blankets in which they'd lain the night before were still there, tumbled into the bushes – but he called for them anyway, again and again, until his throat was raw with shouting.

From somewhere high above him, he heard one of the horns, a long-drawn-out hoot that sounded mocking to his ears.

He understood the present message instantly. *You took two of ours; we have taken two of yours.*

'And you don't think I'll come and get them?' he shouted upward into the dizzying sea of swaying green. 'Tell Captain Accompong I'm coming! I'll have my young men back, and back *safe* – or I'll have his head!'

Blood rose in his face, and he thought he might burst, but had better sense than to punch something, which was his very strong urge. He was alone; he couldn't afford to damage himself. He had to arrive among the maroons with everything that still remained to him, if he meant to rescue Tom and resolve the rebellion – and he did mean to rescue Tom, no matter what. It didn't matter that this might be a trap; he was going.

He calmed himself with an effort of will, stamping round in a circle in his stockinged feet until he had worked off most of his anger. That's when he saw them, sitting neatly side-by-side under a thorny bush.

They'd left him his boots. They did expect him to come.

He walked for three days. He didn't bother trying to follow a trail; he wasn't a particularly skilled tracker, and finding any trace among the rocks and dense growth was a vain hope in any case. He simply climbed, and listened for the horns.

The maroons hadn't left him any supplies, but that didn't matter. There were numerous small streams and pools, and while he was hungry, he didn't starve. Here and there he found trees of the sort he had seen at Twelvetrees, festooned with small yellowish fruits. If the parrots ate them, he reasoned, the fruits must be at least minimally comestible. They were mouth-puckeringly sour, but they didn't poison him.

The horns had increased in frequency since dawn. There were now three or four of them, signalling back and forth. Clearly, he was getting close. To what, he didn't know, but close.

He paused, looking upward. The ground had begun to level out here; there were open spots in the jungle, and in one of these small clearings, he saw what were plainly crops: mounds of curling vines that might be yams, beanpoles, the big yellow flowers of squash or gourds. At the far edge of the field, a tiny curl of smoke rose against the green. Close.

He took off the crude hat he had woven from palm leaves against the strong sun, and wiped his face on the tail of his shirt. That was as much preparation as it was possible to make. The gaudy, gold-laced hat he'd brought was presumably still in its box – wherever that was. He put

221

his palm-leaf hat back on and limped toward the curl of smoke.

As he walked, he became aware of people, fading slowly into view. Dark-skinned people, dressed in ragged clothing, coming out of the jungle to watch him with big, curious eyes. He'd found the maroons.

A small group of men took him further upward. It was just before sunset, and the sunlight slanted gold and lavender through the trees, when they led him into a large clearing, where there was a compound consisting of a number of huts. One of the men accompanying Grey shouted, and from the largest hut emerged a man who announced himself with no particular ceremony as Captain Accompong.

Captain Accompong was a surprise. He was very short, very fat, and hunchbacked, his body so distorted that he did not so much walk as proceed by a sort of sideways lurching. He was attired in the remnants of a splendid coat, now buttonless, and with its gold lace half missing, the cuffs filthy with wear.

He peered from under the drooping brim of a ragged felt hat, eyes bright in its shadow. His face was round and much creased, lacking a good many teeth – but giving the impression of great shrewdness, and perhaps good humour. Grey hoped so.

'Who are you?' Accompong asked, peering up at Grey like a toad under a rock.

Everyone in the clearing very plainly knew his identity; they shifted from foot to foot and nudged each other, grinning. He paid no attention to them, though, and bowed very correctly to Accompong.

'I am the man responsible for the two young men

222

who were taken on the mountain. I have come to get them back – along with my soldiers.'

A certain amount of scornful hooting ensued, and Accompong let it go on for a few moments, before lifting his hand.

'You say so? Why you think I have anything to do with these young men?'

'I do not say that you do. But I know a great leader when I see one – and I know that you can help me to find my young men. If you will.'

'Phu!' Accompong's face creased into a gap-toothed smile. 'You think you flatter me, and I help?'

Grey could feel some of the smaller children stealing up behind him; he heard muffled giggles, but didn't turn round.

'I ask for your help. But I do not offer you only my good opinion in return.'

A small hand reached under his coat and rudely tweaked his buttock. There was an explosion of laughter, and mad scampering behind him. He didn't move.

Accompong chewed slowly at something in the back of his capacious mouth, one eye narrowed.

'Yes? What do you offer, then? Gold?' One corner of his thick lips turned up.

'Do you have any need of gold?' Grey asked. The children were whispering and giggling again behind him, but he also heard shushing noises from some of the women – they were getting interested. Maybe.

Accompong thought for a moment, then shook his head.

'No. What else you offer?'

'What do you want?' Grey parried.

'Captain Cresswell's head!' said a woman's voice, very clearly. There was a shuffle and smack, a man's voice rebuking in Spanish, a heated crackle of women's voices

223

in return. Accompong let it go on for a minute or two, then raised one hand. Silence fell abruptly.

It lengthened. Grey could feel the pulse beating in his temples, slow and labouring. Ought he to speak? He came as a suppliant already; to speak now would be to lose face, as the Chinese put it. He waited.

'The governor is dead?' Accompong asked at last.

'Yes. How do you know of it?'

'You mean, did I kill him?' The bulbous yellowed eyes creased.

'No,' Grey said patiently. 'I mean – do you know how he died?'

'The zombies kill him.' The answer came readily – and seriously. There was no hint of humour in those eyes now.

'Do you know who made the zombies?'

A most extraordinary shudder ran through Accompong, from his ragged hat to the horny soles of his bare feet.

'You do know,' Grey said softly, raising a hand to prevent the automatic denial. 'But it wasn't you, was it? Tell me.'

The captain shifted uneasily from one buttock to the other, but didn't reply. His eyes darted toward one of the huts, and after a moment, he raised his voice, calling something in the maroons' patois, wherein Grey thought he caught the word 'Azeel'. He was puzzled momentarily, finding the word familiar, but not knowing why. Then the young woman emerged from the hut, ducking under the low doorway, and he remembered.

Azeel. The young slave-woman whom the governor had taken and misused, whose flight from King's House had presaged the plague of serpents.

Seeing her as she came forward, he couldn't help but see what had inspired the governor's lust, though it was not a beauty that spoke to him. She was small, but not inconsequential. Perfectly proportioned, she stood like a queen,

224

and her eyes burned as she turned her face to Grey. There was anger in her face – but also something like a terrible despair.

'Captain Accompong says that I will tell you what I know – what happened.'

Grey bowed to her.

'I should be most grateful to hear it, madam.'

She looked hard at him, obviously suspecting mockery, but he'd meant it, and she saw that. She gave a brief, nearly imperceptible nod.

'Well, then. You know that beast—' she spat neatly on the ground, '—forced me? And I left his house?'

'Yes. Whereupon you sought out an Obeah-man, who invoked a curse of snakes upon Governor Warren, am I correct?'

She glared at him, and gave a short nod. 'The snake is wisdom, and that man had none. None!'

'I think you're quite right about that. But the zombies?'

There was a general intake of breath among the crowd. Fear, distaste – and something else. The girl's lips pressed together, and tears glimmered in her large dark eyes.

'Rodrigo,' she said, and choked on the name. 'He— and I—' Her jaw clamped hard; she couldn't speak without weeping, and would not weep in front of him. He cast down his gaze to the ground, to give her what privacy he could. He could hear her breathing through her nose, a soft, snuffling noise. Finally, she heaved a deep breath.

'He was not satisfied. He went to a *houngan*. The Obeah-man warned him, but—' Her entire face contorted with the effort to hold in her feelings. 'The *houngan*. He had zombies. Rodrigo paid him to kill the beast.'

Grey felt as though he had been punched in the chest. Rodrigo. Rodrigo, hiding in the garden shed at the sound of shuffling bare feet in the night – or Rodrigo, warning his fellow servants to leave, then unbolting the doors,

225

following a silent horde of ruined men in clotted rags up the stairs . . . or running up before them, in apparent alarm, summoning the sentries, drawing them outside, where they could be taken.

'And where is Rodrigo now?' Grey asked sharply. There was a deep silence in the clearing. None of the people even glanced at each other; every eye was fixed on the ground. He took a step toward Accompong. 'Captain?'

Accompong stirred. He raised his misshapen face to Grey, and a hand toward one of the huts.

'We do not like zombies, colonel,' he said. 'They are unclean. And to kill a man using them . . . this is a great wrong. You understand this?'

'I do, yes.'

'This man, Rodrigo—' Accompong hesitated, searching out words. 'He is not one of us. He comes from Hispaniola. They . . . do such things there.'

'Such things as make zombies? But presumably it happens here as well.' Grey spoke automatically; his mind was working furiously in light of these revelations. The thing that had attacked him in his room – it would be no great trick for a man to smear himself with grave-dirt and wear rotted clothing . . .

'Not among us,' Accompong said, very firmly. 'Before I say more, my colonel – do you believe what you have heard so far? Do you believe that we – that *I* – had nothing to do with the death of your governor?'

Grey considered that one for a moment. There was no evidence, only the story of the slave-girl. Still . . . he did have evidence. The evidence of his own observations and conclusions, regarding the nature of the man who sat before him.

'Yes,' he said abruptly. 'So?'

'Will your king believe it?'

Well, not as baldly stated, no, Grey thought. The

226

matter would need a little tactful handling . . . Accompong snorted faintly, seeing the thoughts cross his face.

'This man, Rodrigo. He has done us great harm, by taking his private revenge in a way that . . . that . . .' He groped for the word.

'That incriminates you,' Grey finished for him. 'Yes, I see that. What have you done with him?'

'I cannot give this man to you,' Accompong said at last. His thick lips pressed together briefly, but he met Grey's eye. 'He is dead.'

The shock hit Grey like a musket ball. A thump that knocked him off-balance, and the sickening knowledge of irrevocable damage done.

'How?' he said, short and sharp. 'What happened to him?'

The clearing was still silent. Accompong stared at the ground in front of him. After a long moment, a sigh, a whisper, drifted from the crowd.

'Zombie.'

'Where?' he barked. 'Where is he? Bring him to me. Now!'

The crowd shrank away from the hut, and a sort of moan ran through them. Women snatched up their children, pushed back so hastily that they stepped on the feet of their companions. The door opened.

'Anda!' said a voice from inside. 'Walk,' it meant, in Spanish. Grey's numbed mind had barely registered this when the darkness inside the hut changed, and a form appeared at the door.

It was Rodrigo. But then again – it wasn't. The glowing skin had gone pale and muddy, almost waxen. The firm, soft mouth hung loose, and the eyes – oh, God, the eyes! They were sunken, glassy, and showed no comprehension, no movement, not the least sense of awareness. They were a dead man's eyes. And yet . . . he walked.

227

This was the worst of all. Gone was every trace of Rodrigo's springy grace, his elegance. This creature moved stiffly, shambling, feet dragging, almost lurching from foot to foot. Its clothing hung upon its bones like a scarecrow's rags, smeared with clay and stained with dreadful liquids. The odour of putrefaction reached Grey's nostrils, and he gagged.

'*Alto*,' said the voice, softly, and Rodrigo stopped abruptly, arms hanging like a marionette's. Grey looked up, then, at the hut. A tall, dark man stood in the doorway, burning eyes fixed on Grey.

The sun was all but down; the clearing lay in deep shadow, and Grey felt a convulsive shiver go through him. He lifted his chin, and ignoring the horrid thing standing stiff before him, addressed the tall man.

'Who are you, sir?'

'Call me Ishmael,' said the man, in an odd, lilting accent. He stepped out of the hut, and Grey was conscious of a general shrinking, everyone pulling away from the man, as though he suffered from some deadly contagion. Grey wanted to step back, too, but didn't.

'You did . . . this?' Grey asked, flicking a hand at the remnant of Rodrigo.

'I was paid to do it, yes.' Ishmael's eyes flicked toward Accompong, then back to Grey.

'And Governor Warren – you were paid to kill him as well, were you? By this man?' A brief nod at Rodrigo; he could not bear to look directly at him.

The zombies think they're dead, and so does everyone else.

A frown drew Ishmael's brows together, and with the change of expression, Grey noticed that the man's face was scarred, with apparent deliberation, long channels cut in cheeks and forehead. He shook his head.

'No. This—' he nodded at Rodrigo, '—paid me to bring my zombies. He says to me that he wishes to terrify a man. And zombies will do that,' he added, with a wolfish smile. 'But when I brought them into the room and the *buckra* turned to flee, this one—' the flick of a hand toward Rodrigo, 'he sprang upon him and stabbed him. The man fell dead, and Rodrigo then *ordered* me—' his tone of voice made it clear what he thought of anyone ordering him to do anything, 'to make my zombies feed upon him. And I did,' he ended abruptly.

Grey swung round to Captain Accompong, who had sat silently through this testimony.

'And then you paid this— this—'

'*Houngan*,' Ishmael put in helpfully.

'—to do *that*?!' He pointed at Rodrigo, and his voice shook with outraged horror.

'Justice,' said Accompong, with simple dignity. 'Don't you think so?'

Grey found himself temporarily bereft of speech. While he groped for something possible to say, the headman turned to a lieutenant and said, 'Bring the other one.'

'The *other*—' Grey began, but before he could speak further, there was another stir among the crowd, and from one of the huts, a maroon emerged, leading another man by a rope around his neck. The man was wild-eyed and filthy, his hands bound behind him, but his clothes had originally been very fine. Grey shook his head, trying to dispel the remnants of horror that clung to his mind.

'Captain Cresswell, I presume?' he said.

'Save me!' the man panted, and collapsed on his knees at Grey's feet. 'I beg you, sir – whoever you are – save me!'

Grey rubbed a hand wearily over his face, and looked down at the erstwhile superintendent, then at Accompong.

'Does he need saving?' he asked. 'I don't want to – I know what he's done – but it *is* my duty.'

Accompong pursed his lips, thinking.

'You know what he is, you say. If I give him to you, what would you do with him?'

At least there was an answer to that one.

'Charge him with his crimes, and send him to England for trial. If he is convicted, he would be imprisoned – or possibly hang. What would happen to him here?' he asked curiously.

Accompong turned his head, looking thoughtfully at the *houngan*, who grinned unpleasantly.

'No!' gasped Cresswell. 'No, please! Don't let him take me! I can't— I can't— oh, GOD!' He glanced, appalled, at the stiff figure of Rodrigo, then fell face-first onto the ground at Grey's feet, weeping convulsively.

Numbed with shock, Grey thought for an instant that it *would* probably resolve the rebellion . . . but no. Cresswell couldn't, and neither could he.

'Right,' said Grey, and swallowed before turning to Accompong. 'He *is* an Englishman, and as I said, it's my duty to see that he's subject to English laws. I must therefore ask that you give him into my custody, and take my word that I will see he receives justice. Our sort of justice,' he added, giving the evil look back to the *houngan*.

'And if I don't?' Accompong asked, blinking genially at him.

'Well, I suppose I'll have to fight you for him,' Grey said. 'But I'm bloody tired and I really don't want to.' Accompong laughed at this, and Grey followed swiftly up with, 'I will, of course, appoint a new superintendent – and given the importance of the office, I will bring the new superintendent here, so that you may meet him and approve of him.'

'If I don't approve?'

'There are a bloody lot of Englishmen on Jamaica,' Grey said, impatient. 'You're bound to like *one* of them.'

Accompong laughed out loud, his little round belly jiggling under his coat.

'I like you, colonel,' he said. 'You want to be superintendent?'

Grey suppressed the natural answer to this and instead said, 'Alas, I have a duty to the army which prevents my accepting the offer, amazingly generous though it is.' He coughed. 'You have my word that I will find you a suitable candidate, though.'

The tall lieutenant who stood behind Captain Accompong lifted his voice and said something sceptical in a patois that Grey didn't understand – but from the man's attitude, his glance at Cresswell, and the murmur of agreement that greeted his remark, he had no trouble in deducing what had been said.

What is the word of an Englishman worth?

Grey gave Cresswell, grovelling and snivelling at his feet, a look of profound disfavour. It would serve the man right if— then he caught the faint reek of corruption wafting from Rodrigo's still form, and shuddered. No, nobody deserved *that*.

Putting aside the question of Cresswell's fate for the moment, Grey turned to the question that had been in the forefront of his mind since he'd come in sight of that first curl of smoke.

'My men,' he said. 'I want to see my men. Bring them out to me, please. At once.' He didn't raise his voice, but he knew how to make a command sound like one.

Accompong tilted his head a little to one side, as though considering, but then waved a hand, casually. There was a stirring in the crowd, an expectation. A turning of heads, then bodies, and Grey looked toward the rocks where their focus lay. An explosion of shouts, cat-calls, and laughter, and the two soldiers and Tom Byrd came out of the defile. They were roped together by the necks, their ankles hobbled and hands tied, and they shuffled awkwardly, bumping into one another, turning their heads to and fro like chickens, in a vain effort to avoid the spitting and the small clods of earth thrown at them.

Grey's outrage at this treatment was overwhelmed by his relief at seeing Tom and his young soldiers, all plainly scared, but uninjured. He stepped forward at once, so they could see him, and his heart was wrung by the pathetic relief that lighted their faces.

'Now, then,' he said, smiling. 'You didn't think I would leave you, surely?'

'*I* didn't, me lord,' Tom said stoutly, already yanking at the rope about his neck. 'I told 'em you'd be right along, the minute you got your boots on!' He glared at the little boys, naked but for shirts, who were dancing round him and the soldiers, shouting, 'Buckra! Buckra!' and making not-quite-pretend jabs at the men's genitals with sticks. 'Can you make 'em leave off that filthy row, me lord? They been at it ever since we got here.'

Grey looked at Accompong and politely raised his brows. The headman barked a few words of something not quite Spanish, and the boys reluctantly fell back, though they continued to make faces and rude arm-pumping gestures.

Captain Accompong put out a hand to his lieutenant, who hauled the fat little headman to his feet. He dusted fastidiously at the skirts of his coat, then walked slowly around the little group of prisoners, stopping at Cresswell. He contemplated the man, who had now curled himself into a ball, then looked up at Grey.

'Do you know what a *loa* is, my colonel?' he asked quietly.

'I do, yes,' Grey replied warily. 'Why?'

'There is a spring, quite close. It comes from deep in the earth, where the *loas* live, and sometimes they will come forth, and speak. If you will have back your men – I ask

232

you to go there, and speak with whatever *loa* may find you. Thus we will have truth, and I can decide.'

Grey stood for a moment, looking back and forth among the fat old man, Cresswell, his back heaving with silent sobs, and the young girl Azeel, who had turned her head to hide the hot tears coursing down her cheeks. He didn't look at Tom. There didn't seem much choice.

'All right,' he said, turning back to Accompong. 'Let me go now, then.'

Accompong shook his head.

'In the morning,' he said. 'You do not want to go there at night.'

'Yes, I do,' Grey said. 'Now.'

'Quite close' was a relative term, apparently. Grey thought it must be near midnight by the time they arrived at the spring – Grey, the *houngan* Ishmael, and four maroons bearing torches and armed with the long cane-knives called machetes.

Accompong hadn't told him it was a *hot* spring. There was a rocky overhang, and what looked like a cavern beneath it, from which steam drifted out like dragon's breath. His attendants – or guards, as one chose to look at it – halted as one, a safe distance away. He glanced at them for instruction, but they were silent.

He'd been wondering what the *houngan*'s role in this peculiar undertaking was. The man was carrying a battered canteen; now he uncorked this and handed it to Grey. It smelled hot, though the tin of the heavy canteen was cool in his hands. Raw rum, he thought, from the sweetly searing smell of it – and doubtless a few other things.

. . . Herbs. Ground bones – bits o' other things. But the main

thing, the one thing ye must have, is the liver of a fugu fish . . . They don't come back from it, ye ken. The poison damages their brains . . .

'Now we drink,' Ishmael said. 'And we enter the cave.'

'Both of us?'

'Yes. I will summon the *loa*. I am a priest of Damballa.' The man spoke seriously, with none of the hostility or smirking he had displayed earlier. Grey noticed, though, that their escort kept a safe distance from the *houngan*, and a wary eye upon him.

'I see,' said Grey, though he didn't. 'This . . . Damballa. He, or she—?'

'Damballa is the great serpent,' Ishmael said, and smiled, teeth flashing briefly in the torchlight. 'I am told that snakes speak to you.' He nodded at the canteen. 'Drink.'

Repressing the urge to say, 'You first,' Grey raised the canteen to his lips and drank, slowly. It was *very* raw rum, with a strange taste, sweetly acrid, rather like the taste of fruit ripened to the edge of rot. He tried to keep any thought of Mrs Abernathy's casual description of *afile* powder out of mind – she hadn't, after all, mentioned how the stuff might taste. And surely Ishmael wouldn't simply poison him . . . ? He hoped not.

He sipped the liquid until a slight shift of the *houngan*'s posture told him it was enough, then handed the canteen to Ishmael, who drank from it without hesitation. He supposed he should find this comforting, but his head was beginning to swim in an unpleasant manner, his heartbeat throbbing audibly in his ears, and something odd was happening to his vision; it went intermittently dark, then returned with a brief flash of light, and when he looked at one of the torches, it had a halo of coloured rings around it.

He barely heard the *clunk* of the canteen, dropped on

the ground, and watched, blinking, as the *houngan*'s white-clad back wavered before him. A dark blur of face as Ishmael turned to him.

'Come.' The man disappeared into the veil of water.

'Right,' he muttered. 'Well, then . . .' He removed his boots, unbuckled the knee-bands of his breeches and peeled off his stockings. Then shucked his coat and stepped cautiously into the steaming water.

It was hot enough to make him gasp, but within a few moments, he had got used to the temperature, and made his way across a shallow, steaming pool toward the mouth of the cavern, shifting gravel hard under his bare feet. He heard whispering from his guards, but no one offered any alternative suggestions.

Water poured from the overhang, but not in the manner of a true waterfall; slender streams, like jagged teeth. The guards had pegged the torches into the ground at the edge of the spring; the flames danced like rainbows in the drizzle of the falling water as he passed beneath the overhang.

The hot, wet air pressed his lungs and made it hard to breathe. After a few moments, he couldn't feel any difference between his skin and the moist air through which he walked; it was as though he had melted into the darkness of the cavern.

And it *was* dark. Completely. A faint glow came from behind him, but he could see nothing at all before him, and was obliged to feel his way, one hand on the rough rock wall. The sound of falling water grew fainter, replaced by the heavy thump of his own heartbeat, struggling against the pressure on his chest. Once he stopped and pressed his fingers against his eyelids, taking comfort in the coloured patterns that appeared there; he wasn't blind, then. When he opened his eyes again, though, the darkness was still complete.

235

He thought the walls were narrowing – he could touch them on both sides by stretching out his arms – and had a nightmare moment when he seemed to *feel* them drawing in upon him. He forced himself to breathe, a deep, explosive gasp, and forced the illusion back.

'Stop there.' The voice was a whisper. He stopped.

There was silence, for what seemed a long time.

'Come forward,' said the whisper, seeming suddenly quite near him. 'There is dry land, just before you.'

He shuffled forward, felt the floor of the cave rise beneath him, and stepped out carefully onto bare rock. Walked slowly forward until again the voice bade him stop.

Silence. He thought he could make out breathing, but wasn't sure; the sound of the water was still faintly audible in the distance. *All right*, he thought. *Come along, then.*

It hadn't been precisely an invitation, but what came into his mind was Mrs Abernathy's intent green eyes, staring at him as she said, *'I see a great, huge snake, lying on your shoulders, colonel.'*

With a convulsive shudder, he realised that he felt a weight on his shoulders. Not a dead weight, but something live. It moved, just barely.

'Jesus,' he whispered, and thought he heard the ghost of a laugh from somewhere in the cave. He stiffened himself and fought back against the mental image, for surely this was nothing more than imagination, fuelled by rum. Sure enough, the illusion of green eyes vanished – but the weight rested on him still, though he couldn't tell whether it lay upon his shoulders or his mind.

'So,' said the low voice, sounding surprised. 'The *loa* has come already. The snakes *do* like you, *buckra*.'

'And if they do?' he asked. He spoke in a normal tone of voice; his words echoed from the walls around him.

The voice chuckled briefly, and he felt rather than heard

movement nearby, the rustle of limbs and a soft thump as something struck the floor near his right foot. His head felt immense, throbbing with rum, and waves of heat pulsed through him, though the depths of the cave were cool.

'See if this snake likes you, *buckra*,' the voice invited. 'Pick it up.'

He couldn't see a thing, but slowly moved his foot, feeling his way over the silty floor. His toes touched something and he stopped abruptly. Whatever he had touched moved abruptly in turn, recoiling from him. Then he felt the tiny flicker of a snake's tongue on his toe, tasting him.

Oddly, the sensation steadied him. Surely this wasn't his friend, the tiny yellow constrictor – but it was a serpent much like that one in general size, so far as he could tell. Nothing to fear from that.

'Pick it up,' the voice invited him. 'The krait will tell us if you speak the truth.'

'Will he, indeed?' Grey said dryly. 'How?'

The voice laughed, and he thought he heard two or three more chuckling behind it – but perhaps it was only echoes.

'If you die . . . you lied.'

He gave a small, contemptuous snort. There were no venomous snakes on Jamaica. He cupped his hand, and bent at the knee, but hesitated. Venomous or not, he had an instinctive aversion to being bitten by a snake. And how did he know how the man – or men – sitting in the shadows would take it if the thing *did* bite him?

'I trust this snake,' said the voice softly. 'Krait comes with me from Africa. Long time now.'

Grey's knees straightened abruptly. Africa! Now he placed the name, and cold sweat broke out on his face. *Krait*. A fucking *African* krait. Gwynne had had one. Small, no bigger than the circumference of a man's little finger.

237

'Bloody deadly,' Gwynne had crooned, stroking the thing's back with the tip of a goose-quill – an attention to which the snake, a slender, nondescript brown thing, had seemed oblivious.

This one was squirming languorously over the top of Grey's foot; he had to restrain a strong urge to kick it away and stamp on it. What the devil was it about him that attracted *snakes*, of all ungodly things? He supposed it could be worse; it might be cockroaches . . . he instantly felt a hideous crawling sensation upon his forearms, and rubbed them hard, reflexively, seeing, yes, he bloody *saw* them, here in the dark, thorny jointed legs and wriggling, inquisitive antennae brushing his skin.

He might have cried out. Someone laughed.

If he thought at all, he couldn't do it. He stooped and snatched the thing and rising, hurled it into the darkness. There was a yelp and a sudden scrabbling, then a brief, shocked scream.

He stood panting and trembling from reaction, checking and rechecking his hand – but felt no pain, could find no puncture wounds. The scream had been succeeded by a low stream of unintelligible curses, punctuated by the deep gasps of a man in terror. The voice of the *houngan* – if that's who it was – came urgently, followed by another voice, doubtful, fearful. Behind him, before him? He had no sense of direction anymore.

Something brushed past him, the heaviness of a body, and he fell against the wall of the cave, scraping his arm. He welcomed the pain; it was something to cling to, something real.

More urgency in the depths of the cave, sudden silence. And then a swishing *thunk*! as something struck hard into flesh, and the sheared-copper smell of fresh blood came strong over the scent of hot rock and rushing water. No further sound.

He was sitting on the muddy floor of the cave; he could feel the cool dirt under him. He pressed his hands flat against it, getting his bearings. After a moment, he heaved himself to his feet and stood, swaying and dizzy.

'I don't lie,' he said, into the dark. 'And I *will* have my men.'

Dripping with sweat and water, he turned back, toward the rainbows.

The sun had barely risen when he came back into the mountain compound. The smoke of cooking fires hung among the huts, and the smell of food made his stomach clench painfully, but all that could wait. He strode as well as he might – his feet were so badly blistered that he hadn't been able to get his boots back on, and had walked back barefoot, over rocks and thorns – to the largest hut, where Captain Accompong sat placidly waiting for him.

Tom and the soldiers were there, too, no longer roped together, but still bound, kneeling by the fire. And Cresswell, a little way apart, looking wretched, but at least upright.

Accompong looked at one of his lieutenants, who stepped forward with a big cane-knife, and cut the prisoners' bonds with a series of casual but fortunately accurate swipes.

'Your men, my colonel,' he said magnanimously, flipping one fat hand in their direction. 'I give them back to you.'

'I am deeply obliged to you, sir.' Grey bowed. 'There is one missing, though. Where is Rodrigo?'

There was a sudden silence. Even the shouting children hushed instantly, melting back behind their mothers. Grey could hear the trickling of water down the distant rock-face, and the pulse beating in his ears.

239

'The zombie?' Accompong said at last. He spoke mildly, but Grey sensed some unease in his voice. 'He is not yours.'

'Yes,' Grey said firmly. 'He is. He came to the mountain under my protection – and he will leave the same way. It is my duty.'

The squatty headman's expression was hard to interpret. For none of the crowd moved, or murmured, though he caught a glimpse from the corner of his eyes of the faint turning of heads, as folk asked silent questions of one another.

'It is my duty,' Grey repeated. 'I cannot go without him.' Carefully omitting any suggestion that it might not be his choice whether to go or not. Still, why would Accompong return the white men to him, if he planned to kill or imprison Grey?

The headman pursed fleshy lips, then turned his head and said something questioning. Movement, in the hut where Ishmael had emerged the night before. There was a considerable pause, but once more, the *houngan* came out.

His face was pale, and one of his feet was wrapped in a blood-stained wad of fabric, bound tightly. Amputation, Grey thought with interest, recalling the metallic *thunk* that had seemed to echo through his own flesh in the cave. It was the only sure way to keep a snake's venom from spreading through the body.

'Ah,' said Grey, voice light. 'So the krait liked me better, did he?'

He thought Accompong laughed under his breath, but didn't really pay attention. The *houngan*'s eyes flashed hate at him, and he regretted his wit, fearing that it might cost Rodrigo more than had already been taken from him.

Despite his shock and horror, though, he clung to what Mrs Abernathy had told him. The young man was *not* truly dead. He swallowed. Could Rodrigo perhaps be restored? The Scotchwoman had said not – but perhaps she was wrong. Clearly Rodrigo had not been a zombie for more than a few days. And she did say that the drug dissipated over time . . . perhaps . . .

Accompong spoke sharply, and the *houngan* lowered his head.

'*Anda*,' he said sullenly. There was stumbling movement in the hut, and he stepped aside, half-pushing Rodrigo out into the light, where he came to a stop, staring vacantly at the ground, mouth open.

'You want this?' Accompong waved a hand at Rodrigo. 'What for? He's no good to you, surely? Unless you want to take him to bed – he won't say no to you!'

Everyone thought that very funny; the clearing rocked with laughter. Grey waited it out. From the corner of his eye, he saw the girl Azeel, watching him with something like a fearful hope in her eyes.

'He is under my protection,' he repeated. 'Yes, I want him.'

Accompong nodded and took a deep breath, sniffing appreciatively at the mingled scents of cassava porridge, fried plantain, and frying pig-meat.

'Sit down, colonel,' he said, 'and eat with me.'

Grey sank slowly down beside him, weariness throbbing through his legs. Looking round, he saw Cresswell dragged roughly off, but left sitting on the ground against a hut, unmolested. Tom and the two soldiers, looking dazed, were being fed at one of the cook-fires. Then he saw Rodrigo, still standing like a scarecrow, and struggled to his feet.

He took the young man's tattered sleeve and said, 'Come with me.' Rather to his surprise, Rodrigo did, turning like an automaton. He led the young man through the staring crowd to the girl Azeel, and said, 'Stop.' He lifted Rodrigo's hand and offered it to the girl, who, after a moment's hesitation, took firmly hold of it.

'Look after him, please,' Grey said to her. Only as he turned away did it register upon him that the arm he had held was wrapped with a bandage. Ah. Dead men don't bleed.

Returning to Accompong's fire, he found a wooden platter of steaming food awaiting him. He sank down gratefully upon the ground again, and closed his eyes – then opened them, startled, as he felt something descend upon his head, and found himself peering out from under the drooping felt brim of the headman's ragged hat.

'Oh,' he said. 'Thank you.' He hesitated, looking round, either for the leather hat-box, or for his ragged palm-frond hat, but didn't see either one.

'Never mind,' said Accompong, and leaning forward, slid his hands carefully over Grey's shoulders, palm up, as though lifting something heavy. 'I will take your snake, instead. You have carried him long enough, I think.'

AUTHOR'S NOTES

My source for the theoretical basis of making zombies was *The Serpent and the Rainbow: A Harvard Scientist's Astonishing Journey into the Secret Societies of Haitian Voodoo, Zombis, and Magic*, by Wade Davis, which I'd read many years ago. Information on the maroons of Jamaica, the temperament, beliefs, and behaviour of Africans from different regions, and on historical slave rebellions came chiefly from *Black Rebellion: Five Slave Revolts*, by Thomas Wentworth Higginson. This manuscript (originally a series of articles published in *Atlantic Monthly*, *Harper's Magazine*, and *Century*) also supplied a number of valuable details regarding terrain and personalities.

Captain Accompong was a real maroon leader – I took his physical description from this source – and the custom of trading hats upon conclusion of a bargain also came from *Black Rebellion*. General background, atmosphere, and the importance of snakes came from Zora Neale Hurston's *Tell My Horse* and a number of less important books dealing with voodoo. (By the way, I now have most of my reference collection – some 1,500 books – listed on LibraryThing and cross-indexed by topic, in case you're interested in pursuing anything like, say, Scotland, magic, or the American Revolution.)

The Space Between

Introduction to
The Space Between

This is an odd one. I could tell from the final chapters of *An Echo in the Bone*, wherein Michael Murray arrives from France, freshly widowed, to be there for his father's approaching death, that this was a very vulnerable man, and one wide open to the winds of fate. *Echo* wasn't his story, though.

Neither was it Joan's story, though she too is plainly headed for adventure when she masterminds her escape from her mother's Highland home, bound for a convent and determined to become a nun – though she's never seen either a convent *or* a nun.

If you have a widower and a postulant headed off to Paris together, plainly you can expect Something Interesting to happen – and it does, but this story doesn't belong only to Michael and Joan.

Did you ever wonder what happened after the Comte St Germain collapsed in King Louis's Star Chamber, in *Dragonfly in Amber*? Step into the space between and find out.

The Space Between

Paris, June 1778

He still didn't know why the frog hadn't killed him. Paul Rakoczy, Comte St Germain, picked up the vial, pulled the cork and sniffed cautiously for the third time, but then recorked it, still dissatisfied. Maybe. Maybe not. The scent of the dark grey powder in the vial held the ghost of something familiar – but it had been thirty years.

He sat for a moment, frowning at the array of jars, bottles, flasks and pelicans on his workbench. It was late afternoon, and the late spring sun of Paris was like honey, warm and sticky on his face, but glowing in the rounded globes of glass, throwing pools of red and brown and green on the wood from the liquids contained therein. The only discordant note in this peaceful symphony of light was the body of a large rat, lying on its back in the middle of the workbench, a pocket-watch open beside it.

The comte put two fingers delicately on the rat's chest and waited patiently. It didn't take so long this time; he was used to the coldness as his mind felt its way into the body. Nothing. No hint of light in his mind's eye, no warm red of a pulsing heart. He glanced at the watch: half an hour.

He took his fingers away, shaking his head.

'Mélisande, you evil bitch,' he murmured, not without affection. 'You didn't think I'd try anything *you* sent me on myself, did you?'

248

Still . . . he himself had stayed dead a great while longer than half an hour, when the frog had given him the dragon's-blood. It had been early evening when he went into Louis's Star Chamber thirty years before, heart beating with excitement at the coming confrontation – a duel of wizards, with a king's favour as the stakes – and one he'd thought he'd win. He remembered the purity of the sky, the beauty of the stars just visible, Venus bright on the horizon, and the joy of it in his blood. Everything always had a greater intensity, when you knew life could cease within the next few minutes.

And an hour later, he thought his life *had* ceased, the cup falling from his numbed hand, the coldness rushing through his limbs with amazing speed, freezing the words *I've lost*, an icy core of disbelief in the centre of his mind. He hadn't been looking at the frog; the last thing he had seen through darkening eyes was the woman – La Dame Blanche – her face over the cup she'd given him appalled and white as bone. But what he recalled, and recalled again now, with the same sense of astonishment and avidity, was the great flare of blue, intense as the colour of the evening sky beyond Venus, that had burst from her head and shoulders as he died.

He didn't recall any feeling of regret or fear; just astonishment. This was nothing, however, to the astonishment he'd felt when he regained his senses, naked on a stone slab in a revolting subterranean chamber next to a drowned corpse. Luckily, there had been no one alive in that disgusting grotto, and he had made his way – reeling and half-blind, clothed in the drowned man's wet and stinking shirt – out into a dawn more beautiful than any twilight could ever be. So – ten to twelve hours from the moment of apparent death to revival.

He glanced at the rat, then put out a finger and lifted one of the small, neat paws. Nearly twelve hours. Limp, the rigor had already passed; it was warm up here at the top of the house. Then he turned to the counter that ran along the far wall of the laboratory, where a line of rats lay, possibly insensible, probably dead. He walked slowly along the line, prodding each body. Limp, limp, stiff. Stiff. Stiff. All dead, without doubt. Each had had a smaller dose than the last, but all had died – though he couldn't yet be positive about the latest. Wait a bit more, then, to be sure.

He needed to know. Because the Court of Miracles was talking. And they said the frog was back.

The English Channel

They did say that red hair was a sign of the Devil. Joan eyed her escort's fiery locks consideringly. The wind on deck was fierce enough to make her eyes water, and it jerked bits of Michael Murray's hair out of its binding so they danced round his head like flames, a bit. You might expect his face to be ugly as sin if he was one of the Devil's, though, and it wasn't.

Lucky for him, he looked like his mother in the face, she thought. His younger brother Ian wasn't so fortunate, and that without the heathen tattoos. Michael's was just a fairly pleasant face, for all it was blotched with windburn and the lingering marks of sorrow, and no wonder, him having just lost his father, and his wife dead in France no more than a month before that.

But she wasn't braving this gale in order to watch Michael Murray, even if he might burst into tears or turn into Auld Horny on the spot. She touched her crucifix for reassurance, just in case. It was blessed by the priest and her mother'd carried it all the way to St Ninian's Spring and dipped it in the water there, to ask the saint's protection. And it was her mother she wanted to see, as long as ever she could.

She pulled her kerchief off and waved it, keeping a tight grip lest the wind make off with it. Her mother was growing smaller on the quay, waving madly herself, Joey behind her with his arm round her waist to keep her from falling into the water.

Joan snorted a bit at sight of her new stepfather, but then thought better and touched the crucifix again, muttering a quick Act of Contrition in penance. After all, it was she herself who'd made that marriage happen, and a good thing, too. If not, she'd still be stuck to home at Balriggan, not on her way at last to be a Bride of Christ in France.

A nudge at her elbow made her glance aside, to see Michael offering her a handkerchief. Well, so. If her eyes were streaming – aye, *and* her nose – it was no wonder, the wind so fierce as it was. She took the scrap of cloth with a curt nod of thanks, scrubbed briefly at her cheeks, and waved her kerchief harder.

None of his family had come to see Michael off, not even his twin sister, Janet. But they were taken up with all there was to do in the wake of Old Ian Murray's death, and no wonder. No need to see Michael to the ship, either – Michael Murray was a wine merchant in Paris, and a wonderfully well-travelled gentleman. She took some comfort from the knowledge that he knew what to do and where to go, and had said he would see her safely delivered to the convent of the Angels, because the thought of making her way through Paris alone and the streets full of people all speaking French . . . Though she knew French quite well, of course; she'd been studying it all the winter, with Michael's mother helping her. But perhaps she had better not tell the Reverend Mother

251

about the sorts of French novels Jenny Murray had in her bookshelf . . .

'*Voulez-vous descendre, mademoiselle?*'

'Eh?' She glanced at Michael, to see him gesturing toward the hatchway that led downstairs. She turned back, blinking – but the quay had vanished, and her mother with it.

'No,' she said. 'Not just yet. I'll just . . .' She wanted to see the land so long as she could. It would be her last sight of Scotland, ever, and the thought made her wame curl into a small, tight ball. She waved a vague hand toward the hatchway. 'You go, though. I'm all right by myself.'

He didn't go, but came to stand beside her, gripping the rail. She turned away from him a little, so he wouldn't see her weep, but on the whole, she wasn't sorry he'd stayed.

Neither of them spoke, and the land sank slowly, as though the sea swallowed it, and there was nothing round them now but the open sea, glassy grey and rippling under a scud of clouds. The prospect made her dizzy, and she closed her eyes, swallowing.

Dear Lord Jesus, don't let me be sick!

A small shuffling noise beside her made her open her eyes, to find Michael Murray regarding her with some concern.

'Are ye all right, Miss Joan?' He smiled a little. 'Or should I call ye Sister?'

'No,' she said, taking a grip on her nerve and her stomach and drawing herself up. 'I'm no a nun yet, am I?'

He looked her up and down in the frank way Hieland men did, and smiled more broadly.

'Have ye ever *seen* a nun?' he asked.

'I have not,' she said, as starchily as she could. 'I havena seen God or the Blessed Virgin, either, but I believe in them, too.'

Much to her annoyance, he burst out laughing. Seeing

252

the annoyance, though, he stopped at once, though she could see the urge still trembling there behind his assumed gravity.

'I do beg your pardon, Miss MacKimmie,' he said. 'I wasna questioning the existence of nuns. I've seen quite a number of the creatures with my own eyes.' His lips were twitching, and she glared at him.

'Creatures, is it?'

'A figure of speech, nay more, I swear it! Forgive me, Sister – I ken not what I do!' He held up a hand, cowering in mock terror. The urge to laugh herself made her that much crosser, but she contented herself with a simple *mmphm* of disapproval.

Curiosity got the better of her, though, and after a few moments spent inspecting the foaming wake of the ship, she asked, not looking at him, 'When ye saw the nuns, then – what were they doing?'

He'd got control of himself by now, and answered her seriously.

'Well, I see the Sisters of Notre Dame who work among the poor all the time in the streets. They always go out by twos, ken, and both nuns will be carrying great huge baskets, filled with food, I suppose – maybe medicines? They're covered, though – the baskets – so I canna say for sure what's in them. Perhaps they're smuggling brandy and lace down to the docks—' He dodged aside from her upraised hand, laughing.

'Oh, ye'll be a rare nun, Sister Joan! *Terror daemonium, solatium miserorum . . .*'

She pressed her lips tight together, not to laugh. Terror of demons, the cheek of him!

'Not Sister Joan,' she said. 'They'll give me a new name, likely, at the convent.'

'Oh, aye?' He wiped hair out of his eyes, interested. 'D'ye get to choose the name, yourself?'

253

'I don't know,' she admitted.

'Well, though – what name would ye pick, if ye had the choosing?'

'Er . . . well . . .' She hadn't told anyone, but after all, what harm could it do? She wouldn't see Michael Murray again, once they reached Paris. 'Sister Gregory,' she blurted.

Rather to her relief, he didn't laugh.

'Oh, that's a good name,' he said. 'After Saint Gregory the Great, is it?'

'Well . . . aye. Ye don't think it's presumptuous?' she asked, a little anxious.

'Oh, no!' he said, surprised. 'I mean, how many nuns are named Mary? If it's not presumptuous to be named after the Mother o' God, how can it be high-falutin' to call yourself after a mere pope?' He smiled at that, so merrily that she smiled back.

'How many nuns *are* named Mary?' she asked, out of curiosity. 'It's common, is it?'

'Oh, aye, ye said ye'd not seen a nun.' He'd stopped making fun of her, though. 'About half the nuns I've met seem to be called Sister Mary Something – ye ken, Sister Mary Polycarp, Sister Mary Joseph . . . like that.'

'And ye meet a great many nuns in the course o' your business, do ye?' Michael Murray was the junior partner of Fraser et Cie, one of the biggest dealers in wines and spirits in Paris – and from the cut of his clothes, did well enough at it.

His mouth twitched, but he answered seriously.

'Well, I do, really. Not every day, I mean, but the Sisters come round to my office quite often – or I go to them. Fraser et Cie supplies wine to most o' the monasteries and convents in Paris, and some will send a pair of nuns to place an order or to take away something special; otherwise, we deliver it, of course. And even the orders who

254

dinna take wine themselves – and most of the Parisian houses do, they bein' French, aye? – need sacramental wine for their chapels. And the begging orders come round like clockwork to ask alms.'

'Really?' She was fascinated, sufficiently so as to put aside her reluctance to look ignorant. 'I didna ken . . . I mean . . . so the different orders of nuns do quite different things, is that what ye're saying? What other kinds are there?'

He shot her a brief glance, but then turned back, narrowing his eyes against the wind as he thought.

'Well . . . there's the sort of nun that prays all the time – contemplative, I think they're called. I see them in the Cathedral all hours of the day and night. There's more than one order of that sort, though; one kind wears grey habits and prays in the chapel of St Joseph, and another wears black; ye see them mostly in the chapel of Our Lady of the Sea.' He glanced at her, curious. 'Will it be that sort of nun that you'll be?'

She shook her head, glad that the wind-chafing hid her blushes.

'No,' she said, with some regret. 'That's maybe the holiest sort of nun, but I've spent a good bit o' my life being contemplative on the moors, and I didna like it much. I think I havena got the right sort of soul to do it verra well, even in a chapel.'

'Aye,' he said, and wiped back flying strands of hair from his face. 'I ken the moors. The wind gets into your head after a bit.' He hesitated for a moment. 'When my uncle Jamie – your da, I mean – ye ken he hid in a cave after Culloden?'

'For seven years,' she said, a little impatient. 'Aye, everyone kens that story. Why?'

He shrugged.

'Only thinking. I was no but a wee bairn at the time,

but I went now and then wi' my mam, to take him food there. He'd be glad to see us, but he wouldna talk much. And it scared me to see his eyes.'

Joan felt a small shiver pass down her back, nothing to do with the stiff breeze. She saw – suddenly *saw*, in her head – a thin, dirty man, the bones starting in his face, crouched in the dank, frozen shadows of the cave.

'Da?' she scoffed, to hide the shiver that crawled up her arms. 'How could anyone be scairt of him? He's a dear, kind man.'

Michael's wide mouth twitched at the corners.

'I suppose it would depend whether ye'd ever seen him in a fight. But—'

'Have you?' she interrupted, curious. 'Seen him in a fight?'

'I have, aye. BUT—' he said, not willing to be distracted, 'I didna mean *he* scared me. It was that I thought he was haunted. By the voices in the wind.'

That dried up the spit in her mouth, and she worked her tongue a little, hoping it didn't show. She needn't have worried; he wasn't looking at her.

'My own da said it was because Jamie spent so much time alone, that the voices got into his head, and he couldna stop hearing them. When he'd feel safe enough to come to the house, it would take hours sometimes, before he could start to hear *us* again – Mam wouldna let us talk to him until he'd had something to eat and was warmed through.' He smiled, a little ruefully. 'She said he wasna human 'til then – and looking back, I dinna think she meant that as a figure of speech.'

'Well,' she said, but stopped, not knowing how to go on. She wished fervently that she'd known this earlier. Her da and his sister were coming on to France later, but she might not see him. She could maybe have talked to da, asked him just what the voices in his head were like –

256

what they said. Whether they were anything like the ones she heard.

⁂

Nearly twilight, and the rats were still dead. The comte heard the bells of Notre-Dame calling Sext, and glanced at his pocket-watch. The bells were two minutes before their time, and he frowned. He didn't like sloppiness. He stood up and stretched himself, groaning as his spine cracked like the ragged volley of a firing squad. No doubt about it, he *was* ageing, and the thought sent a chill through him.

If. If he could find the way forward, then perhaps . . . but you never knew, that was the devil of it. For a little while, he'd thought – hoped – that travelling back in time stopped the process of ageing. That initially seemed logical, like rewinding a clock. But then again, it *wasn't* logical, because he'd always gone back further than his own lifetime. Only once, he'd tried to go back only a few years, to his early twenties. *That* was a mistake, and he still shivered at the memory.

He went to the tall gabled window that looked out over the Seine.

That particular view of the river had changed barely at all in the last two hundred years; he'd seen it at several different times. He hadn't always owned this house, but it had stood in this street since 1620, and he always managed to get in briefly, if only to re-establish his own sense of reality after a passage.

Only the trees changed in his view of the river, and sometimes a strange-looking boat would be there. But the rest was always the same, and no doubt always would be: the old fishermen, catching their supper off the landing in stubborn silence, each guarding his space with out-thrust elbows, the younger ones, barefoot and slump-shouldered

257

with exhaustion, laying out their nets to dry, naked little boys diving off the quay. It gave him a soothing sense of eternity, watching the river. Perhaps it didn't matter so much if he must one day die?

'The devil it doesn't,' he murmured to himself, and glanced up at the sky. Venus shone bright. He should go.

Pausing conscientiously to place his fingers on each rat's body and ensure that no spark of life remained, he passed down the line, then swept them all into a burlap bag. If he was going to the Court of Miracles, at least he wouldn't arrive empty-handed.

Joan was still reluctant to go below, but the light was fading, the wind getting up regardless, and a particularly spiteful gust that blew her petticoats right up round her waist and grabbed her arse with a chilly hand made her yelp in a very undignified way. She smoothed her skirts hastily and made for the hatchway, followed by Michael Murray.

Seeing him cough and chafe his hands at the bottom of the ladder made her sorry; here she'd kept him freezing on deck, too polite to go below and leave her to her own devices, and her too selfish to see he was cold, the poor man. She made a hasty knot in her handkerchief, to remind her to say an extra decade of the rosary for penance, when she got to it.

He saw her to a bench, and said a few words to the woman sitting next to her, in French. Obviously, he was introducing her, she understood that much – but when the woman nodded and said something in reply, she could only sit there open-mouthed. She didn't understand a word. Not a word!

Michael evidently grasped the situation, for he said

something to the woman's husband that drew her attention away from Joan, and engaged them in a conversation that let Joan sink quietly back against the wooden wall of the ship, sweating with embarrassment.

Well, she'd get into the way of it, she reassured herself. Bound to. She settled herself with determination to listen, picking out the odd word here and there in the conversation. It was easier to understand Michael; he spoke slower and didn't swallow the back half of each word.

She was trying to puzzle out the probable spelling of a word that *sounded* like 'pwufgweemiarniere' but surely couldn't be, when her eye caught a slight movement from the bench opposite, and the gurgling vowels caught in her throat.

A man sat there, maybe close to her own age of twenty-five. He was good-looking, if a bit thin in the face, decently dressed – and he was going to die.

There was a grey shroud over him, the same as if he was wrapped in mist, so his face showed through it. She'd seen that same thing, the greyness lying on someone's face like fog, seen it twice before and knew it at once for Death's shadow. Once it had been on an elderly man, and that might have been only what anybody could see, because Angus MacWheen *was* ill, but then again, and only a few weeks after, she'd seen it on the second of Vhairi Fraser's little boys, and him a rosy-faced wee bairn with dear chubby legs.

She hadn't wanted to believe it. Either that she saw it, or what it meant. But four days later, the wean was crushed in the lane by an ox that was maddened by a hornet's sting. She'd vomited when they told her, and couldn't eat for days after, for sheer grief and terror. Because, could she have stopped it, if she'd said? And what – dear Lord, *what* – if it happened again?

Now it had, and her wame twisted. She leaped to her

259

feet and blundered toward the companionway, cutting short some slowly worded speech from the Frenchman.

Not again, not again! she thought in agony. *Why show me such things? What can I do?*

She pawed frantically at the ladder, climbing as fast as she could, gasping for air, needing to be away from the dying man. How long might it be, dear Lord, until she reached the convent, and safety?

The moon was rising over the Ile de Notre-Dame, glowing through the haze of cloud. He glanced at it, estimating the time; no point in arriving at Madame Fabienne's house before the girls had taken their hair out of curling papers and rolled on their red stockings. There were other places to go first, though; the obscure drinking places where the professionals of the Court fortified themselves for the night ahead. One of those was where he had first heard the rumours – he'd see how far they had spread, and judge the safety of asking openly about *Maître* Raymond.

That was one advantage to hiding in the past, rather than going to Hungary or Sweden – life at this Court tended to be short, and there were not so many who knew either his face or his history, though there would still be stories. Paris held on to its *histoires*. He found the iron gate – rustier than it had been; it left red stains on his palm – and pushed it open with a creak that would alert whatever now lived at the end of the alley.

He had to *see* the frog. Not meet him, perhaps – he made a brief sign against evil – but see him. Above all else, he needed to know: had the man – if he was a man – aged?

'Certainly he's a man,' he muttered to himself, impatient. 'What else could he be, for heaven's sake?'

He could be something like you, was the answering thought, and a shiver ran up his spine. *Fear?* he wondered. *Antici-pation of an intriguing philosophical mystery? Or possibly . . . hope?*

'What a waste of a wonderful arse,' Monsieur Brechin remarked in French, watching Joan's ascent from the far side of the cabin. 'And *mon Dieu*, those legs! Imagine those wrapped around your back, eh? Would you have her keep the striped stockings on? I would.'

It hadn't occurred to Michael to imagine that, but he was now having a hard time dismissing the image. He coughed into his handkerchief to hide the reddening of his face.

Madame Brechin gave her husband a sharp elbow in the ribs. He grunted, but seemed undisturbed by what was evidently a normal form of marital communication.

'Beast,' she said, with no apparent heat. 'Speaking so of a Bride of Christ. You will be lucky if God Himself doesn't strike you dead with a lightning bolt.'

'Well, she isn't His bride yet,' monsieur protested. 'And who created that arse in the first place? Surely God would be flattered to hear a little sincere appreciation of His handiwork. From one who is, after all, a connoisseur in such matters.' He leered affectionately at madame, who snorted.

A faint snigger from the young man across the cabin indicated that monsieur was not alone in his appreciation, and madame turned a reproving glare on the young man. Michael wiped his nose carefully, trying not to catch monsieur's eye. His insides were quivering, and not entirely from amusement or the shock of inadvertent lust. He felt very queer.

Monsieur sighed as Joan's striped stockings disappeared through the hatchway.

'Christ will not warm her bed,' he said, shaking his head.

'Christ will not fart in her bed, either,' said madame, taking out her knitting.

'*Pardonnez-moi . . .*' Michael said in a strangled voice, and, clapping his handkerchief to his mouth, made hastily for the ladder, as though sea-sickness might be catching.

It wasn't *mal de mer* that was surging up from his belly, though. He caught sight of Joan, dim in the evening light at the rail, and turned quickly aside, going to the other side, where he gripped the rail as though it were a life-raft, and let the overwhelming waves of grief wash through him. It was the only way he'd been able to manage, these last few weeks. Hold on as long as he could, keeping a cheerful face, until some small unexpected thing, some bit of emotional debris, struck him through the heart like a hunter's arrow, and then hurry to find a place to hide, curling up on himself in mindless pain until he could get a grip of himself.

This time, it was madame's remark that had come out of the blue, and he grimaced painfully, laughing in spite of the tears that poured down his face, remembering Lillie – that time she'd eaten eels in garlic sauce for dinner; they always made her fart with a silent deadliness, like poison swamp gas. As the ghastly miasma had risen up round him, he'd sat bolt upright in bed, only to find her staring at him, a look of indignant horror on her face.

'How *dare* you?' she'd said, in a voice of offended majesty. '*Really*, Michel.'

'You *know* it wasn't me!'

Lillie's mouth had dropped open, outrage added to horror and distaste.

'Oh!' she gasped, gathering her small pug-dog to

her bosom. 'You not only fart like a rotting whale, you attempt to blame it on my poor puppy! *Cochon!*' Whereupon she had begun to shake the bedsheets delicately, using her free hand to waft the noxious odours in his direction, addressing censorious remarks to Plonplon, who gave Michael a sanctimonious look before turning to lick his mistress's face with great enthusiasm.

'Oh, Jesus,' he whispered, back in the present, and sinking down, pressed his face against the rail. 'Oh, God, lass, I love you!'

He shook, silently, head buried in his arms, aware of sailors passing now and then behind him, but none of them took notice of him in the dark. At last the agony eased a little, and he drew breath.

All right, then. He'd be all right now, for a time. And he thanked God, belatedly, that he had Joan – or Sister Gregory, if she liked – to look after for a bit. He didn't know how he'd manage to walk through the streets of Paris to his house, alone. Go in, greet the servants – would his cousin Jared be there? – face the sorrow of the household, accept their sympathy for his father's death, order a meal, sit down . . . and all the time wanting just to throw himself on the floor of their empty bedroom and howl like a lost soul. He'd have to face it, sooner or later – but not just yet. And right now, he'd take the grace of any respite that offered.

He blew his nose with resolution, tucked away his mangled handkerchief, and went downstairs to fetch the basket his mother had sent. He couldn't swallow a thing, himself, but feeding Sister Joan would maybe keep his mind off things for one minute more.

'That's how ye do it,' his brother Ian had told him, as they leaned together on the rail of their mother's sheep pen, the winter's wind cold on their faces, waiting for their da to find his way through dying. 'Ye find a way to

263

live for just one more minute. And then another. And another.' Ian had lost a wife, too, and knew.

He'd wiped his face – he could weep before Ian, while he couldn't in front of his elder brother or the girls, and certainly not in front of his mother. He'd asked, 'And it gets better after a time; is that what ye're telling me?'

His brother had looked at him straight on, the quiet in his eyes showing through the outlandish Mohawk tattoos.

'No,' he'd said softly. 'But after a time, ye find ye're in a different place than ye were. A different person than ye were. And then ye look about, and see what's there with ye. Ye'll maybe find a use for yourself. *That* helps.'

'Aye, fine,' he said, under his breath, and squared his shoulders. 'We'll see, then.'

To Rakoczy's surprise, there was a familiar face behind the rough bar. If Maximilian the Great was surprised to see him, the Spanish dwarf gave no indication of it. The other drinkers – a pair of jugglers, each missing an arm (but the opposing arm), a toothless hag who smacked and muttered over her mug of arrack, and something that looked like a ten-year-old girl but almost certainly wasn't – turned to stare at him, but seeing nothing remarkable in his shabby clothing and burlap bag, turned back to the business of getting sufficiently drunk as to do what needed to be done tonight.

He nodded to Max and pulled up one of the splintering kegs to sit on.

'What's your pleasure, *señor*?'

Rakoczy narrowed his eyes; Max had never served anything but arrack. But times had changed; there was a stone bottle of something that might be beer, and a dark

264

glass bottle with a chalk scrawl on it, standing next to the keg of rough liquor.

'Arrack, please, Max,' he said – better the devil you know – and was surprised to see the dwarf's eyes narrow in return.

'You knew my honoured father, I see, *señor*,' the dwarf said, putting the cup on the board. 'It's some time since you've been in Paris?'

'*Pardon*,' Rakoczy said, accepting it and tossing it back. If you could afford more than one cup, you didn't let it linger on the tongue. 'Your honoured – late? – father, Max?'

'Maximiliano el Maximo,' the dwarf corrected him firmly.

'To be sure.' Rakoczy gestured for another drink. 'And whom have I the honour to address?'

The Spaniard – though perhaps his accent wasn't as strong as Max's had been – drew himself up proudly. 'Maxim Le Grande, monsieur, *à votre service!*'

Rakoczy saluted him gravely, and threw back the second cup, motioning for a third and with a gesture, inviting Maxim to join him.

'It has been some time since I was last here,' he said. No lie there. 'I wonder if another old acquaintance might be still alive – *Maître* Raymond, otherwise called "the frog"?'

There was a tiny quiver in the air, a barely perceptible flicker of attention, gone almost as soon as he'd sensed it – somewhere behind him?

'A frog,' Maxim said, meditatively pouring himself a drink. 'I don't know any frogs myself, but should I hear of one, who shall I say is asking for him?'

Should he give his name? No, not yet.

'It doesn't matter,' he said. 'But word can be left with Madame Fabienne. You know the place? In the Rue Antoine?'

The dwarf's sketchy brows rose, and his mouth turned up at one corner.

'I know it.'

Doubtless he did, Rakoczy thought. 'El Maximo' hadn't referred to Max's stature, and probably 'Le Grande' didn't, either. God had a sense of justice, as well as a sense of humour.

'*Bon*.' He wiped his lips on his sleeve and put down a coin that would have bought the whole keg. '*Merci*.'

He stood up, the hot taste of the arrack bubbling at the back of his throat, and belched. Two more places to visit, maybe, before he went to Fabienne's. He couldn't visit more than that and stay upright; he *was* getting old.

'Good night.' He bowed to the company and gingerly pushed open the cracked wooden door; it was hanging by one leather hinge, and that looked ready to give way at any moment.

'*Ribbit*,' someone said very softly, just before the door closed behind him.

Madeleine's face lit up when she saw him, and his heart warmed. She wasn't very bright, poor creature, but she was pretty and amiable, and had been a whore long enough to be grateful for small kindnesses.

'Monsieur Rakoczy!' She flung her arms about his neck, nuzzling affectionately.

'Madeleine, my dear.' He cupped her chin and kissed her gently on the lips, drawing her close so that her belly pressed against his. He held her long enough, kissing her eyelids, her forehead, her ears – so that she made high squeaks of pleasure – that he could feel his way inside her, hold the weight of her womb in his mind, evaluate her ripening.

266

It felt warm, the colour in the heart of a dark crimson rose, the kind called 'sang-de-dragon'. A week before, it had felt solid, compact as a folded fist; now it had begun to soften, to hollow slightly as she readied. Three more days? he wondered. Four?

He let her go, and when she pouted prettily at him, he laughed and raised her hand to his lips, feeling the same small thrill he had felt when he first found her, as the faint blue glow rose between her fingers in response to his touch. She couldn't see it – he'd raised their linked hands to her face before and she had merely looked puzzled – but it was there.

'Go and fetch some wine, ma belle,' he said, squeezing her hand gently. 'I need to talk to madame.'

Madame Fabienne was not a dwarf, but she was small, brown and mottled as a toadstool – and as watchful as a toad, round yellow eyes seldom blinking, never closed.

'Monsieur le Comte,' she said graciously, nodding him to a damask chair in her salon. The air was scented with candlewax and flesh – flesh of a far better quality than that on offer in the Court of Miracles. Even so, madame had come from that Court, and kept her connections there alive; she made no bones about that. She didn't blink at his clothes, but her nostrils flared at him, as though she picked up the scent of the dives and alleys he had come from.

'Good evening, madame,' he said, smiling at her, and lifted the burlap bag. 'I brought a small present for Leopold. If he's awake?'

'Awake and irritable,' she said, eyeing the bag with interest. 'He's just shed his skin – you don't want to make any sudden moves.'

Leopold was a remarkably handsome – and remarkably large – python; an albino, quite rare. Opinion of his origins was divided; half Madame Fabienne's clientele

267

held that she had been given the snake by a noble client – some said the late king himself – whom she had cured of impotence. Others said the snake had once *been* a noble client, who had refused to pay her for services rendered. Rakoczy had his own opinions on that one, but he liked Leopold, who was ordinarily tame as a cat and would sometimes come when called – as long as you had something he regarded as food in your hand.

'Leopold! Monsieur le Comte has brought you a treat!' Fabienne reached across to an enormous wicker cage and flicked the door open, withdrawing her hand with sufficient speed as to indicate just what she meant by 'irritable'.

Almost at once, a huge yellow head poked out into the light. Snakes had transparent eyelids, but Rakoczy could swear the python blinked irritably, swaying up a coil of its monstrous body for a moment before plunging out of the cage and swarming across the floor with amazing rapidity for such a big creature, tongue flicking in and out like a seamstress's needle.

He made straight for Rakoczy, jaws yawning as he came, and Rakoczy snatched up the bag just before Leopold tried to engulf it – or Rakoczy – whole. He jerked aside, hastily seized a rat and threw it. Leopold flung a coil of his body on top of the rat with a thud that rattled madame's spoon in her tea-bowl, and before the company could blink, had whipped the rat into a half-hitch knot of coil.

'Hungry as well as ill-tempered, I see,' Rakoczy remarked, trying for nonchalance. In fact, the hairs were prickling over his neck and arms. Normally, Leopold took his time about feeding and the violence of the python's appetite at such close quarters had shaken him.

Fabienne was laughing, almost silently, her tiny sloping

268

shoulders quivering beneath the green Chinese silk tunic she wore.

'I thought for an instant he'd have you,' she remarked at last, wiping her eyes. 'If he had, I shouldn't have had to feed him for a month!'

Rakoczy bared his teeth in an expression that might have been taken for a smile.

'We cannot let Leopold go hungry,' he said. 'I wish to make a special arrangement for Madeleine – it should keep the worm up to his yellow arse in rats for some time.'

Fabienne put down her handkerchief and regarded him with interest.

'Leopold has two cocks, but I can't say I've ever noticed an arse. Twenty écus a day. Plus two extra if she needs clothes.'

He waved an easy hand, dismissing this.

'I had in mind something longer.' He explained what he had in mind, and had the satisfaction of seeing Fabienne's face go quite blank with astonishment. It didn't stay that way more than a few moments; by the time he had finished, she was already laying out her initial demands.

By the time they came to agreement, they had drunk half a bottle of decent wine, and Leopold had swallowed the rat. It made a small bulge in the muscular tube of the snake's body, but hadn't slowed him appreciably; the coils slithered restlessly over the painted canvas floor-cloth, glowing like gold, and Rakoczy saw the patterns of his skin like trapped clouds beneath the scales.

'He *is* beautiful, no?' Fabienne saw his admiration, and basked a little in it. 'Did I ever tell you where I got him?'

'Yes, more than once. And more than one story, too.' She looked startled, and he compressed his lips. He'd been patronising her establishment for no more than a few weeks, this time. He'd known her fifteen years before – though only a couple of months, that time. He hadn't

269

given his name then, and a madam saw so many men that there was little chance of her recalling him. On the other hand, he also thought it unlikely that she troubled to recall to whom she'd told which story, and this seemed to be the case, for she lifted one shoulder in a surprisingly graceful shrug, and laughed.

'Yes, but this one is true.'

'Oh, well, then.' He smiled, and reaching into the bag, tossed Leopold another rat. The snake moved more slowly this time, and didn't bother to constrict its motionless prey, merely unhinging its jaw and engulfing it in a single-minded way.

'He is an old friend, Leopold,' she said, gazing affectionately at the snake. 'I brought him with me from the West Indies, many years ago. He is a *Mystère*, you know.'

'I didn't, no.' Rakoczy drank more wine; he had sat long enough that he was beginning to feel almost sober again. 'And what is that?' He was interested – not so much in the snake, but in Fabienne's mention of the West Indies. He'd forgotten that she claimed to have come from there, many years ago, long before he'd known her the first time.

The *afile* powder had been waiting in his laboratory when he'd come back; no telling how many years it had sat there – the servants couldn't recall. Mélisande's brief note – 'Try this. It may be what the frog used.' – had not been dated, but there was a brief scrawl at the top of the sheet, saying 'Rose Hall, Jamaica.' If Fabienne retained any connections in the West Indies, perhaps . . .

'Some call them *loa*,' her wrinkled lips pursed as she kissed the word, 'but those are the Africans. A *Mystère* is a spirit, one who is an intermediary between the Bondye and us. Bondye is *le bon Dieu*, of course,' she explained to him. 'The African slaves speak very bad French. Give him another rat; he's still hungry, and it scares the girls if I let him hunt in the house.'

The third rat had made another bulge; the snake was beginning to look like a fat string of pearls, and was showing an inclination to lie still, digesting. The tongue still flickered, tasting the air, but lazily now.

Rakoczy picked up the bag again, weighing the risks – but after all, if news came from the Court of Miracles, his name would soon be known in any case.

'I wonder, madame – as you know everyone in Paris – ' he gave her a small bow, which she graciously returned, 'are you acquainted with a certain man known as *Maître* Raymond? Some call him "the frog",' he added.

She blinked, then looked amused.

'You're looking for the frog?'

'Yes. Is that funny?' He reached into the sack, fishing for a rat.

'Somewhat. I should perhaps not tell you, but since you are so accommodating . . .' she glanced complacently at the purse he had put beside her tea-bowl, a generous deposit on account, '*Maître Grenouille* is looking for *you*.'

He stopped dead, hand clutching a furry body.

'What? You've seen him?'

She shook her head, and setting down her empty glass, rang the bell for her maid.

'No, but I've heard the same from two people.'

'Asking for me by name?' Rakoczy's heart beat faster.

'Monsieur le Comte St Germain. That *is* you?' She asked with no more than mild interest; false names were common in her business.

He nodded, mouth suddenly too dry to speak, and pulled the rat from the sack. It squirmed suddenly in his hand, and a piercing pain in his thumb made him hurl the rodent away.

'*Sacrebleu!* It bit me!'

The rat, dazed by impact, staggered drunkenly across the floor toward Leopold, whose tongue began to flicker

271

faster. Fabienne, though, uttered a sound of disgust and threw a silver-backed hairbrush at the rat. Startled by the sudden clatter, the rat leaped convulsively into the air, landed on and raced directly over the snake's astonished head, disappearing through the door into the foyer, where – by the resultant scream – it evidently encountered the maid before making its ultimate escape into the street.

'*Jésus Marie*,' Madame Fabienne said, piously crossing herself. 'A miraculous resurrection. Two months past Easter, too.'

It was a smooth passage; the shore of France came into sight just after dawn next day. Joan saw it, a low smudge of dark green on the horizon, and felt a little thrill at the sight, in spite of her tiredness.

She hadn't slept, though she'd reluctantly gone below after nightfall, there to wrap herself in her cloak and shawl, trying not to look at the young man with the shadow on his face. She'd lain all night, listening to the snores and groans of her fellow-passengers, praying doggedly and wondering in despair whether prayer was the only thing she could do to help.

She often wondered whether it was because of her name. She'd been proud of her name when she was small; it was a heroic name, a saint's name, but also a warrior's name. Her mother'd told her that, often and often. She didn't think her mother had considered that the name might also be haunted.

Surely it didn't happen to everyone named Joan, though, did it? She wished she knew another Joan to ask. Because if it *did* happen to them all, the others would be keeping it quiet, just like she did.

You just didn't go round telling people that you heard

voices that weren't there. Still less, that you saw things that weren't there, either. You just *didn't*.

She'd heard of a seer, of course; everyone in the Highlands had. And nearly everyone she knew at least claimed to have seen the odd fetch or had a premonition that Angus MacWheen was dead when he didn't come home that time last winter. The fact that Angus MacWheen was a filthy auld drunkard and so yellow and crazed that it was heads or tails whether he'd die on any particular day, let alone when it got cold enough that the loch froze, didn't come into it.

But she'd never *met* a seer; there was the rub. How did you get into the way of it? Did you just tell folk, 'Here's a thing . . . I'm a seer,' and they'd nod and say, 'Oh, aye, of course; what's like to happen to me next Tuesday?' More important, though, how the devil—

'Ow!' She'd bitten her tongue fiercely as penance for the inadvertent blasphemy, and clapped a hand to her mouth.

'What is it?' said a concerned voice behind her. 'Are ye hurt, Miss MacKimmie? Er . . . Sister Gregory, I mean?'

'Mm! No. No, I justh . . . bit my tongue.' She turned to Michael Murray, gingerly touching the injured tongue to the roof of her mouth.

'Well, that happens when ye talk to yourself.' He took the cork from a bottle he was carrying and held the bottle out to her. 'Here, wash your mouth wi' that; it'll help.'

She took a large mouthful and swirled it round; it burned the bitten place, but not badly, and she swallowed, as slowly as possible, to make it last.

'Jesus, Mary, and Bride,' she breathed. 'Is that *wine*?' The taste in her mouth bore some faint kinship with the liquid she knew as wine – just like apples bore some resemblance to horse turds.

'Aye, it *is* pretty good,' he said modestly. 'German. Umm . . . have a wee nip more?'

273

She didn't argue, and sipped happily, barely listening to his talk, telling about the wine, what it was called, how they made it in Germany, where he got it . . . on and on. Finally she came to herself enough to remember her manners, though, and reluctantly handed back the bottle, now half-empty.

'I thank ye, sir,' she said primly. ''Twas kind of ye. Ye needna waste your time in bearing me company, though; I shall be well enough alone.'

'Aye, well . . . it's no really for your sake,' he said, and took a reasonable swallow himself. 'It's mine.'

She blinked against the wind. He was flushed, but not from drink or wind, she thought.

She managed a faint interrogative, 'Ah . . . ?'

'Well, what I want to ask,' he blurted, and looked away, cheekbones burning red. 'Will ye pray for me? Sister? And my— my wife. The repose of— of—'

'Oh!' she said, mortified that she'd been so taken up with her own worries as not to have seen his distress. *Think you're a seer, dear Lord, ye dinna see what's under your neb; you're no but a fool, and a selfish fool at that.* She put her hand over his where it lay on the rail and squeezed tight, trying to channel some sense of God's goodness into his flesh.

'To be sure I will!' she said. 'I'll remember ye at every Mass, I swear it!' She wondered briefly whether it was proper to swear to something like that, but after all . . . 'And your poor wife's soul, of course I will! What . . . er . . . what was her name? So as I'll know what to say when I pray for her,' she explained hurriedly, seeing his eyes narrow with pain.

'Lilliane,' he said, so softly that she barely heard him over the wind. 'I called her Lillie.'

'Lilliane,' she repeated carefully, trying to form the syllables like he did. It was a soft, lovely name, she thought,

274

slipping like water over the rocks at the top of a burn. *You'll never see a burn again*, she thought with a sudden pang, but dismissed this, turning her face toward the growing shore of France. 'I'll remember.'

He nodded in mute thanks, and they stood for some little while, until she realised that her hand was still resting on his, and drew it back with a jerk. He looked startled, and she blurted – because it was the thing on the top of her mind – 'What was she like? Your wife?'

The most extraordinary mix of emotions flooded over his face. She couldn't have said what was uppermost, grief, laughter, or sheer bewilderment, and she realised suddenly just how little of his true mind she'd seen before.

'She was . . .' He shrugged, and swallowed. 'She was my wife,' he said, very softly. 'She was my life.'

She should know something comforting to say to him, but she didn't.

She's with God? That was the truth, she hoped, and yet clearly to this young man, the only thing that mattered was that his wife was not with *him*.

'What happened to her?' she asked instead, baldly, only because it seemed necessary to say something.

He took a deep breath and seemed to sway a little; he'd finished the rest of the wine, she saw, and took the empty bottle from his hand, tossing it overboard.

'The influenza. They said it was quick. Didn't seem quick to me – and yet, it was, I suppose it was. It took two days, and God kens well that I recall every second of those days – yet it seems that I lost her between one heartbeat and the next. And I— I keep lookin' for her there, in that space between.'

He swallowed.

'She— she was . . .' The words 'with child' came so quietly that she barely heard them.

'Oh,' Joan said softly, very moved. 'Oh, *a chiusle*.'

275

'Heart's blood', it meant – and what *she* meant was that his wife had been that to him— dear Lord, she hoped he hadn't thought she meant— no, he hadn't, and the tight-wound spring in her backbone relaxed a little, seeing the look of gratitude on his face. He did know what she'd meant, and seemed glad that she'd understood.

Blinking, she looked away – and caught sight of the young man with the shadow on him, leaning against the railing a little way down. The breath caught in her throat at sight of him.

The shadow was darker in the morning light. The sun was beginning to warm the deck, frail white clouds swam in the blue of clear French skies, and yet the mist seemed now to swirl and thicken, obscuring the young man's face, wrapping round his shoulders like a shawl.

Dear Lord, tell me what to do! Her body jerked, wanting to go to the young man, speak to him. But say what? *You're in danger, be careful*? He'd think she was mad. And if the danger was a thing he couldn't help, like wee Ronnie and the ox, what difference might her speaking make?

She was dimly aware of Michael staring at her, curious. He said something to her, but she wasn't listening, listening hard instead inside her head. Where were the damned voices when you bloody *needed* one?

But the voices were stubbornly silent, and she turned to Michael, the muscles of her arm jumping, she'd held so tight to the ship's rigging.

'I'm sorry,' she said. 'I wasna listening properly. I just— thought of something.'

'If it's a thing I can help ye with, Sister, ye've only to ask,' he said, smiling faintly. 'Oh! And speak of that, I meant to say – I said to your mam, if she liked to write to you in care of Fraser et Cie, I'd see to it that ye got the letters.' He shrugged, one-shouldered. 'I dinna ken what

276

the rules are at the convent, aye? About getting letters from outside.'

Joan didn't know that, either, and had worried about it. She was so relieved to hear this that a huge smile split her face.

'Oh, it's that kind of ye!' she said. 'And if I could – maybe write back . . . ?'

He smiled, the marks of grief easing in his pleasure at doing her a service.

'Anytime,' he assured her. 'I'll see to it. Perhaps I could—'

A ragged shriek cut through the air, and Joan glanced up, startled, thinking it one of the sea-birds that had come out from shore to wheel round the ship. But it wasn't. It was the young man, standing on the rail, one hand on the rigging, and before she could so much as draw breath, he let go and was gone.

Paris

Michael was worried for Joan; she sat slumped in the coach, not bothering to look out of the window, until a faint waft of the spring breeze touched her face. The smell was so astonishing that it drew her out of the shell of shocked misery in which she had travelled from the docks.

'Mother o' God!' she said, clapping a hand to her nose. 'What *is* that?'

Michael dug in his pocket and pulled out the grubby rag of his handkerchief, looking dubiously at it.

'It's the public cemeteries. I'm sorry, I didna think—'

'*Moran taing.*' She seized the damp cloth from him and held it over her face, not caring. 'Do the French not *bury* folk in their cemeteries?' Because from the smell, a thousand corpses had been thrown out on wet ground and left to rot, and the sight of darting, squabbling flocks of

277

black corbies in the distance did nothing to correct this impression.

'They do.' Michael felt exhausted – it had been a terrible morning – but struggled to pull himself together. 'It's all marshland over there, though; even coffins buried deep – and most of them aren't – work their way through the ground in a few months. When there's a flood – and there's a flood whenever it rains – what's left of the coffins falls apart, and . . .' He swallowed, just pleased that he'd not eaten any breakfast.

'There's talk of maybe moving the bones at least, putting them in an ossuary, they call it. There are mine workings, old ones, outside the city – over there – ' he pointed with his chin, 'and perhaps . . . but they havena done anything about it yet,' he added in a rush, pinching his nose fast to get a breath in through his mouth. It didn't matter whether you breathed through your nose or your mouth, though; the air was thick enough to taste.

She looked as ill as he felt, or maybe worse, her face the colour of spoiled custard. She'd vomited when the crew had finally pulled the suicide aboard, pouring grey water and slimed with the seaweed that had wrapped round his legs and drowned him. There were still traces of sick down her front, and her dark hair was lank and damp, straggling out from under her cap. She hadn't slept at all, of course – neither had he.

He couldn't take her to the convent in this condition. The nuns maybe wouldn't mind, but she would. He stretched up and rapped on the ceiling of the carriage.

'Monsieur?'

'Au château, vite!'

He'd take her to his house, first. It wasn't much out of the way, and the convent wasn't expecting her at any particular day or hour. She could wash, have something to eat, and put herself to rights. And if it saved him from walking into his house alone, well, they did say a kind deed carried its own reward.

By the time they'd reached the Avenue Trémoulins, Joan had forgotten – partly – her various reasons for distress, in the sheer excitement of being in Paris. She had never seen so many people in one place at the same time – and that was only the folk coming out of Mass at a parish church! While round the corner, a pavement of fitted stones stretched wider than the whole River Ness, and those stones covered from one side to the other in barrows and wagons and stalls, rioting with fruit and vegetables and flowers and fish and meat . . . she'd given Michael back his filthy handkerchief and was panting like a dog, turning her face to and fro, trying to draw all the wonderful smells into herself at once.

'Ye look a bit better,' Michael said, smiling at her. He was still pale himself, but he too seemed happier. 'Are ye hungry, yet?'

'I'm famished!' She cast a starved look at the edge of the market. 'Could we stop, maybe, and buy an apple? I've a bit of money . . .' She fumbled for the coins in her stocking-top, but he stopped her.

'Nay, there'll be food a-plenty at the house. They were expecting me this week, so everything will be ready.'

She cast a brief longing look at the market, but turned obligingly in the direction he pointed, craning out the carriage window to see his house as they approached.

'That's the biggest house I've ever seen!' she exclaimed.

'Och, no,' he said, laughing. 'Lallybroch's bigger than that.'

'Well . . . this one's *taller*,' she replied. And it was – a good four storeys, and a huge roof of lead slates and green-coppered seams, with what must be more than a score of glass windows set in, and . . .

She was still trying to count the windows when Michael helped her down from the carriage and offered her his arm to walk up to the door. She was goggling at the big yew trees set in brass pots and wondering how much trouble it must be to keep those polished, when she felt the arm under her hand go suddenly rigid as wood.

She glanced at Michael, startled, then looked where he was looking – toward the door of his house. The door had swung open, and three people were coming down the marble steps, smiling and waving, calling out.

'Who's that?' Joan whispered, leaning close to Michael. The one short fellow in the striped apron must be a butler; she'd read about butlers. But the other man was a gentleman, limber as a willow tree and wearing a coat and waistcoat striped in lemon and pink – with a hat decorated with . . . well, she supposed it must be a feather, but she'd pay money to see the bird it came off of. By comparison, she had hardly noticed the woman, who was dressed in black. But now she saw that Michael had eyes only for the woman.

'Li—' he began, and choked it back. 'L— Léonie. Léonie is her name. My wife's sister.'

She looked sharp then, because from the look of Michael Murray, he'd just seen his wife's ghost. Léonie seemed flesh and blood, though, slender and pretty, though she bore the same marks of sorrow as did Michael, and her face was pale under a small, neat black tricorne with a tiny curled blue feather.

'Michel,' she said, 'Oh, Michel!' And with tears brimming from eyes shaped like almonds, she threw herself into his arms.

Feeling extremely superfluous, Joan stood back a little

and glanced at the gentleman in the lemon-striped waist-coat – the butler had tactfully withdrawn into the house.

'Charles Pépin, mademoiselle,' he said, sweeping off his hat. Taking her hand, he bowed low over it, and now she saw the band of black mourning he wore round his bright sleeve. '*À votre service.*'

'Oh,' she said, a little flustered. 'Um. Joan MacKimmie. *Je suis* . . . er . . . um . . .'

Tell him not to do it, said a sudden small, calm voice inside her head, and she jerked her own hand away as though he'd bitten her.

'Pleased to meet you,' she gasped. 'Excuse me.' And turning, threw up into one of the bronze yew-pots.

Joan had been afraid it would be awkward, coming to Michael's bereaved and empty house, but had steeled herself to offer comfort and support, as became a distant kinswoman and a daughter of God. She might have been miffed, therefore, to find herself entirely supplanted in the department of comfort and support – quite relegated to the negligible position of guest, in fact, served politely and asked periodically if she wished more wine, a slice of ham, some gherkins . . .? but otherwise ignored, while Michael's servants, sister-in-law, and . . . she wasn't quite sure of the position of M. Pépin, though he seemed to have something personal to do with Léonie, perhaps someone had said he was her cousin? – all swirled round Michael like perfumed bathwater, warm and buoyant, touching him, kissing him – well, all right, she'd heard of men kissing one another in France but she couldn't help staring when M. Pépin gave Michael a big wet one on both cheeks – and generally making a fuss of him.

She was more than relieved, though, not to have to

281

make conversation in French, beyond a simple *merci* or *s'il vous plaît* from time to time. It gave her a chance to settle her nerves – and her stomach, and she would say the wine was a wonder for that – and to keep a close eye on Monsieur Charles Pépin.

'*Tell him not to do it.*' And just what d'ye mean by that? she demanded of the voice. She didn't get an answer, which didn't surprise her. The voices weren't much for details.

She couldn't tell whether the voices were male or female; they didn't seem either one, and she wondered whether they might maybe be angels – angels didn't have a sex, and doubtless that saved them a lot of trouble. Joan of Arc's voices had had the decency to introduce themselves, but not hers, oh, no. On the other hand, if they *were* angels, and told her their names, she wouldn't recognise them anyway, so perhaps that's why they didn't bother.

Well, so. Did this particular voice mean that Charles Pépin was a villain? She squinted closely at him. He didn't look it. He had a strong, good-looking face, and Michael seemed to like him – after all, Michael must be a fair judge of character, she thought, and him in the wine business.

What was it Mr Charles Pépin oughtn't to do, though? Did he have some wicked crime in mind? Or might he be bent on doing away with himself, like that poor wee gomerel on the boat? There was still a trace of slime on her hand, from the seaweed.

She rubbed her hand inconspicuously against the skirt of her dress, frustrated. She hoped the voices would stop, in the convent. That was her nightly prayer. But if they didn't, at least she might be able to tell someone there about them without fear of being packed off to a madhouse or stoned in the street. She'd have a confessor, she knew that much. Maybe he could help her discover what God had meant, landing her with a gift like this, and no explanation what she was to do with it.

In the meantime, Monsieur Pépin would bear watching; she should maybe say something to Michael before she left. *Aye, what?* she thought, helpless.

Still, she was glad to see that Michael grew less pale as they all carried on, vying to feed him tidbits, refill his glass, tell him bits of gossip. She was also pleased to find that she mostly understood what they were saying, as she relaxed. Jared – that would be Jared Fraser, Michael's elderly cousin, who'd founded the wine company, and whose house this was – was still in Germany, they said, but was expected at any moment. He had sent a letter for Michael, too, where was it? No matter, it would turn up . . . and La Comtesse de Maurepas had had a fit, a veritable *fit* at court last Wednesday, when she came face to face with Mademoiselle de Perpignan wearing a confection in the particular shade of pea-green that was La Comtesse's alone, and God alone knew why, because she always looked like a cheese in it, and had slapped her own maid so hard for pointing this out that the poor girl flew across the rushes and cracked her head on one of the mirrored walls – and cracked the mirror, too, very bad luck that, but no one could agree whether the bad luck was de La Tour's, the maid's, or La Perpignan's.

Birds, Joan thought dreamily, sipping her wine. *They sound just like cheerful wee birds in a tree, all chattering away together.*

'The bad luck belongs to the seamstress who made the dress for La Perpignan,' Michael said, a faint smile touching his mouth. 'Once La Comtesse finds out who it is.' His eye lighted on Joan, then, sitting there with a fork – an actual fork! and silver, too – in her hand, her mouth

283

half-open in the effort of concentration required to follow the conversation.

'Sister Joan, Sister Gregory, I mean; I'm that sorry, I was forgetting. If ye've had enough to eat, will ye have a bit of a wash, maybe, before I deliver ye to the convent?'

He was already rising, reaching for a bell, and before she knew where she was, a maid-servant had whisked her off upstairs, deftly undressed her, and wrinkling her nose at the smell of the discarded garments, wrapped Joan in a robe of the most amazing green silk, light as air, and ushered her into a small stone room with a copper bath in it, then disappeared, saying something in which Joan caught the word '*eau*'.

She sat on the wooden stool provided, clutching the robe about her nakedness, head spinning with more than wine. She closed her eyes and took deep breaths, trying to put herself in the way of praying. God was everywhere, she assured herself, embarrassing as it was to contemplate Him being with her in a bathroom in Paris. She shut her eyes harder and firmly began the rosary, starting with the Joyful Mysteries.

She'd got through The Visitation before she began to feel steady again. This wasn't quite how she'd expected her first day in Paris to be. Still, she'd have something to write home to Mam about, that was for sure. If they let her write letters in the convent.

The maid came in with two enormous cans of steaming water, and upended these into the bath with a tremendous splash. Another came in on her heels, similarly equipped, and between them, they had Joan up, stripped, and stepping into the tub before she'd so much as said the first word of the Lord's Prayer for the third decade.

They said French things to her, which she didn't understand, and held out peculiar-looking instruments to her in invitation. She recognised the small pot of soap, and pointed at it, and one of them at once poured water on her head and began to wash her hair.

She had for months been bidding farewell to her hair whenever she combed it, quite resigned to its loss, for whether she must sacrifice it immediately, as a postulant, or later, as a novice, plainly it must go. The shock of knowing fingers rubbing her scalp, the sheer sensual delight of warm water coursing through her hair, the soft wet weight of it lying in ropes down over her breasts – was this God's way of asking if she'd truly thought it through? Did she know what she was giving up?

Well, she did, then. And she *had* thought about it. On the other hand . . . she couldn't make them stop, really; it wouldn't be mannerly. The warmth of the water was making the wine she'd drunk course faster through her blood, and she felt as though she were being kneaded like toffee, stretched and pulled, all glossy and falling into languid loops. She closed her eyes and gave up trying to remember how many Hail Marys she had yet to go in the third decade.

It wasn't until the maids had hauled her, pink and steaming, out of the bath and wrapped her in a most remarkable huge fuzzy kind of towel, that she emerged abruptly from her sensual trance. The cold air coalesced in her stomach, reminding her that all this luxury was indeed a lure of the devil – for lost in gluttony and sinful bathing, she'd forgot entirely about the poor young man on the ship, the poor, despairing sinner who had thrown himself into the sea.

The maids had gone for the moment. She dropped at once to her knees on the stone floor and threw off the coddling towels, exposing her bare skin to the full chill of the air in penance.

'*Mea culpa, mea culpa, mea maxima culpa,*' she breathed, knocking a fist against her bosom in a paroxysm of sorrow and regret. The sight of the drowned young man was in her mind, soft brown hair fanned across his cheek, young eyes half-closed, seeing nothing – and what terrible thing was it that he'd seen before he jumped, or thought of, that he'd screamed so?

She thought briefly of Michael, the look on his face when he spoke of his poor wife – perhaps the young brown-haired man had lost someone dear, and couldn't face his life alone?

She should have spoken to him. That was the undeniable, terrible truth. It didn't matter that she didn't know what to say. She should have trusted God to give her words, as He had when she'd spoken to Michael.

'Forgive me, Father!' she said urgently, out loud. 'Please – forgive me, give me strength!'

She'd betrayed that poor young man. And herself. *And* God, who'd given her the terrible gift of Sight for a reason. And the voices . . .

'Why did ye not tell me?' she cried. 'Have ye nothing to say for yourselves?' Here she'd thought the voices those of angels, and they weren't – just drifting bits of bog-mist, getting into her head, pointless, useless . . . useless as she was, oh, Lord Jesus . . .

She didn't know how long she knelt there, naked, half-drunk, and in tears. She heard the muffled squeaks of dismay from the French maids who poked their heads in, and just as quickly withdrew them, but paid no attention. She didn't know if it was right even to pray for the poor young man – for suicide was a mortal sin, and surely he'd gone straight to Hell. But she couldn't give him up; she couldn't. She felt somehow that he'd been her charge, that she'd carelessly let him fall, and surely God would not hold the young man entirely responsible, when it was she who should have been watching out for him?

And so she prayed, with all the energy of body and

mind and spirit, asking mercy. Mercy for the young man, for wee Ronnie and wretched auld Angus – mercy for poor Michael, and for the soul of Lillie, his dear wife, and their babe unborn. And mercy for herself, this unworthy vessel of God's service.

'I'll do better!' she promised, sniffing and wiping her nose on the fluffy towel. 'Truly, I will. I'll be braver. I will.'

Michael took the candlestick from the footman, said goodnight, and shut the door. He hoped Sister Joan-Gregory was comfortable; he'd told the staff to put her in the main guest room. He was fairly sure she'd sleep well. He smiled wryly to himself; unaccustomed to wine, and obviously nervous in company, she'd sipped her way through most of a decanter of Jerez sherry before he noticed, and was sitting in the corner with unfocused eyes and a small inward smile that reminded him of a painting he had seen at Versailles, a thing the steward had called *La Gioconda*.

He couldn't very well deliver her to the convent in such a condition, and had gently escorted her upstairs and given her into the hands of the chambermaids, both of whom regarded her with some wariness, as though a tipsy nun was a particularly dangerous commodity.

He'd drunk a fair amount himself in the course of the afternoon, and more at dinner. He and Charles had sat up late, talking and drinking rum-punch. Not talking of anything in particular; he had just wanted not to be alone. Charles had invited him to go to the gaming rooms – Charles was an inveterate gambler – but was kind enough to accept his refusal and simply bear him company.

The candle flame blurred briefly at thought of Charles's kindness. He blinked and shook his head, which proved a mistake; the contents shifted abruptly, and his stomach rose in protest at the sudden movement. He barely made it to the chamber pot in time, and once evacuated, lay numbly on the floor, cheek pressed to the cold boards.

It wasn't that he couldn't get up and go to bed. It was that he couldn't face the thought of the cold white sheets, the pillows round and smooth, as though Lillie's head had never dented them, the bed never known the heat of her body.

Tears ran sideways over the bridge of his nose and dripped on the floor. There was a snuffling noise, and Plonplon came squirming out from under the bed and licked his face, whining anxiously. After a little while, he sat up, and leaning against the side of the bed with the dog in one arm, reached for the decanter of port that the butler had left – by instruction – on the table beside it.

The smell was appalling. Rakoczy had wrapped a woollen comforter about his lower face, but the odour seeped in, putrid and cloying, clinging to the back of the throat, so that even breathing through the mouth didn't preserve you from the stench. He breathed as shallowly as he could, though, picking his way carefully past the edge of the cemetery by the narrow beam of a dark lantern. The mine lay well beyond it, but the stench carried amazingly, when the wind lay in the east.

The chalk mine had been abandoned for years; it was rumoured to be haunted. It was. Rakoczy knew what haunted it. Never religious – he was a philosopher and a natural scientist, a rationalist – he still crossed himself by reflex at the head of the ladder that led down the shaft into those spectral depths.

At least the rumours of ghosts and earth-demons and

288

the walking dead would keep anyone from coming to investigate strange light glowing from the subterranean tunnels of the workings, if it was noticed at all. Though just in case . . . he opened the burlap bag, still redolent of rats, and fished out a bundle of pitchblende torches and the oiled-silk packet that held several lengths of cloth saturated with *salpêtre*, salts of potash, blue vitriol, verdigris, butter of antimony, and a few other interesting compounds from his laboratory.

He found the blue vitriol by smell, and wrapped the cloth tightly around the head of one torch, then – whistling under his breath – did three more, impregnated with different salts. He loved this part. It was so simple, and so astonishingly beautiful.

He paused for a minute to listen, but it was well past dark and the only sounds were those of the night itself – frogs chirping and bellowing in the distant marshes by the cemetery, wind stirring the leaves of summer. A few hovels a half-mile away, only one with firelight glowing dully from a smoke-hole in the roof.

Almost a pity there's no one but me to see this. He took the little clay firepot from its wrappings and touched a coal to the cloth-wrapped torch. A tiny green flame flickered like a serpent's tongue, then burst into life in a brilliant globe of ghostly colour.

He grinned at the sight, but there was no time to lose; the torches wouldn't last for ever, and there was work to be done. He tied the bag to his belt and with the green fire crackling softly in one hand, climbed down into darkness.

He paused at the bottom, breathing deep. The air was clear, the dust long-settled. No one had been down here recently. The dull white walls glowed soft, eerie under the green light, and the passage yawned before him, black as a murderer's soul. Even knowing the place as well as he did,

289

and with light in his hand, it gave him a qualm to walk into it.

Is that what death is like? he wondered. A black void, that you walked into with no more than a feeble glimmer of faith in your hand? His lips compressed. Well, he'd done *that* before, if less permanently. But he disliked the way that the notion of death seemed always to be lurking in the back of his mind these days.

The main tunnel was large, big enough for two men to walk side by side, and the roof was high enough above him that the roughly excavated chalk lay in shadow, barely touched by his torch. The side-tunnels were smaller, though. He counted the ones on the left, and despite himself, hurried his step a little as he passed the fourth. That was where *it* lay, down the side-tunnel, a turn to the left, another to the left – was it 'widdershins' the English called it, turning against the direction of the sun? He thought that was what Mélisande had called it when she'd brought him here . . .

The sixth. His torch had begun to gutter already, and he pulled another from the bag and lit it from the remains of the first, which he dropped on the floor at the entrance to the side-tunnel, leaving it to flare and smoulder behind him, the smoke catching at his throat. He knew his way, but even so, it was as well to leave landmarks, here in the realm of everlasting night. The mine had deep rooms, one far back that showed strange paintings on the wall, of animals that didn't exist, but had an astonishing vividness, as though they would leap from the wall and stampede down the passages. Sometimes – rarely – he went all the way down into the bowels of the earth, just to look at them.

The fresh torch burned with the warm light of natural fire, and the white walls took on a rosy glow. So did the painting at the end of the corridor, this one different: a crude but effective rendering of the Annunciation. He didn't know who had made the paintings that appeared unexpectedly here and there in the mines – most were of religious subjects, a few most emphatically *not* – but they were useful. There was an iron ring in the wall by the picture, and he set his torch into it.

Turn back at the Annunciation, then three paces . . . he stamped his foot, listening for the faint echo, and found it. He'd brought a trowel in his bag, and it was the work of a few moments to uncover the sheet of tin that covered his cache.

The cache itself was three feet deep and three feet square – he found satisfaction in the knowledge of its perfect cubicity whenever he saw it; any alchemist was by profession a numerologist as well. It was half-full, the contents wrapped in burlap or canvas – not things he wanted to carry openly through the streets. It took some prodding and unwrapping to find the pieces he wanted. Madame Fabienne had driven a hard bargain, but a fair one: two hundred écus a month times four months, for the guaranteed exclusive use of Madeleine's services.

Four months would surely be enough, he thought, feeling a rounded shape through its wrappings. In fact, he thought one night would be enough, but his man's pride was restrained by a scientist's prudence. And even if . . . there was always some chance of early miscarriage; he wanted to be sure of the child before he undertook any more personal experiments with the space between times. If he knew that something of himself – someone with his peculiar abilities – might be left, just in case *this* time . . .

He could feel *it* there, somewhere in the smothered dark behind him. He knew he couldn't hear it now; it was silent, save on the days of solstice and equinox, or when you actually walked into it . . . but he felt the sound of it in his bones, and it made his hands tremble on the wrappings.

The gleam of silver, of gold. He chose two gold snuffboxes, a filigree necklace, and – with some hesitation – a small silver salver. Why did the void not affect metal? he wondered, for the thousandth time. In fact, carrying gold or silver eased the passage – or at least he thought so. Mélisande had told him it did. But jewels were always destroyed by the passage, though they gave the most control and protection.

That made some sense; everyone knew that gemstones had a specific vibration that corresponded to the heavenly spheres, and the spheres themselves of course affected the earth – 'As above, so below.' He still had no idea exactly *how* the vibrations should affect the space, the portal . . . *it*. But thinking about it gave him a need to touch them, to reassure himself, and he moved wrapped bundles out of the way, digging down to the left-hand corner of the wood-lined cache, where pressing on a particular nailhead caused one of the boards to loosen and turn sideways, rotating smoothly on spindles. He reached into the dark space thus revealed and found the small wash-leather bag, feeling his sense of unease dissipate at once when he touched it.

He opened it and poured the contents into his palm, glittering and sparking in the dark hollow of his hand. Reds and blues and greens, the brilliant white of diamonds, the lavender and violet of amethyst, and the golden glow of topaz and citrine. Enough?

Enough to travel back, certainly. Enough to steer himself with some accuracy, to choose how far he went. But enough to go forward?

He weighed the glittering handful for a moment, then poured them carefully back. Not yet. But he had time to find more; he wasn't going anywhere for at least four months. Not until he was sure that Madeleine was well and truly with child.

'Joan.' Michael put his hand on her arm, keeping her from leaping out of the carriage. 'Ye're *sure*, now? I mean, if ye didna feel quite ready, ye're welcome to stay at my house until—'

'I'm ready.' She didn't look at him, and her face was pale as a slab of lard. 'Let me go, please.'

He reluctantly let go of her arm, but insisted upon getting down with her, and ringing the bell at the gate, stating their business to the portress. All the time, though, he could feel her shaking, quivering like a blancmange. Was it fear, though, or just understandable nerves? He'd feel a bit cattywumpus, himself, he thought with sympathy, were he making such a shift, beginning a new life so different from what had gone before.

The portress went away to fetch the mistress of postulants, leaving them in the little enclosure by the gatehouse. From here, he could see across a sunny courtyard with a cloister walk on the far side, and what looked like extensive kitchen gardens to the right. To the left was the looming bulk of the hospital run by the order, and beyond that, the other buildings that belonged to the convent. It was a beautiful place, he thought – and hoped the sight of it would settle her fears.

She made an inarticulate noise, and he glanced at her, alarmed to see what looked like tears slicking her cheeks.

'Joan,' he said more quietly, and handed her his fresh handkerchief. 'Dinna be afraid. If ye need me, send for me, anytime; I'll come. And I meant it, about the letters.'

He would have said more, but just then the portress reappeared, with Sister Eustacia, the postulant mistress,

293

who greeted Joan with a kind motherliness that seemed to comfort her, for the girl sniffed and straightened herself, and reaching into her pocket, pulled out a little folded square, obviously kept with care through her travels.

'*J'ai une lettre*,' she said, in halting French. '*Pour Madame le ... pour ...* Reverend Mother?' she said, in a small voice. 'Mother Hildegarde?'

'*Oui?*' Sister Eustacia took the note with the same care with which it was proffered.

'It's from ... her,' Joan said to Michael, having plainly run out of French. She still wouldn't look at him. 'Da's ... er ... wife. You know. Claire.'

'Jesus Christ!' Michael blurted, making both the portress and the postulant mistress stare reprovingly at him.

'She said she was a friend of Mother Hildegarde. And if she was still alive ...' She stole a look at Sister Eustacia, who appeared to have followed this.

'Oh, Mother Hildegarde is certainly alive,' she assured Joan, in English. 'And I'm sure she will be most interested to speak with you.' She tucked the note into her own capacious pocket, and held out a hand. 'Now, my dear child, if you are quite ready ...'

'*Je suis prête*,' Joan said, shaky, but dignified. And so Joan MacKimmie of Balriggan passed through the gates of the convent of Our Lady Queen of Angels, still clutching Michael Murray's clean handkerchief and smelling strongly of his dead wife's scented soap.

Michael had dismissed his carriage, and wandered restlessly about the city after leaving Joan at the convent, not wanting to go home. He hoped they would be good to her, hoped that she'd made the right decision.

Of course, he comforted himself, she wouldn't actually

be a nun for some time. He didn't know quite how long it took, from entering as a postulant to becoming a novice, to taking the final vows of poverty, chastity, and obedience, but at least a few years. There would be time for her to be sure. And at least she was in a place of safety; the look of terror and distress on her face as she'd shot through the gates of the convent still haunted him. He strolled toward the river, where the evening light glowed on the water like a bronze mirror. The deckhands were tired and the day's shouting had died away. In this light, the reflections of the boats gliding homeward seemed more substantial than the boats themselves.

He'd been surprised at the letter, and wondered whether that had anything to do with Joan's distress. He'd had no notion that his uncle's wife had anything to do with the Convent des Anges – though now that he cast his mind back, he did recall Jared mentioning that Uncle Jamie had worked in Paris in the wine business for a short time, back before the Rising. He supposed Claire might have met Mother Hildegarde then . . . but it was all before he himself was born.

He felt an odd warmth at the thought of Claire; he couldn't really think of her as his auntie, though she was. He'd not spent much time with her alone at Lallybroch – but he couldn't forget the moment when she'd met him, alone at the door. Greeted him briefly and embraced him in impulse. And he'd felt an instant sense of relief, as though she'd taken a heavy burden from his heart. Or maybe lanced a boil on his spirit, as she might one on his bum.

That thought made him smile. He didn't know what she was – the talk near Lallybroch painted her as everything from a witch to an angel, with most of the opinion hovering cautiously around 'faery' – for the Auld Ones were dangerous, and you didn't talk too much about them

– but he liked her. So did Da and Young Ian, and that counted for a lot. And Uncle Jamie, of course . . . though everyone said, very matter-of-fact, that Uncle Jamie was bewitched. He smiled wryly at that. Aye, if being mad in love with your wife was bewitchment.

If anyone outside the family kent what she'd told them – he cut that thought short. It wasn't something he'd forget, but it wasn't something he wanted to think about just yet, either. The gutters of Paris running with blood . . . he glanced down, involuntarily, but the gutters were full of the usual assortment of animal and human sewage, dead rats, and bits of rubbish too far gone to be salvaged for food even by the street beggars.

He got up and walked, making his way slowly through the crowded streets, past La Chapelle and Montmartre. If he walked enough, sometimes he could fall asleep without too much wine.

He sighed, elbowing his way through a group of buskers outside a tavern, turning back toward the Avenue Trémoulins. Some days, his head was like a bramble patch, thorns catching at him no matter which way he turned, and no path leading out of the tangle.

Paris wasn't a large city, but it was a complicated one; there was always somewhere else to walk. He crossed the Place de la Concorde, thinking of what his uncle's wife had told them, seeing there in his mind the tall shadow of a terrible machine.

Joan had had her dinner with Mother Hildegarde, a lady so ancient and holy that Joan had feared to breathe too heavily, lest Mother Hildegarde fragment like a stale croissant and go straight off to Heaven in front of her. Mother Hildegarde had been delighted with the letter

296

Joan had brought, though; it brought a faint flush to her face.

'From my— er . . .' Martha, Mary, and Lazarus, what was the French word for stepmother? 'Ahh . . . the wife of my . . .' Fittens, she didn't know the word for stepfather, either! 'The wife of my father,' she ended, weakly.

'You are the daughter of my good friend Claire!' Mother had exclaimed. 'And how is she?'

'Bonny, er . . . *bon*, I mean, last I saw her,' said Joan, and then tried to explain, but there was a lot of French being talked very fast, and she gave up and accepted the glass of wine that Mother Hildegarde offered her. She was going to be a sot long before she took her vows, she thought, trying to hide her flushed face by bending down to pat Mother's wee dog, a fluffy, friendly creature the colour of burned sugar, named Bouton.

Whether it was the wine or Mother's kindness, though, her wobbly spirit steadied. Mother had welcomed her to the community and kissed her forehead at the end of the meal, before sending her off in the charge of Sister Eustacia to see the convent.

Now she lay on her narrow cot in the dormitory, listening to the breathing of a dozen other postulants. It sounded like a byre full of cows, and had much the same warm, humid scent – bar the manure. Her eyes filled with tears, the vision of the homely stone byre at Balriggan sudden and vivid in her mind. She swallowed them back, though, pinching her lips together. A few of the girls sobbed quietly, missing home and family, but she wouldn't be one of them. She was older than most – a few were nay more than fourteen – and she'd promised God to be brave.

It hadn't been bad during the afternoon. Sister Eustacia had been very kind, taking her and a couple of other new postulants round the walled estate, showing them the big

297

gardens where the convent grew medicinal herbs and fruit and vegetables for the table, the chapel where devotions were held six times a day, plus Mass in the mornings, the stables and kitchens, where they would take turns working – and the great Hôpital des Anges, the order's main work. They had only seen the Hôpital from the outside, though; they would see the inside tomorrow, when Sister Marie-Amadeus would explain their duties.

It was strange, of course – she still understood only half what people said to her, and was sure from the looks on their faces that they understood much less of what she tried to say to *them* – but wonderful. She loved the idea of spiritual discipline, the hours of devotion, with the sense of peace and unity that came upon the Sisters as they chanted and prayed together. Loved the simple beauty of the chapel, amazing in its clean elegance, the solid lines of granite and the grace of carved wood, a faint smell of incense in the air, like the breath of angels.

The postulants prayed with the others, but did not yet sing. They would be trained in music, though, such excitement! Mother Hildegarde had been a famous musician in her youth, it was rumoured, and considered it one of the most important forms of devotion.

The thought of the new things she'd seen, and the new things to come, distracted her mind – a little – from thoughts of her mother's voice, the wind off the moors . . . She shoved these hastily away, and reached for her new rosary, this a substantial thing with smooth wooden beads, lovely and comforting in the fingers.

Above all, there was peace. She hadn't heard a word from the voices, hadn't seen anything peculiar or alarming. She wasn't foolish enough to think she'd escaped her dangerous gift, but at least there might be help at hand if – when – it came back.

And at least she already knew enough Latin to say her

rosary properly; Da had taught her the proper words. *'Ave, Maria,'* she whispered, *'gratia plena, Dominus tecum,'* and closed her eyes, the sobs of the homesick fading in her ears as the beads moved slow and silent through her fingers.

The Next Day

Michael Murray stood in the aisle of the ageing-shed, feeling puny and unreal. He'd waked with a terrible headache, the result of having drunk a great deal of mixed spirits on an empty stomach, and while the headache had receded to a dull throb at the back of his skull, it had left him feeling trampled and left for dead.

His cousin Jared, owner of Fraser et Cie, looked at him with the cold eye of long experience, shook his head and sighed deeply, but said nothing, merely taking the list from his nerveless fingers and beginning the count on his own.

He wished Jared had rebuked him. Everyone still tip toed round him, careful of him. And like a wet dressing on a wound, their care kept the wound of Lillie's loss open and weeping. The sight of Léonie didn't help, either – so much like Lillie to look at, so different in character. She said they must help and comfort one another, and to that end, came to visit every other day, or so it seemed. He really wished she would . . . just go away, though the thought shamed him.

'How's the wee nun, then?' Jared's voice, dry and matter-of-fact as always, drew him out of his bruised and soggy thoughts. 'Give her a good send-off to the convent?'

'Aye. Well – aye. More or less.' Michael mustered up a feeble smile. He didn't really want to think about Sister Joan-Gregory this morning, either.

'What did ye give her?' Jared handed the check-list to Humberto, the Italian shed-master, and looked Michael

299

over appraisingly. 'I hope it wasna the new Rioja that did that to ye.'

'Ah . . . no.' Michael struggled to focus his attention. The heady atmosphere of the shed, thick with the fruity exhalations of the resting casks, was making him dizzy. 'It was Moselle. Mostly. Jerez sherry. And a bit of rum punch.'

'Oh, I see.' Jared's ancient mouth quirked up on one side. 'Did I never tell ye not to mix wine wi' rum?'

'Not above two hundred times, no.' Jared was moving, and Michael followed him perforce down the narrow aisle, the casks in their serried ranks rising high above on either side.

'Rum's a demon. But whisky's a virtuous dram,' Jared said, pausing by a rack of small, blackened casks. 'So long as it's a good make, it'll never turn on ye. Speakin' of which . . .' He tapped the end of one cask, which gave off the resonant deep *thongk* of a full barrel, 'what's this? It came up from the docks this morning.'

'Oh, aye.' Michael stifled a belch, and smiled painfully. 'That, cousin, is the Ian Alastair Robert MacLeod Murray Memorial *uisge-baugh*. My da and Uncle Jamie made it during the winter. They thought ye might like a wee cask for your personal use.'

Jared's brows rose and he gave Michael a swift sideways glance. Then he turned back to examine the cask, bending close to sniff at the seam between the lid and staves.

'I've tasted it,' Michael assured him. 'I dinna think it will poison ye. But ye should maybe let it age a few years.'

Jared made a rude noise in his throat, and his hand curved gently over the swell of the staves. He stood thus for a moment as though in benediction, then turned suddenly and took Michael into his arms. His own breathing was hoarse, congested with sorrow. He was years older than Da and Uncle Jamie, but had known the two of them all their lives.

'I'm sorry for your faither, lad,' he said, after a moment, and let go, patting Michael on the shoulder. He looked at the cask and sniffed deeply. 'I can tell it will be fine.' He paused, breathing slowly, then nodded once, as though making up his mind to something.

'I've a thing in mind, *a charaid.* I'd been thinking, since ye went to Scotland – and now that we've a kinswoman in the church, so to speak . . . come back to the office with me, and I'll tell ye.'

It was chilly in the street, the leaning buildings shutting out the sun, but the goldsmith's back room was cosy as a womb, with a porcelain stove throbbing with heat and woven wool hangings on the walls. Rakoczy hastily unwound the comforter about his neck; it didn't do to sweat indoors; the sweat chilled the instant one went out again, and next thing you knew, it would be *la grippe* at the best, pleurisy or pneumonia at the worst.

Rosenwald himself was comfortable in shirt and waistcoat, without even a wig, only a plum-coloured turban to keep his polled scalp warm. The goldsmith's stubby fingers traced the curves of the octafoil salver, turned it over – and stopped dead. Rakoczy felt a tingle of warning at the base of his spine, and deliberately relaxed himself, affecting a nonchalant self-confidence.

'Where did you get this, monsieur, if I may ask?' Rosenwald looked up at him, but there was no accusation in the goldsmith's aged face – only a wary excitement.

'It was an inheritance,' Rakoczy said, glowing with earnest innocence. 'An elderly aunt left it – and a few

301

other pieces – to me. Is it worth anything more than the value of the silver?'

The goldsmith opened his mouth, then shut it, glancing at Rakoczy. Was he honest? Rakoczy wondered with interest. *He's already told me it's something special. Will he tell me why, in hopes of getting other pieces? Or lie, to get this one cheap?* Rosenwald had a good reputation, but he was a Jew.

'Paul de Lamerie,' Rosenwald said reverently, his index finger tracing the hallmark. 'This was made by Paul de Lamerie.'

A shock ran up Rakoczy's backbone. *Merde!* He'd brought the wrong one!

'Really?' he said, striving for simple curiosity. 'Does that mean something?'

It means I'm a fool, he thought, and wondered whether to snatch the thing back and leave instantly. The goldsmith had carried it away, though, to look at it more closely under the lamp.

'De Lamerie was one of the very best goldsmiths ever to work in London – perhaps in the world,' Rosenwald said, half to himself.

'Indeed,' Rakoczy said politely. He was sweating freely. *Nom d'un chameau!* Wait, though – Rosenwald had said 'was'. De Lamerie was dead, then, thank God. Perhaps the Duke of Sandringham, from whom he'd stolen the salver, was dead, too? He began to breathe more easily.

He never sold anything identifiable within a hundred years of his acquisition of it; that was his principle. He'd taken the other salver from a rich merchant in a game of cards in the Low Countries in 1630; he'd stolen this one in 1745 – much too close for comfort. Still . . .

His thoughts were interrupted by the chime of the silver bell over the door, and he turned to see a young man come in, removing his hat to reveal a startling head of dark red

302

hair. He was dressed *à la mode*, and addressed the goldsmith in perfect Parisian French, but he didn't look French. A long-nosed face with faintly slanted eyes. There was a slight sense of familiarity about that face, yet Rakoczy was sure he'd never seen this man before.

'Please, sir, go on with your business,' the young man said with a courteous bow. 'I meant no interruption.'

'No, no,' Rakoczy said, stepping forward. He motioned the young man toward the counter. 'Please, go ahead. Monsieur Rosenwald and I are merely discussing the value of this object. It will take some thought.' He snaked out an arm and seized the salver, feeling a little better with it clasped to his bosom. He wasn't sure; if he decided it was too risky to sell, he could slink out quietly while Rosenwald was busy with the red-headed young man.

The Jew looked surprised, but after a moment's hesitation, nodded and turned to the young man, who introduced himself as one Michael Murray, partner in Fraser et Cie, the wine merchants.

'I believe you are acquainted with my cousin, Jared Fraser?'

Rosenwald's round face lit up at once.

'Oh, to be sure, sir! A man of the most exquisite taste and discrimination. I made him a wine-cistern with a motif of butterflies and carnations, not a year past!'

'I know.' The young man smiled, a smile that creased his cheeks and narrowed his eyes, and that small bell of recognition rang again. But the name held no familiarity to Rakoczy – only the face, and that only vaguely.

'My uncle has another commission for you, if it's agreeable?'

'I never say no to honest work, monsieur.' From the pleasure apparent on the goldsmith's rubicund face, honest work that paid very well was even more welcome.

'Well, then – if I may?' The young man pulled a folded

303

paper from his pocket, but half-turned toward Rakoczy, eyebrow cocked in inquiry. Rakoczy motioned him to go on, and turned himself to examine a music-box that stood on the counter – an enormous thing the size of a cow's head, crowned with a nearly naked nymph, festooned with the airiest of gold draperies and dancing on mushrooms and flowers, in company with a large frog.

'A chalice,' Murray was saying, the paper laid flat on the counter. From the corner of his eye, Rakoczy could see that it held a list of names. 'It's a presentation to the chapel of des Anges, to be given in memory of my late father. A young cousin of mine has just entered the convent there as a postulant,' he explained. 'So Monsieur Fraser thought that the best place.'

'An excellent choice.' Rosenwald picked up the list. 'And you wish all of these names inscribed?'

'Yes, if you can.'

'Monsieur!' Rosenwald waved a hand, professionally insulted. 'These are your father's children?'

'Yes, these at the bottom.' Murray bent over the counter, his finger tracing the lines, speaking the outlandish names carefully. 'At the top, these are my parents' names: Ian Alastair Robert MacLeod Murray, and Janet Flora Arabella Fraser Murray. Now, also, I – we, I mean – we want these two names as well: James Alexander Malcolm MacKenzie Fraser, and Claire Elizabeth Beauchamp Fraser. Those are my uncle and aunt; my uncle was very close to my father,' he explained. 'Almost a brother.'

He went on saying something else, but Rakoczy wasn't listening. He grasped the edge of the counter, vision flickering so that the nymph seemed to leer at him.

Claire Fraser. That had been the woman's name, and her husband, James, a Highland Lord from Scotland. That was who the young man resembled, though he was not so

304

imposing as . . . but La Dame Blanche! It was her, it had to be.

And in the next instant, the goldsmith confirmed this, straightening up from the list with an abrupt air of wariness, as though one of the names might spring off the paper and bite him.

'That name – your aunt, you say? Did she and your uncle live in Paris at one time?'

'Yes,' Murray said, looking mildly surprised. 'Maybe thirty years ago – only for a short time, though. Did you know her?'

'Ah. Not to say I was personally acquainted,' Rosenwald said, with a crooked smile. 'But she was . . . known. People called her La Dame Blanche.'

Murray blinked, clearly surprised to hear this.

'Really?' He looked rather appalled.

'Yes, but it was all a long time ago,' Rosenwald said hastily, clearly thinking he'd said too much. He waved a hand toward his back room. 'If you'll give me a moment, monsieur, I have a chalice actually here, if you would care to see it – and a paten, too; we might make some accommodation of price, if you take both. They were made for a patron who died suddenly, before the chalice was finished, so there is almost no decoration – plenty of room for the names to be applied, and perhaps we might put the, um, aunt and uncle on the paten?'

Murray nodded, interested, and at Rosenwald's gesture, went round the counter and followed the old man into his back room. Rakoczy put the octafoil salver under his arm and left, as quietly as possible, head buzzing with questions.

305

Jared eyed Michael over the dinner table, shook his head and bent to his plate.

'I'm not drunk!' Michael blurted, then bent his own head, face flaming. He could feel Jared's eyes boring into the top of his head.

'Not now, ye're not.' Jared's voice wasn't accusing. In fact, it was quiet, almost kindly. 'But ye have been. Ye've not touched your dinner, and ye're the colour of rotten wax.'

'I—' The words caught in his throat, just as the food had. Eels in garlic sauce. The smell wafted up from the dish, and he stood up suddenly, lest he either vomit or burst into tears.

'I've nay appetite, cousin,' he managed to say, before turning away. 'Excuse me.'

He would have left, but he hesitated that moment too long, not wanting to go up to the room where Lillie no longer was, but not wanting to look petulant by rushing out into the street. Jared rose and came round to him with a decided step.

'I'm nay verra hungry myself, *a charaid*,' Jared said, taking him by the arm. 'Come sit wi' me for a bit and take a dram. It'll settle your wame.'

He didn't much want to, but there was nothing else he could think of doing, and within a few moments, he found himself in front of a fragrant applewood fire, with a glass of his father's whisky in hand, the warmth of both easing the tightness of chest and throat. It wouldn't cure his grief, he knew, but it made it possible to breathe.

'Good stuff,' Jared said, sniffing cautiously, but approvingly. 'Even raw as it is. It'll be wonderful, aged a few years.'

'Aye. Uncle Jamie kens what he's about; he said he'd made whisky a good many times, in America.'

Jared chuckled.

'Your uncle Jamie usually kens what he's about,' he said. 'Not that knowing it keeps him out o' trouble.' He shifted, making himself more comfortable in his worn leather chair. 'Had it not been for the Rising, he'd likely have stayed here wi' me. Aye, well . . .' The old man sighed with regret and lifted his glass, examining the spirit. It was still nearly as pale as water – it hadn't been casked above a few months – but had the slightly viscous look of a fine strong spirit, like it might climb out of the glass if you took your eye off it.

'And if he had, I suppose I'd not be here myself,' Michael said dryly.

Jared glanced at him, surprised.

'Och! I didna mean to say ye were but a poor substitute for Jamie, lad.' He smiled crookedly, and his hooded eyes grew moist. 'Not at all. Ye've been the best thing ever to come to me. You and dear wee Lillie, and . . .' He cleared his throat. 'I . . . well, I canna say anything that will help, I ken that. But . . . it won't always be like this.'

'Won't it?' Michael said bleakly. 'Aye, I'll take your word for it.' A silence fell between them, broken only by the hissing and snap of the fire. The mention of Lillie was like an awl digging into his breastbone, and he took a deeper sip of the whisky to quell the ache. Maybe Jared was right to mention the drink to him. It helped, but not enough. And the help didn't last. He was tired of waking to grief and headache both.

Shying away from thoughts of Lillie, his mind fastened on Uncle Jamie instead. He'd lost his wife, too, and from what Michael had seen of the aftermath, it had torn his soul in two. Then she'd come back to him by some miracle, and he was a man transformed. But in between . . . he'd managed. He'd found a way to be.

Thinking of Auntie Claire gave him a slight feeling of comfort – as long as he didn't think too much about what she'd told the family . . . Who – or what – she was, and where she'd been while she was gone those twenty years. The brothers and sisters had talked among themselves about it afterward; Young Jamie and Kitty didn't believe a word of it, Maggie and Janet weren't sure – but Young Ian believed it, and that counted for a lot with Michael. And she'd looked at him – right at him – when she said what was going to happen in Paris.

He felt the same small thrill of horror now, remembering. *The Terror. That's what it will be called, and that's what it will be. People will be arrested for no cause and beheaded in the Place de la Concorde. The streets will run with blood, and no one – no one – will be safe.*

He looked at his cousin; Jared was an old man, though still hale enough. He knew there was no way he could persuade Jared to leave Paris and his wine business. But it would be some time yet – if Auntie Claire was right. No need to think about it now. But she'd seemed so sure, like a seer, talking from a vantage point after everything had happened, from a safer time.

And yet she'd come back from that safe time, to be with Uncle Jamie again.

For a moment, he entertained the wild fantasy that Lillie wasn't dead, but only swept away by the faeries into a distant time. He couldn't see or touch her, but the knowledge that she was doing things, was alive . . . maybe it was knowing that, thinking that, that had kept Uncle Jamie whole. He swallowed, hard.

'Jared,' he said, clearing his own throat. 'What did ye think of Auntie Claire? When she lived here?'

Jared looked surprised, but lowered his glass to his knee, pursing his lips in thought.

'She was a bonny lass, I'll tell ye that,' he said. 'Verra bonny. A tongue like the rough side of a rasp, if she took against something, though – and decided opinions.' He nodded, twice, as though recalling a few, and grinned suddenly. 'Verra decided indeed!'

'Aye? The goldsmith – Rosenwald, ye ken? – mentioned her, when I went to commission the chalice and he saw her name on the list. He called her La Dame Blanche.' This last was not phrased as a question, but he gave it a slight rising inflection, and Jared nodded, his smile widening into a grin.

'Oh, aye, I mind that! 'Twas Jamie's notion. She'd find herself now and then in dangerous places without him – ken how some folk are just the sort as things happen to – so he put it about that she was La Dame Blanche. Ken what a White Lady is, do ye?'

Michael crossed himself, and Jared followed suit, nodding.

'Aye, just so. Make any wicked sod with villainy in mind think twice. A White Lady can strike ye blind or shrivel a man's balls, and likely a few more things than that, should she take the notion. And I'd be the last to say that Claire Fraser couldn't, if she'd a mind to.'

Jared raised the glass absently to his lips, took a bigger sip of the raw spirit than he'd meant to and coughed, spraying droplets of memorial whisky halfway across the room. Rather to his own shock, Michael laughed.

Jared wiped his mouth, still coughing, but then sat up straight and lifted his glass, which still held a few drops.

'To your da. *Sláinte mhath!*'

'*Sláinte mhath!*' Michael echoed, and drained what remained in his own glass. He set it down with finality, and rose. He'd drink nay more tonight.

'*Oidche mhath, a charaid.*'

'Goodnight, lad,' said Jared. The fire was burning low, but still cast a warm ruddy glow on the old man's face. 'Fare ye well.'

The Next Night

Michael dropped his key several times before finally managing to turn it in the old-fashioned lock. It wasn't drink; he'd not had a drop since the wine at supper. Instead, he'd walked the length of the Ile de Paris and back, accompanied only by his thoughts; his whole body quivered and he felt mindless with exhaustion, but he was sure he would sleep. Jean-Baptiste had left the door unbarred, according to his orders, but one of the footmen was sprawled on a settle in the entryway, snoring. He smiled a little, though it was an effort to raise the corners of his mouth.

'Bolt the door and go to bed, Paul,' he whispered, bending and shaking the man gently by the shoulder. The footman stirred and snorted, but Michael didn't wait to see whether he woke entirely. There was a tiny oil-lamp burning on the landing of the stairs, a little round glass globe in the gaudy colours of Murano. It had been there since the first day he came from Scotland to stay with Jared, years before, and the sight of it soothed him and drew his aching body up the wide, dark stair.

The house creaked and talked to itself at night; all old houses did. Tonight, though, it was silent, the big copper-seamed roof gone cold and its massive timbers settled into somnolence.

He flung off his clothes and crawled naked into bed, head spinning. Tired as he was, his flesh quivered and twitched, his legs jerking like a spitted frog's, before he finally relaxed enough to fall headfirst into the seething cauldron of dreams that awaited him.

She was there, of course. Laughing at him, playing with her ridiculous pug. Running a hand filled with desire across his face, down his neck, easing her body close, and closer. Then they were somehow in bed, with the wind blowing cool through gauzy curtains, too cool, he felt cold,

310

but then her warmth came close, pressed against him. He felt a terrible desire, but at the same time feared her. She felt utterly familiar, utterly strange – and the mixture thrilled him.

He reached for her, and realised that he couldn't raise his arms, couldn't move. And yet she was against him, writhing in a slow squirm of need, greedy and tantalising. In the way of dreams, he was at the same time in front of her, behind her, touching, and seeing from a distance. Candle-glow on naked breasts, the shadowed weight of solid buttocks, falling drapes of parting white, one round, firm leg protruding, a pointed toe rooting gently between his legs. Urgency.

She was curled behind him then, kissing the back of his neck, and he reached back, groping, but his hands were heavy, drifting; they slid helpless over her. Hers on him were firm, more than firm; she had him by the cock, was working him. Working him hard, fast and hard. He bucked and heaved, suddenly released from the dream-swamp of immobility. She loosed her grip, tried to pull away, but he folded his hand round hers and rubbed their folded hands hard up and down with joyous ferocity, spilling himself convulsively, hot wet spurts against his belly, running thick over their clenched knuckles.

She made a sound of horrified disgust and his eyes flew open. A pair of huge, bugging eyes stared into his, over a gargoyle's mouth full of tiny, sharp teeth. He shrieked.

Plonplon leaped off the bed and ran to and fro, barking hysterically. There was a body behind him in bed. Michael flung himself off the bed, tangled in a winding-sheet of damp, sticky bedclothes, fell and rolled in panic.

'Jesus, Jesus, Jesus!'

On his knees, he gaped, shook his head. Could *not* make sense of it, couldn't.

'Lillie,' he gasped. 'Lillie!'

But the woman in his bed, tears running down her face, wasn't Lillie; he realised it with a wrench that made him groan, doubling up in the desolation of fresh loss.

'Oh, Jesus!'

'Michel, Michel, please, please forgive me!'

'You . . . what . . . for God's *sake* . . . !' Belatedly, he seized a sheet and hastily wiped himself.

Léonie was weeping frantically, reaching out toward him.

'I couldn't help it. I'm so lonely, I wanted you so much!'

Plonplon had ceased barking and now came up behind Michael, nosing his bare backside with a blast of hot, moist breath.

'*Va-t'en!*'

The pug backed up and started barking again, eyes bulging with offence.

Unable to find any words suitable to the situation, he grabbed the dog and muffled it with a handful of sheet. He got unsteadily to his feet, still holding the squirming pug.

'I—' he began. 'You— I mean . . . oh, Jesus Christ!' He leaned over and put the dog carefully on the bed. Plonplon instantly wriggled free of the sheet and rushed to Léonie, licking her solicitously. Michael had thought of giving her the dog after Lillie's death, but for some reason this had seemed a betrayal of the pug's former mistress, and brought Michael near to weeping.

'I can't,' he said simply. 'I just can't. You go to sleep now, lass. We'll talk about it later, aye?'

He went out, walking carefully, as though very drunk, and closed the door gently behind him. He got halfway down the main stair before realising he was naked. He just stood there, his mind blank, watching the colours of the Murano lamp fade as the daylight grew outside, until Paul saw him and ran up to wrap him in a cloak and lead him off to a bed in the guest rooms.

❦

Rakoczy's favourite gaming club was the Golden Cockerel, and the wall in the main salon was covered by a tapestry featuring one of these creatures, worked in gold thread, wings spread and throat swollen as it crowed in triumph at the winning hand of cards laid out before it. It was a cheerful place, catering to a mix of wealthy merchants and lesser nobility, and the air was spicy with the scents of candlewax, powder, perfume, and money.

He'd thought of going to the offices of Fraser et Cie, making some excuse to speak to Michael Murray, and manoeuvre his way into an inquiry about the whereabouts of the young man's aunt. Upon consideration, though, he thought such a move might make Murray wary – and possibly lead to word getting back to the woman, if she was somewhere in Paris. That was the last thing he wanted to happen.

Better, perhaps, to instigate his inquiries from a more discreet distance. He'd learned that Murray occasionally came to the Cockerel, though he himself had never seen him there. But if he was known . . .

It took several evenings of play, wine, and conversation, before he found Charles Pépin. Pépin was a popinjay, a reckless gambler, and a man who liked to talk. And to drink. He was also a good friend of the young wine merchant's.

'Oh, the nun!' he said, when Rakoczy had – after the second bottle – mentioned having heard that Murray had a young relative who had recently entered the convent. Pépin laughed, his handsome face flushed.

'A less likely nun I've never seen – an arse that would

313

make the Archbishop of Paris forget his vows, and he's eighty-six if he's a day. Doesn't speak any sort of French, poor thing – the girl, not the Archbishop. Not that I for one would be wanting to carry on a lot of conversation if I had her to myself, you understand . . . she's Scotch, terrible accent . . .'

'Scotch, you say.' Rakoczy held a card consideringly, then put it down. 'She is Murray's cousin – would she perhaps be the daughter of his uncle James?'

Pépin looked blank for a moment.

'I don't really— oh, yes, I do know!' He laughed heartily, and laid down his own losing hand. 'Dear me. Yes, she did say her father's name was Jay-mee, the way the Scotches do; that must be James.'

Rakoczy felt a ripple of anticipation go up his spine. *Yes!* This sense of triumph was instantly succeeded by a breathless realisation. The girl was the daughter of La Dame Blanche.

'I see,' he said casually. 'And which convent did you say the girl has gone to?'

To his surprise, Pépin gave him a suddenly sharp look.

'Why do you want to know?'

Rakoczy shrugged, thinking fast.

'A wager,' he said, with a grin. 'If she is as luscious as you say . . . I'll bet you five hundred louis that I can get her into bed before she takes her first vows.'

Pépin scoffed.

'Oh, never! She's tasty, but she doesn't know it. And she's virtuous, I'd swear it. And if you think you can seduce her inside the convent . . . !'

Rakoczy lounged back in his chair, and motioned for another bottle.

'In that case . . . what do you have to lose?'

314

The Next Day

Joan could smell the Hôpital, long before the small group of new postulants reached the door. They walked two by two, practising custody of the eyes – that meant looking where you were told to and not gawking about like a chicken – but she couldn't help a quick glance upward at the building, a three-storey chateau, originally a noble house that had – rumour said – been given to Mother Hildegarde by her father, as part of her dowry when she joined the church. It had become a convent house, and then gradually been given over more and more to the care of the sick, the nuns moving to the new chateau built in the park.

It was a lovely old house – on the outside. The odour of sickness, of urine and shit and vomit, hung about it like a cloying veil, though, and she hoped she wouldn't vomit, too. The little postulant next to her, Sister Miséricorde de Dieu (known to all simply as Mercy), was as white as her veil, eyes fixed on the ground, but obviously not seeing it, as she stepped smack on a slug and gave a small cry of horror as it squished under her sandal.

Joan looked hastily away; she would never master custody of the eyes, she was sure. Nor yet custody of thought.

It wasn't the notion of sick people that troubled her. She'd seen sick people before, and they wouldn't be expecting her to do more than wash and feed them; she could manage that easily. It was fear of seeing those who were about to die – for surely there would be a great many of those in a hospital. And what might the voices tell her about *them*?

As it was, the voices had nothing to say. Not a word, and after a little, she began to lose her nervousness. She *could*

315

do this, and in fact – to her surprise – quite enjoyed the sense of competence, the gratification of being able to ease someone's pain, give them at least a little attention – and if her French made them laugh (and it did), that at least took their minds off of pain and fear for a moment.

There were those who lay under the veil of death. Only a few, though, and it seemed somehow much less shocking here than when she had seen it on Vhairi's lad or the young man on the ship. Maybe it was resignation, perhaps the influence of the angels for whom the Hôpital was named . . . Joan didn't know, but she found that she wasn't afraid to speak to or touch the ones she knew were going to die. For that matter, she observed that the other sisters, even the orderlies, behaved gently toward these people, and it occurred to her that no particular Sight was needed to know that the man with the wasting sickness, whose bones poked through his skin, was not long for this world.

Touch him, said a soft voice inside her head. *Comfort him*.

'All right,' she said, taking a deep breath. She had no idea how to comfort anyone, but bathed him, as gently as she could, and coaxed him to take a few spoonfuls of porridge. Then she settled him in his bed, straightening his nightshirt and the thin blanket over him.

'Thank you, Sister,' he said, and taking her hand, kissed it. 'Thank you for your sweet touch.'

She went back to the postulants' dormitory that evening feeling thoughtful, but with a strange sense of being on the verge of discovering something important.

That Night

Rakoczy lay with his head on Madeleine's bosom, eyes closed, breathing the scent of her body, feeling the whole of her between his palms, a slowly pulsing entity of light.

She was a gentle gold, traced with veins of incandescent blue, her heart deep as lapis beneath his ear, a living stone. And deep inside, her warm red womb, open, soft. Refuge and succour. Promise.

Mélisande had shown him the rudiments of sexual magic, and he'd read about it with great interest in some of the older alchemical texts. He'd never tried it with a whore, though – and in fact, hadn't been trying to do it this time. And yet it had happened. Was happening. He could see the miracle unfolding slowly before him, under his hands.

How odd, he thought dreamily, watching the tiny traces of green energy spread upward through her womb, slowly but inexorably. He'd thought it happened instantly, that a man's seed found its root in the woman and there you were. But that wasn't what was happening, at all.

There were *two* types of seed, he now saw. She had one; he felt it plainly, a brilliant speck of light, glowing like a fierce, tiny sun. His own – the tiny green animalculae – were being drawn toward it, bent on immolation.

'Happy, *Chéri*?' she whispered, stroking his hair. 'Did you have a good time?'

'Most happy, sweetheart.' He wished she wouldn't talk, but an unexpected sense of tenderness toward her made him sit up and smile at her. She also began to sit up, reaching for the clean rag and douching syringe, and he put a hand on her shoulder, urging her to lie back down.

'Don't douche this time, *ma belle*,' he said. 'A favour to me.'

'But—' She was confused; usually he was insistent upon cleanliness. 'Do you *want* me to get with child?' For he had stopped her using the wine-soaked sponge before-hand, too.

'Yes, of course,' he said, surprised. 'Did Madame Fabienne not tell you?'

317

Her mouth dropped open.

'She did *not*. What— why, for God's sake?' In agitation, she squirmed free of his restraining hand and swung her legs out of bed, reaching for her wrapper. 'You aren't – what do you mean to do with it?'

'Do with it?' he said, blinking. 'What do you mean, "Do with it"?'

She had the wrapper on, pulled crookedly round her shoulders, and had backed up against the wall, hands plastered against her stomach, regarding him with open fear.

'You're a *magicien*, everyone knows that. You take newborn children and use their blood in your spells!'

'What?' he said, rather stupidly. He reached for his breeches, but changed his mind. He got up and went to her instead, putting his hands on her shoulders.

'No,' he said, bending down to look her in the eye. 'No, I do no such thing. Never.' He used all the force of sincerity he could summon, pushing it into her, and felt her waver a little, still fearful, but less certain. He smiled at her.

'Who told you I was a *magicien*, for heaven's sake? I am a *philosophe*, *Chérie* – an inquirer into the mysteries of nature, no more. And I can swear to you, by my hope of Heaven—' this being more or less nonexistent, but why quibble? '—that I have never, not once, used anything more than the water of a man-child in any of my investigations.'

'What, little boys' piss?' she said, diverted. He let his hands relax, but kept them on her shoulders.

'Certainly. It's the purest water one can find. Collecting it is something of a chore, mind you.' She smiled at that; good. 'But the process does not the slightest harm to the infant, who will eject the water whether anyone has a use for it or not.'

318

'Oh.' She was beginning to relax a little, but her hands were still pressed protectively over her belly, as though she felt the imminent child already. *Not yet*, he thought, pulling her against him and feeling his way gently into her body. *But soon!* He wondered if he should remain with her until it happened; the idea of feeling it as it happened inside her – to be an intimate witness to the creation of life itself! – but there was no telling how long it might take. From the progress of his animalculae, it could be a day, even two.

Magic, indeed.

Why do men never think of that? he wondered. Most men – himself included – regarded the engendering of babies as necessity, in the case of inheritance, or nuisance – but *this* . . . But then, most men would never know what he now knew, or see what he had seen.

He had only once before felt this sense of closeness to a woman. That was Amelie, lost these many years . . . He felt a sudden thump as his heart skipped a beat. Had she been with child? Was that the reason he had felt so? But there was nothing to be done about it now.

Madeleine had begun to relax against him, her hands at last leaving her belly. He kissed her, with a real feeling of affection.

'It will be beautiful,' he whispered to her. 'And once you are well and truly with child, I will buy your contract from Fabienne and take you away. I will buy you a house.'

'A *house*?' Her eyes went round. They were green, a deep, clear emerald, and he smiled at her again, stepping back.

'Of course. Now, go and sleep, my dear. I shall come again tomorrow.'

She flung her arms around him, and he had some difficulty in extracting himself, laughing, from her embraces. Normally, he left a whore's bed with no feeling save physical relief. But what he had done had made a connection with Madeleine that he had not experienced with any woman save Amelie. Well . . . and Mélisande, too, now that he thought . . .

Mélisande. A sudden thought ran through him like the spark from a Leyden jar. *Mélisande*.

He looked hard at Madeleine, now crawling happily naked and white-rumped into bed, her wrapper thrown aside. That bottom . . . the eyes, the soft blonde hair, the gold-white of fresh cream.

'*Chérie*,' he said, as casually as he might, pulling on his breeches, 'how old are you?'

'Eighteen,' she said, without hesitation. 'Why, monsieur?'

'Ah. A wonderful age to become a mother.' He pulled the shirt over his head and kissed his hand to her, relieved. He had known Mélisande Robicheaux in 1744. He had not, in fact, just committed incest with his own daughter.

It was only as he passed Madame Fabienne's parlour on his way out that it occurred to him that Madeleine *might* possibly still be his granddaughter. That thought stopped him short, but he had no time to dwell on it, for Fabienne appeared in the doorway and motioned to him.

'A message, monsieur,' she said, and something in her voice touched his nape with a cold finger.

'Yes?'

'Monsieur Grenouille begs the favour of your company, at midnight tomorrow. In the square before Notre Dame de Paris.'

They didn't have to practise custody of the eyes in the market. In fact, Sister George-Mary, the stout nun who oversaw these expeditions, warned them in no uncertain

320

terms to keep a sharp eye out for short weight and uncivil prices, to say nothing of pickpockets.

'Pickpockets, Sister?' Mercy had said, her blonde eyebrows all but vanishing into her veil. 'But we are nuns – more or less,' she added hastily. 'We have nothing to steal!'

Sister George's big red face got somewhat redder, but she kept her patience.

'Normally, that would be true,' she agreed. 'But we – or I, rather – have the money with which to buy our food, and once we've bought it, you will be carrying it. A pickpocket steals to eat, *n'est-ce pas*? They don't care whether you have money or food, and most of them are so depraved that they would willingly steal from God himself, let alone a couple of chick-headed postulants.'

For Joan's part, she wanted to see *everything*, pickpockets included. To her delight, the market was the one she'd passed with Michael, on her first day in Paris. True, the sight of it brought back the horrors and doubts of that first day, too – but for the moment, she pushed those aside and followed Sister George into the fascinating maelstrom of colour, smells, and shouting.

Filing away a particularly entertaining expression that she planned to make Sister Philomène explain to her – Sister Philomène was a little older than Joan, but painfully shy and with such delicate skin that she blushed like an apple at the least excuse – she followed Sister George and Sister Mathilde through the fishmongers' section, where Sister George bargained shrewdly for a great quantity of sand dabs, scallops, tiny grey translucent shrimp, and an enormous sea-salmon, the pale spring light shifting through its scales in colours that faded so subtly from pink to blue to silver and back that some of them had no name at all – so beautiful even in its death that it made Joan catch her breath with joy at the wonder of creation.

'Oh, *bouillabaisse* tonight!' said Mercy, under her breath. '*Délicieuse!*'

'What is *bouillabaisse*?' Joan whispered back.

'Fish stew – you'll like it, I promise!' Joan had no doubt of it; brought up in the Highlands during the poverty-stricken years following the Rising, she'd been staggered by the novelty, deliciousness and sheer abundance of the convent's food. Even on Fridays, when the community fasted during the day, supper was simple but mouthwatering, toasted sharp cheese on nutty brown bread with sliced apples.

Luckily, the salmon was so huge that Sister George arranged for the fish-seller to deliver it to the convent, along with the other briny purchases, and so they had room in their baskets for fresh vegetables and fruit, and so passed from Neptune's realm to that of Demeter. Joan hoped it wasn't sacrilegious to think of Greek gods, but she couldn't forget the book of myths that Da had read to her and Marsali when they were young, with wonderful hand-coloured illustrations.

After all, she told herself, you needed to know about the Greeks, if you studied medicine. She had some trepidation still at the thought of working in the hospital, but God called people to do things, and if it was His will, then—

The thought stopped short as she caught sight of a neat dark tricorne with a curled blue feather, bobbing slowly through the tide of people. Was it— it was! Léonie, the sister of Michael Murray's dead wife. Moved by curiosity, Joan glanced at Sister George, who was engrossed in a huge display of fungus – dear God, people *ate* such things? – and slipped round a barrow billowing with green sallet herbs.

She'd meant to speak to Léonie, ask her to tell Michael that she needed to talk to him. Postulants were permitted to write letters to their families only twice a year, at Christmas and Easter, but he could send a note to her mother, reassuring her that Joan was well and happy.

Surely Michael could contrive a way to visit the convent . . . but before she could get close enough, Léonie looked furtively over her shoulder, as though fearing discovery, then ducked behind a curtain that hung across the back of a small caravan.

Joan had seen gypsies before, though not often. A dark-skinned man loitered nearby, talking with a group of others; their eyes passed over her habit without pausing, and she sighed with relief. Being a nun was as good as having a cloak of invisibility in most circumstances, she thought.

She looked round for her companions, and saw that Sister Mathilde had been called into consultation regarding a big warty lump of something that looked like the excrement of a seriously diseased hog. Good, she could wait for a minute longer.

In fact, it took very little more than that, before Léonie slipped out from behind the curtain, tucking something into the small basket on her arm. For the first time, it struck Joan as unusual that someone like Léonie should be shopping without a servant to push back crowds and carry purchases – or even to be in a public market. Michael had told her about his own household during the voyage – how Madame Hortense, the cook, went to the markets at dawn, to be sure of getting the freshest things. What would a lady like Léonie be buying, alone?

Joan slithered as best she could through the rows of stalls and wagons, following the bobbing blue feather. A sudden stop allowed her to come up behind Léonie, who had paused by a flower stall, fingering a bunch of white roses.

It occurred suddenly to Joan that she had no idea what

Léonie's last name was, but she couldn't worry about politeness now.

'Ah . . . madame?' she said tentatively. 'Mademoiselle, I mean?' Léonie swung round, eyes huge and face pale. Finding herself faced with a nun, she blinked, confused.

'Er . . . it's me,' Joan said, diffident, resisting the impulse to pull off her veil. 'Joan MacKimmie?' It felt odd to say it, as though 'Joan MacKimmie' was truly someone else. It took a moment for the name to register, but then Léonie's shoulders relaxed a little.

'Oh.' She put a hand to her bosom, and mustered a small smile. 'Michael's cousin. Of course. I didn't . . . er . . . how nice to see you!' A small frown wrinkled the skin between her brows. 'Are you . . . alone?'

'No,' Joan said hurriedly. 'And I mustn't stop. I only saw you, and I wanted to ask—' It seemed even stupider than it had a moment ago, but no help for it. 'Would you tell Monsieur Murray that I must talk to him? I have something – something important – that I have to tell him.'

'*Soeur Gregory?*' Sister George's stentorian tones boomed through the higher-pitched racket of the market, making Joan jump. She could see the top of Sister Mathilde's head, with its great white sails, turning to and fro in vain search.

'I have to go,' she said to the astonished Léonie. 'Please. Please tell him!' Her heart was pounding, and not only from the sudden meeting. She'd been looking at Léonie's basket, where she caught the glint of a brown glass bottle, half-hidden beneath a thick bunch of what even Joan recognised as black hellebores. Lovely, cup-shaped flowers of an eerie greenish-white – and deadly poison.

She dodged back across the market to arrive breathless and apologising at Sister Mathilde's side, wondering if . . . She hadn't spent much time at all with Da's wife – but she

324

had heard her talking with Da as she wrote down receipts in a book, and she'd mentioned black hellebore as something women used to make themselves miscarry. If Léonie were pregnant . . . Holy Mother of God, could she be with child by *Michael*? The thought struck her like a blow in the stomach.

No. No, she couldn't believe it. He was still in love with his wife, anyone could see that, and even if not, she'd swear he wasn't the sort to . . . but what did she ken about men, after all?

Well, she'd ask him when she saw him, she decided, her mouth clamping tight. And 'til then . . . Her hand went to the rosary at her waist and she said a quick, silent prayer for Léonie. Just in case.

As she was bargaining doggedly in her execrable French for six aubergines (wondering meanwhile what on earth they were for, medicine, or food?), she became aware of someone standing at her elbow. A handsome man of middle age, taller than she was, in a well-cut dove-grey coat. He smiled at her, and touching one of the peculiar vegetables, said in slow, simple French, 'You don't want the big ones. They're tough. Get small ones, like that.' A long finger tapped an aubergine half the size of the ones the vegetable-seller had been urging on her, and the vegetable-seller burst into a tirade of abuse that made Joan step back, blinking.

Not so much because of the expressions being hurled at her – she didn't understand one word in ten – but because a voice in plain English in her head had just said clearly, *'Tell him not to do it.'*

She felt hot and cold at the same time.

'I . . . er . . . *je suis* . . . um . . . *merci beaucoup, monsieur!*' she blurted, and turning, ran, scrambling back between piles of paper narcissus bulbs and fragrant spikes of hyacinth, her shoes skidding on the slime of trodden leaves.

'*Soeur* Gregory!' Sister Mathilde loomed up so suddenly in front of her that she nearly ran into the massive nun. 'What are you doing? Where is Sister Miséricorde?'

'I . . . oh.' Joan swallowed, gathering her wits. 'She's— over there.' She spoke with relief, spotting Mercy's small head in the forefront of a crowd by the meat-pie wagon. 'I'll get her!' she blurted, and walked hastily off before Sister Mathilde could say more.

'*Tell him not to do it.*' That's what the voice had said about Charles Pépin. What was going on? She thought wildly. Was Monsieur Pépin engaged in something awful with the man in the dove-grey coat?

As though thought of the man had reminded the voice, it came again.

Tell him not to do it, the voice repeated in her head, with what seemed like particular urgency. *Tell him he must not!*

'Hail Mary, full of grace, the Lord is with thee, blessed art thou among women . . .' Joan clutched at her rosary and gabbled the words, feeling the blood leave her face. There he was, the man in the dove-grey coat, looking curiously at her over a stall of Dutch tulips and sprays of yellow freesias.

She couldn't feel the pavement under her feet, but was moving toward him. *I have to*, she thought. *It doesn't matter if he thinks I'm mad . . .*

'Don't do it,' she blurted, coming face to face with the astonished gentleman. 'You mustn't do it!'

And then she turned and ran, rosary in hand, apron and veil flapping like wings.

Rakoczy couldn't help thinking of the cathedral as an entity. An immense version of one of its own gargoyles, crouched over the city. In protection, or threat?

326

Notre-Dame de Paris rose black above him, solid, obliterating the light of the stars, the beauty of the night. Very appropriate. He'd always thought that the Church blocked one's sight of God. Nonetheless, the sight of the monstrous stone creature made him shiver as he passed under its shadow, despite the warm cloak.

Perhaps it was the cathedral's stones themselves that gave him the sense of menace? He stopped, paused for a heartbeat, and then strode up to the church's wall and pressed his palm flat against the cold limestone. There was no immediate sense of anything, just the inert roughness of the rock. Impulsively, he shut his eyes and tried to feel his way into the rock. At first, nothing. But he waited, pressing with his mind, a repeated question: *Are you there*?

He would have been terrified to get an answer, and felt something that was much more relief than disappointment when he didn't. Even so, when he finally opened his eyes and took his hands away, he saw a trace of blue light, the barest trace, glow briefly between his knuckles. That frightened him, and he hurried away, hiding his hands beneath the shelter of the cloak.

Surely not, he assured himself. He'd done that before, made the light happen when he held the jewels he used for travel and said the words over them – his own version of consecration, he supposed. He didn't know if the words were necessary, but Mélisande had used them; he was afraid not to.

And yet. He had felt *something* here. The sense of something heavy, inert. Nothing resembling thought, let alone speech, thank God. By reflex, he crossed himself, then shook his head, rattled and irritated.

But *something*. Something immense, and very old. Did God have the voice of a stone? He was further unsettled by the thought. The stones there in the chalk mine, the noise they made – was it, after all, God that he glimpsed, there in that terrifying space between?

A movement in the shadows banished all such thoughts in an instant. The frog! Rakoczy's heart clenched like a fist.

'Monsieur le Comte,' said an amused, gravelly voice. 'I see the years have been kind to you.'

Raymond stepped into the starlight, smiling. The sight of him was disconcerting; Rakoczy had imagined this meeting for so long that the reality seemed oddly anti-climactic. Short, broad-shouldered, with long, loose hair that swept back from a massive forehead. A broad, almost lipless mouth. Raymond the frog.

'Why are you here?' Rakoczy blurted.

Maître Raymond's brows were black – surely they had been white, thirty years ago? One of them lifted in puzzlement.

'I was told that you were looking for me, monsieur.' He spread his hands, the gesture graceful. 'I came!'

'Thank you,' Rakoczy said dryly, beginning to regain some composure. 'I meant, why are you in Paris?'

'Everyone has to be somewhere, don't they? They can't be in the same place.' This should have sounded like badinage, but didn't. It sounded serious, like a statement of scientific principle, and Rakoczy found it unsettling.

'Did you come looking for me?' he asked boldly. He moved a little, trying to get a better look at the man. He was nearly sure that the frog looked *younger* than he had when last seen. Surely his flowing hair was darker, his step more elastic? A spurt of excitement bubbled in his chest.

'For you?' The frog looked amused for a moment, but then the look faded. 'No. I'm looking for a lost daughter.'

Rakoczy was surprised and disconcerted.

'Yours?'

328

'More or less.' Raymond seemed uninterested in explaining further. He moved a little to one side, eyes narrowing as he sought to make out Rakoczy's face in the darkness. 'You can hear stones, then, can you?'

'I— what?'

Raymond nodded at the façade of the cathedral. 'They do speak. They move, too, but very slowly, as one might expect.'

An icy chill shot up Rakoczy's spine, at thought of the grinning gargoyles perched high above him and the implication that one might at any moment choose to spread its silent wings and hurtle down upon him, teeth still bared in carnivorous hilarity. Despite himself, he looked up, over his shoulder.

'Not that fast.' The note of amusement was back in the frog's voice. 'You would never see them. It takes them millennia to move the slightest fraction of an inch – unless of course they are propelled or melted. But you don't want to see them do that, of course. Much too dangerous.'

This kind of talk seemed frivolous, and Rakoczy was bothered by it, but for some reason, not irritated. Troubled, with a sense that there was something under it, something that he simultaneously wanted to know – and wanted very much to avoid knowing. The sensation was novel, and unpleasant.

He cast caution to the wind, and demanded boldly, 'Why did you not kill me in the Star Chamber?'

Raymond grinned at him; he could see the flash of teeth, and felt yet another shock: he was sure – almost sure – that the frog had *had* no teeth when last seen.

'If I had wanted you dead, son, you wouldn't be here talking to me,' he said. 'I wanted you to be out of the way, that's all; you obliged me by taking the hint and leaving Paris.'

'And just why did you want me "out of the way"?' Had

329

he not needed to find out, Rakczoy would have taken offence at the man's tone.

The frog lifted one shoulder.

'You were something of a threat to the lady.'

Sheer astonishment brought Rakoczy to his full height.

'The lady? You mean the woman – La Dame Blanche?'

'They did call her that.' The frog seemed to find the notion amusing.

It was on the tip of Rakoczy's tongue to tell Raymond that La Dame Blanche still lived, but he himself hadn't lived as long as he had by blurting out everything he knew – and he didn't want Raymond thinking that he himself might still be a threat to her.

'What is the ultimate goal of an alchemist?' the frog said, very seriously.

'To transform matter,' Rakoczy replied automatically.

The frog's face split in a broad amphibian grin.

'Exactly!' he said. And vanished.

He *had* vanished. No puffs of smoke, no illusionist's tricks, no smell of sulphur . . . the frog was simply gone. The square stretched empty under the starlit sky; the only thing that moved was a cat that darted mewing out of the shadows and brushed past Rakoczy's leg.

Rakoczy was so shaken – and so excited – by the encounter that he wandered without knowing where he was going, crossed bridges without noticing, lost his way among the maze of twisting streets and *allées* on the Left Bank and did not reach his house 'til nearly dawn, footsore and exhausted, but with his mind buzzing with speculation.

Younger. He was sure of it. Raymond the frog was

younger than he had been thirty years before. So it could be done – somehow.

He was convinced now that Raymond was indeed a traveller, like him. It had to be the travel; specifically, travelling forward in time. But how? He'd tried, more than once. To go back was dangerous, and the journey depleted you physically, but it was possible. If you had the right combinations of stones, you could even arrive at a certain time – more or less. But you needed also a focus; someone or something upon which to fix the mind; without that, you might still end up at some random point. And that, he thought, was the problem in going forward: it wasn't possible to focus on something you didn't know was there.

But Master Raymond had done it.

How, then, to persuade the frog to share the secret? Raymond did not seem to be hostile to him, but neither did he seem friendly; Rakoczy would hardly have expected him to be.

A lost daughter, the frog had said. And he had poisoned Rakoczy to remove him as a threat to the Fraser woman, La Dame Blanche. And the woman had glowed with blue light – because she had touched him, when handing him the cup? He couldn't remember. But she had glowed, he was positive.

So. If he was right, then she too was a traveller.

'*Merveilleuse*,' he whispered. He had already been interested in the woman; now he was possessed. Not only did he want – need – to know what she knew; she was important to Raymond in some way, perhaps connected with the lost daughter – perhaps she *was* the lost daughter?

If he could but lay hands on her . . . He had made a few cautious inquiries, but no one in the Court of Miracles, or among his more respectable connections, had heard anything of Claire Fraser in the last thirty years. Her husband had been political, had died, he thought, in Scotland. But if she had gone to Scotland with him, how did Raymond come to be searching for her in Paris?

These thoughts, and many more like them, ran round in his head like a pack of fleas, raising itching welts of curiosity.

The sky had begun to lighten, though the stars still burned dimly above the rooftops. The scent of fresh woodsmoke touched him, and a whiff of yeast: the boulangeries firing their ovens for the day's bread. A distant clop of hooves, as the farmers' wagons came in from the country, full of vegetables, fresh meat, eggs and flowers. The city was beginning to stir.

His own house, his own bed. His mind had slowed now, and the thought of sleep was overwhelming. There was a grey cat sitting on the stoop of his house, washing its paws.

'*Bonjour,*' he said to it, and in his drowsy, exhausted state, almost expected it to answer him. It didn't, though, and when the butler opened the door it vanished, so quickly that he wondered whether it had ever really been there.

Worn out with constant walking, Michael slept like the dead these days, without dreams or motion, and woke when the sun came up. His valet, Robert, heard him stir and came in at once, one of the *femmes de chambre* on his heels with a bowl of coffee and some pastry.

He ate slowly, suffering himself to be brushed, shaved, and tenderly tidied into fresh linen. Robert kept up a soothing murmur of the sort of conversation that doesn't require response, and smiled encouragingly when presenting the mirror. Rather to Michael's surprise, the image

332

in the mirror looked quite normal. Hair neatly clubbed – he wore his own, without powder – suit modest in cut but of the highest quality. Robert hadn't asked him what he required, but had dressed him for an ordinary day of business.

He supposed that was all right. What, after all, did clothes matter? It wasn't as though there was a costume *de rigueur* for calling upon the sister of one's deceased wife, who had come uninvited into one's bed in the middle of the night.

He had spent the last two days trying to think of some way never to see or speak to Léonie again, but really, there was no help for it. He'd have to see her.

But what was he to say to her? he wondered, as he made his way through the streets toward the house where Léonie lived with an aged aunt, Eugenie Galantine. He wished he could talk the situation over with Sister Joan, but that wouldn't be appropriate, even were she available.

He'd hoped that walking would give him time to come up at least with a *point d'appui*, if not an entire statement of principle, but instead, he found himself obsessively counting the flagstones of the market as he crossed it, counting the bongs of the public *horloge* as it struck the hour of three, and – for lack of anything else to count – counting his own footsteps as he approached her door. *Six hundred and thirty-seven, six hundred and thirty-eight . . .*

As he turned into the street, though, he stopped counting abruptly. He stopped walking, too, for an instant – then began to run. Something was wrong at the house of Madame Galantine.

He pushed his way through the crowd of neighbours and vendors clustered near the steps, and seized the butler, whom he knew, by a sleeve.

'What?' he barked. 'What's happened?' The butler, a

tall, cadaverous man named Hubert, was plainly agitated, but settled a bit on seeing Michael.

'I don't know, sir,' he said, though a sideways slide of his eyes made it clear that he did. 'Mademoiselle Léonie . . . she's ill. The doctor . . .'

He could smell the blood. Not waiting for more, he pushed Hubert aside and sprinted up the stairs, calling for Madame Eugenie, Léonie's aunt.

Madame Eugenie popped out of a bedroom, her cap and wrapper neat in spite of the uproar.

'Monsieur Michel!' she said, blocking him from entering the room. 'It's all right, but you must not go in.'

'Yes, I must.' His heart was thundering in his ears and his hands felt cold.

'You may *not*,' she said firmly. 'She's ill. It isn't proper.'

'Proper? A young woman tries to make away with herself and you tell me it isn't *proper*?'

A maid appeared in the doorway, a basket piled with blood-stained linen in her arms, but the look of shock on Madame Eugenie's broad face was more striking.

'Make away with herself?' The old lady's mouth hung open for a moment, then snapped shut like a turtle's. 'Why would you think such a thing?' She was regarding him with considerable suspicion. 'And what are you doing here, for that matter? Who told you she was ill?'

A glimpse of a man in a dark robe, who must be the doctor, decided Michael that little was to be gained by engaging further with Madame Eugenie. He took her gently but firmly by the elbows, picked her up – she uttered a small shriek of surprise – and set her aside.

He went in and shut the bedroom door behind him.

'Who are you?' The doctor looked up, surprised. He was wiping out a freshly used bleeding-bowl, and his case lay open on the boudoir's settee. Léonie's bedroom must

334

lie beyond; the door was open, and he caught a glimpse of the foot of a bed, but could not see the bed's inhabitant.

'It doesn't matter. How is she?'

The doctor eyed him narrowly, but after a moment, nodded.

'She will live. As for the child . . .' He made an equivocal motion of the hand. 'I've done my best. She took a great deal of the—'

'The *child*?' The floor shifted under his feet, and the memory of the dream flooded him, that queer sense of something half-wrong, half-familiar. It was the feeling of a small, hard swelling, pressed against his bum; that's what it was. Lillie had been only two months gone with child, but he remembered all too well the feeling of a woman's body in early pregnancy.

'It's yours? I beg your pardon, I shouldn't ask.' The doctor put away his bowl and fleam, and shook out his black velvet turban.

'I want— I need to talk to her. Now.'

The doctor opened his mouth in automatic protest, but then glanced thoughtfully over his shoulder.

'Well . . . you must be careful not to—' But Michael was already inside the bedroom, standing by the bed.

She was pale. They had always been pale, Lillie and Léonie, with the soft glow of cream and marble. This was the paleness of a frog's belly, of a rotting fish, blanched on the shore.

Her eyes were ringed with black, sunk in her head. They rested on his face, flat, expressionless, as still as the ringless hands that lay limp on the coverlet.

'Who?' he said quietly. 'Charles?'

'Yes.' Her voice was as dull as her eyes, and he wondered whether the doctor had drugged her.

'Was it his idea – to try to foist the child off on me? Or yours?'

335

She did look away then, and her throat moved.

'His.' The eyes came back to him. 'I didn't want to, Michel. Not – not that I find you disgusting, not that . . .'

'*Merci*,' he muttered, but she went on, disregarding him.

'You were Lillie's husband. I didn't envy her you,' she said frankly, 'but I envied what you had together. It couldn't be like that between you and me, and I didn't like betraying her. But—' her lips, already pale, compressed to invisibility, 'I didn't have much choice.'

He was obliged to admit that she hadn't. Charles couldn't marry her; he had a wife – and children. Bearing an illegitimate child was not a fatal scandal in high Court circles, but the Galantines were of the emerging bourgeoisie, where respectability counted for almost as much as money. Finding herself pregnant, she would have had two alternatives: find a complaisant husband quickly, or . . . he tried not to see that one of her hands rested lightly across the slight swell of her stomach.

The child . . . He wondered what he would have done, had she come to him and told him the truth, if she had asked him to marry her for the sake of the child. But she hadn't. And she wasn't asking now. He couldn't bring himself to offer.

It would be best – or at least easiest – were she to lose the child. And she might yet.

'I couldn't wait, you see,' she said, as though continuing a conversation. 'I would have tried to find someone else, but I thought she knew. She'd tell you as soon as she could manage to see you. So I had to, you see, before you found out.'

'She? Who? Tell me what?'

'The nun,' Léonie said, and sighed deeply, as though losing interest. 'She saw me in the market, and rushed up to me. She said she had to talk to you – that she had something important to tell you. I saw her look into

336

my basket, though, and her face . . . thought she must realise . . .'

Her eyelids were fluttering, whether from drugs or fatigue. She smiled faintly, but not at him; she seemed to be looking at something a long way off.

'So funny,' she murmured. 'Charles said it would solve everything, that the comte would pay him such a lot for her, it would solve everything. But how can you solve a baby?'

Michael jerked as though her words had stabbed him.

'What? Pay for whom?'

'The nun. I told Charles that you woke, and it wouldn't work, but he said it didn't matter, because the comte would pay him for finding the nun, and—'

He grabbed her by the shoulders.

'The nun? Sister Joan? What do you mean, pay for her? What did Charles tell you?'

She made a whiny sound of protest. Michael wanted to shake her hard enough to break her neck, but forced himself to withdraw his hand. She settled into the pillow like a bladder losing air, flattening under the bedclothes. Her eyes were closed, but he bent close, speaking directly into her ear.

'This comte, Léonie. What is his name? Tell me his name.'

A faint frown rippled the flesh of her brow, then passed.

'St Germain,' she murmured, scarcely loud enough to be heard. 'The Comte St Germain.'

Michael went instantly to Rosenwald, and by dint of badgering and the promise of extra payment, got him to finish the engraving on the chalice at once. He waited impatiently while it was done, and scarcely waiting for

337

the cup and paten to be wrapped in brown paper, flung money to the goldsmith and made for the Convent des Anges, almost running.

With great difficulty, he restrained himself while making the presentation of the chalice, and with great humility, inquired whether he might ask the great favour of seeing Sister Gregory, that he might convey a message to her from her family in the Highlands. Sister Eustacia looked surprised and somewhat disapproving – postulants were not normally permitted visits – but after all . . . in view of Monsieur Murray's and Monsieur Fraser's great generosity to the convent . . . perhaps just a few moments, in the visitor's parlour, and in the presence of Sister herself . . .

Michael turned, and blinked once, his mouth opening a little. He looked shocked. Did she look so different in her robe and veil?

'It's me,' Joan said, and tried to smile reassuringly. 'I mean . . . still me.'

His eyes fixed on her face, and he let out a deep breath and smiled, like she'd been lost and he'd found her again.

'Aye, so it is,' he said softly. 'I was afraid it was Sister Gregory. I mean, the . . . er . . .' He made a sketchy, awkward gesture indicating her grey robes and white postulant's veil.

'It's only clothes,' she said, and put a hand to her chest, defensive.

'Well, no,' he said, looking her over carefully, 'I dinna think it is, quite. It's more like a soldier's uniform, no? Ye're doing your job when ye wear it, and everybody as sees it kens what ye are and knows what ye do.'

338

Kens what I am. I suppose I should be pleased it doesn't *show*, she thought, a little wildly.

'Well . . . aye, I suppose.' She fingered the rosary at her belt. She coughed. 'In a way, at least.'

Ye've got to tell him. It wasn't one of the voices, just the voice of her own conscience, but that was demanding enough. She could feel her heart beating, so hard that she thought the bumping must show through the front of her habit.

He smiled encouragingly at her.

'Léonic told me ye wanted to see me.'

'Michael . . . can I tell ye something?' she blurted. He looked surprised.

'Well, of course ye can,' he said. 'Whyever not?'

'Whyever not,' she said, half under her breath. She glanced over his shoulder, but Sister Eustacia was on the far side of the room, talking to a very young, frightened-looking French girl and her parents.

'Well, it's like this, see,' she said, in a determined voice. 'I hear voices.'

She stole a look at him, but he didn't look shocked. Not yet.

'In my head, I mean.'

'Aye?' He looked cautious. 'Um . . . what do they say, then?'

She realised she was holding her breath, and let a little of it out.

'Ah . . . different things. But they now and then tell me something's going to happen. More often, they tell me I should say thus-and-so to someone.'

'Thus and so,' he repeated attentively, watching her face. 'What . . . *sort* of thus-and-so?'

'I wasna expecting the Spanish Inquisition,' she said, a little testily. 'Does it matter?'

His mouth twitched.

339

'Well, I dinna ken, now, do I?' he pointed out. 'It might give a clue as to who's talkin' to ye, might it not? Or do ye already know that?'

'No, I don't,' she admitted, and felt a sudden lessening of tension. 'I— I was worrit – a bit – that it might be demons. But it doesna really . . . well, they dinna tell me *wicked* sorts of things. Just . . . more like, when something's going to happen to a person. And sometimes it's no a good thing – but sometimes it is. There was wee Annie MacLaren, her wi' a big belly by the third month, and by six, lookin' as though she'd burst, and she was frightened she was goin' to die come her time, like her ain mother did, wi' a babe too big to be born – I mean, *really* frightened, not just like all women are. And I met her by St Ninian's spring one day, and one of the voices said to me, *Tell her it will be as God wills and she will be delivered safely of a son.*'

'And ye did tell her that?'

'Yes. I didna say how I knew, but I must have sounded like I *did* know, because her poor face got bright all of a sudden, and she grabbed onto my hands and said, 'Oh! From your lips to God's ear!''

'And was she safely delivered of a son?'

'Aye – and a daughter, too. It was twins.' Joan smiled, remembering the glow on Annie's face.

Michael glanced aside at Sister Eustacia, who was bidding farewell to the new postulant's family. The girl was white-faced and tears ran down her cheeks, but she clung to Sister Eustacia's sleeve as though it were a lifeline.

'I see,' he said slowly, and looked back at Joan. 'Is that why— is it the voices told ye to be a nun, then?'

She blinked, surprised by his apparent acceptance of what she'd told him, but more so by the question.

'Well . . . no. They never did. Ye'd think they would have, wouldn't ye?'

340

He smiled a little.

'Maybe so.' He coughed, then looked up, a little shyly. 'It's no my business, but what *did* make ye want to be a nun?'

She hesitated, but why not? She'd already told him the hardest bit.

'Because of the voices. I thought maybe— maybe I wouldna hear them in here. Or . . . if I still did, maybe somebody – a priest, maybe? – could tell me what they were, and what I should do about them.'

Sister Eustacia was comforting the new girl, half-sunk on one knee to bring her big, homely, sweet face close to the girl's. Michael glanced at them, then back at Joan, one eyebrow raised.

'I'm guessing ye havena told anyone yet,' he said. 'Did ye reckon ye'd practise on me, first?'

Her own mouth twitched.

'Maybe.' His eyes were dark, but had a sort of warmth to them, like they drew it from the heat of his hair. She looked down; her hands were pleating the edge of her blouse, which had come untucked. 'It's no just that, though.'

He made the sort of noise in his throat that meant, 'Aye, then, go on.' Why didn't French people do like that? she wondered. So much easier. But she pushed the thought aside; she'd made up her mind to tell him, and now was the time to do it.

'I told ye because— your friend,' she blurted. 'The one I met at your house. Monsieur Pépin,' she added impatiently, when he looked blank.

'Aye?' He sounded as baffled as he looked.

'Aye. When I met him, a voice said, "*Tell him not to do it.*" And I didn't – I was frightened.'

'I would ha' been a bit disturbed myself,' he assured her. 'It didna say what he oughtn't to do, though?'

341

She bit her lip.

'No, it didn't. And then, two days ago, I saw the man – the comte, Sister Mercy said he was, the Comte St Germain – in the market, and the voice said the same thing, only a good bit more urgent. *"Tell him not to do it. Tell him he must not do it!"* '

'It did?'

'Aye, and it was verra firm about it. I mean – they are, usually. It's no just an opinion, take it or leave it. But this one truly meant it.' She spread her hands, helpless to explain the feeling of dread and urgency.

Michael's thick red eyebrows drew together.

'D'ye think it's the same thing they're not supposed to do?' He sounded startled. 'I didna ken they even knew each other.'

'Well, I don't know, now, do I?' she said, a little exasperated. 'The voices didn't say. But I saw that the man on the ship was going to die, and I didna say anything, because I couldn't think what to say. And then he *did* die, and maybe he wouldn't, if I'd spoken . . . so I— well, I thought I'd best say something to someone, and at least ye ken Monsieur Pépin.'

He thought about that for a moment, then nodded uncertainly.

'Aye. All right. I'll— well, I dinna ken what to do about it either, to be honest. But I'll talk to them both and I'll have that in my mind, so maybe I'll think of something. D'ye want me to tell them, "Don't do it"?'

She grimaced, and looked at Sister Eustacia. There wasn't much time.

'I already told the comte. Just— maybe. If ye think it might help. Now—' Her hand darted under her apron and she passed him the slip of paper, fast. 'We're only allowed to write to our families twice a year,' she said, lowering her voice. 'But I wanted Mam to know I was all right.

342

Could ye see she gets that, please? And— and maybe tell her a bit, yourself, that I'm weel and— and happy. Tell her I'm happy,' she repeated, more firmly.

Sister Eustacia had come back, and was standing by the door, emanating an intent to come and tell them it was time for Michael to leave.

'I will,' he said. He couldn't touch her, he knew that, so bowed instead, and bowed deeply to Sister Eustacia, who came toward them, looking benevolent.

'I'll come to Mass at the chapel on Sundays, how's that?' he said rapidly. 'If I've a letter from your mam, or ye have to speak to me, gie me a wee roll of the eyes or something. I'll figure something out.'

The Next Day

Sister Joan-Gregory, postulant of Our Lady Queen of Angels, regarded the bum of a large cow. The cow in question was named Mirabeau, and was of uncertain temper, as evidenced by the nervously lashing tail.

'She's kicked three of us this week,' said Sister Anne-Joseph, eyeing the cow resentfully. '*And* spilled the milk twice. Sister Jeanne-Marie was most upset.'

'Well, we canna have that now, can we?' Joan murmured in English. '*N'inquiétez-vous pas*,' she added in French, hoping that was at least vaguely grammatical. 'Let me do it.'

'Better you than me,' Sister Anne-Joseph said, crossing herself, and vanished before Sister Joan might think better of the offer.

A week spent working in the cow-shed was intended as punishment for her flighty behaviour in the marketplace, but Joan was grateful for it. There was nothing better for steadying the nerves than cows.

Granted, the convent's cows were not quite like her

mother's sweet-tempered, shaggy red Hieland coos, but if you came right down to it, a cow was a cow, and even a French-speaking wee besom like the present Mirabeau was no match for Joan MacKimmie, who'd driven kine to and from the shielings for years, and fed her mother's kine in the byre beside the house with sweet hay and the leavings from supper.

With that in mind, she circled Mirabeau thoughtfully, eyeing the steadily champing jaws and the long slick of blackish-green drool that hung down from slack pink lips. She nodded once, slipped out of the cow-shed, and made her way down the *allée* behind it, picking what she could find. Mirabeau, presented with a bouquet of fresh grasses, tiny daisies, and – delicacy of all delicacies – fresh sorrel, bulged her eyes half out of her head, opened her massive jaw, and inhaled the sweet stuff. The ominous tail ceased its lashing and the massive creature stood as if turned to stone, aside from the ecstatically grinding jaws.

Joan sighed in satisfaction, sat down, and resting her head on Mirabeau's monstrous flank, got down to business. Her mind, released, took up the next worry of the day.

Had Michael spoken to his friend Pépin? And if so, had he told him what she'd said, or just asked whether he kent the Comte St Germain? Because if *tell him not to do it* referred to the same thing, then plainly the two men must be acquent with each other.

She had got thus far in her ruminations, when Mirabeau's tail began to switch again. She hurriedly stripped the last of the milk from Mirabeau's teats and snatched the bucket out of the way, standing up in a hurry. Then she saw what had disturbed the cow.

The man in the dove-grey coat was standing in the door to the shed, watching her. She hadn't noticed before, in the market, but he had a handsome dark face, though rather hard about the eyes, and with a chin that brooked no opposition. He smiled pleasantly at her, though, and bowed.

'Mademoiselle. I must ask you, please, to come with me.'

Michael was in the warehouse, stripped to his shirtsleeves and sweating in the hot, wine-heady atmosphere, when Jared appeared, looking disturbed.

'What is it, cousin?' Michael wiped his face on a towel, leaving black streaks; the crew were clearing the racks on the southeast wall, and there were years of filth and cobwebs behind the most ancient casks.

'Ye haven't got that wee nun in your bed, have ye, Michael?' Jared lifted a beetling grey brow at him.

'Have I what?'

'I've just had a message from the Mother Superior of the Convent des Anges, saying that one Sister Gregory appears to have been abducted from their cow-shed, and wanting to know whether you might possibly have anything to do with the matter.'

Michael stared at his cousin for a moment, unable to take this in.

'Abducted?' he said stupidly. 'Who would be kidnapping a nun? What for?'

'Well, now, there ye have me.' Jared was carrying Michael's coat over his arm, and at this point, handed it to him. 'But maybe best ye go to the convent and find out.'

'Forgive me, Mother,' Michael said carefully. Mother Hildegarde looked fragile and transparent, as though a breath would make her disintegrate. 'Did ye think— is it

345

possible that Sister J— Sister Gregory might have . . . left of her own accord?'

The old nun gave him a look that revised his opinion of her state of health instantly.

'We did,' she said. 'It happens. However—' She raised one stick-like finger. 'One: there were signs of a considerable struggle in the cow-shed. A full bucket of milk not merely spilled, but apparently *thrown* at something, the manger overturned, the door left open and two of the cows escaped into the herb garden.' Another finger. 'Two: had Sister Gregory experienced doubt regarding her vocation, she was quite free to leave the convent after speaking with me, and she knew that.'

One more finger, and the old nun's black eyes bored into his. 'And three: had she felt it necessary to leave suddenly and without informing us, where would she go? To you, Monsieur Murray. She knows no one else in Paris, does she?'

'I— well, no, not really.' He was flustered, almost stammering, confusion and a burgeoning alarm for Joan making it difficult to think.

'But you have not seen her since you brought us the chalice and paten – and I thank you and your cousin with the deepest sentiments of gratitude, monsieur – that would be two days ago?'

'No.' He shook his head, trying to clear it. 'No, Mother.'

Mother Hildegarde nodded, her lips nearly invisible, pressed together amid the lines of her face.

'Did she say anything to you on that occasion? Anything that might assist us in discovering her?'

'I— well . . .' Jesus, should he tell her what Joan had said about the voices she heard? It couldn't have anything to do with this, surely, and it wasna his secret to share. On

346

the other hand, Joan *had* said she meant to tell Mother Hildegarde about them . . .

'You'd better tell me, my son.' The Mother Superior's voice was somewhere between resignation and command. 'I see she told you *something*.'

'Well, she did, then, Mother,' he said, rubbing a hand over his face in distraction. 'But I canna see how it has anything to do— she hears voices,' he blurted, seeing Mother Hildegarde's eyes narrow dangerously.

The eyes went round.

'She what?'

'Voices,' he said helplessly. 'They come and say things to her. She thinks maybe they're angels, but she doesn't know. And she can see when folk are going to die. Sometimes,' he added dubiously. 'I don't know whether she can always say.'

'*Par le sang sacré de Jésus-Christ,*' the old nun said, sitting up straight as an oak sapling. 'Why did she not— well, never mind about that. Does anyone else know this?'

He shook his head.

'She was afraid to tell anyone. That's why – well, one reason why – she came to the convent. She thought you might believe her.'

'I might,' Mother Hildegarde said dryly. She shook her head rapidly, making her veil flap. '*Nom de nom!* Why did her mother not tell me this?'

'Her mother?' Michael said stupidly.

'Yes! She brought me a letter from her mother, very kind, asking after my health and recommending Joan to me – but surely her mother would have known!'

'I don't think she— wait.' He remembered Joan fishing out the carefully folded note from her pocket. 'The letter she brought – it was from Claire Fraser. That's the one you mean?'

'Of course!'

347

He took a deep breath, a dozen disconnected pieces falling suddenly into a pattern. He cleared his throat, and raised a tentative finger.

'One point: Claire Fraser is the wife of Joan's stepfather. But she's not Joan's mother.'

The sharp black eyes blinked once.

'And a second point: my cousin Jared tells me that Claire Fraser was known as a— a White Lady, when she lived in Paris many years ago.'

Mother Hildegarde clicked her tongue angrily.

'She was no such thing. Stuff! But it is true that there was a common rumour to that effect,' she admitted grudgingly. She drummed her fingers on the desk; they were knobbed with age, but surprisingly nimble, and he remembered hearing that Mother Hildegarde had been a famous musician in her youth.

'Mother . . .'

'Yes?'

'I don't know if it has anything to do— do you know of a man called the Comte St Germain?'

The old nun was already the colour of parchment; at this, she went white as bone and her fingers gripped the edge of the desk.

'I do,' she said. 'Tell me – and quickly – what he has to do with Sister Gregory.'

Joan gave the very solid door one last kick, for form's sake, then turned and collapsed with her back against it, panting. The room was huge, extending across the entire top floor of the house, though pillars and joists here and there showed where walls had been knocked down. It smelled peculiar, and looked even more peculiar.

'*A Dhia, cuidich mi,*' she whispered to herself, reverting

348

to the Gaelic in her agitation. There was a very fancy bed in one corner, piled with feather pillows and bolsters, with writhing corner-posts and heavy swags and curtains of cloth embroidered in what looked like gold and silver thread. Did the comte haul young women up here for wicked ends on a regular basis? For surely he hadn't set up this establishment solely in anticipation of her arrival . . . the area near the bed was equipped with all kinds of solid, shiny furniture with marble tops and alarming gilt feet that looked like they'd come off some kind of beast or bird with great curving claws.

He'd told her in the most matter-of-fact way that he was a sorcerer, too, and not to touch anything. She crossed herself, and averted her gaze from the table with the nastiest-looking feet; maybe he'd charmed the furniture, and it came to life and walked around after dark. The thought made her move hastily off to the farther end of the room, rosary clutched tight in one hand.

This side of the room was scarcely less alarming, but at least it didn't look as though any of the big coloured glass balls and jars and tubes could move on their own. It *was* where the worst smells were coming from, though; something that smelled like burned hair and treacle, and something else very sharp that curled the hairs in your nose, like it did when someone dug out a jakes for the saltpetre. But there *was* a window near the long table where all this sinister stuff was laid out, and she went to this at once.

The big river – the Seine, Michael had called it – was right there, and the sight of boats and people made her feel a bit steadier. She put a hand on the table to lean closer, but set it on something sticky and jerked it back. She swallowed, and leaned in more gingerly. The window was barred on the inside. Glancing round, she saw that all the others were, too.

What in the name of the Blessed Virgin did that man expect would try to get in? Gooseflesh raced right up the curve of her spine and spread down her arms, her imagination instantly conjuring a vision of flying demons hovering over the street in the night, beating leathery wings against the window. *Or – dear Lord in heaven! – was it to keep the furniture from getting* out?

There was a fairly normal-looking stool; she sank down on this and, closing her eyes, prayed with great fervour. After a bit, she remembered to breathe, and after a further bit, began to be able to think again, shuddering only occasionally.

He hadn't *exactly* threatened her. Nor had he hurt her, really – just put a hand over her mouth and his other arm round her body, and pulled her along, then boosted her into his coach with a shockingly familiar hand under her bottom, though it hadn't been done with any sense that he was wanting to interfere with her.

In the coach, he'd introduced himself, apologised briefly for the inconvenience – *inconvenience? The cheek of him* – and then had grasped both her hands in his, staring intently into her face as he clasped them tighter and tighter. He'd raised her hands to his face, so close she'd thought he meant to smell them or kiss them, but then had let go, his brow deeply furrowed.

He'd ignored all her questions and her insistence upon being returned to the convent. In fact, he almost seemed to forget she was there for a moment, leaving her huddled back in the corner of the seat while he thought intently about something, lips pursing in and out. She'd thought of jumping out – had almost got up her nerve to reach for the door handle, though the coach was rattling on at such a pace she was almost sure to be killed – but then his eyes had fastened on her again, pinning her to the seat as though he'd stabbed her through the chest with a knitting-needle.

'The frog,' he'd said, intent. 'You know the frog, don't you?'

'Any number of them,' she'd said, thinking that if he was mad, she'd best humour him. 'Green ones, mostly.'

His nostrils had flared in sudden anger, and she'd shrunk back into the seat. But then he had snorted, and relapsed into a sort of brooding stare, emerging from this only to say, 'The rats didn't all die,' in a sort of accusing tone, as though it were her fault.

Her mouth was so dry that she could barely speak, but had managed to say, 'Oh? Did ye try rat's-bane, then?' But she'd spoken in English, too rattled to summon any French, and he didn't seem to take any note.

And then he had lugged her up here, told her briefly that she wouldn't be hurt, added the bit about being a sorcerer in a very offhand sort of a way, and locked her in!

She was terrified, and indignant, too. But now that she'd calmed down a wee bit . . . she'd believed him when he said he meant her no harm. He hadn't threatened her or tried to frighten her. Well, he'd frightened her, all right, but didn't seem like he'd meant to. But if that was true . . . what could he want of her?

He likely wants to know what ye meant by rushing up to him in the market and telling him not to do it, her common sense – lamentably absent to this point – remarked.

'Oh,' she said aloud. That made some sense. Naturally, he'd be curious about that. But if so, why hadn't he asked her, instead of dragging her off? And what had he gone off to do now?

He had something in mind, and she didn't want to think what.

She got up again, and explored the room, thinking anyway. She couldn't tell him any more than she had, that was the thing. Would he believe her, about the voices? Even if so, he'd try to find out more, and there wasn't any more to find out. What then?

Don't wait about to see, advised her common sense.

Having already come to this conclusion, she didn't bother replying. She'd found a heavy marble mortar and pestle; that might do. Wrapping the mortar in her apron, she went to the window that overlooked the street. She'd break the glass, then shriek 'til she got someone's attention. Even so high up, she thought someone would hear. Pity it was a quiet street. But—

She stiffened like a bird-dog. A coach was stopped outside one of the houses opposite, and Michael Murray was getting out of it! He was just putting on his hat – no mistaking that flaming red hair.

'Michael!' she shouted at the top of her lungs. But he didn't look up; the sound wouldn't pierce glass. She swung the cloth-wrapped mortar at the window, but it bounced off the bars with a ringing *clang!* She took a deep breath and a better aim; this time, she hit one of the panes and cracked it. Encouraged, she tried again, with all the strength of muscular arms and shoulders, and was rewarded with a small crash, a shower of glass, and a rush of mud-scented air from the river.

'*Michael!*' But he had disappeared. A servant's face showed briefly in the open door of the house opposite, then vanished as the door closed. Through a red haze of frustration, she noticed the swag of black crepe hanging from the knob. Who was dead?

Charles's wife, Berthe, was in the small parlour, surrounded by a huddle of women. All of them turned to see who had come, many of them lifting their handkerchiefs

352

automatically in preparation for a fresh outbreak of tears. All of them blinked at Michael, then turned to Berthe, as though for an explanation.

Berthe's eyes were red, but dry. She looked as though she had been dried in an oven, all the moisture and colour sucked out of her, her face paper-white and drawn tight over her bones. She too looked at Michael, but without much interest. He thought she was too much shocked for anything to matter much. He knew how she felt.

'Monsieur Murray,' she said tonelessly, as he bowed over her hand. 'How kind of you to call.'

'I— offer my condolences, madame, mine and my cousin's. I hadn't . . . heard. Of your grievous loss.' He was almost stuttering, trying to grasp the reality of the situation. What the devil had happened to Charles?

Berthe's mouth twisted.

'Grievous loss,' she repeated. 'Yes. Thank you.' Then her dull self-absorption cracked a little and she looked at him more sharply. 'You hadn't heard. You mean— you didn't know? You came to see Charles?'

'Er . . . yes, madame,' he said awkwardly. A couple of the women gasped, but Berthe was already on her feet.

'Well, you might as well see him, then,' she said, and walked out of the room, leaving him with no choice but to follow her.

'They've cleaned him up,' she remarked, opening the door to the large parlour across the hall. She might have been talking about a messy domestic incident in the kitchen.

Michael thought it must in fact have been very messy. Charles lay on the large dining table, this adorned with a cloth and wreaths of greenery and flowers. A woman clad in grey was sitting by the table, weaving more wreaths from a basket of leaves and grasses; she glanced up, her eyes going from Berthe to Michael and back.

353

'Leave,' said Berthe with a flip of the hand, and the woman got up at once and went out. Michael saw that she'd been making a wreath of laurel leaves, and had the sudden absurd thought that she meant to crown Charles with it, in the manner of a Greek hero.

'He cut his throat,' Berthe said. 'The coward.' She spoke with an eerie calmness, and Michael wondered what might happen when the shock that surrounded her began to dissipate.

He made a respectful sort of noise in his throat, and touching her arm gently, went past her to look down at his friend.

Don't do it. That's what Joan said the voices had told her. Was this what they'd meant?

The dead man didn't look peaceful. There were lines of stress in his countenance that hadn't yet smoothed out, and he appeared to be frowning. The undertaker's people had cleaned the body and dressed him in a slightly worn suit of dark blue; Michael thought that it was probably the only thing Charles had owned that was in any way appropriate in which to appear dead, and suddenly missed his friend's frivolity with a surge that brought unexpected tears to his eyes.

Don't do it. He hadn't come in time. *If I'd come right away, when she told me – would it have stopped him?*

He could smell the blood, a rusty, sickly smell that seeped through the freshness of the flowers and leaves. The undertaker had tied a white neckcloth for Charles – he'd used an old-fashioned knot, nothing that Charles himself would have worn for a moment. The black stitches showed above it, though, the wound harsh against the dead man's livid skin.

Michael's own shock was beginning to fray, and stabs of guilt and anger poked through it like needles.

'Coward?' he said softly. He didn't mean it as a

354

question, but it seemed more courteous to say it that way. Berthe snorted and looking up, he met the full charge of her eyes. No, not shocked any longer.

'You'd know, wouldn't you,' she said, and it wasn't at all a question, the way she said it. 'You knew about your slut of a sister-in-law, didn't you? And his other mistresses?' Her lips curled away from the word.

'I— no. I mean . . . Léonie told me yesterday. That was why I came to talk to Charles.' Well, he would certainly have mentioned Léonie. And he wasn't going anywhere near the mention of Babette, whom he'd known about for quite some time. But Jesus, what did the woman think he could have done about it?

'Coward,' she said, looking down at Charles's body with contempt. 'He made a mess of everything – everything! – and then couldn't deal with it, so he runs off and leaves me alone, with children, penniless!'

Don't do it.

Michael looked to see if this was an exaggeration, but it wasn't. She was burning now, but with fear as much as anger, her frozen calm quite vanished.

'The . . . house . . .' he began, with a rather vague wave around the expensive, stylish room. He knew it was her family house; she'd brought it to the marriage.

She snorted.

'He lost it in a card game last week,' she said bitterly. 'If I'm lucky, the new owner will let me bury him before we have to leave.'

'Ah.' The mention of card games jolted him back to an awareness of his reason for coming here. 'I wonder, madame, do you know an acquaintance of Charles's – the Comte St Germain?' It was crude, but he hadn't time to think of a graceful way to come to it.

Berthe blinked, nonplussed.

'The comte? Why do you want to know about *him*?'

355

Her expression sharpened into eagerness. 'Do you think he owes Charles money?'

'I don't know, but I'll certainly find out for you,' Michael promised her. 'If you can tell me where to find Monsieur le Comte.'

She didn't laugh, but her mouth quirked in what might, in another mood, have been humour.

'He lives across the street.' She pointed toward the window. 'In that big pile of— where are you going?'

But Michael was already through the door and into the hallway, bootheels clattering on the parquet in his haste.

There were footsteps coming up the stairs; Joan started away from the window, but then craned back, desperately willing the door across the street to open and let Michael out. What was he *doing* there?

That door didn't open, but a key rattled in the lock of the door to the room. In desperation, she tore the rosary from her belt and pushed it through the hole in the window, then dashed across the room and threw herself into one of the repulsive chairs.

It was the comte. He glanced round, worried for an instant, and then his face relaxed when he saw her. He came toward her, holding out his hand.

'I'm sorry to have kept you waiting, mademoiselle,' he said, very courtly. 'Come, please. I have something to show you.'

'I don't want to see it.' She stiffened a little and tucked her feet under her, to make it harder for him to pick her up. If she could just delay him until Michael came out! But he might well not see her rosary – or, even if he did, know it was hers. Why should he? All nuns' rosaries looked the same!

356

She strained her ears, hoping to hear the sounds of departure on the other side of the street – she'd scream her lungs out. In fact . . .

The comte sighed a little, but bent and took her by the elbows, lifting her straight up, her knees still absurdly bent. He was really very strong. She put her feet down, and there she was, her hand tucked into the crook of his elbow, being led across the room toward the door, docile as a cow on its way to be milked! She made her mind up in an instant, yanked free and ran to the smashed window.

'HELP!' she bellowed through the broken pane. 'Help me, help me! *Au secours*, I mean! *AU SECOU*—' The comte's hand clapped across her mouth, and he said something in French that she was sure must be bad language. He scooped her up, so fast that the wind was knocked out of her, and had her through the door before she could make another sound.

Michael didn't pause for hat or cloak, but burst into the street, so fast that his driver started out of a doze and the horses jerked and neighed in protest. He didn't pause for that, either, but shot across the cobbles and pounded on the door of the house, a big bronze-coated affair that boomed under his fists.

It couldn't have been very long, but seemed an eternity. He fumed, pounded again, and pausing for breath, caught sight of the rosary on the pavement. He ran to catch it up, scratched his hand, and saw that it lay in a scatter of glass fragments. At once he looked up, searching, and saw the broken window just as the big door opened.

He sprang at the butler like a wildcat, seizing him by the arms.

'Where is she? Where, damn you?'

'She? But there is no she, monsieur . . . Monsieur le Comte lives quite alone. You—'

'Where is Monsieur le Comte?' Michael's sense of urgency was so great he felt that he might strike the man. The man apparently felt he might, too, because he turned pale, and wrenching himself loose, fled into the depths of the house. With no more than an instant's hesitation, Michael pursued him.

The butler, his feet fuelled by fear, flew down the hall, Michael in grim pursuit. The man burst through the door into the kitchen; Michael was dimly aware of the shocked faces of cooks and maids, and then they were out into the kitchen-garden. The butler slowed for an instant going down the steps, and Michael launched himself at the man, knocking him flat.

They rolled together on the gravelled path, then Michael got on top of the smaller man, seized him by the shirt-front and shaking him, shouted, 'WHERE IS HE?'

Thoroughly undone, the butler covered his face with one arm and pointed blindly toward a gate in the wall.

Michael leaped off the supine body and ran. He could hear the rumble of coach-wheels, the rattle of hooves – he flung open the gate in time to see the back of a coach rattling down the *allée*, and a gaping servant, paused in the act of sliding to the doors of a carriage house. He ran, but it was clear that he'd never catch the coach on foot.

'JOAN!' he bellowed after the vanishing equipage. 'I'm coming!'

He didn't waste time in questioning the servant, but ran back, pushing his way through the maids and footmen gathered round the cowering butler, and burst out of the house, startling his own coachman afresh.

'That way!' he shouted, pointing toward the distant

358

conjunction of the Rue St André and the *allée*, where the comte's coach was just emerging. 'Follow that coach! *Vite!*'

'*Vite!*' Rakoczy urged his coachman on, then sank back, letting fall the hatch in the roof. The light was fading; his errand had taken longer than he'd expected, and he wanted to be out of the city before night fell. The city streets were dangerous at night.

His captive was staring at him, her eyes enormous in the dim light. She'd lost her postulant's veil and her dark hair was loose on her shoulders. She looked charming, but very scared. He reached into the bag on the floor and pulled out a flask of brandy.

'Have a little of this, *Chérie.*' He removed the cork and handed it to her. She took it, but looked uncertain what to do with it, nose wrinkling at the hot smell.

'Really,' he assured her. 'It will make you feel better.'

'That's what they all say,' she said in her slow, awkward French.

'All of whom?' he asked, startled.

'The Old Ones. I don't know what you call them in French, exactly. The folk that live in the hills – *souterrain*?' she added doubtfully. 'Underground?'

'Underground? And they give you brandy?' He smiled at her, but his heart gave a sudden thump of excitement. Perhaps she *was*. He'd doubted his instincts, when his touch failed to kindle her, but clearly she was *something*.

'They give you food and drink,' she said, putting the flask down into the space between the squab and the wall. 'But if you take any, you lose time.'

The spurt of excitement came again, stronger. *She knows! She is!*

359

'Lose time?' he repeated, encouraging. 'How do you mean?'

She struggled to find words, smooth brow furrowed with the effort.

'They – you – one who is enchanted by them . . . he, it? . . . no, he— goes into the hill and there's music and feasting and dancing. But in the morning, when he goes . . . back . . . it's two hundred years later than it was when he went to feast with the— the— Folk. Everybody he knew has turned to dust.' Her throat moved as she swallowed, and her eyes glistened a little.

'How interesting!' he said. It was. He also wondered, with a fresh spasm of excitement, whether the old paintings, the ones far back in the bowels of the chalk mine, might have been made by these Folk, whoever they were.

She observed him narrowly, apparently looking for an indication that he was a faery. He smiled at her, though his heart was now thumping audibly in his ears. *Two hundred years!* For that was what Mélisande had told him was the usual period, when one travelled through stone. It could be changed by use of gemstones, or of blood, she said, but that was the usual. And it had been, the first time he went back.

'Don't worry,' he said to the girl, hoping to reassure her. 'I only want you to look at something. Then I'll take you back to the convent – assuming that you still want to go there?' He lifted an eyebrow, half-teasing. It really wasn't his intent to frighten her, though he already had, and he feared that more fright was unavoidable. He wondered just what she might do, when she realised that he was in fact planning to take her underground.

360

Michael kneeled on the seat, his head out the window of the coach, urging it on by force of will and muscle. It was nearly full dark, and the comte's coach was visible only as a distantly moving blot. They were out of the city, though; there were no other large vehicles on the road, nor likely to be – and there were very few turnings where such a large equipage might leave the main road.

The wind blew in his face, tugging strands of hair loose so they beat about his face. It blew the faint scent of decay, too – they'd pass the cemetery in a few minutes.

He wished passionately that he'd thought to bring a pistol, a smallsword – anything! But there was nothing in the coach with him, and he had nothing on his person save his clothes and what was in his pockets, this consisting, after a hasty inventory, of a handful of coins, a used handkerchief – the one Joan had given back to him, in fact, and he crumpled it tightly in one hand – a tinderbox, a mangled paper spill, a stub of sealing-wax, and a small stone he'd picked up in the street, pinkish with a yellow stripe – perhaps he could improvise a sling with the handkerchief, he thought wildly, and paste the comte in the forehead with the stone, *à la* David and Goliath. And then cut off the comte's head with the pen-knife he discovered in his breast pocket, he supposed.

Joan's rosary was also in that pocket; he took it out and wound it round his left hand, holding the beads for comfort – he was too distracted to pray, beyond the words he repeated silently over and over, hardly noticing what he said.

'Let me find her in time!'

'Tell me,' the comte asked curiously, 'why did you speak to me in the market that day?'

361

'I wish I hadn't,' Joan replied briefly. She didn't trust him an inch; still less, since he'd offered her the brandy. It hadn't struck her before that he really *might* be one of the Auld Ones. They could walk about, looking just like people. Her own mother had been convinced for years – and even some of the Murrays thought so – that Da's wife Claire was one. She herself wasn't sure; Claire had been kind to her, but no one said the Folk *couldn't* be kind if they wanted to.

Da's wife. A sudden thought paralysed her; the memory of her first meeting with Mother Hildegarde, when she'd given the Mother Superior Claire's letter. She'd said, '*ma mère*,' unable to think of a word that might mean 'stepmother'. It hadn't seemed to matter; why should anyone care?

'Claire Fraser,' she said aloud, watching the comte carefully. 'Do you know that name?'

His eyes widened, showing white in the gloaming. Oh, aye, he kent her, all right!

'I do,' he said, leaning forward. 'Your mother, is she not?'

'No!' Joan said, with great force, and repeated it in French, several times for emphasis. 'No, she's not!'

But she observed, with a sinking heart, that her force had been misplaced. He didn't believe her; she could tell by the eagerness in his face. He thought she was lying to put him off. *Jesus, Lord, deliver me . . .*

'I told you what I did in the market because the voices told me to!' she blurted, desperate for anything that might distract him from the horrifying notion that she was one of the Folk. Though if *he* was one, her common sense pointed out, he ought to be able to recognise her. Oh, Jesus, Lamb of God . . . that's what he'd been trying to do, holding her hands so tight and staring into her face. And now she'd told him . . .

362

'Voices?' he said, looking rather blank. 'What voices?'

'The ones in my head,' she blurted. 'They tell me things now and then. About other people, I mean. You know,' she went on, encouraging him, hoping to convince him that she wasn't whatever he thought she was. 'I'm a— a—' St Jerome on a bannock, what was the *word*? '. . . someone who sees the future,' she ended weakly. 'Er . . . some of it. Sometimes. Not always.'

The comte was rubbing a finger over his upper lip; she didn't know if he was expressing doubt or trying not to laugh, but either way, it made her angry.

'So one of them told me to tell ye that, and I did!' she said, lapsing into Scots. 'I dinna ken what it is ye're no supposed to do, but I'd advise ye not to do it!'

It occurred to her belatedly that perhaps killing her was the thing he wasn't supposed to do, and she was about to put this notion to him, but by the time she had disentangled enough French grammar to have a go at it, the coach was slowing, bumping from side to side as it turned off the main road. A sickly smell seeped into the air, and she sat up straight, her heart in her throat.

'Mary, Joseph, and Bride,' she said, her voice no more than a squeak. 'Where *are* we?'

Michael leaped from the coach almost before it had stopped moving. He daren't let them get too far ahead of him; his driver had nearly missed the turning as it was, and the comte's coach had come to a halt minutes before his own reached it.

'Talk to the other driver,' he shouted at his own, half-visible on the box. 'Find out why the comte has come here! Find out what he's doing!'

Nothing good. He was sure of that. Though he couldn't

363

imagine why anyone would kidnap a nun and drag her out of Paris in the dark, only to stop at the edge of a public cemetery. Unless . . . half-heard rumours of depraved men who murdered and dismembered their victims, even those who *ate* . . . his wame rose and he nearly vomited, but it wasn't possible to vomit and run at the same time, and he could see a pale splotch on the darkness that he thought – he hoped, he feared – must be Joan.

Suddenly, the night burst into flower. A huge puff of green fire bloomed in the darkness, and by its eerie glow, he saw her clearly, her hair flying in the wind.

He opened his mouth to shout, to call out to her, but he had no breath, and before he could recover it, she vanished into the ground, the comte following her, torch in hand.

He reached the mineshaft moments later, and below, he saw the faintest green glow, just vanishing down a white chalk tunnel. Without an instant's hesitation, he flung himself down the ladder.

'Do you hear anything?' the comte kept asking her, as they stumbled along the white-walled tunnels, he grasping her so hard by the arm that he'd surely leave bruises on her skin.

'No,' she gasped. 'What— am I listening for?'

He merely shook his head in a displeased way, but more as though he were listening for something himself, than because he was angry with her for not hearing it.

She still had a faint hope that he'd meant what he said, and would take her back. He did mean to go back himself; he'd lit several torches and left them burning along their way. So he wasn't about to disappear into the hill altogether, taking her with him to the lighted ballroom where people danced all night with the Fine Folk, unaware that their own world slipped past beyond the stones of the hill.

The comte stopped abruptly, hand squeezing harder round her arm.

'Be still,' he said, very quietly, though she wasn't making any noise. 'Listen.'

She listened as hard as possible – and thought she did hear something. What she thought she heard, though, was footsteps, far in the distance. Behind them. Her heart seized up for a moment.

'What— what do *you* hear?' she thought of asking. He glanced down at her, but not as though he really saw her.

'Them,' he said. 'The stones. They make a buzzing sound, most of the time. If it's close to a fire-feast or a sun-feast, though, they begin to sing.'

'Do they?' she said faintly. He was hearing *something*, and evidently it wasn't the footsteps she'd heard. They'd stopped now, as though whoever followed was waiting, maybe stealing along, one step at a time, careful now to make no sound.

Was it another of the Auld Ones? If it was, it didn't want to be heard. It was cold here underground, but sweat crawled down the crease of her back, and her nape prickled, imagining something ancient and sharp-toothed, leaping out of the dark just behind . . .

'Yes,' he said, and his face was intent. He looked at her sharply again, and this time, he saw her.

'You don't hear them,' he said, with certainty, and she shook her head.

'No,' she whispered. Her lips felt stiff. 'I don't— I don't hear anything.'

He pressed his lips tight together, but after a moment, lifted his chin, gesturing toward another tunnel, where there seemed to be something painted on the chalk.

He paused there to light another torch – this one

burned a brilliant yellow, and stank of sulphur – and she saw by its light the wavering shape of the Virgin and an angel. Her heart lifted a little at the sight, for surely faeries would have no such thing in their lair.

'Come,' he said, and now took her by the hand. His own was cold.

❧

Michael caught a glimpse of them as they moved into a side tunnel. The comte had lit another torch, a red one this time – how did he do that? – and it was easy to follow its glow.

How far down in the bowels of the earth were they? He had long since lost track of the turnings, though he might be able to get back by following the torches – assuming they hadn't all burned out.

He still had no plan in mind, other than to follow them until they stopped. Then he'd make himself known, and . . . well, take Joan away, by whatever means proved necessary.

Swallowing hard, rosary still wrapped around his left hand and pen-knife in his right, he stepped into the shadows.

❧

The chamber was round, and quite large. Big enough that the torchlight didn't reach all the edges, but it lit the pentagram inscribed into the floor in the centre.

The noise was making Rakoczy's bones ache, and often as he had heard it, it never failed to make his heart race and his hands sweat. He let go of the nun's hand for a moment, to wipe his palm on the skirts of his coat, not wanting to disgust her. She looked scared, but not

366

terrified, and if she heard it, surely she— Her eyes widened suddenly and she let out a small yelp.

'Who's *that*?' she said.

He whirled, to see Raymond, apparently come out of nowhere, standing tranquilly in the centre of the pentagram.

'*Bonsoir, mademoiselle*,' the frog said, bowing politely.

'Ah . . . *bonsoir*,' the girl replied faintly. She made to back away, and Rakoczy seized her by the wrist.

'What the devil are you doing here?' Rakoczy interposed his body between Raymond and the nun.

'Very likely the same thing you are,' the frog replied. 'Might you introduce your *petite amie*, sir?'

Shock, anger, and sheer confusion robbed Rakoczy of speech for a moment. What was the infernal creature *doing* here? Wait— the girl! The lost daughter he'd mentioned; the nun was the daughter! *Tabernac*, had the frog sired this girl on La Dame Blanche?

In any case, he'd plainly discovered the nun's whereabouts, and somehow had followed them to this place. He took hold of the girl's arm again, firmly.

'She is a Scotch,' he said. 'And as you see, a nun. No concern of yours.'

The frog looked amused, cool and unruffled. Rakoczy was sweating, the noise beating against his skin in waves. He could feel the little bag of stones in his pocket, a hard lump against his heart. They seemed to be warm, warmer even than his skin.

'I doubt that she is, really,' said Raymond. 'Why is she a concern of yours, though?'

'That's also none of your business.' He was trying to think. He couldn't lay out the stones, not with the damned frog standing there. Could he just leave with the girl? But if the frog meant him harm . . . and if the girl truly wasn't . . .

367

Raymond ignored the incivility, and bowed again to the girl.

'I am Master Raymond, my dear,' he said. 'And you?'

'Joan Mac—' she said. 'Er . . . Sister Gregory, I mean.' She pulled hard against Rakoczy's grip. 'Um. If I'm not the concern of either of you gentlemen . . .'

'She's my concern, gentlemen.' The voice was high with nerves, but firm. Rakoczy looked round, shocked to see the young wine merchant walk into the chamber, dishevelled and dirty, but eyes fixed on the girl. At his side, the nun gasped.

'Sister.' The merchant bowed. He was white-faced, but not sweating. He looked as though the chill of the cavern had seeped into his bones, but put out a hand from which the beads of a wooden rosary swung. 'You dropped your rosary.'

Joan thought she might faint from sheer relief. Her knees wobbled from terror and exhaustion, but she summoned enough strength to wrench free of the comte and run, stumbling, into Michael's arms. He grabbed her and hauled her away from the comte, half-dragging her.

The comte made an angry sound and took a step in her direction, but Michael said, 'Stop right there, ye wicked bugger!' just as the little froggy-faced man said sharply, 'Stop!'

The comte swung first toward one and then the other. He looked . . . crazed. Joan swallowed and nudged Michael, urging him toward the chamber's door, only then noticing the pen-knife in his hand.

'What were ye going to do wi' *that*?' she whispered, half-hysterical. 'Shave him?'

'Let the air out of him,' Michael muttered. He lowered

his hand, but didn't put the knife away, and kept his eyes on the two men.

'Your daughter,' the comte said hoarsely to the man who called himself Master Raymond. 'You were looking for your lost daughter. I've found her for you.'

Raymond's brows shot up, and he glanced at Joan.

'Mine?' he said, astonished. 'She isn't one of mine. Can't you tell?'

The comte drew a breath so deep it cracked in his throat.

'Tell? But—'

The frog looked impatient.

'Can you not see auras? The electrical fluid that surrounds people,' he elucidated, waving a hand around his own head. The comte rubbed a hand hard over his face.

'I can't— she doesn't—'

'For goodness sake, come in here!' Raymond stepped to the edge of the star, reached across and seized the comte's hand.

Rakoczy stiffened at the touch. Blue light exploded from their linked hands, and he gasped, feeling a surge of energy such as he had never before experienced. It ran like water, like lightning! through his veins. Raymond pulled hard, and he stepped across the line into the pentagram.

Silence. The buzzing had stopped. He nearly wept with the relief of it.

'I— you—' he stammered, looking at the linked hands, where the blue light now pulsed gently, with the rhythm of a beating heart. *Connection.* He felt the other. Felt him in his own blood, his bones, and astonished exaltation filled him. Another. By God, another!

369

'You didn't know?' Raymond looked surprised.

'That you were a—' He waved at the pentagram. 'I thought you might be.'

'Not that,' Raymond said, almost gently. 'That you were one of mine.'

'Yours?' Rakoczy looked down again at their linked fingers, bathed in blue.

'Everyone has an aura of some kind,' Raymond said. 'But only my . . . people – my sons and daughters – have *this*.'

In the blessed silence, it was possible to think again. And the first thing that came to mind was the Star Chamber, the king looking on as they had faced each other over a poisoned cup. And now he knew why the frog hadn't killed him.

Rakoczy's mind bubbled with questions. La Dame Blanche, blue light, Mélisande and Madeleine . . . The thought of Madeleine and what grew in her womb nearly stopped him asking, but the urge to find out, to *know* at last, was too strong.

'Can you— can we— go forward?'

Raymond hesitated a moment, then nodded.

'Yes. But it's not safe. Not safe at all.'

'Will you show me?'

'I mean it.' The frog's grip tightened on his. 'It's not a safe thing to know, let alone to do.'

Rakoczy laughed, exhilarated, full of joy. Why should he fear knowledge? Perhaps the passage would kill him – but he had a pocket full of gems, and besides, what was the point of waiting to die slowly?

'Tell me!' he said, squeezing the other's hand. 'For the sake of our shared blood!'

Joan stood stock-still, amazed. Michael's arm was still around her, but she scarcely noticed.

'He *is*!' she whispered. 'He truly is! They both are!'

'Are what?' Michael gaped at her.

'Auld Folk! Faeries!'

He looked wildly back at the scene before them. The two men stood face to face, hands locked together, their mouths moving in animated conversation – in total silence. It was like watching mimes, but even less interesting.

'I dinna care *what* they are. Loons, criminals, demons, angels . . . come on!' He dropped his arm and seized her hand, but she was planted solid as an oak sapling, her eyes growing wider and wider.

She gripped his hand hard enough to grind the bones and shrieked at the top of her lungs, *'Don't do it!'*

He whirled round just in time to see the front of the comte's coat explode in a fountain of sparks. And then they vanished.

They stumbled together down the long pale passages, bathed in the flickering light of dying torches, red, yellow, blue, green, a ghastly purple that made Joan's face look drowned.

'*Des feux d'artifice,*' Michael said. His voice sounded queer, echoing in the empty tunnels. 'A conjuror's trick.'

'What?' Joan looked drugged, her eyes black with shock.

'The fires. The . . . colours. Have ye never heard of fireworks?'

'No.'

371

'Oh.' It seemed too much a struggle to explain, and they went on in silence, hurrying as much as they could, to reach the shaft before the light died entirely.

At the bottom, he paused to let her go first, thinking too late that he should have gone first – she'd think he meant to look up her dress . . . he turned hastily away, face burning.

'D'ye think he was? That *they* were?' She was hanging onto the ladder, a few feet above him. Beyond her, he could see the stars, serene in a velvet sky.

'Were what?' He looked at her face, so as not to risk her modesty. She was looking better now, but very serious.

'Were they Auld Folk? Faeries?'

'I suppose they must ha' been.' His mind was moving very slowly; he didn't want to have to try to think. He motioned to her to climb, and followed her up, his eyes tightly shut. If they were Auld Ones, then likely so was Auntie Claire. He truly didn't want to think about *that*.

He drew the fresh air gratefully into his lungs. The wind was toward the city now, coming off the fields, full of the resinous cool scent of pine trees and the breath of summer grass and cattle. He felt Joan breathe it in, sigh deeply, and then she turned to him, put her arms around him, and rested her forehead on his chest. He put his arms round her and they stood for some time, in peace.

Finally, she stirred and straightened up.

'Ye'd best take me back, then,' she said. 'The Sisters will be half out o' their minds.'

He was conscious of a sharp sense of disappointment, but turned obediently toward the coach, standing in the distance. Then he turned back.

'Ye're sure?' he said. 'Did your voices tell ye to go back?'

She made a sound that wasn't quite a rueful laugh.

'I dinna need a voice to tell me that.' She brushed a

372

hand through her hair, smoothing it off her face. 'In the Highlands, if a man's widowed, he takes another wife as soon as he can get one; he's got to have someone to mend his shirt and rear his bairns. But Sister Philomène says it's different in Paris; that a man might mourn for a year.'

'He might,' he said, after a short silence. Would a year be enough, he wondered, to heal the great hole where Lillie had been? He knew he would never forget – never stop looking for her in that space between heartbeats – but he didn't forget what Ian had told him, either: *But after a time, ye find ye're in a different place than ye were. A different person than ye were. And then ye look about, and see what's there with ye. Ye'll maybe find a use for yourself.*

Joan's face was pale and serious in the moonlight, her mouth gentle.

'It's a year before a postulant makes up her mind. Whether to stay and become a novice, or . . . or leave. It takes time. To know.'

'Aye,' he said softly. 'Aye, it does.'

He turned to go, but she stopped him, a hand on his arm.

'Michael,' she said. 'Kiss me, aye? I think I should maybe know *that*, before I decide.'

AUTHOR'S NOTES

You'll doubtless have noticed the links between 'Mrs Abernathy' in *Plague of Zombies*, and the comte's lady-friend, Mélisande. You also doubtless recall Claire meeting Mrs Abernathy in *Voyager* – twice. But you may or may not recall that Mélisande Robicheaux was the *nom de guerre* under which Geillis Duncan lived in Paris, following her escape from Scotland after the witch-trial in *Outlander*.

Chronology of the Outlander Series

The Outlander series includes three kinds of stories:

- The Big, Enormous Books (BEBs) that have no discernible genre (or all of them)

- The Shorter, Less Indescribable Novels (SLINs) that are more or less historical mysteries (though dealing also with battles, eels, and mildly deviant sexual practices)

And,

- The Bulges – these being short(er) pieces that fit somewhere inside the storylines of the BEBs and SLINs, much in the nature of squirming prey swallowed by a large snake. These deal frequently but not exclusively – with secondary characters, are prequels or sequels, and/or fill some lacunae left in the original storylines

Now, most of the SLINs (so far) fit within a large lacuna left in the middle of *Voyager*, from 1757–1761. Some of the Bulges also fall in this period; others don't.

So for the reader's convenience, here is a detailed Chronology, showing the sequence of the various elements in terms of the storyline. *HOWEVER, it should be noted that the SLINs and Bulges are all designed suchly that they may be read alone*, without reference either to each other, or to the BEBs – should you be in the mood for a light literary snack instead of the nine-course meal with wine-pairings and dessert trolley.

Outlander (aka *Cross Stitch*) (BEB) – If you've never read any of the series, I'd suggest starting here. If you're unsure about it, open the book anywhere and read three pages; if you can put it down again, I'll give you a dollar.

Dragonfly in Amber (BEB) – It doesn't start where you think it's going to. And it doesn't end how you think it's going to, either. Just keep reading; it'll be fine.

Voyager (BEB) – This one won an award from *EW* magazine for 'Best Opening Line'. (To save you having to find a copy just to read the opening, it was: 'He was dead. However, his nose throbbed painfully, which he thought odd, in the circumstances.') If you're reading the series in order, rather than piece-meal, you do want to read this book before tackling the SLINs and Bulges.

Lord John and the Hand of Devils ('Hell-Fire Club') (Bulge) – Just to add an extra layer of confusion, this (*Hand of Devils*) is a SLIN that includes three Bulges (novellas). The first story in this book, 'Hell-fire Club', is set in London in 1757, and deals with a red-haired man who approaches Lord John Grey with an urgent plea for help, just before dying in front of him. [Originally published in the anthology PAST POISONS (ed. Maxim Jakubowski, 1998).]

Lord John and the Private Matter (SLIN) – Set in London, 1757, this is a historical mystery steeped in blood and even less-savoury substances, in which Lord John meets (in short order) a valet, a traitor, an apothecary with a sure cure for syphilis, a bumptious German, and an unscrupulous merchant prince.

Hand of Devils ('Succubus') (Bulge) – The second novella in the *Hand of Devils* collection finds Lord John in Germany, having unsettling dreams about Jamie Fraser, unsettling encounters with Saxon princesses, night-hags, and a really disturbing encounter with a big, blond Hanoverian graf. [Originally published in the anthology LEGENDS II, ed. Robert Silverberg, 2004.]

Lord John and the Brotherhood of the Blade (SLIN) – The second full-length novel focused on Lord John (but it does include Jamie Fraser) is set in 1759, deals with a twenty-year-old family scandal, and sees Lord John engaged at close range with exploding cannon and even more dangerously explosive emotions.

Hand of Devils ('Haunted Soldier') (Bulge) – 1759, London and the Woolwich Arsenal. In which Lord John faces a court of inquiry into the explosion of a cannon, and learns that there are more dangerous things in the world than gunpowder.

The Scottish Prisoner (SLIN) – This one's set in 1760, in the Lake District, London, and Ireland. A sort of hybrid novel, it's divided evenly between Jamie Fraser and Lord John Grey, who are recounting their different perspectives on a tale of politics, corruptions, murder, opium dreams, horses and illegitimate sons.

Drums of Autumn (BEB) – This one begins in 1766, in the New World, where Jamie and Claire find a foothold in the mountains of North Carolina, and their daughter Brianna finds a whole lot of things she didn't expect, when a sinister newspaper clipping sends her in search of her parents.

The Fiery Cross (BEB) – Late 1760s. The historical background to this one is the War of the Regulation in North

Carolina, which was more or less a dress rehearsal for the oncoming Revolution. In which Jamie Fraser becomes a reluctant Rebel, his wife Claire becomes a conjure-woman, and meets a ghost. Something Much Worse happens to Brianna's husband Roger, but I'm not telling you what. This one's won several awards for 'Best Last Line', but I'm not telling you that, either.

A Breath of Snow and Ashes (BEB) – Early-to-mid 1770s. Winner of the 2006 Corine International Prize for Fiction, and a Quill Award (this book beat books by both George R.R. Martin *and* Stephen King, which I thought Very Entertaining Indeed). All the books have an internal 'shape' that I see while I'm writing them. This one looks like the Hokusai print titled 'The Great Wave Off Kanagawa'. Think *tsunami* – twice.

An Echo in the Bone (BEB) – 1777–1778, America, London, Canada, and Scotland. The cover image on this reflects the internal shape of the book: a caltrop. That's an ancient military weapon that looks like a child's jack with sharp points; the Romans used them to deter elephants, and the Highway Patrol still uses them to stop fleeing perps in cars. This book has four major storylines: Jamie and Claire; Roger and Brianna (and family); Lord John and William; and Young Ian, all intersecting in the nexus of the American Revolution – and all of them with sharp points.

Written in My Own Heart's Blood (BEB) – The eighth of the Big Enormous Books, this will probably be published in 2013. It begins where *An Echo in the Bone* leaves off, in summer of 1778 (and the autumn of 1974).

A Leaf on the Wind of All Hallows (Bulge) – Set (mostly) in 1940/42, this is the story of What Really Happened to

378

Roger MacKenzie's parents. [Originally published in the anthology *Songs of Love and Death* (ed. George R.R. Martin and Gardner Dozois, 2010).]

The Space Between (Bulge) – Set mostly in Paris, 1778, this novella deals with Michael Murray (Young Ian's elder brother), Joan MacKimmie (Marsali's younger sister), the Comte St Germain (who is Not Dead After All), Mother Hildegarde, and a few other persons of interest. The space between *what?* It depends who you're talking to. [To be published in early 2013 in the anthology THE MAD SCIENTIST'S GUIDE TO WORLD DOMINATION, ed. John Joseph Adams.]

Virgins (Bulge) – Set in 1740, in France. In which Jamie Fraser (aged 19) and his friend Ian Murray (aged 20) become young mercenaries. [To be published in late 2012, in the anthology DANGEROUS WOMEN, ed. George R.R. Martin and Gardner Dozois.]

NOW REMEMBER . . .

You can read the SLINs and Bulges by themselves, or in any order you like. I would recommend reading the BEBs in order, though.

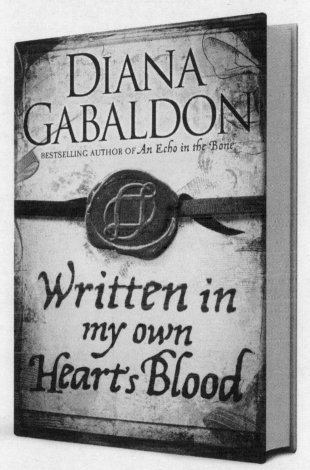

CHAPTER ONE:
A HUNDREDWEIGHT OF STONES

June 16, 1778
The forest between Philadelphia and Valley Forge

Ian Murray stood with a stone in his hand, eyeing the ground he'd chosen. A small clearing, out of the way, up among a scatter of great lichened boulders, under the shadow of firs, and at the foot of a big red cedar; a place where no casual passerby would go, but not inaccessible. He meant to bring them up here—the family.

Fergus, to begin with. Maybe just Fergus, by himself. Mam had raised Fergus from the time he was ten, and he'd had no mother before that. Ian himself had been born about that same time, so Fergus had known Mam as long as he had, and loved her as much. *Maybe more*, he thought, his grief aggravated by guilt. Fergus had stayed with her at Lallybroch, helped to take care of her and the place; he hadn't. He swallowed hard and, walking into the small clear space, set his stone in the middle, then stood back to look.

Even as he did so, he found himself shaking his head. No, it had to be two cairns. His mam and Uncle Jamie were brother and sister, and the family could mourn them here together—but there were others he might bring, maybe, to remember and pay their respects. And those were the folk who would have known Jamie Fraser and loved him well

3

but wouldn't ken Jenny Murray from a hole in the—

The image of his mother *in* a hole in the ground stabbed him like a fork, retreated with the recollection that she wasn't after all in a grave, and stabbed again all the harder for that. He really couldn't bear the vision of them drowning, maybe clinging to each other, struggling to keep—

"*A Dhia!*" he said violently, and dropped the stone, turning back at once to find more. He'd seen people drown.

Tears ran down his face with the sweat of the summer day; he didn't mind it, only stopping now and then to wipe his nose on his sleeve. He'd tied a rolled kerchief round his head to keep the hair and the stinging sweat out of his eyes; it was sopping before he'd added more than twenty stones to each of the cairns.

He and his brothers had built a fine cairn for their father, at the head of the carved stone that bore his name—all his names, in spite of the expense—in the burying ground at Lallybroch. And all the family, followed by the tenants and then at the funeral later, the servants would have come one by one to add a stone each to the weight of remembrance.

Fergus, then. Or . . . no, what was he thinking? Auntie Claire must be the first he brought here. She wasn't Scots herself, but she kent fine what a cairn was and would maybe be comforted a bit to see Uncle Jamie's. Aye, right. Auntie Claire, then Fergus. Uncle Jamie was Fergus's foster father; he had a right. And then maybe Marsali and the children. But maybe Germain was old enough to come with Fergus? He was almost eleven, near enough to being a man to understand, to be treated like a man. And Uncle Jamie was his grandsire; it was proper.

He stepped back again and wiped his face, breathing heavily. Bugs whined and buzzed past his ears and hovered

4

over him, wanting his blood, but he'd stripped to a loin-cloth and rubbed himself with bear grease and mint in the Mohawk way; they didn't touch him.

"Look over them, O spirit of red cedar," he said softly in Mohawk, looking up into the fragrant branches of the tree. "Guard their souls and keep their presence here, fresh as thy branches."

He crossed himself and bent to dig about in the soft leaf mold. A few more rocks, he thought. In case they might be scattered by some passing animal. Scattered like his thoughts, which roamed restless to and fro among the faces of his family, the folk of the Ridge—God, might he ever go back there? Brianna. Oh, Jesus, Brianna . . .

He bit his lip and tasted salt, licked it away and moved on, foraging. She was safe with Roger Mac and the weans. But, Jesus, he could have used her advice—even more, Roger Mac's.

Who was left for him to ask, if he needed help in taking care of them all?

Thought of Rachel came to him, and the tightness in his chest eased a little. Aye, if he had Rachel . . . She was younger than him, nay more than nineteen, and, being a Quaker, had very strange notions of how things should be, but if he had her, he'd have solid rock under his feet. He hoped he *would* have her, but there were still things he must say to her, and the thought of that conversation made the tightness in his chest come back.

The picture of his cousin Brianna came back, too, and lingered in his mind: tall, long-nosed, and strong-boned as her father . . . and with it rose the image of his *other* cousin, Bree's half brother. Holy God, William. And what ought he to do about William? He doubted the man kent

5

the truth, kent that he was Jamie Fraser's son—was it Ian's responsibility to tell him so? To bring him here and explain what he'd lost?

He must have groaned at the thought, for his dog, Rollo, lifted his massive head and looked at him in concern.

"No, I dinna ken that, either," Ian told him. "Let it bide, aye?" Rollo laid his head back on his paws, shivered his shaggy hide against the flies, and relaxed in boneless peace.

Ian worked awhile longer and let the thoughts drain away with his sweat and his tears. He finally stopped when the sinking sun touched the tops of his cairns, feeling tired but more at peace. The cairns rose knee-high, side by side, small but solid.

He stood still for a bit, not thinking anymore, just listening to the fussing of wee birds in the grass and the breathing of the wind among the trees. Then he sighed deeply, squatted, and touched one of the cairns.

"Tha gaol agam oirbh, a Mhàthair," he said softly. *My love is upon you, Mother.* Closed his eyes and laid a scuffed hand on the other heap of stones. The dirt ground into his skin made his fingers feel strange, as though he could maybe reach straight through the earth and touch what he needed.

He stayed still, breathing, then opened his eyes.

"Help me wi' this, Uncle Jamie," he said. "I dinna think I can manage, alone."

6

CHAPTER TWO:
SCHMUTZIGER BASTARD

William Ransom, Ninth Earl of Ellesmere, Viscount Ashness, and Baron Derwent, shoved his way through the crowds on Market Street, oblivious to the complaints of those rebounding from his impact.

He didn't know where he was going, or what he might do when he got there. All he knew was that he'd burst if he stood still.

His head throbbed like an inflamed boil. Everything throbbed. His hand—he'd probably broken something, but he didn't care. His heart, pounding and sore inside his chest. His foot, for God's sake—what, had he kicked something? He lashed out viciously at a loose cobblestone and sent it rocketing through a crowd of geese, who set up a huge cackle and lunged at him, hissing and beating at his shins with their wings.

Feathers and goose shit flew wide, and the crowd scattered in all directions.

"Bastard!" shrieked the goose-girl, and struck at him with her crook, catching him a shrewd thump on the ear. "Devil take you, *schmutziger Bastard!*"

This sentiment was echoed by a number of other angry voices, and he veered into an alley, pursued by shouts and honks of agitation.

He rubbed his throbbing ear, lurching into buildings as he passed, oblivious to everything but the one word throbbing ever louder in his head. *Bastard.*

"Bastard!" he said out loud, and shouted, "Bastard, bastard, *bastard!!*" at the top of his lungs, hammering at the brick wall next to him with a clenched fist.

"Who's a bastard?" said a curious voice behind him. He swung round to see a young woman looking at him with some interest. Her eyes moved slowly down his frame, taking note of the heaving chest, the bloodstains on the facings of his uniform coat, and the green smears of goose shit on his breeches. Her gaze reached his silver-buckled shoes and returned to his face with more interest.

"I am," he said, hoarse and bitter.

"Oh, really?" She left the shelter of the doorway in which she'd been standing and came across the alley to stand right in front of him. She was tall and slim and had a very fine pair of high young breasts—which were clearly visible under the thin muslin of her shift, because, while she had a silk petticoat, she wore no stays. No cap, either—her hair fell loose over her shoulders. A whore.

"I'm partial to bastards myself," she said, and touched him lightly on the arm. "What kind of bastard are you? A wicked one? An evil one?"

"A sorry one," he said, and scowled when she laughed. She saw the scowl, but didn't pull back.

"Come in," she said, and took his hand. "You look as though you could do with a drink." He saw her glance at his knuckles, burst and bleeding, and she caught her lower lip behind small white teeth. She didn't seem afraid, though, and he found himself drawn, unprotesting, into the shadowed doorway after her.

What did it matter? he thought, with a sudden savage weariness. *What did anything matter?*

8

CHAPTER THREE:
IN WHICH THE WOMEN, AS USUAL, PICK UP THE PIECES

No. 17 Chestnut Street, Philadelphia
The residence of Lord and Lady John Grey

William had left the house like a thunderclap, and the place looked as though it had been struck by lightning. I certainly felt like the survivor of a massive electrical storm, hairs and nerve endings all standing up straight on end, waving in agitation.

Jenny Murray had entered the house on the heels of William's departure, and while the sight of her was a lesser shock than any of the others so far, it still left me speechless. I goggled at my erstwhile sister-in-law—though, come to think, she still *was* my sister-in-law . . . because Jamie was alive. *Alive.*

He'd been in my arms not ten minutes before, and the memory of his touch flickered through me like lightning in a bottle. I was dimly aware that I was smiling like a loon, despite massive destruction, horrific scenes, William's distress—if you could call an explosion like that "distress"—Jamie's danger, and a faint wonder as to what either Jenny or Mrs. Figg, Lord John's cook and housekeeper, might be about to say.

Mrs. Figg was smoothly spherical, gleamingly black, and inclined to glide silently up behind one like a menacing ball bearing.

9

"What's *this*?" she barked, manifesting herself suddenly behind Jenny.

"Holy Mother of God!" Jenny whirled, eyes round and hand pressed to her chest. "Who in God's name are you?"

"This is Mrs. Figg," I said, feeling a surreal urge to laugh, despite—or maybe because of—recent events. "Lord John Grey's cook. And Mrs. Figg, this is Mrs. Murray. My, um . . . my . . ."

"Your good-sister," Jenny said firmly. She raised one black eyebrow. "If ye'll have me still?" Her look was straight and open, and the urge to laugh changed abruptly into an equally strong urge to burst into tears. Of all the unlikely sources of succor I could have imagined . . . I took a deep breath and put out my hand.

"I'll have you." We hadn't parted on good terms in Scotland, but I had loved her very much, once, and wasn't about to pass up any opportunity to mend things.

Her small firm fingers wove through mine, squeezed hard, and, as simply as that, it was done. No need for apologies or spoken forgiveness. She'd never had to wear the mask that Jamie did. What she thought and felt was there in her eyes, those slanted blue cat-eyes she shared with her brother. She knew the truth now of what I was, and she knew I loved and always had loved her brother with all my heart and soul—despite the minor complications of my being presently married to someone else.

She heaved a sigh, eyes closing for an instant, then opened them and smiled at me, mouth trembling only a little.

"Well, fine and dandy," said Mrs. Figg shortly. She narrowed her eyes and rotated smoothly on her axis, taking in the panorama of destruction. The railing at the top of the stair had been ripped off, and cracked banisters, dented walls, and bloody smudges marked the path of William's descent. Shattered crystals from the chandelier littered the floor, glinting festively in the light from the open front door, the door itself cracked through and hanging drunkenly from one hinge.

"*Merde* on toast," Mrs. Figg murmured. She turned abruptly to me, her small blackcurrant eyes still narrowed. "Where's his lordship?"

"Ah," I said. This was going to be rather sticky, I saw. While deeply disapproving of most people, Mrs. Figg was devoted to John. She wasn't going to be at all pleased to hear that he'd been abducted by—

"For that matter, where's my brother?" Jenny inquired, glancing round as though expecting Jamie to appear suddenly out from under the settee.

"Oh," I said. "Hmm. Well . . ." Possibly worse than sticky. Because . . .

"And where's my sweet William?" Mrs. Figg demanded, sniffing the air. "He's been here; I smell that stinky cologne he puts on his linen." She nudged a dislodged chunk of plaster disapprovingly with the toe of her shoe.

I took another long, deep breath and a tight grip on what remained of my sanity.

"Mrs. Figg," I said, "perhaps you would be so kind as to make us all a cup of tea?"

We sat in the parlor, while Mrs. Figg came and went to the cookhouse, keeping an eye on her terrapin stew.

"You don't want to scorch turtle, no, you don't," she said severely to us, setting down the teapot in its padded yellow cozy on her return. "Not with so much sherry as his

11

lordship likes in it. Almost a full bottle—terrible waste of good liquor, that would be."

My insides turned over promptly. Turtle soup—with a lot of sherry—had certain strong and private associations for me, these being connected with Jamie, feverish delirium, and the way in which a heaving ship assists sexual intercourse. Contemplation of which would *not* assist the impending discussion in the slightest. I rubbed a finger between my brows, in hopes of dispelling the buzzing cloud of confusion gathering there. The air in the house still felt electric.

"Speaking of sherry," I said, "or any other sort of strong spirits you might have convenient, Mrs. Figg . . ."

She looked thoughtfully at me, nodded, and reached for the decanter on the sideboard.

"Brandy is stronger," she said, and set it in front of me.

Jenny looked at me with the same thoughtfulness and, reaching out, poured a good-sized slug of the brandy into my cup, then a similar one into her own.

"Just in case," she said, raising one brow, and we drank for a few moments. I thought it might take something stronger than brandy-laced tea to deal with the effect of recent events on my nerves—laudanum, say, or a large slug of straight Scotch whisky—but the tea undeniably helped, hot and aromatic, settling in a soft trickling warmth amidships.

"So, then. We're fettled, are we?" Jenny set down her own cup and looked expectant.

"It's a start." I took a deep breath and gave her a *précis* of recent events.

Jenny's eyes were disturbingly like Jamie's. She blinked at me once, then twice, and shook her head as though to clear it, accepting what I'd just told her.

12

"So Jamie's gone off wi' your Lord John, the British army is after them, the tall lad I met on the stoop wi' steam comin' out of his ears is Jamie's son—well, of course he is; a blind man could see that—and the town's aboil wi' British soldiers. Is that it, then?"

"He's not exactly *my* Lord John," I said. "But, yes, that's essentially the position. I take it Jamie told you about William?"

"Aye, he did." She grinned at me over the rim of her teacup. "I'm that happy for him. But what's troubling his lad, then? He looked like he wouldna give the road to a bear."

"What did you say?" Mrs. Figg's voice cut in abruptly. She set down the tray she had just brought in, the silver milk jug and sugar basin rattling like castanets. "William is *whose* son?"

I took a fortifying gulp of tea. Mrs. Figg did know that I'd been married to—and theoretically widowed from—one James Fraser. But that was all she knew.

"Well," I said, and paused to clear my throat. "The, um, tall gentleman with the red hair who was just here—you saw him?"

"I did." Mrs. Figg eyed me narrowly.

"Did you get a good look at him?"

"Didn't pay much heed to his face when he came to the door and asked where you were, but I saw his backside pretty plain when he pushed past me and ran up the stairs."

"Possibly the resemblance is less marked from that angle." I took another mouthful of tea. "Um . . . that gentleman is James Fraser, my . . . er . . . my—" "First husband" wasn't accurate, and neither was "last husband"—or even, unfortunately, "most recent husband." I settled for

13

the simplest alternative. "My husband. And, er . . . William's father."

Mrs. Figg's mouth opened, soundless for an instant. She backed up slowly and sat down on a needlework ottoman with a soft *phumph*.

"William know that?" she asked, after a moment's contemplation.

"He does *now*," I said, with a brief gesture toward the devastation in the stairwell, clearly visible through the door of the parlor where we were sitting.

"*Merde* on—I mean, Holy Lamb of God preserve us." Mrs. Figg's second husband was a Methodist preacher, and she strove to be a credit to him, but her first had been a French gambler. Her eyes fixed on me like gun-sights.

"You his mother?"

I choked on my tea.

"No," I said, wiping my chin with a linen napkin. "It isn't quite *that* complicated." In fact, it was more so, but I wasn't going to explain just how Willie had come about, either to Mrs. Figg or to Jenny. Jamie had to have told Jenny who William's mother was, but I doubted that he'd told his sister that William's mother, Geneva Dunsany, had forced him into her bed by threatening Jenny's family. No man of spirit likes to admit that he's been effectively blackmailed by an eighteen-year-old girl.

"Lord John became William's legal guardian when William's grandfather died, and at that point, Lord John also married Lady Isobel Dunsany, Willie's mother's sister. She'd looked after Willie since his mother's death in childbirth, and she and Lord John were essentially Willie's parents since he was quite young. Isobel died when he was eleven or so."

14

Mrs. Figg took this explanation in stride, but wasn't about to be distracted from the main point at issue.

"James Fraser," she said, tapping a couple of broad fingers on her knee and looking accusingly at Jenny. "How comes he not to be dead? News was he drowned." She cut her eyes at me. "I thought his lordship was like to throw himself in the harbor, too, when he heard it."

I closed my own eyes with a sudden shudder, the salt-cold horror of that news washing over me in a wave of memory. Even with Jamie's touch still joyful on my skin and the knowledge of him glowing in my heart, I relived the crushing pain of hearing that he was dead.

"Well, I can enlighten ye on that point, at least."

I opened my eyes to see Jenny drop a lump of sugar into her fresh tea and nod at Mrs. Figg. "We were to take passage on a ship called *Euterpe*—my brother and myself—out o' Brest. But the blackhearted thief of a captain sailed without us. Much good it did him," she added, frowning.

Much good, indeed. The *Euterpe* had sunk in a storm in the Atlantic, lost with all hands. As I—and John Grey—had been told.

"Jamie found us another ship, but it landed us in Virginia, and we'd to make our way up the coast, partly by wagon, partly by packet boat, keepin' out of the way of the soldiers. Those wee needles ye gave Jamie against the seasickness work most o' the time," she added, turning approvingly to me. "He showed me how to put them in for him. But when we came to Philadelphia yesterday," she went on, returning to her tale, "we stole into the city by night, like a pair o' thieves, and made our way to Fergus's printshop. Lord, I thought my heart would stop a dozen times!"

15

She smiled at the memory, and I was struck by the change in her. The shadow of sorrow still lay on her face, and she was thin and worn by travel, but the terrible strain of her husband Ian's long dying had lifted. There was color in her cheeks again, and a brightness in her eyes that I had not seen since I had first known her thirty years before. She had found her peace, I thought, and felt a thankfulness that eased my own soul.

". . . so Jamie taps on the door at the back, and there's no answer, though we can see the light of a fire comin' through the shutters. He knocks again, makin' a wee tune of it—" She rapped her knuckles lightly on the table, *bump-ba-da-bump-ba-da-bump-bump-bump*, and my heart turned over, recognizing the theme from *The Lone Ranger*, which Brianna had taught him.

"And after a moment," Jenny went on, "a woman's voice calls out fierce, 'Who's there?' And Jamie says in the *Gaidhlig*, 'It is your father, my daughter, and a cold, wet, and hungry man he is, too.' For it was rainin' hammer handles and pitchforks, and we were both soaked to the skin."

She rocked back a little, enjoying the telling.

"The door opens then, just a crack, and there's Marsali wi' a horse pistol in her hand, and her two wee lasses behind her, fierce as archangels, each with a billet of wood, ready to crack a thief across his shins. They see the firelight shine on Jamie's face then, and all three of them let out skellochs like to wake the dead and fall upon him and drag him inside and all talkin' at once and greetin', askin' was he a ghost and why was he not drowned, and that was the first we learned that the *Euterpe* had sunk." She crossed herself. "God rest them, poor souls," she said, shaking her head.

16

I crossed myself, too, and saw Mrs. Figg look sideways at me; she hadn't realized I was a Papist.

"I've come in, too, of course," Jenny went on, "but everyone's talkin' at once and rushin' to and fro in search of dry clothes and hot drinks and I'm just lookin' about the place, for I've never been inside a printshop before, and the smell of the ink and the paper and lead is a wonder to me, and, sudden-like, there's a tug at my skirt and this sweet-faced wee mannie says to me, 'And who are you, madame? Would you like some cider?'"

"Henri-Christian," I murmured, smiling at the thought of Marsali's youngest, and Jenny nodded.

"'Why, I'm your grannie Janet, son,' says I, and his eyes go round, and he lets out a shriek and grabs me round the legs and gives me such a hug as to make me lose my balance and fall down on the settle. I've a bruise on my bum the size of your hand," she added out of the corner of her mouth to me.

I felt a small knot of tension that I hadn't realized was there relax. Jenny did of course know that Henri-Christian had been born a dwarf—but knowing and seeing are sometimes different things. Clearly they hadn't been, for Jenny.

Mrs. Figg had been following this account with interest, but maintained her reserve. At mention of the printshop, though, this reserve hardened a bit.

"These folk—Marsali is your daughter, then, ma'am?" I could tell what she was thinking. The entire town of Philadelphia knew that Jamie was a rebel—and, by extension, so was I. It was the threat of my imminent arrest that had caused John to insist upon my marrying him in the wake of the tumult following Jamie's presumed death. The mention of printing in British-occupied Philadelphia was

17

bound to raise questions as to just *what* was being printed, and by whom.

"No, her husband is my brother's adopted son," Jenny explained. "But I raised Fergus from a wee lad myself, so he's my foster son, as well, by the Highland way of reckoning."

Mrs. Figg blinked. She had been gamely trying to keep the cast of characters in some sort of order to this point, but now gave it up with a shake of her head that made the pink ribbons on her cap wave like antennae.

"Well, where the devil—I mean, where on earth has your brother gone with his lordship?" she demanded. "To this printshop, you think?"

Jenny and I exchanged glances.

"I doubt it," I said. "More likely he's gone outside the city, using John—er, his lordship, I mean—as a hostage to get past the pickets, if necessary. Probably he'll let him go as soon as they're far enough away for safety."

Mrs. Figg made a deep humming noise of disapproval.

"And maybe he'll make for Valley Forge and turn him over to the rebels instead."

"Oh, I shouldna think so," Jenny said soothingly. "What would they want with him, after all?"

Mrs. Figg blinked again, taken aback at the notion that anyone might not value his lordship to the same degree that she did, but after a moment's lip-pursing allowed as this might be so.

"He wasn't in his uniform, was he, ma'am?" she asked me, brow furrowed. I shook my head. John didn't hold an active commission. He was a diplomat, though technically still lieutenant-colonel of his brother's regiment, and therefore wore his uniform for purposes of ceremony or

20

intimidation, but he was officially retired from the army, not a combatant, and in plain clothes he would be taken as citizen rather than soldier—thus of no particular interest to General Washington's troops at Valley Forge.

I didn't think Jamie was headed for Valley Forge in any case. I knew, with absolute certainty, that he would come back. Here. For me.

The thought bloomed low in my belly and spread upward in a wave of warmth that made me bury my nose in my teacup to hide the resulting flush.

Alive. I caressed the word, cradling it in the center of my heart. Jamie was alive. Glad as I was to see Jenny—and gladder still to see her extend an olive branch in my direction—I really wanted to go up to my room, close the door, and lean against the wall with my eyes shut tight, reliving the seconds after he'd entered the room, when he'd taken me in his arms and kissed me, the simple, solid, warm fact of his presence so overwhelming that I might have collapsed onto the floor without his arms' support.

Alive, I repeated silently to myself. *He's alive*.

Nothing else mattered. Though I did wonder briefly what he'd done with John.